A TALENT
FOR WAR

Jack McDevitt

ACE BOOKS, NEW YORK

A TALENT FOR WAR

Portions of chapter 15 originally appeared in the March 1988 issue of *Isaac Asimov's Science Fiction Magazine* under the title "Sunrise."

Portions of chapters 9, 22, 23, and 24 are adapted from "Dutchman," which appeared in *Isaac Asimov's Science Fiction Magazine*, February 1987.

An Ace Book / published by arrangement with the author

PRINTING HISTORY
Ace mass market edition / February 1989

Copyright © 1989 by Jack McDevitt.
Cover art by Darrell K. Sweet.
Cover design by Rita Frangie.

ISBN: 0-441-01217-5

ACE®
Ace Books are published by The Berkley Publishing Group, a division of Penguin Group (USA) Inc., 375 Hudson Street, New York, New York 10014.
ACE and the "A" design are trademarks belonging to Penguin Group (USA) Inc.

PRINTED IN THE UNITED STATES OF AMERICA

10 9 8 7 6

For Joseph H. Parroff, Rev. L. Richard Casavant,
m.s., and Rev. Robert E. Carson, O. Praem.,
to mark debts I can never pay.

ACKNOWLEDGMENTS

I am indebted for the technical assistance of James H. Sharp of the Albert Einstein Planetarium at the Smithsonian Institution. I'd also like to express my appreciation to Lewis Shiner for his suggestions and time; to Ginjer Buchanan, for her assistance with the manuscript; and to Maureen McDevitt, whose presence is felt throughout Christopher Sim's world.

PROLOGUE

THE AIR WAS heavy with incense and the sweet odor of hot wax.

Cam Chulohn loved the plain stone chapel. He knelt on the hard bench and watched the crystal water dribble across Father Curry's fingers into the silver bowl held by the postulant. The timeless symbol of man's effort to evade responsibility, it had always seemed to Chulohn the most significant of all the ancient rituals. There, he thought, is the essence of our nature, displayed endlessly throughout the ages for all who can see.

His gaze lingered in turn on the Virgin's Alcove (illuminated by a few flickering candles) and the Stations of the Cross, on the simple altar, on the hewn pulpit with its ponderous Bible. It was modest by the opulent standards of Rimway and Rigel III and Taramingo. But somehow the magnificence of the architecture in those sprawling cathedrals, the exquisite quality of the stained glass windows, the satisfying bulk of marble columns, the sheer angelic power of the big organs, the sweeping choir lofts: it all got in the way. Here, halfway up a mountainside, he could look out over the river valley that the early fathers, in a burst of enthusiasm, had dedicated to St. Anthony of Toxicon. There was only the river, and the ridges, and the Creator.

Chulohn's visit to the Abbey was the first by a presiding bishop (so far as he could determine) during the entire existence of the community. Albacore, this snowbound, cold world at the farthest extreme of the Confederacy's influence, was home to few other than the fathers. But it was not difficult—enjoying its massive

1

silence, listening for the occasional distant rumble of a rockslide, taking the cold vigorous air into his lungs—to understand how it was that it had housed, at one time or another, the finest scholars the Order had known. Martin Brendois had written his great histories of the Time of Troubles in a cubicle just above the chapel. Albert Kale had completed his celebrated study of transgalactic strings, and Morgan Ki had composed the essays that would link his name irrevocably to classic economic theory.

Yes, there was something about this place that called forth greatness.

After mass, he walked along the parapet with Mark Thasangales, the Abbot. They were wrapped in coats, and their breath hung before them. Thasangales had much in common with St. Anthony's Valley: no one in the Order could remember when he had been young. His features were as uncompromising and lined as the limestone walls and snowswept crags. He was a tower of faith: Chulohn could not imagine those dark blue eyes beset by the doubts that harried ordinary men.

They were reminiscing about better times—as middle-aged men who have not seen each other for a long time will—when the Abbot shook off the past. "Cam," he said, raising his voice slightly to get above the wind, "you've done well."

Chulohn smiled. Thasangales was talented: his capability for raising and managing funds in no way diminished his certifiable aura of sanctity. He was a superb administrator and a persuasive speaker, precisely the sort of man to represent the Church and the Order. But he had always lacked ambition. And so he had returned to St. Anthony's when the opportunity offered. And he had stayed a lifetime. "The Church has been good to me, Mark. As it has been to you." They looked down from the mountaintop on which the Abbey stood. The floor of the valley was brown with approaching winter. "I've always thought I would have liked to come here for a couple of years. Maybe teach theology. Maybe just put my life in order."

"The Church needed you for more important things."

"Perhaps." Chulohn studied his ring, the emblem of his office, and sighed. "I traded a great deal for *this*. Maybe the price has been too high."

The Abbot neither agreed nor disagreed, but merely stood his ground, awaiting his bishop's pleasure. Chulohn sighed. "You don't really approve of the path I've taken."

"I didn't say that."

"Your eyes did." Chulohn smiled.

A sudden burst of wind raked the trees, and snowflakes flew. "First of the year," Thasangales announced.

St. Anthony's Valley is located in the high country of the smaller of Albacore's two continents. (There are those who say the small, compact world consists almost exclusively of high country.) But, in Chulohn's eyes, it was one of God's special places, a corrugated land of forest and limestone and snowcap. The Bishop had grown up in this kind of country, on rugged Dellaconda, whose sun was too distant to be seen from St. Anthony's.

Standing in that ancient wilderness, he felt emotions he had not known for thirty years. The thoughts of youth. Why was it they were so much more real than anything that would follow after? How had it happened that he'd fulfilled his earliest ambitions, had in fact far exceeded them, and found it all so unsatisfying?

He drew his coat around him, fending off a sudden icy gust.

It was disquieting here, among the cold still peaks. Somehow, in a way he couldn't grasp, they challenged the warm comfort of the tiny chapel. There was a movement back home, a group of zealots who pretended to speak for Christ, who wanted him to sell off the churches, and give the proceeds to the poor. But Chulohn, who loved the bleak places of the worlds *because* they were fearful, understood that churches are shelters against the intimidating majesty of the Almighty.

He watched the snow gathering force.

Several seminarians boiled out of the refectory and hurried noisily toward the gym. The sudden activity shook Chulohn from his reverie. He glanced at Thasangeles. "Are you cold?" he asked.

"No."

"Then let's see the rest of the grounds."

Little had changed since the Bishop had been ordained here: stone grottos and sweeping lawns and gray somber church buildings compressed the decades. Had the midnight beer raids on the refectory really been half a lifetime ago? Was it really so long since the forays into Blasinwell and the innocent flirtations with the young women there? Since those naked dips into mountain pools? (My God, how did it happen he could still feel the delicious bite of cool currents along his flanks?)

It had all seemed deliciously sinful then.

The stone chip walkways, which were covered lightly by snow, crunched pleasantly underfoot. Chulohn and Thasangales circled the library. Its antenna, mounted at the peak of the sharply sloping roof, turned slowly, tracking one or another of the orbiters. The flakes were wet in Chulohn's eyes, and his feet were getting cold.

The Fathers' quarters were located in the rear of the complex of buildings, safely away from the distractions of visitors and novices. They paused at the entrance, a simple bilious green metal door that had been built to withstand the ages, and threatened to do so. But Chulohn was looking away, up the gently rising slope that dominated the ground behind the abbey. At its crest, almost invisible against the gathering storm, were an arch, an iron fence, and several long rows of white crosses.

The place of honor for those who had persevered.

Thasangales had pulled open the door and waited patiently for the Bishop to enter.

"A moment," said Chulohn, brushing the snow from his shoulders, drawing his collar about his neck, and continuing to stare thoughtfully at the ridge.

"Cam, it's cold." There was a hint of irritation in Thasangales' voice.

Chulohn gave no appearance of having heard. "I'll be back in a few minutes," he said presently. And, without another word, he set off at a brisk pace up the slope.

The Abbot let go of the door, and fell in behind with a suggestion of resignation that a casual observer might have missed.

The walkway to the cemetery had vanished beneath the snow, but Chulohn paid no attention and, bent against the incline, he made directly uphill. A pair of stone angels, heads bowed, wings spread, guarded the approach. He passed between them and paused to read the legend carved into the face of the arch: *He that would teach men to die must know how to live.*

The crosses were arranged in precise rows, the oldest in front and to the left, proceeding in somber sequence through the years across the top of the ridge and down the opposite slope. Each displayed a name, the proud designation of the Order, *O. D. J.*, and the date of death stated in standard years of the Christian Era.

Toward the rear, he discovered Father Brenner. Brenner had been redheaded, robust, overweight. But he was young in the days when Chulohn had been young. His class was History of the Church during the Great Migration.

"Surely, you knew . . ." said the Abbot, noting the Bishop's reaction.

"Yes. But hearing that a man is dead is not quite the same as standing at his grave."

There was a painful number of familiar names along that back row. They were, at first, his instructors: Philips and Mushallah and Otikapa. Mushallah had been a silent moody man with quick eyes and relentless conviction who loved to duel with any student who dared question the sophisticated reasoning that demonstrated God's existence through logic.

Further on, he found John Pannell and Crag Hover and others. Dust now. All the theology in the world didn't change that.

He looked curiously at Thasangales, standing patiently in the falling snow, hands pushed deep into his pockets, apparently untouched by it all. Did he understand anything of what it meant to walk through such a place? The Abbot's expression showed no trace of pain. Chulohn was uncertain whether he would really wish his own faith so strong. . . .

Uncomfortable notion: the sinner clasping the sin.

There were numerous stones, dating back several centuries. And there were many here to whom he should pay his respects; but he wished ardently to turn back, perhaps because of the deteriorating weather, perhaps because he wished to see no more. And it happened that as he turned, intending to retreat, his gaze fell across one of the stones, and he saw that something was wrong, though he was not immediately sure what it might be. He walked toward the marker, and peered at its inscription:

Jerome Courtney
Died 11,108 A.D.

The grave was a hundred sixty standard years old. Relatively recent by St. Anthony standards. But the inscription was incomplete. The sign of the Order was missing.

The Bishop squinted at the marker, and brushed at the stone, to clear away a few flakes that might have obscured the designation.

"Don't bother, Cam," said the Abbot. "It's not there."

"Why not?" He straightened, his obvious perplexity giving way to displeasure. "Who is he?"

"He is not one of us. In any narrow sense."

"He is not a Disciple?"

"He's not even a Catholic, Cam. I don't think he was a believer at all."

Chulohn took a step forward, crowding his subordinate. "Then what in God's name is he doing here? Among the Fathers?" It was not a place for shouting, but the Bishop's effort to control his voice produced a modulated rasp that embarrassed him.

Thasangeles' eyes were round and blue. "He's been here a long time, Cam. He came to us for refuge, and lived with the Community for almost forty years."

"That doesn't explain why he lies here."

"He lies here," the Abbot said, "because the men among whom he lived and died loved him, and decreed that he should remain among them."

I.

She passed Awinspoor in the dead of night, lights blazing. The cloud of relay shuttles which had raced through the system with her fell rapidly behind. Many persons later claimed to have picked up broadcasts from the onboard radio station, featuring a popular nightclub comic of the period. She approached jump status near the outermost rocky world shortly after breakfast, and entered Armstrong space precisely on schedule. She carried twenty-six hundred souls, passengers and crew, with her.

—Machias,
Chronicles, XXII

ON THE NIGHT we heard that the *Capella* had slipped into oblivion, I was haggling with a wealthy client over a collection of four-thousand-year-old ceramic pots. We stopped to watch the reports. There was little to say, really, other than that the *Capella* had not re-entered linear space as expected, that the delay was now considerable, and an announcement declaring the ship officially lost was expected momentarily.

The names of prominent passengers followed: a few diplomats were on board, some sports figures, a musician who had clearly lost his mind years before but whose work seemed only to have prospered by the experience, a group of students who had won some sort of competition, and a well-heeled mystic with her male retinue.

The loss of the *Capella* entered almost immediately into the rarefied atmosphere of legend. Certainly there have been far worse disasters. But the twenty-six hundred people riding with the big interstellar had not died in any ordinary sense. They might, in fact, not have died at all. No one knows. And therein lies the fascination of the event.

The client, whose name I no longer recall, shook his head sadly at the hazards of life, and returned quickly to the artifacts at hand. We compromised nearer his end than mine.

The *Capella* had been the flagship of the newest class of interstellars, equipped with every conceivable sort of safety device, piloted by a captain of documented ingenuity. It was painful to think of it reduced quietly to the stature of a ghost.

It's happened before. But never to anything so big. And with so many people. Almost immediately, we had a hit song. And theories.

The vessel had struck a time node, some said, and would emerge at a future date, with the passengers and crew unaware that anything unusual had happened. Of course, we'd been losing ships for a hell of a long time now, and none has ever reappeared. So if they're going uptime, it must be a considerable distance.

The idea most widely held was that the Armstrongs had simultaneously failed, leaving the ship to wander forever, unseen, unheard. (That, it struck me, was a wonderful thing to tell the families of the travelers.)

There was a host of other ideas. The *Capella* had emerged in another universe. Or there'd been a glitch that had propelled her to another galaxy (or more likely, into the gulfs between the galaxies). The one that seemed most likely to me was the boulder theory: Armstrong space is *not* a perfect vacuum, and the *Capella* had struck something too big for its deflectors.

Of course I have no more idea than anyone else. But it was unnerving all the same. And it was just one more reason why I didn't ride the damned things unless I absolutely had to.

During the days that followed, the net was filled with the usual human interest stories. The man who had overslept, missed the shuttle, and thereby missed the flight, mentioned his appreciation to an Almighty who, apparently, was less indulgent to the twenty-six hundred others. The captain was on her last cruise, and was to have retired when the ship reached Saraglia Station, the final port of call. A woman on Rimway claimed to have dreamt, on the night before the disaster, of the loss of the *Capella*. (She eventually parlayed that claim into a lucrative career, and became one of the leading seers of the age.)

And so on. We heard that an inquiry would be conducted, but of course that was likely to lead to nothing. There was, after all, little to examine, other than passenger and cargo manifests, shipping schedules, and the like.

The carriers released fresh statistics that demonstrated people were safer traveling between Rigel and Sol than tooling around the average city.

About ten days after the loss, I received a transmission from a cousin on Rimway with whom I'd had no communication in years. *In case you haven't heard*, he said, *Gabe was on the Capella. I'm sorry. Let me know if there's anything I can do.*

That brought it home.

In the morning, an electronic package containing two sponders arrived from the law firm of Brimbury & Conn, which, according to the routing information, was also located on Rimway. I fed it into the system, dropped into a chair, and put on the headband. The standing image of a woman formed, about a half-meter off the floor, and angled at maybe thirty degrees. The tone wasn't quite right either. I could have compensated easily enough, but I knew I wasn't going to like this, so I didn't bother. The woman was talking to the floor. A library tried to take shape around her. I screened it out.

The woman was attractive, in a bureaucratic, well-pressed sort of way. "Mr. Benedict, please allow us to extend our condolences on the loss of your uncle." Pause. "He was a valued customer here at Brimbury & Conn, and a friend as well. We'll miss him."

"As will we all," I said.

The image nodded. The woman's lips trembled, and when she spoke again there was enough uncertainty in her voice to persuade me that, despite the canned speech, there had been some genuine feeling. "We wanted to inform you that you have been named sole heir of his estate. You will need to file the necessary documents as outlined in the appendix to this transmission." She seemed to flounder a little. "We have started procedures to have Gabriel declared officially dead. There will be some delay, of course. The courts are not anxious to move in the case of a missing person, even in this type of situation. However, we will want to be prepared to act on your behalf at the earliest opportunity. Consequently, you should forward the documents to us without delay.'' She sat down and arranged her skirt. ''Your uncle also left in our custody a sealed communication for you, to be delivered in the event of his death. It will be activated at the conclusion of this message by your voice. Say anything. Please do not hesitate to inform us if we can be of further assistance. And, Mr. Benedict—'' her voice fell to a whisper, ''—I really will miss him.''

I stopped it, ran a test, and adjusted the picture. Then I went back to my chair, but I sat a long time before putting the headband back on.

''Gabe.''

The lights dimmed, and I was in the old second-floor study back home, seated in a thickly cushioned chair that had once been my favorite. Nothing seemed to have changed: the paneled walls were familiar, and the ancient heavy furniture, and the mahogany-colored drapes. A fire crackled in the grate. And Gabriel stood at my side.

He was barely an arm's length away, tall, thin, grayer than I remembered, his face partially in shadow. Without a word, he touched my shoulder, pressed down on it. ''Hello, Alex.''

This was all simulation. But I knew in that moment how much I would miss the old bastard. I had mixed emotions about this. And it surprised me: I'd have expected Gabe to accept his misfortune without subjecting anyone to a maudlin farewell. It was unlike him.

I wanted to break the illusion, to just sit and watch, but you have to respond, or the image reacts to your silence by telling you to speak up, or by reassuring you everything's okay. I didn't need that. ''Hello, Gabe.''

''Since I'm here,'' he said ruefully, ''I guess things must have gone wrong.''

''I'm sorry,'' I said.

He shrugged. ''It happens. Timing could hardly have been worse, but you don't always have control of everything. I assume you have the details. Though possibly not, now that I think of it. Where I'm going, there's a chance we'll just disappear and never be heard from again.''

Yes, I thought. But not in the way you expect. "Where are you going?"

"Hunting. Into the Veiled Lady." He shook his head; and I could see he was full of regret. "It is a son of a bitch, Alex, the way things turn out sometimes. I hope that, whatever happened, it happened on the way back. I would not want to die before I find out about this."

The plea—for that is what it was—hung there. "You never made it to Saraglia Station," I said.

"Oh." His brow furrowed, and his frame seemed to collapse. He turned away from me, circled a coffee table that had been in the house for years, and eased himself stiffly into a chair opposite mine. "Pity."

He'd slowed down: his movements were more deliberate now, and the quixotic face had sobered. It was difficult to judge whether he was showing the effects of age, or simply responding to the news of his death. In any case, there was a grayness about the conversation, a quivery uncertainty, and a sense of things undone.

"You look good," I said, emptily. It was, under the circumstances, an eerie remark. He seemed not to notice.

"I'm sorry we didn't get a chance to talk together at least one more time. This is a poor substitute."

"Yes."

"I wish things had been better between us."

There was no easy way to respond to that. He'd been the only parent I'd known, and we had suffered the usual strains. But there had been more: Gabe was an idealist. "You made it very difficult," he continued. What he meant was that I'd made a comfortable living selling rare artifacts to private collectors. An activity he considered immoral.

"I broke no law," I said. Arguing was pointless: nothing I could say would be carried back to the sender. Gabe was beyond this sort of communication now. The illusion was all that remained.

"You'd have broken a few *here*. No enlightened society allows the sort of thing you do to go unregulated." He took a deep breath, and exhaled slowly. "Let it go. I paid a higher price for my principles than I would have wished, Alex. It's been a long time."

The figure before me was nothing more than software, knew only what my uncle had known at the moment of storage. It had no grasp of the principles of which it spoke, no real sense of the regret that I felt. But it allowed him to do something that I would have liked very much to have done: "I'm sorry," he said. "If I had it to do over, I would have let it go."

"But you would still have disapproved."

"Of course."

"Good."

He smiled, and repeated my comment with satisfaction. "There's hope for you yet, Alex." He pushed himself to his feet, opened a liquor cabinet, and extracted a bottle and two glasses. "Mindinmist," he said. "Your favorite."

It was good to be home.

I violated a personal rule with *that* sponder: I gave in to the images and allowed myself to accept the illusion as real. And I realized how much I'd missed the paneled, book-lined study at the back of the house. It had always been one of my two favorite rooms. (The other was in the attic, a magic place from which I'd watched the forest many times for the approach of dragons or enemy soldiers.) It smelled of pine and fresh cloth drapes and casselate book covers and scorched wood. It was filled with exotic photos: an abandoned vine-strangled temple guarded by an obscene idol that seemed to be mostly belly and teeth, a broken column in an otherwise empty desert, a small group gathered before a step pyramid under a pair of moons. A reproduction of Marcross's portrait of the immortal warship *Corsarius* hung on one wall, with plyseal sketches of men and women with whom Gabe had worked. (Plyseal had been one of his hobbies. There was one of me, at about four years old, in my old bedroom.)

And there were always artifacts: toys, computers, lamps, statuary that Gabe had recovered from various field sites. Even now, I could see a cylindrical, studded object in a glass display.

I raised my drink to him. He lifted his own, and our eyes locked briefly. I could almost believe that Gabe and I were making it right, at long last. The liquor was warm, very smooth, and it tasted of other days.

"There's something you'll have to do," he said.

He was standing before VanDyne's depiction of the ruins at Point Edward. You know the one: blackened wreckage beneath red-gold rings and a cluster of silver moons. The way they found it after the attack.

The chair was comfortable. Supernaturally so, in fact, just as the Mindinmist was supremely good. You get that kind of effect with objects that don't really exist. Some people say perfection spoils the illusion, and that sponders would work better if the physical sensations were muted, or flawed. Like the real thing.

"What's that?" I asked, thinking he was going to ask me to administer the estate in some meaningful way. See that the money went to a good cause. Not spend it all on skimmers and women.

He poked at the fire. It popped, and a log fell heavily off the grate. A cloud of sparks swirled and died. I could feel the heat on my face. "How did it happen? Heart attack? Problem with the leased ship? Hell, was I run down by a taxi on my way to the spaceport?"

I couldn't suppress a smile at the notion that the simulacrum was curious. "Gabe," I said, "the flight never came out of the jump."

"Isn't that a son of a bitch?" A chuckle forced its way out, and then he dissolved in gales of laughter. "I died on the goddam *commercial* leg." I started to laugh too. The Mindinmist was warm in my stomach, and I refilled our glasses.

"Ridiculous," he said.

"Safest form of travel per passenger-kilometer," I observed.

"Well, I'm damned if I'll make *that* mistake again." But the laughter died into a long silence. "Still, I'd have liked to see it."

I expected him to say more. When he didn't, I prompted him. "See what? What were you looking for?"

He waved the question away. "To be honest with you, I don't feel very comfortable doing this. I mean, it seems only decent that people shouldn't hang around after they've—" he shook one hand idly, looking for the expression he wanted, "—gone to a happier world." He sounded uncertain. Lost. "But I had to guard against this possibility." His eyes fastened on mine and grew very round. "Do you remember Hugh Scott?"

I considered it. "No," I said at last.

"No reason why you should, I suppose. How about Terra Nuela? Do you remember *that*?"

Sure. Terra Nuela was the first habitation built outside the solar system. It was constructed on a hot, rocky world circling Beta Centauri, and it was, of course, little more now than a hole in the desert. It was the first excavation Gabe had taken me to. "Yes," I said. "Hottest place I've ever seen."

"Scott was along on that trip. I thought you might have remembered him. He used to take you for walks after sundown."

"Okay," I said, calling up a vague recollection of a big,

bearded, dark-skinned man. Of course, I was at an age when everyone was big.

"If you had known Scott a few years ago, known him as I did, you wouldn't recognize him now."

"Health?" I asked. "Marital problems?"

"No. Nothing like that. He came back from a mission with Survey about three years ago. He came back somber, preoccupied, disoriented. Not at all like his old self. In fact, I suspect a psychiatrist would conclude that he's undergone a fundamental personality change. You would not have found him a desirable companion."

"And?"

"He was on board the *Tenandrome*, one of the big new survey ships. They saw something very strange in the Veiled Lady."

"What?"

"He wouldn't tell me, Alex. Wouldn't admit to anything."

"Then you're guessing—?"

"I know what they saw. Or at least I think I do. I was on my way out there when—" He stopped, unable to continue, and waved one hand at the ceiling.

"What do you think they saw?"

"I'm not sure how much I can tell you," he said. "There's always a security problem about these transmissions. And you won't want this to get around."

"Why not?" I asked.

"Take my word for it." He was back in his chair again, kneading his forehead in the way that he did when he was trying to count something out. "You'll have to come home. I'm sorry about that, but it can't be helped. Jacob has everything you'll need. It's in the 'Leisha Tanner' file. The lawyers will provide the access code." He looked suddenly very tired. But he stayed on his feet. "Missing this one is a son of a bitch, Alex. I envy you."

"Gabe, I have a business here. I can't just pick up and leave."

"I understand. It would have been easier for me, I suppose, to go elsewhere for help. I have several colleagues who would trade their souls for this. But I wanted to compensate *us* for lost years. My gift and your reward, Alex. Do as I ask: you'll never regret it. At least, I don't think you will."

"You can't tell me anything now?"

"No more than I have. It's all waiting for you at home."

"Who's Leisha Tanner?"

He disregarded the question. "You'll want to keep this to yourself. At least until you know what it's about. Alex, I should also tell you that time is of the essence. The offer will go elsewhere unless you present yourself at the offices of Brimbury and Conn within thirty standard days. I'm sorry about that, but I can't risk having this get away from us."

"Gabe, you are still a son of a bitch." I said it lightly and he smiled.

"I'll tell you this much." He looked smug. "I've got the truth about Talino."

"Who the hell is Talino?"

He pursed his lips. "*Ludik* Talino."

"Oh," I said. "The traitor."

He nodded. "Yes." He spoke the word dreamily. "Christopher Sim's navigator. Perhaps one of the most unfortunate men who ever lived."

"*Infamous* would be a better word."

"Yes. Good. He still arouses passions after two centuries." He was moving swiftly around the room now, a fountain of energy. "Did you know that he always claimed to be innocent?"

I shrugged. "All that's dead a long time, Gabe. I can understand your interest, but I can't imagine why there'd be a security risk with anything concerning Ludik Talino. Would you want to explain a bit further?"

"I'd rather not pursue the issue, Alex. You have no idea how much is at stake. Come as quickly as you can."

"Okay. I'll do it." I was finding it increasingly hard to speak. I really didn't give a damn about the collection of clay pots or whatever it was he thought he had hold of this time. In a sense, these were our last moments together, and that was all I could think about. "I'll inform the lawyers I'm on my way. But I have a few things to clear up here. Will they hold me to the thirty days? I mean, whatever you've got has kept for two centuries. Surely a few more months won't make any difference."

"No." He leaned toward me, bracing his chin on one fist. There was a hint of amusement in his eyes. "Perhaps not. I don't suppose a little delay would matter much now. But you'll have to ask Brimbury and Conn. I left them some discretion to act. I suppose it will come down to whether they feel you're reliable." He winked. "After you've read the file, you may conclude that I have proceeded improperly. I have no sure way of judging your reaction.

I must admit that I'm of several minds about my own conduct in this matter. But I leave everything to you, with confidence. I'm sorry I won't be with you at the end."

"You'll be there," I said.

He laughed. "Sentimental nonsense, Alex. I'm gone already, past caring about any of this, really. But if you want to do something for me: when everything's over, send an appropriate souvenir to the Center for Accadian Studies." He beamed with pleasure at the prospect. "Those bastards have always called me an amateur."

He held his hands out, palms wide. "I guess that's all, Alex. I love you. And I'm glad you were along for the ride."

We embraced. "Thanks, Gabe."

"It's okay. I want this one in the family. One way or another." I was standing, but he still looked down into my eyes. "Handle this right, and they'll be naming universities for us."

"I never knew you cared about stuff like that."

His lips curled in amusement. "I'm dead now, Alex. I have to take the long view."

II.

---

talinian (tal iń ē ən), adj. 1. pertaining to withdrawal under pressure. 2. contemptibly timid. 3. characteristic of, or suggesting, a coward. (See *cowardly.)*
—*SYN*. craven, fainthearted, pusillanimous, fearful, unreliable, weak-kneed.

Ludik Talino: what a wealth of contempt and pity that name generated over two centuries. It had always lacked the power of a Judas or an Arnold, who had wantonly betrayed their trusts, who had actively engaged to ruin the men to whom they owed their loyalty. Talino was never a traitor in that sense. The universal view was that his courage rather than his moral sense had faltered. No one ever believed he would have sold his captain over to his enemies. But the act of which he stood accused, and for which his name became a synonym, was in its way even more despicable: at the critical moment he had fled.

I entered *Talino* into the library, and spent the evening reading accounts of the old story.

Contemporary records were fragmentary. None of the original Dellacondan ships were known to have survived the Resistance, whole data networks were wiped out, and few witnesses from the early years were still alive at the end.

Little is known about the man himself. He might have been a Dellacondan, but there's evidence he was born in the City on the Crag, and at least one major historian claims he grew up on Rimway. What *is* known is that he was already a certified technician on one of Dellaconda's dozen frigates at the outbreak of

17

the war. He served almost two years as a weapons specialist and navigator on the *Proctor* before assuming the latter post on board Sim's celebrated *Corsarius*.

Apparently, he fought with distinction. There's a tradition that he was commended by Sim personally after Grand Salinas, though the records have been lost and confirmation has never been possible. In any case, he remained on that fabled vessel through the great days of the Resistance, when the *Corsarius* spearheaded the allied band of sixty-odd frigates and destroyers holding off the massive fleets of the Ashiyyur. Eventually, of course, Rimway and Toxicon and the other inner systems recognized the common danger, buried their old quarrels, and joined the war. But by then, Christopher Sim and the *Corsarius* were gone.

After Grand Salinas, when the Dellacondans and their allies were reduced to a desperate few and had given up hope, Sim withdrew the remnants of his fleet to Abonai for refitting and rearming. But the Ashiyyur, seizing the opportunity to destroy their old enemy, pressed him hard; and the Dellacondans prepared for an engagement that they were certain would be their last.

And then, on the eve of battle, something happened which provoked historical debate for two centuries.

Most accounts maintained that Talino and the other six crewmen of the *Corsarius*, discouraged, and seeing no escape, tried to persuade their captain to give up the suicidal struggle and to make terms with their relentless enemy; that, when he refused to do so, they abandoned him. They are said to have left a message damning him and the war, and fled to the surface of Abonai.

Others have it that Sim, himself convinced of the futility of further resistance, called his crew together and released them from their obligations. I've always felt less comfortable with this version than the others. I suppose it's easy to sit in a warm room and condemn actions taken under extreme duress; but somehow the notion that Talino and his comrades would have taken advantage of his generosity, and left their captain at such a moment, seemed even more contemptible than the honest cowardice of slinking off into the dark.

However it may have occurred, this was the event that triggered a legend: Sim's descent to Abonai; the trek through the bars and dives of that dismal place; the appeal for help to deserters, derelicts, and convicts who had escaped, or been driven, to that frontier world; and ultimately, of course, his immortal sally with them against an overwhelming enemy.

It was a time fashioned for greatness. Every child in the Confederacy knew the story of the seven nameless men and women from that grim world who agreed to join him, and who thereby rode into history. And of how they died with Sim a few hours later, during the final encounter with the Ashiyyur, wedding themselves irrevocably to his legend. Most researchers agreed that they must have had naval backgrounds, but some maintained that a few technicians would have done as well. However that might have been, they were a popular subject for doctoral theses, novels, the fine arts, and serious drama.

There was little of a factual nature concerning Talino. Birth and death. Engineering degree, Schenk University, Toxicon. Abandoned his captain. No charges filed, because the navy in which he served ceased to exist shortly after the offense.

I called up Barcroft's impressionistic tragedy, *Talinos*. (He adds the final *s* to lend the name an aristocratic aura, and for dramatic effect.) I'd intended to scroll through, but I got hooked in the first act. That surprised me, because I'm not usually strong on classical theater.

Talino was played as a driven, melancholy figure by a rangy, bearded simulat of considerable physical presence. He is consumed with rage against the Ashiyyur, and against the powerful worlds that blindly stand by while the small force of allies are gradually reduced to impotence. His loyalty to Christopher Sim; and his passion for Inaissa, the young bride whose marriage has never known peace, fuel the action. The drama is set on the eve of the climactic engagement off Rigel.

Sim has given up hope of personal survival, but intends to save his crew. He will take *Corsarius* out alone, deliver what blows he can, and accept a death that may rally the human worlds. "If not," he tells Talino, "if still they do not come, then it will be up to you to salvage what you can. Disengage. Retreat to the Veiled Lady. In time, Earth and Rimway will be forced to fight. Then, perhaps, you can return and teach the damned fools how to beat the mutes . . ."

The gray, shadowy sets breathe gloom and despair. There is much of the medieval fortress about the orbiting station at Abonai: its ponderous weapons, the long curving walkways, the occasional guard, the hushed tones in which passersby converse, the heavy air. Over all, one senses transience and tragedy. The course of events has passed beyond the control of any human agency.

But Talino refuses his captain's orders. "Send someone else to rally the survivors," he argues. "My place is with you."

Sim, in a moment of weakness, is grateful. He hesitates. Talino presses the point: "Do not humiliate me in this way." And Sim reluctantly accedes. They will make the final assault together.

But Talino must break the news to Inaissa. She has been hoping for a general retreat, and she is outspoken about Sim's determination to kill himself, "and take you along." She does not ask her husband to break faith, knowing that, to do so, and succeed, would destroy any future for them.

Consequently, she goes to Sim, arguing that his death would so demoralize the Dellacondans that the cause would be lost. When that effort fails, she asks to man one of the weapon's consoles, to be with her husband at the end.

Sim is so moved by her appeal that he orders Talino off the ship. When the navigator objects, he is confined to the orbiting station, from which he is able to watch the technicians completing repairs on *Corsarius*, preparing her for battle. And he observes also the arrival of the crew, summoned at this unusual hour by their commander. He tries to link into the shipboard systems to follow the conversations there, but someone has cut the external feed. And a few minutes after boarding, they leave, heads lowered, faces hard.

Moments later, they come to release him. Sim has freed the crew from their obligations. Talino tries to persuade them to return to their ship, but they know what the next day will bring. "If by staying," says one, "we could save him, then we would stay. But there is no sense to it: he is determined to die."

Free now, Talino goes to Inaissa, intending to take his farewell and return to his captain's side. When she refuses to leave without him, he orders her put forcibly groundside. But his own resolve fails shortly thereafter, and he sends word to Sim that, "I accept my captain's generous offer; I can do no other, God help me. . . ."

But Inaissa, determined to accompany her husband, conceals herself in a cloak and succeeds in procuring a place among the Seven. Thus, Talino loses both his honor and his wife.

The notion that Inaissa was one of the volunteers was a part of the myth I'd not heard before. There are two beam sculptures by period artists showing her onboard the *Corsarius*. One places her at a console with Sim visible at her left; and the other depicts the moment of recognition between her and the captain.

There were a hundred variations of the story, and countless shadings of Talino's character and motivation. Sometimes he is perceived as a man loaded down with gambling debts, who accepted money from mute agents; sometimes he is disgruntled at not having received his own command; sometimes he is Sim's rival for an illicit love, deliberately arranging his commander's death.

Where in all the enormous body of myth and literature was the truth? What had Gabe meant?

Other aspects of the event also received considerable attention. Arven Kimonides' novel *Marvill* recounts the experience of a young man who is present at the gathering of the Seven, but who stands aside and lives guilt-ridden thereafter. Tradition holds that Mikal Killian, the great constitutional arbiter, who would have been about 18 at the time of the Rigel Action, tried to volunteer, and was refused. Wightbury placed his famous cynic Ed Barbar on the scene. (Ed not only did *not* volunteer, but held aside a willing young woman who was, he felt, destined for better things.) At least a dozen other novels and dramas which enjoyed some reputation in their times have featured characters who either witnessed Sim's appeal, or who found themselves among the Seven.

There are also numerous lightcuts, photo constructs, and at least one major symphony. Three of the unknown heroes stand at the great captain's side in Sanrigal's masterpiece, *Sim at the Hellgate*. Talino's wife is portrayed among the drug addicts and derelicts in Tchigorin's *Inaissa*. And in Mommsen's *Finale*, a ragged man helps Sim battle the controls of the stricken *Corsarius*, while a wounded crewman lies prostrate on the deck, and a woman who must have earned her living in the streets of Abonai squeezes the triggers in the weapons cradle.

I suspected that Sim would have cleaned up his new crew, and that the end, when it came, would have been sudden and total. But what the hell: it was good art, if unlikely history.

The deserters dropped out of sight, to become objects of scorn. Talino lived almost a half century after his captain's death. It was said of him that his conscience gave him no rest, and that he was driven from world to world by an outraged public. He died on Rimway, apparently very close to madness.

I could find no record of Inaissa in the histories. Barcroft insists that she existed, but cites no source. (He claims to have spoken with Talino, but that assertion also stands unsupported.) Talino himself is not known to have mentioned her.

Historians entertained themselves for two centuries trying to put names to the volunteers, and even arguing over whether there were not really six, or eight, who took the final ride. Over the years, however, the Seven transcended their status as military heroes. They came eventually to symbolize the noblest sentiments of the Confederacy: the mutual commitment between government and its most desperate citizens.

I made arrangements to go home.

Fortunately, my connections with the world on which I'd been living for the preceding three years were tenuous. I had little trouble dissolving my business interests, after which I made arrangements to sell off most of my property, and packed the rest. I said good-bye to the couple of people who mattered to me (promising, as we always do, to exchange visits). That was a joke, considering how far Rambuckle was from Rimway, and how much I hated starships.

On the day that I was to leave, a second communication arrived from Brimbury & Conn. This one was hardcopy:

We regret to inform you there has been a break-in at Gabriel's home. Thieves took some electronic equipment, silverware, a few other items. Nothing of substantial value. They missed the artifacts. We have initiated steps to see there is no recurrence.

That seemed a suspicious coincidence. I wondered about the security of the Tanner file, and considered asking the lawyers about it before committing myself to travel to Rimway. But owing to the distances involved, I couldn't hope for an answer inside twenty days. So I dismissed the notion as overactive imagination, and headed home.

As I mentioned, I abhor starflight, and I avoided it when I could. A lot of people get nauseated during the transitions between Armstrong and linear space, but it seems to hit me especially hard. I also have trouble adjusting to changes in gravity, time, and climate.

Moreover, there was the sheer uncertainty and inconvenience of it all. In those days, you never knew when you'd arrive at a destination. Vessels traveling through Armstrong space could not determine their position with regard to the outside world. That made navigation a trifle uncertain. Everything was done on dead reckoning, which is to say that the computers measured onboard elapsed time, tried to compensate for the uncertainties of entry, and everyone hoped for the best. Occasionally, vectors got displaced and vessels materialized a thousand light years from their destinations.

The most unnerving possibility, though, was that of re-entering linear space inside a physical object. If the odds were heavily against such an occurrence, it was nevertheless something I always thought of when a vessel was preparing to make its return jump. You never really knew where you were going to come out.

There is, in fact, evidence that this is what happened to the *Hampton* almost a century ago. The *Hampton* was a small freighter which, like *Capella*, disappeared in nonlinear. She was carrying a cargo of manufactured goods to a mining colony in the Marmichon System. At about the time the vessel was to have made the jump from hyper, an outer planet—the gas giant Marmichon VI—blew up. No one has ever advanced an explanation of how a world can explode without help. Speculation at the time held that the vessel materialized inside the iron core, and that the antimatter fuel in the Armstrong drive unit initiated the explosion.

Armstrong generators were equipped with deflector units, which created a field strong enough to clear a few atoms and make room for the ship's transition into linear. Anything bigger wandering into the area at that critical phase put the vessel at risk. There was little real danger, of course. Ships were required to materialize well outside star systems. That bought relative safety, but left the traveler with a long ride to his destination. Usually, you could expect that the voyage from the Armstrong emergence point to the place you wanted to go would take roughly twice as long as the actual travel time between stars. I'd never gone anywhere that I could guess within five days when I would be arriving.

My flight to Rimway was no exception. I got deathly ill making the jump both ways. The carriers pass out drugs to help people through all that, but none of it's ever worked for me. I've learned to rely on alcohol.

All the same, it was good to see Rimway again. We approached from the dark side, so I could see the blazing splinters of light that marked the cities. The sun illuminated a gauzy arc of atmosphere along the rim. Through the opposite window, the moon was pale brown and turbulent. Storm-laden.

We slipped into orbit, crossed the terminator into daylight, and, a few hours later, rode down sun-washed skies toward Andiquar, the planetary capital. It was an exhilarating approach. But all the same, I promised myself that my interstellar days were over. I was home, and I was by God going to stay there.

We ran into snow over the city. The sun was low in the west, and it cast a thousand hews against frosted towers, and the peaks to the east. The capital's extensive parks had all but vanished in the storm. In the Confederate Triangle, the monuments to the two great brothers were blue and timeless: Christopher Sim's Doric pyramid, its illuminated apex glowing steadily against the encroaching dark; and, across the White Pool, Tarien Sim's Omni, a ghostly globe, symbol of the statesman's dream of a united human family.

I checked in at a hotel, logged onto the net in case anyone wanted to reach me, and took a shower. It was early evening, but I was tired. Nevertheless I couldn't sleep. After an hour or so of staring at the ceiling, I wandered downstairs, had a sandwich, and contacted Brimbury & Conn. "I'm in town," I said.

"Welcome home, Mr. Benedict," said their AI. "Is there any way we can be of assistance?"

"I need a skimmer."

"On the roof of your hotel, sir. I am clearing it for you now. Will you be communicating with us tomorrow?"

"Yes," I said. "Probably late morning. And thanks."

I went up and collected my aircraft, punched in the location code of Gabe's house, and five minutes later I was lifting out over the city, headed west.

The malls and avenues were crowded with sightseers, shielded from the falling snow by gantner light. Tennis courts were filled, and kids paddled in pools. Andiquar has always been lovely at night, its gardens, towers, and courtyards softly illuminated, the winding Narakobo silent and deep.

While I floated over that pacific scene, the newsnet reported a mute attack on a communications research ship which had wandered too close to the Perimeter. Five or six dead. No one was sure yet.

I flew out over the western fringes of Andiquar. Snow was falling heavily now, and I tilted the back of the seat and settled into the warmth of the cockpit. The landscape unrolled a few hundred meters below, leaving its trace on the thermals: the suburbs broke up into small towns, hills rose, forests appeared. Occasionally a road wandered through the display and, about twenty minutes out, I crossed the Melony, which had more or less marked the limits of human habitation when I was a boy.

You can see the Melony from the attic bedroom at Gabriel's house. When I first went to live there, it twisted through mysterious, untamed country. A refuge for ghosts, robbers, and dragons.

The amber warning lamp signaled arrival. I banked and dropped lower. The dark forest was harmless now, curbed by athletic fields and pools and curving walkways. I'd watched the retreat of the wilderness over the years, counted the parks and homes and hardware stores. And on that snowy night, I flew above it and knew that Gabe was gone, and that much of what he loved was also gone.

I switched to manual and drifted in over the treetops, watching the house itself materialize out of the storm. There was already a skimmer on the pad (Gabe's, I assumed), so I set down on the front lawn.

Home.

It was probably the only real home I'd known, and I was saddened to see it standing stark and empty against the pale, sagging sky. According to tradition, Jorge Shale and his crew had crashed nearby. Only an historian can tell you now who first set foot on Rimway, but everybody on the planet knows who died in the attempt. Finding the wreckage had been the first major project of my life. But, if it existed out there at all, it had eluded me.

The house had once been a country inn, catering to hunters and travelers. Most of the woodland had been replaced by large glass homes and square lawns. Gabe had done what he could to hold onto the wilderness area. It had been a losing fight, as struggles against progress always are. During my last years with him, he'd grown increasingly irascible with the unfortunates who moved into the neighborhood. And I doubt that many among his neighbors were sorry to see him go.

The attic bedroom was at the top of the house, on the fourth floor. The louvers on its twin windows were shut. A pair of idalia trees reached toward them: the branches of one twisted into a king's seat which I'd loved to climb, thereby scaring the blazes out of Gabe. Or so at least he'd allowed me to think.

I opened the cockpit and stepped down from the skimmer. Snow continued to whisper out of the sky. Somewhere, out of sight, children were playing. Excited shrieks echoed from an illuminated avenue a few houses over, and I could hear the smooth hiss of runners across white lawns and streets.

A sodium postlight beneath an oak threw a soft glow over the skimmer, and against the melancholy front windows. A familiar voice said, "Hello, Alex. Welcome home."

The lamp at the front door blinked on.

"Hello, Jacob," I said. Jacob wasn't really an AI. He was a sophisticated data response network, whose chief responsibility, at least in the old days, had been to maintain whatever conversational level Gabe felt up to, on whatever subject Gabe wished, at any given time. That would have been cruel and unusual treatment for a real AI. But it was sometimes hard to keep Jacob's true nature in mind.

"It's good to see you again," he said. "I'm sorry about Gabe."

The snow was ankle deep. I hadn't dressed for it, and the stuff was already into my shoes. "Yes. I am too." The front door opened, and the living room filled with light. Somewhere in back, music stopped. *Stopped.* That was the sort of thing that gave life to Jacob. "It was unexpected. I'll miss him."

Jacob was silent. I stepped inside, past a scowling stone demon that had been in the house long before I came to it, removed my jacket, and went into the den, the same room from which Gabe had recorded his final message. There was a sharp crack, as of a branch snapping, and flames appeared in the fireplace. It had been a long time. Rambuckle had been a cylinder world, and there had never been wood for burning. Nor any need to. (How long had it been since I'd seen snow? Or experienced inclement weather?)

I was back, and it felt suddenly as though I'd never been away.

"Alex?" There was something almost plaintive in his tone.

"Yes, Jacob. What is it?"

"There is something you need to know." In the back of the house, a clock ticked.

"Yes?"

"I don't remember you."

I paused in the middle of lowering myself into the padded armchair I'd occupied in the sponder. "What do you mean?"

"The lawyers informed you there was a robbery?"

"Yes, they told me."

"Apparently the thief tried to copy my core unit. The basal memory. It must have been a possibility that concerned Gabriel. The system was programmed, in such an eventuality, to do a complete wipe. I have no recollection of anything prior to being reactivated by the authorities."

"Then how——"

"Brimbury and Conn programmed me to recognize you. What I'm trying to tell you is that I know *about* us, but I have no direct recollection."

"Isn't that the same thing?"

"It leaves a few holes." I thought he was going to say something more, but he didn't.

Jacob had been around for twenty years. He'd been there when I was a kid. We'd played chess, and refought the major campaigns of half a dozen wars, and talked about the future while rain had splattered down the big windows. We'd planned to sail together around the world, and later, when my ambitions grew, we'd talked of the stars.

"How about Gabe? You remember *him*, right?"

"I know I would have liked him. His house indicates that he had many interests, and I feel safe in concluding he was worth knowing. I console myself that I *did* know him. But, no: I don't remember him."

I sat for some minutes, listening to the fire, and the sound of the snow at the windows. Jacob was not alive. The only feelings involved here were my own. "How about the data files? I understand something was taken from them."

"I checked the index. It's rather strange, really. They took a data crystal. But it could not have been of any use to the thief. He would need to know the security code to get access to it."

"The Tanner file," I said, with sudden certainty.

"Yes. How did you know?"

"I guessed."

"It seems very odd to steal something one cannot use."

"The rest of it, the silverware, and whatever else they took, was a blind," I said. "They knew precisely what they were after. How many of them were there? Did you recognize anyone?"

"They knocked out the power before they came in, Alex. I wasn't functioning."

"How did they do that?" I asked.

"It was easy. They simply broke a window, got into the utility area, and cut some cables. I do not have visuals down there."

"Damn. Wasn't there some sort of burglar alarm? Something to prevent this?"

"Oh, yes. But do you know how long it's been since there was a felony in this area?"

"No," I said.

"Decades. Literally decades. The police assumed it was only a malfunction. They were slow to respond. Even had they been more prompt, a single thief, if he was familiar with the premises and knew precisely what he was after, could have accomplished it all inside three minutes."

"Jacob, what was Gabe working on when he died?"

"I don't know whether I ever had that information, Alex. Certainly I don't now."

"How good is the security on the Tanner file? Are you sure the thief can't get at it?"

"In maybe twenty years. It requires your voice, using a security code that is in the possession of Brimbury and Conn."

"It'll be easy for the thief to get a recording of my voice to duplicate. We'd better notify the lawyers to take precautions with the code."

"That's already been done, Alex."

"Maybe the lawyers are involved."

"*They* do not have access to the code. They can only turn it over to you."

"What kind was it?"

"A sequence of digits, which have to be spoken by you, or a reasonable facsimile thereof, during a time period no shorter than a full minute. That prevents a high-speed computer attack. Any attempt to circumvent the precautions results in immediate destruction of the file."

"How many digits?"

"The recommended standard is fourteen. I don't know how many Gabe used."

I sat quietly, watching the fire. The street lamps were yellow blobs, and the wind shook the trees. Snow was piling up against the skimmer. "Jacob, who's Leisha Tanner?"

"Just a moment." The roomlights dimmed.

Outside somewhere, a metal door rattled shut.

A holo formed near the window, a woman in evening dress, her face angled away from me, as though her attention were fixed on the storm. In the uncertain light of the fireplace and the sodium postlamp, she was achingly lovely. She appeared to be lost in thought, her eyes reflecting, but not seeing, the snowscape.

"She's in her mid-thirties here. When this was taken, she was an instructor at Tielhard University on Earth. It's dated circa 1215, our time.''

Six years after the Resistance. ''My God,'' I said, ''I assumed she was someone I was going to be able to talk to.''

''Oh, no, Alex. She's been dead quite a long time. Over a century, in fact.''

''What's her connection with the project Gabe was working on?''

''Impossible to say.''

''Is there anyone else who might know?''

''No one that I know of.''

I poured myself a drink, a real one, of the Mindinmist. ''Tell me about Tanner. Who was she?''

''Scholar. Teacher. She's best known for her translations of the Ashiyyurean philosopher Tulisofala. They are still available, and some authorities consider them to be definitive. She's produced other works, but most are no longer in circulation. She was an instructor in Ashiyyurean philosophy and literature for forty standard years at several universities. Born on Khaja Luan, 1179. Married. Possibly one child.''

''That it?''

''She was a star pilot, certified for small craft. A peace activist during the war. The records also show that she served as an intelligence officer and a diplomat for the Dellacondans.''

''A peace activist and an intelligence officer.''

''That is what the records say. I don't understand it either.''

Jacob rotated the image. Her eyes brushed past mine. The jawline had a tilt that almost implied arrogance. Her lips were slightly parted, revealing even white teeth (but no smile); and a forehead possibly a shade too broad concealed by thick auburn hair.

''During the war, was she on the *Corsarius?*''

Pause. ''There's not much information in the general files, Alex. But I don't think so. She seems to have been attached to *Mercuriel*, the Dellacondan flagship.''

''I thought *Corsarius* was the flagship?''

''No. *Corsarius* was only a frigate. Sim used it to lead his units into combat, but it wasn't really adequate for staffing and planning functions. The Dellacondans used two different vessels for that purpose. The *Mercuriel* was donated to them by rebels on Toxicon midway through the war. It was especially adapted for command and control, and it was named for a Toxi volunteer who died in the Slot.''

"Do you know any more about her?''

"I believe I can give you rank, date of discharge, and so on.''

"That it?''

"There may be something else of interest.''

"What's that?''

"Just a moment. You understand that I'm scanning all this myself while we're talking?''

"Okay.''

"Yes. Well, you should also be aware that she's an obscure figure, and there's not much on her.''

"Okay. What are you leading up to?''

"She apparently returned from the war in a deep state of depression.''

"Nothing unusual about that.''

"No. I would react that way myself. But she did not improve for a long time. Years, in fact. There is also an indication that she visited Maurina Sim about 1208, the year after Christopher Sim died at Rigel. No record that I can find on what they talked about. Now the odd thing is that Tanner tended to drop from sight for long periods of time. On one occasion, for almost two years. No one knows why.

"This went on until about 1217, after which there are no more reports of unusual behavior. Which of course is not to say there was none.''

I gave up for the night. I had a snack, and picked out a room on the second floor. Gabe's bedroom was on the same floor, at the front of the building. I went in there, perhaps out of curiosity, but ostensibly because I was looking for comfortable pillows.

There were photos everywhere: mostly from the excavations, but there were also a couple of me as a child, and one of a woman he had once, apparently, loved. Her name was Ria, and she had died in an accident twenty years before I'd come to live with him. I'd forgotten about her during my long years away, but she still held her honored place on a table between two exquisite vases that were probably middle-European. I took a moment to study the image as I had not done since I was a child, and had never done with mature eyes. She was almost boyish in aspect: her frame was slim, her

brown hair was cut short, and she sat with her hands hugging her
knees to her breast in a pose that implied uninhibited exuberance.
But her glance suggested deeper waters, and caused me to linger a
long time. To my knowledge, Gabe had never been emotionally
involved with another woman.

There was a book on the side table: a volume of poetry by
Walford Candles. The title was *Rumors of Earth*, and though I'd
never heard of it, I knew Candles's reputation. He was one of the
people that no one really reads, but that you were supposed to if
you were going to call yourself educated.

The book aroused my curiosity though, for several reasons: Gabe
had never shown much inclination toward poetry; Candles had been
a contemporary of Christopher Sim and Leisha Tanner; and, when I
picked it up, the book fell open to a poem titled "Leisha"!

> *Lost pilot,*
> *She rides her solitary orbit*
> *Far from Rigel,*
> *Seeking by night*
> *The starry wheel.*
> *Adrift in ancient seas,*
> *It marks the long year round,*
> *Nine on the rim,*
> *Two at the hub.*
> *And she,*
> *Wandering,*
> *Knows neither port,*
> *Nor rest,*
> *nor me.*

Footnotes dated it 1213, two years before Candles's death, and
four years after the war's end. There was some discussion of style,
and the editors commented that the subject was "believed to be
Leisha Tanner, who alarmed her friends by periodically dropping
out of sight between 1208 and 1216. No explanation was ever
advanced."

III.

They sent a single ship across the rooftops of the world. And when they saw that the Ilyandans had fled, a terrible anger came over them. And they burned everything: the empty houses and the deserted parks and the silent lakes. They burned it all.

> —Akron Garrity,
> *Armageddon*

I SPENT THE night at the house, enjoyed a leisurely breakfast, and retired afterward to the big armchair in the study. Sunlight streamed through the windows, and Jacob announced that he was pleased to see me up and about so early. "Would you like to talk politics this morning?" he asked.

"Later." I was looking around for a headband.

"In the table drawer," offered Jacob. "Where are you going?"

"The offices of Brimbury and Conn." I tried the unit on, and it slid down over my ears.

"When you're ready," he said drily, "I have a channel."

The light shifted, and the study was gone, replaced by a modern crystalline conference room. There was a background of soft music, and I was able to look through one wall at Andiquar from a height that far exceeded the altitude of any structure in the city.

The woman from the transmission, tall, dark and now of oppressive appearance, materialized near the door. She smiled, approached with aggressive cordiality, and extended her hand.

"Mr. Benedict," she said. "I'm Capra Brimbury, the junior partner." That provided my first inclination that Gabe's estate was worth considerably more than I had imagined. I was beginning to feel it was going to be a pretty good day.

Her tone was hushed and confidential. An attitude one adopts with a person who is temporarily an equal. Her manner throughout the interview was one of studied enthusiasm, of welcoming a new member to an exclusive club. "We'll never be able to replace him," she observed. "I wish there were something I could say."

I thanked her, and she continued: "We will do everything we can to make the transition easier for you. I believe we can get a very good price on the estate. Assuming, of course, that you wish to sell."

Sell the house? "I hadn't considered it," I said.

"It would bring quite a lot of money, Alex. Whatever you choose to do, let us know, and we will be happy to handle it for you."

"Thank you."

"We have not yet been able to set a precise value to the estate. There are, you understand, a number of intangibles, artwork, antiques, artifacts and whatnot, which complicate the equation. Not to mention fairly extensive commodity holdings, whose worth fluctuates from hour to hour. I assume you will wish to retain your uncle's investment broker?"

"Yes," I said. "Of course."

"Good." She made a note, as though the decision were a matter of little consequence.

"What about the burglary?" I asked. "Have we learned anything?"

"No, Alex." Her voice trailed off. "Strange thing that was. I mean, you don't really expect that sort of behavior, people breaking into someone else's home. They actually used a torch to cut a hole in the back door. We were outraged."

"I have no doubt."

"So were the police. But they are looking into it."

"What exactly was stolen?" I asked.

"Difficult to say. If your uncle kept an inventory, it was lost when the central memory banks were erased. We know they took a holo projector and some silverware. They may also have got some rare books. We've had a few of his friends look at the property and try to make a determination. And maybe jewelry. There's simply no way to check his jewelry."

"I doubt if he had much," I said. "But there are some extremely valuable artifacts in there."

"Yes, we know. We compared them with the insurance listings. They are all accounted for."

She steered the conversation back to financial matters, and in the end I complied with her wishes pretty much down the line. When I asked for the security code, she produced a lockbox, of the sort that destroys the lock when it is opened. "It's voice-operated," she said. "But you need to tell it your birthday."

I did, lifted the lid, and extracted an envelope. It was signed by Gabe across the flap. Inside, I found the security code. It was thirty-one digits long.

He was taking no chances.

"I leave everything to you, with confidence."

It was a hell of a way to treat a worthless nephew.

Gabe had been disappointed in me. He'd never said anything. But his early satisfaction at my interest in antiquities had given way to reluctant tolerance when I failed to pursue a career in field work. He'd shown up at the graduations, had dutifully encouraged me, and had been openly enthusiastic about my academic "achievements." But beneath all that, I knew what he thought: the child who'd camped with him by the shattered walls of half a hundred civilizations was, in the end, more at home in a commodities exchange. Worse yet, the commodities were relics of a past which, he argued, grew constantly more vulnerable to our heat sensors and laser drills.

He had damned me for a philistine. Not in so many words, but I'd seen it in his eyes, heard it in the things he had *not* said, felt it in his gradual withdrawal. And yet, despite the existence of a small horde of professionals with whom he'd dug his way through countless sites, he'd turned to *me* with the *Tenandrome* discovery. I felt good about that. I even felt a vague sense of satisfaction that he'd played fast and loose with security, and allowed the Tanner file to be taken. Gabe was no less fallible than the rest of us.

I went next to the police station, and talked to an officer who said they were hard at work on the case, but that there was no progress to report as yet. She assured me they'd be in touch as soon as they had something. I thanked her, feeling no confidence that there would be any movement by the authorities, and was reaching for my headband, about to break the link, when a plump short man in uniform hurried through a double door, and waved in my direction. "Mr. Benedict?" He nodded, as though he understood I was in severe difficulty. "My name's Fenn Redfield. I'm an old friend of your uncle's." He took my hand, and pumped it vigorously. "Delighted to meet you. You look like Gabe, you know."

"So I've been told."

"Terrible loss, that was. Please come inside. Back to my office."

He turned away, and retreated through the double doors. I waited for the data exchange. The light shifted again, brightened. Heavy sunshine fell through grimy windows. I was seated in a small office, riddled with the smell of alcohol.

Redfield dropped into a stiff, uncomfortable-looking couch. His desk was surrounded by a battery of terminals, monitors, and consoles. The walls were covered with certificates, awards, and official seals of various sorts. There were some trophies, and numerous photographs: Redfield standing beside a sleek police skimmer; Redfield shaking hands with an important-looking woman; Redfield standing oil-streaked at a disaster site, with a child in his arms. That last one held center stage. The trophies were all grouped off to one side. And I decided I liked Fenn Redfield. "I'm sorry we haven't been able to do more," he said. "There really hasn't been much to work with."

"I understand," I said.

He waved me to a chair, and seated himself in *front* of the desk. "It's like a fortress," he chuckled. "Puts people off. I've been meaning to get rid of it, but it's been with me a long time. We *did* find the silver, by the way. Or at least some of it. We can't be certain, but I have a feeling we've got it all. Just this morning. It's not in the system yet, so the officer you spoke with had no way of knowing."

"Where was it?"

"In a creek about a kilometer from the house. It was in a plastic bag, pushed back out of sight in a place where the watercourse goes under a gravel footpath. Some kids found it."

"Strange," I said.

"I thought so too. It's not *extremely* valuable, but it would have been worthwhile holding on to. It suggests that the thief had no way to dispose of it, and no easy way to hold onto it."

"The silver was a blind," I said.

"Oh?" Redfield's eyes flashed interest. "What makes you say so?"

"You said you were a friend of Gabe's."

"Yes. I was. We used to go out together when our schedules permitted. And we played a lot of chess."

"Did he ever talk to you about his work?"

Redfield regarded me shrewdly. "Now and then. May I ask where we're headed, Mr. Benedict?"

"The thieves made off with a data file. Just took one, which happened to be a project that Gabe was working on when he died."

"And I take it you don't know much about it?"

"That's right. I was hoping you might have some information."

"I see." He pushed back in his chair, draped one arm over the desk, and drummed his fingers nervously against its surface. "You're saying that the silver, and whatever else they took, was intended to distract attention from the file."

"Yes."

He raised himself from the chair, circled the desk, and went to the window. "I can tell you that your uncle's been preoccupied during the last three months or so. His game went to hell, by the way."

"But you don't know why?"

"No. No, I don't. I didn't see much of him recently. He did tell me he was engaged in a project, but he never said what it was. We used to get together regularly once a week, but that stopped a few months back. After that, he just didn't seem to be around much."

"When was the last time you saw him?"

Redfield thought about it. "Maybe six weeks before we heard that he'd died. We got an evening of chess in. But I knew something was bothering him."

"He looked worried?"

"His game was off. I hammered him that night. Five or six times, which was unusual. But I could see his mind wasn't on what he was doing. He told me to enjoy myself while I could. He'd get me next time." Redfield stared at the floor. "That was it."

He produced a glass of lime-colored punch from somewhere

behind the desk. "Part of my regimen," he said. "Would you like some?"

"Sure."

"I wish I could help you, uh, Alex. But I just don't know what he was doing. I can tell you what he talked about all the time though."

"What was that?"

"The Resistance. Christopher Sim. He was a nut on the subject, the chronology of the naval actions, who was there, with what, how things turned out. I mean, I'm as interested as anybody, but he'd go on and on. It's tough in the middle of a game. You know what I mean?"

"Yes," I said.

"He wasn't always like that." He filled a second glass and handed it to me. "You play chess, Alex?"

"No. I learned the moves once, a long time ago. But I was never any good at the game."

Redfield's features softened, as though he had recognized the presence of a social disability.

At home, I caught up on the news. There were reports of another clash with the mutes. A ship had been damaged, and there'd been some casualties. A statement was expected from the government any time.

On Earth, they were conducting a referendum on the matter of secession. The voting was still a few days away, at last word, but apparently several political heavyweights had thrown their support behind the movement, and analysts now concluded that approval was likely.

I scanned the other items to see if there was much of interest, while Jacob commented that the real question was what the central government would do if Earth actually tried to secede. "They couldn't simply stand by and let them go," he observed, gloomily.

"It'll never happen," I said. "All that stuff is for home consumption. Local politicians looking tough by attacking the Director." I opened a beer. "Let's get to business."

"Okay."

"Query the main banks. What do they have on Leisha Tanner?"

"I've already looked, Alex. There's apparently relatively little on Rimway. There are three monographs, all dealing with her achievements in translating and commenting on Ashiyyurean literature. All three are available for your inspection. I should observe that I've reviewed them, and found nothing that would seem to be helpful, although there is much of general interest.

"You're aware that Ashiyyurean civilization is older than our own by almost sixty thousand years? In all that time, they have produced no thinker to surpass Tulisofala, or at least none who possesses her reputation. She appeared quite early in their development, and formulated many of their ethical and political attitudes. Tanner was inclined to assign her the place that Plato holds for us. She has, by the way, drawn some fascinating conclusions from this parallel—"

"Later, Jacob. What else is there?"

"Two other monographs are known, but they are no longer indexed. Consequently, they will be difficult to locate, if indeed they exist at all. One apparently concerns her ability as a translator. The other, however, is titled "Diplomatic Initiatives of the Resistance." "

"When was it published?"

"1330. Eighty-four years ago. It went off-line in 1342, and the last copy I can trace disappeared about 1381. The owner died; the estate went up for auction; and there's no record of general disposition. I'll keep trying.

"There may be other off-line materials available locally. Esoteric collector's items, obscure treatises, and so on, frequently never make the index. Unfortunately, our record-keeping procedures are not what they could be.

"Some journals and memorabilia have been maintained on Khaja Luan, where she was an instructor before and after the war. The Confederate Archives have her notebooks, and the Hrinwhar Naval Museum owns a fragmentary memoir. They're both located on Dellaconda, by the way. And the memoir, according to my sources, is *exceedingly* fragmentary."

"Named after the battle," I said.

"Hrinwhar? Yes. Wonderful tactic, that was. Sim was brilliant. Absolutely brilliant."

Next day, I visited half a dozen universities, the Quelling Institute, the Benjamin Maynard Historical Association, and the meeting rooms of the Sons of the Dellacondans. I was naturally interested in anything connecting Tanner with Talino or, more broadly, the Resistance. There wasn't much. I found a few references to her in private documents, old histories, and so on. I copied everything, and settled in for a long evening.

Little of the material seemed to have much to do with Tanner herself. She appears peripherally in discussions of Sim's staff, and of his intelligence gathering methods. I found only one document in which she could be said to be prominent: an obscure doctoral thesis, written forty years before, discussing the destruction of Point Edward.

"Jacob?"

"Yes. I've been reading it. It *has* always been a mystery, you know."

"What has?"

"Point Edward. Why the Ashiyyur destroyed it. I mean, it was empty at the time."

I remembered the story: during the first year of the war, both sides had discovered that population centers could not be protected. Consequently, a tacit agreement came into being, in which tactical targets would not be located near populated areas, and cities became immune to attack. The Ashiyyur violated that understanding at Point Edward. No one knew why.

"But Sim found out what was coming," continued Jacob. "And he evacuated twenty thousand people."

"There were only twenty thousand people?" I asked. I'd always assumed there'd been a lot more.

"Ilyanda was settled by the Cortai. A religious group that never cared much for outsiders. Controlled immigration rigidly, so much so that they'd stagnated, culturally and economically. That's all changed now. But during the Resistance, the city was a theocracy, and virtually everyone on the planet lived there. Communal life was very important to them."

According to the document, Sim compromised his entire intelligence network by reacting the way he did. The Ashiyyur immediately understood that their communications were being intercepted and read, and they changed everything: hardware, cryptosystems, transmission schedules, and routes. Not until the advent of Leisha Tanner eight months later did the Dellacondans begin to recover what had been lost. "Is that possible?" I asked.

"She was evidently a highly intelligent young lady. And you will note that the Ashiyyur responded to their own crisis without imagination. The changes in their cryptosystems were inadequate, and they knew it. So they tried to compensate by using an ancient form of their base language. You haven't got to that yet, but it's in there.''

"I thought they had no language. They're telepaths.''

"No *spoken* language, Alex. But they require a system for the permanent storage of data and concepts. A *written* language. The one they used was of classical origin. It was one every educated Ashiyyurean knew.''

"And Leisha.''

"And Leisha.''

"Now we know, at least, why Sim would have tried to recruit her.''

"It's curious, though,'' said Jacob.

"What's that?''

"Not about Tanner. But Point Edward. The mutes destroyed the city even though it was empty when they arrived. They must have known no one was there. Why would they bother?''

"Military target of some kind,'' I suggested.

"Maybe so. But if it was, nothing ever came out. And another strange thing is that there was no retaliation. Sim could have appeared off one of the Ashiyyurean worlds and smashed flat any city he chose. Why didn't he do so?''

"Maybe because they got everybody out at Point Edward, and he didn't want to start a series of reprisals.''

We found a holo of Tanner tucked away with those of a group of staff officers in Rohrien's *Sword of the Confederacy*. She was about twenty-seven at the time, and lovely even in the dark and light blue Dellacondan uniform. But her amiable expression was clearly out of place among the glowering, hostile males gathered round her.

I tried to read meaning into her eyes: had she known something that sent Gabe tracking off into the Veiled Lady two centuries later? I was sprawled on the downstairs sofa, her image soft and close. Pity that the sponder technique had not been in existence then: how much easier it would be to simply link with her and ask a few questions.

I was still staring at it when Jacob quietly informed me we had a visitor.

A skimmer was descending onto the back ramp. Tanner's image vanished, and the aircraft appeared on the overhead monitor. It was late by then, and dark. Jacob turned on the outside lamps, illuminating the walkway. I watched the pilot lift the canopy, and drop lightly to the ground.

"Jacob, who is she?"

"I don't know."

She knew where the cameras were. She looked directly into one as she strolled past, pulled off her hat, and shook out long black hair. Then she strode purposefully around to the front porch, and mounted the steps.

I was waiting for her. "Good evening," I said.

She was tall, gray-eyed, long-legged, wrapped in an olive cloak which fell almost to her knees. Her features were partially concealed by shadows. The wind had picked up, and the snow swirled round her. "You must be the nephew," she said, in a tone that suggested vague disapproval. "I assume he *was* on the *Capella?*" Her voice was husky, and the fluttering light from the streetlamp caught in her eyes.

"Please come in," I said.

She stepped inside, glanced quickly around, her eyes gliding over the stone demon. "I thought he must have been." She removed her cloak, and hung it by the door in a gesture that implied familiarity. She was not unattractive. But there was no discernible softness in those features. The eyes were penetrating, and the thrust of the jaw was aggressive. Her diction and tone stopped just short of arrogance. "My name's Chase Kolpath."

She said it in a way that suggested I should recognize it. "I'm Alex Benedict," I said.

She appraised me quite frankly, canted her head slightly, and shrugged. I could see she was disappointed. "I was in your uncle's employment," she said. "He owes me a considerable amount of money." She shifted her weight uncomfortably. "I'm sorry to bring up this sort of subject at a difficult time, but I think you should know."

She turned away, terminating further discussion of the matter, and led the way into the study. She took a chair near the fire, and said hello to Jacob, who replied smoothly and without hesitation that she looked well. He produced warm fruit drinks, laced with rum. She sipped hers, put it down, and held her hands out to the blaze. "Feels strange here without him."

"Yes. I thought that too."

"What was it about?" she asked suddenly. "What was he looking for?"

The question startled me. It wasn't an encouraging beginning. "Were you working with him on the project?"

"Yes," she said.

"Let me ask you the same question. What was he looking for?"

She laughed. It was a clean, liquid sound. "He didn't tell you either, I take it?"

"No."

"And he didn't tell anybody else?"

"Not that I know of."

"Jacob would know at least some of it."

"Jacob has been lobotomized."

She glanced with amusement at the monitor, which still carried the image of her skimmer. "You mean no one has any idea what he's been up to these last few months?"

"Not as far as I can tell," I said, with growing irritation.

"Records," she said, in the way one explains things to a child. "There'll be some records."

"They've got lost."

That broke her up. She laughed like a young Viking, throwing shoulders and throat into it, shaking her head, and trying to talk all at the same time. "Well," she got out between spasms, "I'll be damned. But it's just like him."

"Do you know anything? Anything at all?"

"It had something to do with the *Tenandrome*. He told me I'd get rich. And he said that everything else he'd done during his life was trivial by contrast. 'It'll shake the Confederacy,' he said." She pressed her palms to her jaws and shook her head. "Well, that is the dumbest thing I've ever been involved in."

"But you were a part of it. What were you supposed to do to earn your share?"

"I'm a class III pilot. Small craft, interstellar. He hired me to do some research, and to take him somewhere. I don't know where. Listen, I'm a little uncomfortable with all this. But the truth is that he left me sitting out on Saraglia after I'd spent a considerable amount of my own money."

"Saraglia. That's where the *Capella* was headed when it vanished."

"That's right. I was supposed to meet him there."

"And you don't know where he wanted to go afterward?"

"He didn't say."

"Seems odd." I didn't make much effort to mask the suspicion that she might be trying to take personal advantage of Gabe's death. "He had a license himself. He's had it for forty years, and I've never known him to let anybody else do his piloting.''

She shrugged. ''I can't answer that. I don't know. But that was our understanding. Counting travel time, minus an advance, he owed me two months pay plus expenses. I have it all documented.''

''Is there a contract somewhere?''

''No,'' she said. ''We had an agreement.''

''But nothing in writing?''

''Listen, Mr. Benedict.'' Her voice tightened. ''Try to understand. Your uncle and I have done a substantial amount of business over the past few years. We trusted each other. And we got along fine. We had no reason to resort to formal contracts.''

''What sort of research?'' I asked. ''Having to do with the *Tenandrome*?''

''Yes.'' One of the logs gave way and fell into the fire. ''It's a Survey ship. It was out in the Veiled Lady a few years ago, and apparently they saw something.'' She allowed her head to fall back on the chair. Her eyes slid shut. ''Gabe wanted to know *what*, but I never could find out.''

Saraglia is on the edge of the Veiled Lady, a remote, modular world of enormous dimensions, and varying gravities, last point of departure for the big Survey ships that continue to map and probe the vast Trantic Arm. ''And you were going to take him somewhere from there?''

''Yes. Somewhere.'' She shrugged.

''What did you know about your destination? You must have had some information. Range. How long you'd be gone. Something. Were you leasing a ship?''

She glanced down at the statement she'd written out for me. ''Is there going to be any quarrel about money?''

''No,'' I said.

''Okay.'' She smiled roguishly. ''I'd already arranged for a ship. I asked where we were going, but he said he'd tell me when he got there. To Saraglia, that is.''

''Did he expect to leave Saraglia immediately on arrival?''

''Yes,'' she said, ''I think so. I had instructions to have the ship ready to go. It was an old patrol boat, by the way. Hell of a ship.'' She shook her head sadly. ''He also told me we'd be out five to seven months.''

''How far does that put the target?''

''It's hard to say. If he's going to abide by the regulations, less than half that time would actually be spent in stardrive. Say three months, going both ways, the destination is about eight hundred light years. But if he's going to ignore the regs—which aren't really applicable anyhow out there—and make the jump as close as he can get to his target, then we're talking, say five months in hyper, a maximum of fifteen hundred light years.''

"What did you find out about the *Tenandrome?*"

"Not much. Other than that it's a spooky business."

"How do you mean?"

"The Survey ships, the big ones, usually go out for four- or five-year missions. The *Tenandrome* came back after a year and a half. And nobody got off."

"Is Saraglia the first stop on the return flight?"

"For that sector, yes. They traditionally stop there, and the captain files a report personally with the port director. They tend to logistical details, submit to Hazard Control inspections, and then turn everyone loose for a few days. It's a carnival atmosphere. But when the *Tenandrome* came in, things were different.

"The official report, according to the one or two port officials who would talk to me, was beamed in. Nobody got off; nobody got on. Crowds came down, the way they always do, and stood off the exit ramp. I don't know whether you know anything about Saraglia or not, but the ships come right into downtown bays. The walls are transparent, so the people who'd brought their kids for the holiday could stand in the street and see the *Tenandrome*, floating on its cables. The ship's interior lights were on, and it was possible to see the crew moving around inside. But nobody ever came down the tubes. That had never happened before.

"Everyone was upset, especially the business community. They felt they'd been snubbed. It's a big part of local income, when the ships come in."

"But not that time," I said.

"Not that time." She shivered a little. "Eventually, rumors started."

"Like what?"

"That it was a plague ship. But if that were the case, they wouldn't have let them off at Fishbowl, which is the second stop."

"And they *did* disembark at Fishbowl?"

"According to Gabe. He said they cleared the ship routinely."

"That was the final destination?"

"Survey maintains its regional headquarters there. Yes: that's where they go for general refitting, debriefing, and mounting new expeditions.''

"How many were on board?''

"Crew of six. Eighteen on the research teams.'' Chase's expression grew thoughtful. "The *Westover* came in while I was on Saraglia, and they all had a pretty good time. Stayed a little over a week, which I understand is about average. Lot of women and alcohol running loose: it's a wonder to me anyone *ever* goes home. The *Tenandrome* was gone within a day.''

"Did Survey explain why the mission was aborted?''

"They said there was a flaw in the Armstrong drive, that the problem was beyond the repair capabilities on Saraglia—not an unreasonable assertion, by the way—and that nobody got off because time was of the essence.''

"Maybe they were telling the truth.''

"Maybe. The ship went into maintenance at Fishbowl, and Gabe told me the records indicate that the drive did require an extensive overhaul.''

"Then where's the problem?''

"Gabe couldn't find anyone who'd actually worked on the Armstrong units. And Survey got upset when they found out he was asking questions. He was formally denied access to their facilities.''

"How the hell could they do that?''

"Easy. They declared him a safety hazard. I'd have liked to have seen that.'' She smiled. "I was on Saraglia when that happened. Judging from the tone of his messages, he was having apoplexy. But then he told me that Machesney had come through, and that he was on his way out to meet me. And for me to get a ship.''

"Machesney?''

"That's what he said.''

"Who the hell is Machesney?''

"I don't know. All this stuff about Christopher Sim. Maybe he meant Rashim Machesney.''

I shook my head. "Is there anyone at all involved with this who hasn't been dead over a hundred years?'' Rashim Machesney: the grand old man of the Resistance. Genial, fat, brilliant, expert in gravity wave theory, touring the planetary legislatures with Tarien Sim and throwing his enormous influence behind the Confederate cause. How could *he* have "come through''?

"I don't know any other Machesneys," said Chase. "Incidentally, once repairs were completed, Survey wasted no time shipping the *Tenandrome* out again. They had a mission set up and ready to go. The captain and most of the original crew went with her."

"Could it have been a return flight? Were they going back?"

"No," said Chase. "At least I don't think so. Their destination was an area eighteen hundred light years out. Too far. If we can assume that Gabe *did* know where they'd been, and that was where he was headed."

"What about the ship's logs? Don't they routinely become part of the public record? I'm sure I've seen them published."

"Not this time. Everything was classified."

"On what grounds?"

"I don't know. Do they have to tell you? I just know that Gabe couldn't get access to them."

"Jacob? Are you there?"

"Yes," he said.

"Please comment."

"It's not all that unusual to withhold information if, in someone's judgment, its release would damage the public interest. For example, if someone gets eaten, the details would not be made available. A recent example of nondisclosure occurred on the *Borlanget* flight, when a symbolist was seized and carried off by some sort of flying carnivore. But even then, only that part of the record dealing with the specific incident was held back. With the *Tenandrome*, it's almost as if the mission never happened."

"Do you have any idea," I asked Chase, "what they might have seen?"

She shrugged. "I think Gabe knew. But he never told me. And if anybody on Saraglia knew what it was about, they weren't saying."

"It might have been a biological problem," I suggested. "Something they were worried about, but had settled by the time they got to Fishbowl."

"I suppose it's possible. But if they'd put their minds at ease, why are they still hiding information?"

"You said there were rumors."

She nodded. "I told you about the plague. The most interesting one was that there'd been a contact. I heard probably two dozen variations on that, the most common being that they'd barely got away, that the central government was afraid the *Tenandrome* had been followed home, and that the Navy had been called in. Some people said the *Tenandrome* that came home was not the same as the one that went out.''

That was a chilling notion.

"Another story was that there'd been a time displacement, that more than forty years of ship time had passed, and that the crew members had aged severely." She considered the depths of human gullibility. "Gabe was able to talk to one of the members of the research team, and he was perfectly all right. I don't know who that was."

"Hugh Scott," I breathed. "Did *he* say why they aborted the mission?"

"Whoever it was delivered the party line: the ship had problems with its Armstrong units, which they couldn't repair without heavy facilities."

I sighed. "Then that was probably the reason. The fact that Gabe couldn't find anyone who'd actually done the work hardly seems significant. And maybe the captain was anxious to get home for personal reasons. I suspect that this whole business has a series of simple explanations."

"Maybe," she said. "But whoever Gabe talked to—Scott, whoever—refused to tell him who else was on the flight." She pressed her fist against her lower lip. *"That's* strange.''

The conversation wandered a bit, and we went over old ground, as though there might be something there that had been missed. When Machesney's name came up again, she sat up straight. "Gabe had somebody with him on the *Capella*," she said. "Maybe *that* was Machesney."

"Maybe," I said. I listened to the sound of the fire, and the creaking of the old house. "Chase?"

"Yes?"

Jacob had provided some cheese and a fresh round of drinks.

"What do *you* think?"

"About what they saw?"

"Yes."

She exhaled. "If they weren't still sitting on information, I'd be inclined to dismiss the whole business. As it is—they're hiding something. But that's the only real evidence there is. That they won't release the logs.

"Despite that, if I were pinned down, I'd have to think that Gabe's imagination ran away with him." She bit off a piece of cheese, and chewed it slowly. "The romantic thing, of course, is to conclude that there's some sort of threat out there, something rather terrifying. But what could it be? What could possibly scare people at a distance of several hundred light years?''

"How about the Ashiyyur? Maybe they've broken through into the Veiled Lady.''

"So what? I suppose that would cost the military some sleep, but it's not going to bother me. And anyhow they're no more dangerous out there than they are along the Perimeter.''

Later, when Chase was gone, I called up the passenger list for *Capella*. Gabe's name was there, of course. Gabriel Benedict of Andiquar. There was no Machesney on the flight.

And I wondered, far into the night, why Gabe, who had navigated all kinds of ships among the stars, would want to hire a pilot.

IV.

___

That's a hell of a pile of real estate.

—Chief Counsellor Wrightman Toomey, on hearing that
   there was an estimated 200 million habitable worlds in
   the Veiled Lady.

THE DEPARTMENT OF Planetary Survey and Astronomical Research was a semi-autonomous agency, funded by the central treasury and an army of private foundations. It was controlled by a board of directors representing the associated interests and the academic community. The chairman was a political appointee, responsible to the foundations, but ultimately answerable to the Director herself. All of which is to say that, though Survey was officially a scientific body, it was very sensitive to political pressures.

It maintained administrative offices in Andiquar, for the purposes of recruiting technical personnel to man the big ships, and processing applications from specialists who wanted to join the research teams. There was also a public information branch.

Survey shared its office building with several other agencies. They were all on the upper levels of an old stone structure that had once housed the planetary government in the years before Confederation. The west wall was discolored where an interventionist's

49

bomb had gone off during the early days of the Resistance.

The reception room was depressing: washed-out yellow walls, hard flat furniture, group photos of the crews of a couple of starships, and a portrait of a black hole. Not much of a public relations operation.

I got up from the straight-backed chair into which I'd arrived, as a holo strode efficiently out of an adjoining room. The image was that of a cheerful young man, slender, coolly efficient. A stock character, actually, whom I'd seen before in other situations. The door closed behind him. "Good morning," he said. "Can I be of assistance?"

"Yes," I replied. "I hope so. My name's Hugh Scott, and I flew with the *Tenandrome* on its last mission. Research team. A couple of us would like to put together a reunion. But we've lost touch with most of the others. I was wondering if you could supply a roster, or let me know where I could obtain one."

"The last *Tenandrome* flight? Let's see, that would be XVII?"

"Yes," I said, after hesitating just long enough to suggest I was thinking about it.

The image, in turn, looked thoughtful. He had thick brown hair, a pleasant smile, and a face with a nose that was a trifle too long. Management undoubtedly wanted to project intelligence and congeniality. In some types of businesses, like antique merchandising, it would work well. There, in that bland unimaginative setting, these qualities just clashed with the furniture.

"Checking," he said. He crossed the room and stood inspecting the black hole while he waited for the computers to complete their run. I crossed one leg over the other, and picked up a brochure that invited me to consider a career with the Agency of the Future. Good pay, it said, and adventure in exotic places.

The holo turned abruptly, and pursed his lips, reflecting the imminence of an unpleasant duty. "I'm sorry, Dr. Scott," he said. "That information has been classified. *You*, of course, should have no difficulty obtaining it. I can provide you with a form to complete, if you wish to apply for a waiver. You may do that here, if you desire, and I will see that it gets to the right place." He indicated one of the terminals. "You may use that position. You'll need identification, of course."

"Naturally." I was beginning to feel uncomfortable. Was the interview being recorded? "Why would it be classified?"

"I'm afraid the reason is also classified, Doctor."

"Yes," I said. "It would be. Okay." I sat tentatively at the terminal, and then glanced at an overhead clock as if suddenly remembering a late appointment. "I'm a little pressed just now," I said, reaching toward the headband.

"Fine," he replied amiably, giving me the document code number. "You can call it up anytime. Just follow the instructions."

I gathered from Gabe's comments that he wasn't on the best of terms with the Center for Accadian Studies. Still, most of the archeological work originating out of Andiquar was coordinated from that venerable institution. So I arranged an interview, and linked in to a brisk young woman who smiled tolerantly when I mentioned his name. "You have to understand, Mr. Benedict," she said, pressing her index finger pointedly into her cheek, "that we really had no connection whatever with your father. The Center restricts itself to professionally mounted operations, supported by approved institutions."

"He was my uncle," I said.

"I'm sorry. In any case, we really had no contacts with him."

"You're implying," I remarked casually, "that the level of my uncle's activities does not quite measure up to your standards."

"Not to *my* standards, Mr. Benedict. We're talking about the Center's standards. Please understand that your uncle was an amateur. No one will deny he was talented. But still and all, an amateur."

"Schleimann and Champollion were amateurs," I said, growing somewhat testy. "So were Towerman and Crane. And several hundred others. It's a tradition in archeology. Always has been."

"Of course it is," she said smoothly. "And we understand that. We encourage people like Gabriel Benedict in whatever informal ways we can. And we are gratified by their successes."

That evening, I was sitting lost in thought, listening to the fire, when the lights dimmed and went out. A dazzling white object, about the size of a hand, appeared in the center of the room near the coffee table. It was roughly spherical, I thought, though its exact outline was difficult to perceive. Brilliant jets spouted from either side, fell back toward the object, and enshrouded it. Clouds of blazing light expanded, swirled, reformed. The object lengthened, and took a familiar shape.

The Veiled Lady.

"I thought it seemed appropriate for the occasion, Alex." Jacob's voice sounded curiously distant.

It filled half the room now, turning slowly about its own axis, in a movement that, in real time, would have taken millions of years. Only the most imaginative could make out a female form. Still, there were suggestions of shoulder and eye and trailing folds of gossamer in the vast star-clouds.

It was thought to contain a half-billion suns, mostly young and hot. Habitable worlds appeared to be common, and most planners viewed it as the natural home for the burgeoning population of the near future. The proximity of the stars to each other also suggested that the severity of problems arising from the terrible distances separating the worlds of the Confederacy might be alleviated. Eventually, we suspected, the old capitals would be abandoned, and the centers of power transferred into the nebula.

It was the brightest nighttime object in Rimway's southern skies, brighter even than the giant moon. Although never visible from Andiquar, few winter stars within twenty degrees of the horizon had sufficient magnitude to resist its light.

"That's where we're headed, Jacob," I said. "Eventually."

"I agree," he said, misunderstanding. "It only remains for you to uncover your destination."

That was a startling notion. But it suggested it was time to get back to work. I directed him to collect all the news files he could find relating to the *Tenandrome*.

"I've already been looking," he said. "There's not much." The Veiled Lady vanished, and a few lines of hardcopy appeared on the monitor. "This is the earliest."

Saraglia Station, Mmb 3 (ACS): The CSS Tenandrome, *currently involved in exploration of regions deep in the Veiled Lady, more than a thousand light years from Rimway, was reported to have suffered structural damage to its Armstrong units, according to a Survey spokesman. Although the extent of the damage is as yet unknown, the spokesman indicated that no one had been injured, and there was no immediate danger to the vessel. The Navy released a statement that rescue units are standing by to assist if needed.*

Jacob flashed a few more items: the official announcement that the ship was returning home, a notice in the *Commercial and Shipping Registry* of its arrival at Saraglia, and another recording its formal entry on Fishbowl a few weeks later.

"Is there anything at the other end of the trip? Any details on departure?" I asked.

"Just the standard announcement in the *Registry*," he said. "No itinerary given."

"How about crew names? Or passengers?"

"Only the captain: Sajemon McIras. That's not unusual, by the way. They never publish anything much in the way of details. Sometimes there's feature coverage, but that's rare."

"Maybe there's some off-line material available."

"If so, I have no easy way to find it. And it appears that, if anything unusual was going on, the news services never found out about it."

"Okay. Maybe McIras would be willing to tell us something. Can we get an address?"

"Yes. The Moira Deeps, with her ship. I've been checking the house records. Gabe sent her two sponders. She ignored the first."

"And the second?"

"Just a tachline:"

Dr. Benedict: The voyage of the Tenandrome, *save for the disruption of one of its Armstrong units, was uneventful. Best wishes.*

Saje McIras

"Let's try another approach: take a look at all the flights over the last few years. There should be some sort of pattern to them, and we might be able to figure out at least the general area where the *Tenandrome* was."

So Jacob extracted the records, and we studied the recent missions of *Borlanget, Rapatutu, Westover,* and the rest of Survey's Fishbowl-based fleet. But the pattern, if it existed, never showed itself.

The target area contained approximately three trillion cubic light years. Maybe a little less.

"That leaves Scott."

Jacob was momentarily silent. Then: "Do you wish to prepare a sponder?"

"How long would it take to get an answer?"

"If he replies right away, about ten days. The problem is that his code shows inactive on the last four readouts. He doesn't seem to be answering his mail."

"Book passage," I said, reluctantly. "It's probably just as well to go in person anyhow."

"Very good. I'll try to let him know you're coming."

"No," I said. "Let's keep it a surprise."

V.

One gazes through the walls of Pellinor into the great, curious eyes of the sea beasts, and wonders who indeed is peering out, and who peering in—?

—Tiel Chadwick,
Memoirs

THE WORLD AND the city are both named Pellinor, after the ship captain who first descended onto the few square kilometers of earth that were once the only place in all that global ocean where a man could set foot. But to anyone who has since stood beneath the invisible walls that now hold back the sea, who has looked up at the shadowy forms gliding through bright green water, the name by which the place is commonly known is far more appropriate.

Fishbowl.

A world. A sickle-shaped spate of land hewed from the sea. A state of mind. The inhabitants are fond of saying that no place in or beyond the Confederacy induces a sense of mortality quite like Fishbowl.

Barely half the size of Rimway, the planet is nevertheless massive: its gravity is .92 standard. It orbits the ancient class G sun Gideon, which in turn moves in a centuries-long swing around Heli, a dazzling white giant. Both suns have planetary systems, not

54

unusual in binaries when considerable distances separate the main components. But this binary is unique in a substantial way: it was once the home of an intelligent species. Heli's fourth planet is Belarius, which houses fifty-thousand-year-old ruins, and was—until the coming of the Ashiyyur—humanity's only evidence that anything else had ever gazed at the stars.

Belarius is an incredibly savage place, a world of lush jungles, stifling humidity, corrosive atmospheric gases, strong gravity, highly evolved predators, and unpredictable magnetic storms which raise hell with equipment. It is not the sort of place to take your family.

Fishbowl was the only easily habitable world in either system, and consequently it assumed from the beginning a strategic place in Survey thinking. When Harry Pellinor discovered it three centuries ago, he dismissed it as essentially worthless. But he had not yet found Belarius: that celebrated disaster still awaited him. And it was that latter revelation that assured Fishbowl its historic role as administrative headquarters, supply depot, and R&R retreat for the various missions trying to pry loose its secrets.

Today, of course, investigation of Belarius has long since been given up. But Fishbowl is still prominent in Survey administration, serving as a regional headquarters. A prosperous resort area, it boasts a major university, several interworld industries, and the foremost oceanographic research center in the Confederacy. At the time of my visit, it was home to slightly more than a million people.

One of them was Hugh Scott.

Harry Pellinor's statue stands atop the central spire of the Executive Cluster. It is just high enough to get him above sea level. Local tradition had it that there had been extreme reluctance to honor a man whom the outside world associated primarily with disaster and precipitous retreat, the man whose crew had, by and large, been eaten.

It wasn't, people thought, the proper sort of image they wanted to project.

I suppose not. But the city had prospered anyway.

It was filled with well-heeled tourists, wealthy retirees, and assorted technocrats, the latter employed mostly by the tach communications industry, which was then still in its infancy.

The downside port of entry is located on a floating platform, from which one can get over-water tubular transportation into midtown Pellinor. Or, if the weather is good, one can walk across any of several float bridges. My first act coming down in the shuttle had been to consult the directory. I had Scott's address before we settled onto the pad.

I took a taxi, checked in at my hotel, and showered. It was by then early evening local time. I was exhausted, though. It had been my usual difficult flight: sick during both jumps and most of the time between. So I stood under the cooling spray, feeling sorry for myself, and laying plans: I would pin Scott down, find out what was going on, and return to Rimway. From there I'd hire somebody to accompany Kolpath wherever the hell they'd have to go to locate Gabe's secret, and I myself would never again leave the world of my birth.

No wonder the goddam Confederacy was falling apart. It took weeks to get from one place to another, anywhere from days to weeks to communicate, and travel for most people was physically unpleasant. If the Ashiyyur were smart, they'd declare peace, and back off. I wasn't sure that, with the threat removed, we wouldn't simply disintegrate.

I slept well, rose early, and breakfasted at a small outdoor restaurant in the penthouse. The ocean spread out beneath me, covered with sails. The salt air smelled good, and I ate slowly. Tramways and parks and multi-leveled malls extended above the gantner walls and out over the sea. They're lined with exotic bistros, casinos, art galleries, and souvenir shops. There are beaches and suspension piers and a seaside promenade which circles the city just a few meters above the water.

But many people say that Pellinor is most exquisite at ground level. There, most of the sunlight is filtered through about twenty meters of green ocean water. And it's possible to watch the great leviathans of that watery world drift majestically within an arm's length of one's breakfast table.

I flagged a taxi outside the restaurant, and punched Scott's address into the reader.

I had no idea where I was going. The vehicle rose over the skyline, fell into traffic patterns, and arced out over the ocean. Harry Pellinor's island sank from sight. Only the towers remained visible, rising eerily out of a hole in the ocean. The only land in the archipelago which was actually above sea level was located in two clusters southwest of the city. These hills now resembled a string of small islands.

The taxi turned to run parallel to the coastline. It was a brilliant, summery morning. I retracted the canopy, and luxuriated in that golden climate. I've read since that the atmosphere on Fishbowl is relatively oxygen-rich, inducing a sense of euphoria. I can believe it. By the time the taxi banked and headed inland again, I had acquired a remarkable sense of well-being. Everything's going to be fine.

A few sails tacked gracefully before a light wind out of the west, and a blimp floated listlessly through the sky. Small fountains of spray erupted rhythmically from the surface, but I couldn't see the creatures that produced them.

Land came up quickly, and I soared in over the highlands. There were wide, well-maintained beaches, backed by forest, and a long line of rock and crystal homes. The coastline was scored with piers; pools and cabanas were visible among the trees. Several domes stood in the shallow waters along the coast, supported by glittering struts of articulated gantner light.

The area was dominated by Uxbridge Bay. You've probably seen the masterpiece by Durell Coll which made it famous. Supposedly, it formed during Coll's time, two-and-a-half centuries ago, when one of the gantner projection stations failed, and the ocean rushed in.

The taxi drifted along the bay shore, collecting a few sandmongers that flapped excitedly alongside. It turned inland, proceeding across the neck of the island, passing over heavy forest, and drifted down onto a pad on the side of a hill. The sandmongers crashed into the surrounding branches, where they kicked up a substantial racket.

I hadn't seen a house from the air, and I couldn't see one from the ground. The pad was small, barely big enough for the skimmer. I instructed it to wait, climbed out, and followed a footpath into the woods.

I passed almost immediately out of the sunlight, into a cool green world of thick branches and chittering squirrels. I should note here by the way that Fishbowl has virtually no native land forms, and is stocked heavily from Rimway. Even the trees. I felt right at home.

A permearth bungalow appeared at the crest of the hill, amid ferns, branches, and great white sunblossoms. A single chair stood on a wide deck. The windows were empty, the door shut tight. The walls sagged slightly, and the leafy overhang trailed down onto the roof. The air was warm. It smelled vaguely of decay and old wood.

I knocked.

The house was very still. In one of the trees, something flapped and a limb shook.

I peered through the front window into the living room. It was gloomy in half-light: sofa and two armchairs, an antique desk, and a long glass table. A sweater lay on the table, and a crystal figure of a sea creature which I did not recognize. A doorway led out to another room. Against the doorway was a trophy case. It was filled with rocks of various kinds, all of which were labeled. Samples from the outworlds, probably.

The walls were covered with prints, but I was slow to realize what they were: Sanrigal's *Sim at the Hellgate*, Marcross's *Corsarius*, Isitami's *Maurina*, Toldenya's pensive *On the Rock*. There were others, with which I was not familiar: a portrait of Tarien Sim, several of Christopher Sim, one of the Dellacondan high country at night, with a lonely figure who must have been Maurina surveying it all from beneath a skeletal tree.

The only portrait that did not seem to be associated with Sim hung near the trophy case. It was of a modern starship, ablaze with light, warm and living against strange constellations. I wondered whether it was the *Tenandrome*.

I knew what Scott looked like. In fact, I'd brought a couple of photos with me, though both were old. He was tall, dark-skinned, dark-eyed. But there was a diffidence in his appearance, a suggestion of reluctance that implied he embodied more of the shopkeeper than a leader of research teams onto alien worlds.

The cottage *felt* empty. Not abandoned, exactly. But not lived in, either.

I pushed at the windows, hoping to find one open. They were all secured. I circled the house, looking for an entry, and considered whether I could gain anything by breaking in. Probably not, and if the place took my picture in the act, I could be assured of losing Scott's cooperation, and possibly end with a hefty fine as well.

I took to the air and circled the area. There were maybe a dozen houses within a kilometer or so of Scott's property. One by one, I descended on them and asked questions, representing myself as a cousin who had found himself unexpectedly on Fishbowl. It appeared that hardly anyone knew Scott by name, and several said they'd wondered who lived in his house.

No one admitted to being more than a casual acquaintance. Pleasant man, they said of him. Quiet. Minds his business. Not easy to get to know.

A woman whom I found pottering about in the garden of an ultra-modern slab-glass house partially supported by gantner light added an ominous note. "He's changed," she said, her eyes clouding.

"You know him, then?"

"Oh, yes," she said. "We've known him for years." She invited me up into a sitting room, disappeared momentarily into her kitchen, and returned with iced herbal drinks. "All we have," she said. "Sorry."

Her name was Nasha. She was a tiny creature, soft-spoken, with luminous eyes, and a fluttery manner that reminded me vaguely of the sandmongers. It was easy to see she'd been beautiful once. But it fades quickly in some people. I thought she seemed pleased to have someone to talk with. "In what way did he change?"

"How well do you know your cousin?" she asked.

"I haven't seen him in years. Since we were both quite young."

"I haven't known him *that* long." She smiled. "But you're probably aware that Hugh was never much for socializing."

"That's true," I said. "But he wasn't really unfriendly," I hazarded. "Just shy."

"Yes," she said. "Though I'm not sure all of his neighbors would agree, I do. He seemed all right to me, solitary if you know what I mean. Kept to himself. Read a lot. Most of the people he worked with would tell you he always seemed pressed for time, or preoccupied. But once you get to know him, he loosens up. He has a wonderful sense of humor, kind of dry, and not everybody appreciates it. My husband thinks he's one of the funniest people he's ever known."

• "Your husband—"

"—was with him on the *Cordagne*." She squinted out into the double sunlight. "I've always liked Hugh. God knows he's been good to me. I met him when Josh—my husband—and he were training for the *Cordagne* flight. We had our kids with us, and we were new to Fishbowl then. We started having power problems. The house was owned by Survey, but their maintenance people couldn't seem to get things working, particularly the video, and the kids were upset. Going through withdrawal, you know? I don't know how Hugh found out, but he insisted on switching quarters.'' She noted that I'd finished the drink, and hurried to refill my glass. ''He was like that.''

''In what way did he change?''

''I don't know how to describe it exactly. All the characteristics that used to be eccentricities became extreme. His sense of humor took on a bitter flavor. He used to be somber; but we watched him slip into depression. And if it used to be that he kept to himself, he eventually became a hermit. I doubt many of the people around here have even seen him to talk to in the last couple of years.''

''That seems to be true.''

''Only the people who worked with him. But there was more. He developed a mean streak. Like when Harv Killian donated half his money to the hospital to get a room named after him. Scott thought that was pathetic. I still remember his remark: 'He wants to buy what he could never earn.' ''

''Immortality,'' I said.

She nodded. ''He told Killian that to his face. Harv never spoke to him again.''

''Seems cruel.''

''There was a time Scott wouldn't have done that. Told him, that is. He'd have thought it, because he was always like that. But he wouldn't have said anything.

''But these last couple of years—'' Small fine lines appeared around her lips and eyes.

''Do you see much of him anymore?''

''Not for months. He went someplace. I have no idea where.''

''Might Josh know? Your husband?''

She shook her head. ''No. Maybe somebody down at Survey could help you.''

We sat for a bit. I shooed off a couple of insects. ''I don't suppose,'' I said, ''that your husband was ever on the *Tenandrome?*''

''He only made the one flight,'' she said. ''That was enough.''

''Yes, I suppose it was. Do you know anyone who *was* on a *Tenandrome* mission?''

She shook her head. ''They'd be able to tell you in Pellinor. Try there.'' She looked thoughtful. ''He's traveled a lot the last couple of years. This isn't the first time he's just taken off.''

''Where did he go on those other trips? Did he ever tell you?''

''Yes,'' she said. ''He's become a history buff. He spent a

couple of weeks at Grand Salinas. There's some sort of museum in orbit out there.''

Salinas was the scene of Christopher Sim's first defeat, the place where the Dellacondan resistance very nearly died.

"Maybe he went to Hrinwhar," she said suddenly.

"Hrinwhar?" The famous raid. But Hrinwhar was no more than an airless moon.

"Yes." She shook her head vehemently up and down. "Now that I think of it: he's said any number of times that he wanted to visit Hrinwhar."

Scott's house wasn't visible from her front porch, but the hill on which it rested was. She shielded her eyes from the sunlight, and looked toward it. "To tell you the truth," she said, "I think Josh is just as glad he's gone. We'd reached a point where we got pretty uncomfortable when Scott was around."

Her voice had gone brittle. Cold. I could sense a thin red line of anger just below the surface. "Thanks," I said.

"It's all right."

I asked everyone I spoke with to let me know when Scott returned. Then, disappointed, I returned to Pellinor.

Survey's Regional Headquarters complex consists of half a dozen buildings of radically different architectural styles, old and modern, imported and native. A crystal tower stands next to a purely functional block of offices; a quadripar geodesic occupies a site adjacent to a gothic temple. The overall effect is, according to the guide books, that of an academic contempt for the order and form of the mundane mind: the casual motifs of the scholar created in glass and permearth. I suppose that, by the time I'd arrived at this point in my journeys, I'd been thinking too much about Christopher Sim's war; but *my* impression of the place was that it looked as if it had been assembled under enemy fire.

The library was located on the ground level of the dome. It was named the Wicker Closure for an early administrator. (I was struck by the fact that all the buildings, wings, and laboratories memorialized bureaucrats or fund-raisers. The people who had gone out to the stars had to settle for a few plaques and mementoes in the museum. A couple of dozen, who had been killed, got their names carved into a slab in the main lobby.)

It was late when I got there. The library was almost empty. A few people who appeared to be graduate students sat at terminals or wandered quietly through the files. I picked out a booth, went in, closed the door, and sat down.

"*Tenandrome*," I said. "Background material."

"Please put on your headband." The voice came out of a speaker atop the monitor. It was masculine, erudite, middle-aged.

I complied. The illumination softened to the color of the nighttime sky, in the manner of a planetarium. A splinter of light appeared in the darkness, grew into a pattern of boxes and rods. It was slowly spinning about its own axis.

"*Tenandrome*," said the narrator, "was built eighty-six standard years ago on Rimway, specifically for deep space exploration. It is one of the *Cordagne* class of survey ships. Hyperspace transition is provided by twin Armstrong-drive units, recharge time between jumps estimated at approximately forty hours. Ship is powered by accelerated fusion thermals, capable of generating 80,000 megawatts under normal running conditions." The ship continued to grow until it occupied half the booth. It was gray, utilitarian, uninteresting, two groups of boxes built along parallel spines, connected in the after section by a magnetic propulsion system (for linear space maneuvering), and forward by the bridge.

I cut the description short.

"History," I said, "of most recent mission."

The ship floated in the dark.

"I am sorry. That information is not available."

"Why not?"

"Ship's log has been impounded pending outcome of judicial matters arising from alleged irregularities in equipment. Liability considerations preclude further release of data at this time."

"What sort of alleged irregularities?"

"That information is not currently available."

"Was the mission cut short?"

"Yes."

"Why?"

"That information is not currently available."

"When will further information *be* available?"

"I regret that I do not have data to answer that question."

"Can you tell me what the planned itinerary of *Tenandrome* was?"

"No," it said after a moment.

"But wouldn't the itinerary be a matter of public record?"

"Not anymore. It has been removed."

"There must be a copy somewhere."

"I do not have that information."

Schematics of the *Tenandrome* were flickering across the monitor, as though the system had become distracted. "Where is the *Tenandrome* now?"

"It is in the second year of a six-year mission in the Moira Deeps."

"Can you give me a list of crew and research team members from *Tenandrome?*"

"For which voyage?"

"For any of the last four."

"I can supply the information for missions XV and XVI, and also the current voyage."

"What about XVII?"

"Not available."

"Why not?"

"It is classified."

I pulled off the headband, and squinted out through the windows at an illuminated park. In the distance, lights reflected off the ocean wall.

What the hell were they hiding? What could they *possibly* be hiding?

Somebody knew.

Somewhere, somebody knew.

I took to stalking Survey bureaucrats and researchers. I hunted them in bars, at the Field Museum, on benches in the malls, on the beaches, in the gleaming corridors of the Operational Headquarters, in the city's theaters and restaurants, and in its athletic and chess clubs.

Approached obliquely, almost everyone was willing to speculate on the *Tenandrome*. The most widespread theory, one that amounted among many to a conviction, was Chase Kolpath's notion that the ship had found aliens. Some claimed to know for certain that naval vessels had been dispatched to the discovery site, and almost everyone had heard that several young crewmembers had returned with white hair.

There was a variation of this story: *Tenandrome* had found an ancient fleet adrift, and had attempted to investigate. But there was something among the encrusted ships that had discouraged further examination, forcing the captain to break off the mission and return home. One bearded endocrinologist told me, in dead earnestness, that the vessel had found a ghost. But he could not, or would not, elaborate.

An elderly systems analyst with whom I fell in one evening on a ramp overlooking the sea told me she'd heard there was an alien enclave out there, a cluster of turrets on an airless moon. But the aliens were long dead, she said, perfectly preserved within their shelters. "What I heard," she added, "is that all the turrets had been opened to the void. From the *inside*."

The wildest account came from a skimmer rental agent who said the ship had found a vehicle full of humans who spoke no known language, who could not be identified, who were identical with us in every fundamental way—which was to say, he whispered, that their sexual organs complemented ours—but that they were not of common origin.

There was a young woman who had known Scott: there always is, I suppose, if you look long enough. She was a sculptor, slim and attractive, with a good smile.

She had just broken off with someone (or he with her: it's often hard to tell), and we ended in a small bar on one of the piers. Her name was Ivana, and she was vulnerable that night. I could have taken her to bed, but she seemed so desolated that I could not bring myself to take advantage of her.

"Where is he?" I asked. "Do you know where he went?"

She was drinking too much, but it didn't seem to affect her.

"Off-world," she said. "Somewhere. But he'll be back."

"How do you know?"

"He always comes back." There was a trace of venom in her voice.

"He's taken these trips before?"

"Oh, yes," she said. "He's not one for hanging around."

"Why? Where does he go?"

"He gets bored, I guess. And where he goes is battle sites, from the Resistance. Or memorials, I'm not sure which."

It was getting loud in the bar, so I steered her outside, where I thought the fresh air might help us both. "Ivana, what does he tell you when he comes back? About what he's seen?"

"He doesn't really talk about it, Alex. I never really thought to ask him."

"Have you ever heard of Leisha Tanner?"

She started to say no, and changed her mind. "Yes," she said, lighting up. "He's mentioned her a couple of times."

"What did he say about her?"

"That he was trying to find out things about her. She's an historical character of some sort." The ocean crouched out there beneath us like a dark beast. "He's a strange one. Makes me feel uncomfortable sometimes."

"How did you meet him?"

"I don't remember anymore. At a party, I think. Why? Why do you care?"

"No reason," I said.

That brought a lovely, rueful smile. And then she surprised me: "I mean, why do you care about Scott?"

I told my cover story, and she sympathized that I'd missed him. "When I see him again," she said, "I'll tell him you were here."

We drank some more, and walked some more. The night had a bite to it, and I was conscious of her hips as we strolled along the skyway. "He's become very strange," she said again. It was an observation she made several times during the evening. "You wouldn't know him."

"Since the *Tenandrome?*"

"Yes." We stopped, and she leaned against the rail, looking out to sea. She looked lost. The wind whipped at her jacket, and she pulled it tightly about herself. "It's lovely out here." Fishbowl has no satellite; but on clear nights the sky is dominated by the Veiled Lady, which is far more luminous—and intoxicating—than Rimway's full moon. "They brought something back. The *Tenandrome*. Did you know that?"

"No," I said.

"Nobody seems to know what it was. But there was something. Nobody wanted to talk about it. Not even McIras."

"The captain?"

"Yes. A cold-blooded bitch if I've ever seen one." Her eyes hardened. "They were in, and then they were gone again. Out on another long mission. The crew was gone almost before anyone knew they were here."

"How about the research team?"

"They went home. Usually they go home and then come back here for a debriefing. Not this time. We never saw any of them again. Except, of course, Hugh."

We were walking again. Pellinor's waterfront was brilliant and inviting, its dazzling lights floating on the water. "In a sense, he never really came home. At least not to stay. He's always away somewhere. Like now."

"You say he goes to battle sites. Where, for example?"

"The City on the Crag last time. Ilyanda. Randin'hal. Grand Salinas."

It was a roll call of celebrated names from the Resistance.

"Yes," she said, reading my reaction. "He's got a fixation about the Sims. I don't know what it is, but he's looking for something. He comes home after weeks or months away somewhere, and he comes back to Survey for a couple of days, and then next thing we know he's gone again. He was never like that before." Her voice shook. "I don't understand it."

Lest anyone think I wasn't making a serious effort, I have to tell you I also tried a direct approach. Toward the end, after my informal inquiries had taken me as far as they could, I walked through the front doors of the administration building, which they call the Annex, and asked to see the Director of Special Operations. His name was Jemumba.

I was referred to a secretary. State your business please, we'll get back to you, maybe six months. I was eventually able to talk to one of his flunkies, who denied that anything unusual had happened. Yes, he'd heard the rumors, but in this business there were always rumors. He could assure me, unequivocally, that no aliens existed out there, at least not on or around any of the worlds Survey had visited. Also, the notion that there had been any casualties of any sort on the *Tenandrome* was simply untrue.

He explained that withholding the log and other information regarding the flight was standard operating procedure when litigation was involved. And there was a great deal of litigation over *Tenandrome XVII*. "The failure of a major drive unit is no small matter, Mr. Benedict," he explained pointedly, and not without passion. "The Service has incurred considerable expense, and the liability position is quite tangled. Nevertheless, we anticipate that everything will be settled within a year or so. When that happens, you may have access to whatever information on the flight you wish, other than crew and research team data, which of course is never made public. Privacy considerations, you understand.

"Please leave your name and code. We'll get back to you."

* * *

So I had no choice but to go to Hrinwhar. There are no regular flights, of course. I leased a Centaur and hired Chase to pilot the damned thing. The jump is even tougher in a small craft, and I got sicker than usual going out and coming back, and I swore again that that was the end.

There was no need to land. Hrinwhar was a cratered, airless, nickel-iron rock located just inside the rings of a gas giant, which I suppose is why the Ashiyyur thought it would make a good naval base. Some say the assault against it was Sim's finest moment. The Dellacondans lured off the defenders, and literally took the base apart. They left here with some of the enemy's most closely guarded secrets.

The physical evidence of the raid remains: a few holed domes, a gaping shaft which had once been a recovery area for warships, and chunks of metal and plastic strewn across the surface. Probably exactly as it looked when Christopher Sim and his men withdrew two centuries ago.

Chase didn't say much. I got the impression she was watching me more than the moonscape. "Enough?" she asked after we'd made several passes.

"He couldn't be down there," I said.

"No. There's no one here."

"Why would he come out to this barren place?"

VI.

Call forth the fire—!

—The Condor-ni, II, 1

Sim is a son of a bitch: fourteen thousand years of history to learn from, and it's still the same old blood and bluster.

—Leisha Tanner,
Notebooks

WHO HAD GABE'S traveling companion been on the *Capella?*

Sixty-three others had boarded the vessel from the Rimway shuttle, of whom twenty were bound for Saraglia Station. (The big interstellars, of course, never actually stop at ports of call. Too much time and energy would be wasted fighting inertia, so they skim planetary systems at high velocity. Passengers and cargo are transferred in flight from local vehicles.) It seemed likely that his companion had been among the twenty.

I scanned their death notices looking for a likely prospect. The group included elderly vacationers, naval personnel on leave, three sets of newlyweds, a sprinkling of businessmen. Four were from

Andiquar: a pair of import/export brokers, a child being shuttled between relatives, and a retired law enforcement officer. Nothing very promising, but I got lucky right away with John Khyber, the law enforcement guy.

I secured the code of his next of kin from the announcement, and linked in. "I'm Alex Benedict," I said. "May I speak with Mrs. Khyber?"

"I'm Jana Khyber." I waited for her to materialize, but nothing happened.

"I'm sorry to bother you. My uncle was on the *Capella*. I believe he was traveling with your husband."

"Oh?" There was a sea change in the voice: softer, interested, pained. "I'm sorry about your uncle." I heard Jacob's projector switch on. There was a flutter of color in the air, and she appeared: dignified, a trifle matronly, attentive. Perhaps irritated, though with me, or Gabe, or her husband, I could not tell. "I'm glad to have a chance to talk to someone about it. Where were they going?"

"You don't know, Jana?"

"How would *I* know? Trust me, he said."

Son of a bitch. "Did you know Gabe Benedict?"

"No," she said, after a pause. "I didn't know my husband was traveling with anybody." She frowned, and her bosom, which was substantial, rose and fell. "I didn't know he was traveling at all. I mean off-world."

"Had he ever been to Saraglia before?"

"No." She crossed her arms. "He'd never been off Rimway before. At least not that I know of. Now I'm not so sure."

"But you knew he was going to be away for a while?"

"Yes. I knew."

"No explanation?"

"None," she said, biting off a sob. "My God, we've never had a problem of any kind, Mr. Benedict. Not really. He told me he was sorry, that he couldn't explain, that he'd be away six months."

"*Six months?* You must have questioned him."

"Of course I did. *They've called me back,* he said. *They need me, and I've got to go.*"

"Who were *they?*"

"The Agency. He was a security officer. Retired, but it didn't really make any difference. He's still a consultant." She hesitated over the statement, but didn't correct herself. "He specialized in commercial fraud, and you know how much of that there is these days." She sounded close to tears. "I just don't know what it was about, and that's what hurts so much. He's dead and I don't know why."

"Did you check with his agency?"

"They claim they don't know anything about it." She stared at me. "Mr. Benedict, he never gave me any reason to distrust him. We had a lot of years together, and it's the only time he's ever lied to me."

That you know of, I thought. But I said: "Did he have any interest in archeology?"

"I don't think so. No. Is this Gabriel an archeologist?"

"Yes."

"I can't imagine any kind of connection."

Nor could I.

Her voice quivered. "The truth is," she continued, struggling to maintain her composure, "I don't know what he was doing on that damned ship, where he was going, or what he planned to do when he got there. And if *you* have any ideas, I'd be grateful to know what they are. What sort of man was he, your uncle?"

I smiled, to assuage her fears. "One of the best I have ever known, Mrs. Khyber. He would not willingly have led your husband into danger. Or anything else that would have troubled you." Why would a retired police officer have been along? Bodyguard, perhaps? That hardly seemed likely. "Was he a pilot?"

"No."

"Tell me, Mrs. Khyber, did he have any interest in history? In the Resistance, particularly?"

A puzzled expression flickered across her features. "Yes," she said. "He was interested in anything that was old, Mr. Benedict. He collected antique books, was fascinated by old naval vessels, and he belonged to the Talino Society."

Bingo. "And what," I asked eagerly, "is the Talino Society?"

She looked steadily at me. "I don't think this is getting us anywhere."

"Please," I said. "You've already been of some help. Tell me about the Talino Society. I've never heard of it."

"A drinking club, really. They masquerade as historians, but mostly what they do is go down there—they meet on the final weeknight of each month at the Collandium—and they have a good time." She looked very tired. "He was a member for twenty years."

"Did you belong?"

"Yes, I usually went with him."

"Why was it called the 'Talino' Society?"

She smiled. Finally. "Mr. Benedict, you'll want to go down there and find out for yourself."

Two other things happened on the day I talked to Jana Khyber. Brimbury & Conn sent a statement of my assets. There was considerably more than I'd suspected, and I realized that I would never have to work again. Not ever. Oddly, I felt guilty about that. It was, after all, Gabe's money. And I had been less than gentle with him.

The other piece of news was that Jacob discovered a library halfway around the world that had a copy of Leisha Tanner's *Notebooks*. He promptly requested a transmission, and it arrived by lunchtime.

I'd been receiving calls all along from assorted thieves and bunkum artists purporting to have been business associates of my uncle, and wanting to "continue" rendering some high-priced service or other. There were wine brokers, realtors, an individual who described himself as a foundation attempting to erect monuments to prominent business executives, and several portfolio managers. And so on. I'd expected them to trail off, but they were becoming more, rather than less, frequent.

"From now on," I told Jacob, "they are yours. Put them off. Discourage them."

"How?"

"Use your imagination. Tell them we're contributing the money to a worthy cause, make one up, and that I'm retiring to a mountaintop."

Then I settled in with Leisha Tanner.

The *Notebooks* cover five years during which she was an instructor at the University of Khaja Luan on the world of that name. The first entries are dated from about the time she met the poet Walford Candles, and the last conclude with her resignation, in the third year of the Resistance. They were originally intended to be remarks on the progress of her students; but with the beginnings of tension on Imarios, the subsequent revolt, and Cormoral's catastrophic intervention, they widen into a graphic portrayal of social and political upheaval on a small world which was struggling to maintain its neutrality, and thereby its survival, at a time when Christopher Sim and his band of heroes needed every assistance.

Some of the portraits are unsettling. We're accustomed to thinking of those who actively opposed the onslaught of the Ashiyyur as patriots: valiant men and women who risked life and fortune across a hundred worlds to persuade reluctant governments to intervene during the crisis. But here is Tanner on the reaction to the mute assault against the City on the Crag:

Downtown today, speaker after speaker blasted the government and urged immediate intervention. There were some from the University, even old Angus Markham, whom I've never before seen angry. They were joined by some out-of-power politicians, and some entertainers, who seriously believe we ought to send off the entire fleet to make war on the Ashiyyur. I read yesterday that the "fleet" consists of two destroyers and one frigate. One of the destroyers is undergoing major repairs, and all three vessels are obsolete.

There were others present whom I took to be members of the Friends of the Confederacy. They stirred up the mob, which in turn clubbed a few people who didn't share their point of view, and probably a couple who did but didn't move quickly enough. Then they set off across town to march on the Council chambers. But Grenville Park is a long walk from Balister Avenue, and along the way they overturned some vehicles, attacked the police, and broke into a few bars.

A patriot is someone who's prepared to sacrifice anything, even other people's children, for a just cause.

Damn Sim anyhow! The war goes on and on, and everyone knows it's futile. There's a rumor that the Ashiyyur have asked us for the Amorda. For God's sake, I hope the Council is wise enough to comply.

I looked up *Amorda*. It was a guarantee of peace and autonomy to anyone who would accept Ashiyyurean suzerainty. I was surprised to discover that, for every human world that joined the Resistance, two remained neutral. A few even threw their support to the invaders.

The *Amorda*. It was a simple offering: a few cubic centimeters of earth from one's capital, encased in an urn of pure silver, signifying fidelity.

I scrolled ahead: while the Council debated its action, the hour struck for the City on the Crag. The Ashiyyur destroyed her defenses, and her orbiting factories. That center of culture, the longtime symbol of literature, democracy, and progress along the Frontier, was occupied at leisure. *It's a blunder of incredible dimensions*, wrote Tanner. *One almost wonders whether the Ashiyyur are deliberately trying to create the conditions for Tarien Sim to complete his alliance against them. In any case, the moment for the government of Khaja Luan to declare its neutrality, if indeed it ever existed at all, has passed. We will join the war. The only issue now is when.*

The attack is a surprise to no one. The City on the Crag, and her small group of allies, was technically neutral, but it was no secret that her volunteers have been fighting actively with the Dellacondans. It's also common knowledge that Sim has been getting strategic supplies from her orbiting factories. The Ashiyyur were justified; but I wish they could have shown some restraint. This may be enough to bring Earth or Rimway into the war. If that happens, God knows where it will end.

Tanner had been conducting a comparative ethics class when the first reports arrived. *Discussing the good and the beautiful*, she comments sadly, *while the children of Plato and Tulisofala cut one another's throats.* The target was assaulted by a force of several hundred ships that swept its hastily constructed defenses aside. Collapse had followed within hours. And that night, *while most of us concentrated on our steak and wine, the damned fools compounded the felony by shooting some hostages. How can a race of telepaths misjudge so completely the nature of their enemy?*

Tanner's images of the time are unbearably poignant: an enraged citizenry demanding war; a pompous university president leading a community prayer; an exchange student from the fallen world fighting back tears; and her own pangs of guilt at *the perverse way of such things, in which those of us who argue for a rational course, appear so cowardly.*

Again and again, she put the question to her journal, and eventually, I suppose, to us: *How does one account for the fact that a race can espouse the ideals of a Tulisofala, can compose great music, and create exquisite rock gardens, and still behave like barbarians?*

She doesn't record an answer.

Elsewhere in her journals, on a similar occasion (the collapse of the defenders at Randin'hal, I believe), she refers angrily to the Bogolyubov Principle.

I looked that up too. Andrey Bogolyubov lived a thousand years ago on Toxicon. He was an historian, and he specialized in trying to convert history into an exact science, with the predictability that is the hallmark of all the exact sciences. He never succeeded, of course.

His primary area of interest was the process by which reluctant powers become entangled in conflict. His thesis is that potential antagonists engage in a kind of diplomatic war dance, with specific articulable characteristics. The war dance phase creates a psychology which ultimately guarantees an armed clash, because it tends to take over the momentum of events. This is particularly true, he says, in democracies. This process, once begun, is not easily interrupted. Once the first blood is spilt, it becomes almost impossible to draw back. Original ambitions and objectives get lost, each side comes to believe its own propaganda, economies become dependent on the hostile environment, and political careers are built around the common danger. Consequently the cycle of war-making tightens and will not stop until one side or the other is exhausted.

Unless leaders emerge simultaneously *on both sides* who recognize the situation for what it is, and possess the character and the internal support to act, there can be no solution other than a military one. Unfortunately, political systems are seldom designed to produce policymakers capable of even conceiving, much less implementing, a strategy of disengagement. The odds against two such persons stepping forward at the moment of crisis are, to say the least, rather high.

It's hard from this distance to understand the dismay that accompanied the fall of the City on the Crag, which for us is only a symbol of lost greatness, an Atlantis. But among the inhabitants of the Frontier worlds two centuries ago, she was a living force: in a sense they were *all* her citizens; her music and her artists and her political theorists belonged to everyone; and the blow struck against her was an attack against all. Tanner reports Walford Candles's remark that *we've all sat at her sun-splashed tables on wide boulevards sipping expensive wine*. It must have been painful to think of that lovely place under the whip of a conqueror.

Several of Tanner's students announced their intention to leave school, and to join the war. Her friends were deeply divided. *He walked out of his class yesterday afternoon,* she reports of Matt Olander, a middle-aged physicist, whose wife and daughter had died two years earlier on Cormoral. *For several hours, we didn't know where he was. The security people found him just before midnight, slumped on a bench in Southpool. This morning, he told me he's going to offer his services to the Dellacondans. I think he'll be okay when he's had a chance to calm down.*

Bannister tried to point out the dangers of intervention yesterday during a meeting of one of the various war committees that we have these days. "Stand firm," he told them. "Give way to mob emotions now, and Khaja Luan will not survive two weeks." They stoned him.

Olander never did calm down. He submitted his resignation, took Tanner to dinner a few nights later, and said goodby. She gives no other details of the departure.

But Khaja Luan, despite everything, held onto its neutrality. Unrest continued, usually intensified by war news or the occasional reports of volunteer citizens who'd died alongside the Dellacondans. It was a wrenching period, and Tanner's anger mounted against both sides, *whose intransigence kills so many, and threatens us all.*

The small circle of faculty friends dissolves in bitterness and dispute. Walford Candles wanders the grim nights, a cold, familiar wraith. The others speak and write for or against the war and each other.

Occasionally, there is word from Olander.

He sits atop a rail, somewhere, on a wooden pier, framed against sails and nets. Or he stands beside a vegetative growth that is maybe a tree and maybe not. Always, there is a bottle in his hand, and a woman at his side. It is never the same woman, Tanner observes, with a trace of regret.

(The transmissions from Olander were not, of course, modern interactive sponders. He simply talked, and everyone listened.)

I was sorry she hadn't preserved some of the Olander holos. I've learned since that Walford Candles (who twenty years earlier had fought against Toxicon, and so knew firsthand about combat conditions) was so struck by them, by the contrast between Olander's cheerful generalities on local liquor, theater, and mating habits, and the grim reality of the war, that he began writing the great poetry of his middle period. That first collection was named for Olander's dispatches: *News from the Front.*

His references to the long struggle (Tanner reports), *were always vague. "Don't worry about me," he'd say. "We're doing all right." Or: "We lost a few people the other day."*

Occasionally, he speaks of the ships: of the Straczynski *and the* Morimar *and the* Povis *and the others: sleek, deadly, remorseless, and the affection in his voice and in his eyes chilled us all. Sometimes I think there's no hope for any of us.*

As time and the war dragged on, and early hopes that the Ashiyyur would bow to the first serious resistance faded, a little reality slipped through the stern brickwork of the warrior he had become: there were bleak portraits of the men and women who fought with him. "When we are gone," Tanner reports his saying, "who will take our place?"

It's a question to which she responds in a spasm of rage and grief: *Nobody! Nobody, because it's a damn fool war that neither side wants, and the only reason the Ashiyyur are conducting it at all is that we have challenged them!*

"She may have been correct," observed Jacob. "After all, we were on Imarios by their leave to begin with; and the revolt by that colony was not really justified. One has to wonder what the course of history would have been had Cormoral not intervened."

There's no record that any of the witnesses on Khaja Luan responded to Matt Olander. One assumes they must have done so, but there is no direct evidence. It leaves me to wonder whether Leisha Tanner ever voiced those angry sentiments to him. . . .

Candles, whose masterpieces at this time lie just before him, begins to retreat often to the Inner Room. Tanner comes under pressure from interventionists' to restructure her courses in Ashiyyurean philosophy and literature. Students and faculty members take up silent stations outside her classroom to protest the content of her programs. She receives death threats.

Meantime, the Board of Trustees, whose finances depend on an increasingly desperate government, wants to demonstrate its loyalty by supporting the official policy of neutrality. They do this by insisting that the Ashiyyurean studies program not only be maintained, but expanded.

Tension mounts: Randin'hal is occupied when her defenders, reinforced by four Dellacondan frigates, are overwhelmed after a short, desperate defense. The government acts to prohibit private citizens from engaging in foreign wars; and a prominent interventionist is assassinated in the middle of a speech on the Council floor. Three days after news comes of the fall of Randin'hal, there is an unauthorized public broadcast of a recording of radio transmissions among the ships that defended her. Tanner describes it as *heartbreaking*. A meeting called to demand intervention turns into a riot, and a Conciliar no-confidence vote miscarries by a margin of one!

Then Sim and a handful of Dellacondans surprise and rout a large enemy fleet off Eschalet!

In the midst of all this, news comes that Matt Olander is dead. *There are no words,* Tanner writes.

"Killed during the action off Randin'hal, while serving on board the Confederate frigate Straczynski," *the official dispatch says. We watched the statement on Candles's projector, which doesn't work very well. The spokesman was a bilious green. "He performed with valor, in the defense of people he did not know, and in the highest traditions of the Service. Please be assured that you are not alone in mourning his loss. His sacrifice will not be forgotten." It was addressed to the physics department.*

So Matt will not come home to us. I remember those last conversations, when he only shook his head while I argued the pointlessness of it all. "You're wrong, Leisha," he'd said. "This is not a war in the casual human context. It's a watershed. An evolutionary crossroad. Two technological cultures, certainly the only ones in the Arm, possibly in the entire Milky Way. If I were religiously inclined, I would tell you that we've been specifically prepared by nature . . . blah, blah, blah."

Goddam.

It's been raining most of the day. The campus is heavy and sodden under the best of conditions. But tonight the trees and obelisks and giant afolia bushes are shadows from another world, a place without Matt, and without order. The few persons I can see hurry along wrapped in heavy jackets.

Death at a distance.

A few days later the Dellacondans ambush and scatter an Ashiyyurean battle fleet in the Slot. It is their second major victory in a week, and their biggest ever in terms of casualties inflicted: two capital ships, half a dozen escorts; while Sim's small force loses only a frigate.

Then came the enigma.

It started innocently, and painfully. Personal holos inbound from the war zones were relatively low priority on the communication systems, so no one was surprised when another transmission arrived from Olander. They assembled at the Inner Room, Leisha

and Candles and the others, many no longer on speaking terms, but
drawn together by the common grief.

*They were having a party, a bunch of officers, all young (except
Matt), both sexes, in the light and dark blue uniforms of the
Dellacondans. Smoky dancers gyrated through the background, and
everyone was having a pretty good time. Matt kept trying to talk to
us, through the noise and the laughter, telling us they'd all be home
soon. And then there was the line that no one picked up at first, but
which has since kept me awake at night: "You will by now," he said,
speaking over a glass of bubbling wine, "know about Eschalet and
the Slot. We've turned this damned thing around at last. Tell Leisha
the sons of bitches are on the run!"*

*It was a few minutes later, when the holo had ended, that Candles
grunted and glanced at me with a puzzled expression on his blunt
face. "The Slot," he said. "Matt died during the defense of
Randin'hal. The Slot hadn't been fought yet!"*

In effect, it ends there. The *Notebooks* restrict themselves
afterward to the relatively mundane: a breakdown by a gardener
who is employed by the University; an interview with Candles that
would be of some literary interest; and some self-doubt resulting
from Tanner's lack of patience with a difficult student. *My God*, she
complains, *the world's coming apart, and this kid's upset because
she has to try to comprehend how life and death appears to a
telepath. But how else is she to understand Ashiyyurean literature?*

A few weeks later, she records her resignation, and makes her
final entry. It is a single word: *Millenium!*

Millenium: it was Sim's first ally. The world that sent its ships to
Chippewa and Grand Salinas and Rigel. The arsenal of the
Confederacy during the great days of the Dellacondans. It was to
Millenium that Sim took the refugees after his celebrated evacua-
tion of Ilyanda.

So great is the affection on that world for Christopher Sim that
the *Corsarius* is still carried on the rolls as an active warship. All
fleet communications show her call sign.

I requested from the source library a list of others who had got
access to the *Notebooks*. The information was on Jacob's display
before I retired for the evening. Six people over the last five years.
I'd expected to find Hugh Scott's name. I didn't.

But I did find Gabe's.

VII.

In a sense, the raid (on Hrinwhar) constituted a victory far out of proportion to its direct military value. The myth of enemy invulnerability was forever shattered, and the Ashiyyur learned they could not continue their relentless advance without pausing occasionally to look back over their shoulders.

— *The Machesney Review, LXIV, No. 7*

THE HALL OF THE PEOPLE is the center of human government. The Council meets there; the executive offices are located, symbolically, on the lower levels; and the Court convenes in the West Wing. It dominates all surrounding structures, even the Silver Tower of the Confederacy at the opposite end of the White Pool.

Adjacent to the Court, and physically accessible only on foot, the Confederate Archive sprawls across almost a square kilometer of prime parkland. It is a Romanesque structure, guarded by the celebrated Sharpley bronze of Tarien Sim, the scroll of the Instrument (which, in fact, he never lived to see completed) in his extended hand.

The snow had vanished, the weather had turned unseasonably warm, and the assorted flags of the worlds snapped in the breeze, dominated by the green and white banner of Man. It was far too pleasant a day to spend within four walls, so I abandoned the headband and joined the considerable crowds that were taking advantage of the sunshine.

Tourists lined the walks, and clustered around the monuments. One of the tour guides was holding forth on the Archive, which was the oldest government building in Andiquar, dating from the end of the Time of Troubles. It had been restored on several occasions, most recently four years before, during the summer of 1410. It was an antiquarian's treasure trove: people were always finding valuable, long-lost documents in obscure places.

Inside, the main gallery was relatively empty. A small knot of school children and a teacher hovered round the marble and glass case which contains the Instrument of Confederation and a few related documents. A few others from the group stared up at the Declaration of Intent, the joint decision by Rimway and Earth to join the war against the Ashiyyur. I passed the uniformed Companion, stationed at the South Arch, and descended into the library.

Simulations of the major actions of the Resistance were available there. The Spinners. Vendicari. Black Adrian. Grand Salinas. The Slot. Rigel. Tippimaru. And finally Triflis, where, for the first time, the human race drew together.

After two centuries, they were still names to conjure by. The stuff of legend.

I checked out five: Eschaton, Sanusar, the Slot, Rigel, and the Spinners. The latter, of course, is the classic raid that some say turned the course of the war.

On the way home, drifting lazily over the capital, I wondered what it had been like to live in a world of organized mayhem. There was still tension, and occasional shooting, but it was remote, far-off: it was hard to imagine an existence incorporating active everyday institutionalized slaughter. And it struck me that the last conflict fought exclusively among humans had occurred at the height of the Resistance. While the series of critical battles were being fought in the Slot, Toxicon, whose powerful fleets Sim desperately needed and courted, had seized the opportunity to attack the Dellacondan ally, Muri. Later, Sim would call it the darkest hour of the war.

Today, for perhaps the first time in history, there is no man living who knows from personal experience what it is to make war on his brothers. And that happy fact is the *real* legacy of Tarien and Christopher Sim.

Though no one realized it at the time, the attack on Muri might have been the best thing that could have happened, because it so outraged public opinion on Toxicon that, within a year, that world's autocratic government collapsed. The interventionists, heartily supported by a rare alliance between the general population and the military, seized power, broke off the assault against their embattled victims, and promptly announced an intention to support the Dellacondans. Tragically, Toxicon's ringing declaration of war was followed within hours by news of Christopher Sim's death off Rigel.

I went home to a leisurely dinner, and drank a little more wine than usual. Jacob was quiet. It had turned cold outside, and blustery. The wind shook the trees and the house.

I wandered from room to room, paging through Gabe's books, old histories and archeology texts mostly, accounts of excavations on the twenty-five or thirty worlds whose settlements had occurred deep enough in the past to allow for the collapse and interment of cultures.

There were some biographies, a few manuals on planetary sciences, a scattering of mythological texts, and a few general reference books.

Gabe had never shown much interest in literature for its own sake. He'd read Homer before we went to Hissarlik, Kachimonda before Battle Key, and so on. Consequently, when I came across additional volumes of Walford Candles in a remote corner of the house, I pulled them down, and stacked them alongside the material I'd brought from the Archive, added the volume of *Rumors of Earth* that had been in Gabe's bedroom, and retreated with everything to the upstairs study.

I didn't know much then about Candles's literary reputation. But I was learning quickly. He was preoccupied with fragility and transience: passions too easily dissipated; youth too easily lost in the trauma of war. The most fortunate, in his view, are those who die heroically for a principle. The rest of us are left to outlive our friends, to watch love cool, and to feel the lengthening winter in our vitals.

It made for a depressing evening, but the books were well thumbed. Eventually, I went back and reread the "Leisha."

> *Lost pilot,*
> *She rides her solitary orbit*
> *Far from Rigel,*
> *Seeking by night*
> *The starry wheel.*
> *Adrift in ancient seas,*
> *It marks the long year round,*
> *Nine on the rim,*
> *Two at the hub.*
> *And she,*
> *Wandering,*
> *Knows neither port,*
> *Nor rest,*
> *Nor me.*

Rigel had only one association: Sim's death. But what did the rest of it mean? The notes suggested that the poet had considered the work completed. And there was no evidence that the editors found anything baffling about it. Of course, one almost expects to be puzzled by great poetry, I suppose.

According to the introduction to *Dark Stars*, the first volume of the series, Walford Candles had been a professor of classical literature, had never married, and was not appreciated in his own time. A minor talent, his contemporaries had agreed.

To us, he is a different matter altogether.

The poignancy of the sacrifices required by the men and women who fought with Christopher Sim shines everywhere in his work. Most of the poems in *Dark Stars*, *News from the Front*, and *On the Walls* purport to have been written in the Inner Room on Khaja Luan, while he waited to hear the inevitable about old friends who had gone to help the Dellacondans. Candles himself claimed to have offered his services, and been refused. No usable skills. Instead of fighting, his part became merely

> *To stand and count the names of those*
> *Whose dust circles the gray worlds of Chippewa*
> *And Cormoral.*

Candles watches from a dark-lit corner while young volunteers hold a farewell party. One raises an eye to the middle-aged poet, nods, and Candles inclines his head in silent salute.

On the night that they learned about Chippewa, a prosperous

physician who had never before been seen at the Inner Room, enters, and buys drinks for all. His daughter, Candles learns, has been lost on a frigate.

In "Rumors of Earth," the title work from his fourth volume, he describes the effect of reports that the home world is about to intervene. *Who, then,* he asks, *will dare stand aside?*

But it does not happen, and despite Chippewa, despite a hundred small victories, the battered force is pushed relentlessly back, into the final, fatal trap at Rigel.

The poems are dated, and there is a gap beginning at about the time of Sim's death, extending for almost a year, during which Candles appears to have written nothing. And then comes his terrible indictment of Earth, and Rimway, and the others, which had delayed so long:

> *Our children will face again their silent fury,*
> *And they will do it without the Warrior,*
> *Who walks behind the stars*
> *On far Belmincour.*

"There is no 'Belmincour' listed in the catalogs," said Jacob. "It is apparently a literary reference, which might mean 'enthusiastic war,' or 'beautiful place of the heart.' Difficult to be sure: human languages are not very precise."

I agreed.

"Several towns on various worlds," he continued, "and one city on Earth, share the name. But it is not likely the poet refers to any of these."

"Then what?"

"It has been a subject of dispute. Taken within its context, it appears to refer to a kind of Valhalla. Armand Halley, a prominent Candles scholar, argues that it is a classical reference to a better past, the world where Sim—in his words—would have preferred to live."

"Seems odd to use a place name, or a term, that no one understands."

"Poets do it all the time, Alex. It allows the reader's imagination freer play."

"Sure," I grumbled. We were beginning to get some light in the east. And I was weary. But every time I closed my eyes, questions jabbed at me. Olander's name rang a bell, but I couldn't remember where (or if) I'd heard of him before.

And always, the supreme puzzle: what had Hugh Scott and the men of the *Tenandrome* seen?

I picked idly through the crystals I'd brought back from the Conciliar Library, selected one, and inserted it into Jacob's reader.

"The Spinners, sir?" he asked.

"Yes," I said. "Scott was supposed to have gone to Hrinwhar. Let's see what it looked like to Sim."

"It's very late, Alex."

"I know. Please run the simulation."

"If you insist. To opt out, you need, of course, only remove the headband." I sat down in the overstuffed chair, took the control packet from the equipment drawer in the coffee table, and inserted the jack into Jacob. "The program has a monitor. Do you wish me to sit in?"

"I don't think that'll be necessary." I pulled the headband into place, and switched it on.

"Activating," said Jacob.

A feminine voice, whiskey-flavored, flat, asked my name.

"Alex," I said.

Alex, close your eyes. When you open them you will be on board the Pauline Stein. *Do you wish a detailed review of the war to this point?*

"No, thank you."

The Stein *will be functioning as the command and control ship during this operation. Do you wish to participate in the ground raid, or do you prefer to ride with the command ship?*

"The command ship," I answered.

Alex, you are now on the bridge of the Stein. *This program is designed to allow you simply to observe while the battle, as it has been reconstructed from available evidence, plays itself out. Or, if you prefer, we offer other options. You may take command of one of the frigates, or even assume flag responsibility and direct overall strategy, thereby possibly changing history. Which do you prefer?*

"I will watch."

An excellent choice, she said.

I was alone in a forward cockpit with several battle displays. Voices crackled out of hidden speakers. The bridge opened out below me, and I could see occasional movement. A white-bearded, heavy man occupied a central seat. His face was turned away, but I could see the gleam of gold on his uniform. His posture and tone radiated command. The air was filled with voices speaking in hushed, unemotional tones.

I sat on a swivel chair within a plastic bubble. A dark, amorphous landscape moved beneath us, around us, gloomily illuminated by spasms of electricity. There was no sky, no stars, no steady light. It was a fearful place, and I was glad for the solid reassurance of the ship's interior, the voices, the consoles, the chairpads. *We are in the upper atmosphere of the super gas giant Masipol,* said the Monitor. *Sixth planet of Windyne. The mission target is Masipol's eleventh moon, Hrinwhar, which orbits at a range of almost three-quarters of a million kilometers. Although the Ashiyyur do not anticipate an attack, there are major naval units in the area.*

Occasionally, through what I presumed were breaks in heavy clouds, I glimpsed silver and green bands of light, a broad luminous arc that seemed to be traveling with us. Then it was gone, and in the brief glow of its passing, a universal gloom closed in.

The planetary rings, explained the Monitor. *We're climbing into orbit. They should be completely visible shortly.*

Yes: moments later, shadows leaped from the surreal cloudscape. Wedges of soft radiance, and a dozen glittering belts of ice-hard light emerged.

It might have been the rainbow bridge of northern European folklore, risen from the mist, joining the horizons, overwhelming the starfields. Scarlet, yellow, and green planks were supported by a wide violet buttress. Blue and silver ribbons heightened the illusion of solidity by twisting round each other.

A few stars were scattered to the extreme north and south. And two shrunken suns were barely discernible in the glare. *Coreopholi and Windyne,* said the Monitor. *They are known jointly as the Spinners, because both have an extremely high rotation rate. We are on the edge of the Arm, by the way, looking away from the Galaxy. This is the point of Sim's deepest penetration into Ashiyyurean space.*

Christopher Sim's force consists of six frigates. And he has a problem: his ships have emerged from hyper within the past eight hours, and the Armstrong units are depleted. Little is known of the Dellacondan propulsion systems, but at best they will require the better part of a day before they can be used again. And he does not have time to wait.

An order of battle scrolled across my central display: the aliens have one heavy cruiser, two, and possibly three, light cruisers, seven destroyers, and thirteen to sixteen frigates. In addition there are several fleet escort vessels. The heavy cruiser itself is known to be in one of the orbiting docks, from which it can do no damage.

I knew we'd won at the Spinners, and I knew it had been against heavy odds. But that had been electronic knowledge: now I sat and watched an analysis of enemy firepower that should have utterly discouraged the Dellacondans.

"What's it about? What was Sim trying to accomplish?"

This system attracted his interest for a variety of reasons. It houses a major enemy base, which serves as a center for logistical coordination, communications, intelligence gathering, and long range strategic planning. This facility is believed to be ill-prepared to withstand an attack, both because of its distance from the fighting, and because of Ashiyyurean psychology. At this point the war is still young, and the enemy has not yet grown accustomed to human methods. Warfare among the aliens has traditionally been carried out on a formal, ritualistic basis. Opposing forces are expected to announce their intentions well in advance, draw up on opposite sides of the battle zone, exchange salutes, and, at an agreed-upon moment, commence hostilities. Sim, of course, fights in the classical human mode. Which is to say that he cannot be trusted. He ambushes lone warships, strikes supply points, attacks without warning, and, perhaps most outrageous of all, refuses to commit himself to formal battle. In the eyes of the Ashiyyur, he is unethical.

It's always the side with the firepower that expects everybody to line up.

The base is constructed in the center of a crater, and is difficult to detect visually. It is actually an underground city of substantial size. Population at this time is believed to be on the order of eight thousand.

Sim anticipates that a successful raid here will have highly desirable long range consequences: he expects to gain access to detailed information on enemy warships, tactical capabilities, strategic plans. Furthermore, he hopes to disrupt enemy logistics, possibly compromise communications and cryptosystems, and maybe even carry off a few high-ranking prisoners. But his primary goal is to shatter the myth of Ashiyyurean invulnerability, and thereby encourage some of the worlds who have hung back to join the cause.

Outside, against the peaceful incandescence of the rings, Sim's gray wolves swam into view. They were long and tapered and lovely. (What had Leisha Tanner said of them? When she measured her own reaction to these instruments of war, she despaired that any of us would survive.) Clusters of beam and particle weapons projected from a dozen stations. Emblazoned on the prow of each ship was the black harridan, pinions spread in flight, eyes narrowed, claws thrust forward.

On the inmost vessel, the device stood within a silver crescent: and I could not resist a surge of pride. It was the *Corsarius,* Sim's own ship, whose likeness hangs now in Marcross's brilliant oil in the Hall of the People. (The same print, by the way, that dominated one of Hugh Scott's walls.) The artist hadn't done her justice, and I don't suppose any representation could. She was magnificent: a blue and silver bullet, her sleek hull bristling with weapons clusters and communications pods. A sunburst expanded across her parabolic prow. And she looked capable of damned near anything.

You can see two other frigates, said the Monitor. *They are the Straczynski and the Rappaport. Straczynski has already earned a host of commendations, but she will be destroyed, with all her crew, four days from now during the defense of Randin'hal. Rappaport will be the only known Dellacondan vessel to survive the war. She is currently maintained as the centerpiece of the Hrinwhar Naval Museum on Dellaconda.*

I sat, fascinated by the power and grace of the ships. They were silver and deadly in the cold illumination cast by the two suns. The bridge of the *Corsarius* spilled yellow light into the void: I could make out figures moving about inside. And the voices on the commlinks changed subtly, grew charged with tension.

I watched *Straczynski* lift gradually out of formation. She hovered a few moments, apparently falling behind; and then her engines flared, and she dropped away.

She is going to take out a communications relay station, said the Monitor. *Rappaport will follow directly.*

"Monitor," I said, "We seem to have only four ships. Where are the other two? And where are the enemy defenses?"

Two frigates have re-entered linear space in a manner that allows them to approach from a different direction. One of the two, the Korbal, has been altered to put out the electronic "fingerprint" of the Corsarius. *Hrinwhar's defenders have scrambled to attack the intruders.*

"All of them?"

A few units remain. But the light cruisers are gone!

I tried to recall the details of the raid on Hrinwhar, and was dismayed at how little I knew, other than that it had marked the first time the Confederates had seized the initiative.

Korbal and its companion vessel have already taken out a picket, and engaged in a brief exchange of fire with another frigate. This has given the enemy's intelligence analysts time to draw false conclusions about the identity of their attacker, whom they now believe to be Sim. In addition, Ashiyyurean ships tracking the diversionary force have noted an anomaly in the thrust pattern of the vessel they think to be the Corsarius. They believe that Sim has engine trouble. Their great enemy seems to be helpless.

In the fragmented chatter of the ship's intercom, I was able to pick up a running description of the action: "They are still pursuing *Korbal* toward Windyne. *Korbal* will stay in the sun to prevent visual inspection."

"*Straczynski* reports Alpha destroyed."

Alpha's a communications relay station, designated on your display, said the Monitor. *Sim hopes to cut off all communications between the base and its defenders.*

"They're not very bright," I said. "The Ashiyyur."

They're not accustomed to this sort of warfare. It is one of the reasons they hold us in contempt. They don't expect an opponent to be dishonest. In their view, Sim should come forward, without stealth, without deceit, and fight like a man.

"They don't understand war," I grumbled.

A new voice, obviously accustomed to command: "Go to attack mode. Prepare to execute Windsong."

They would reply that the brutality of armed combat demands a sense of ethics. A person who cheats in matters of life and death is perceived as a barbarian.

"This is *Corsarius:* preliminary scan shows a cruiser in the area. It is escorted by two—no, make that three—frigates. Cruiser is Y-class, and is in geosynchronous orbit over base. Two of the frigates appear to be responding to *Straczynski*."

"*Rappaport* approaching Beta."

"Execute Windsong."

Acceleration pressed me gently back into my seat. The cloudscape fell swiftly away. *Corsarius* rose and arced toward the rings, and rapidly dwindled to a triangle of lights moving against the sky.

"This is *Rappaport*. Beta is dead. Communications should be out."

"We are now over the curve of the horizon, within view of enemy scans. Assume that *Corsarius* and *Stein* have been sighted."

"One frigate on intercept vector. No reaction yet from the cruiser."

Targeting information flowed across the screens: schematics of the incoming frigate appeared, rotated. I could hear hatches closing throughout the ship. Below me, all activity seemed to have ceased. I reached up and increased the flow of cool air into the cockpit.

"Cruiser getting underway."

"*Corsarius* will handle. *Stein* take the frigate."

The lights of Sim's ship blinked out. We kept on: the enemy vessel appeared on the short range scopes, a black sphere gliding toward us between the stars.

White light flared on its surface.

At the same instant, we turned a hard bone-crunching left.

I'd belted myself down. But I got thrown around pretty well anyway, and I managed to crack myself in the jaw. There was a brief spurt of nausea, and I would have touched the headband for reassurance except that I didn't dare let go of the webbing until we straightened out.

"Firing NDL," said the intercom. A shudder ran through the bulkheads, and lightning squirted toward the oncoming sphere.

"On track."

"Another incoming." We swung violently in the opposite direction, and dived. I left my stomach behind, and started thinking about terminating. Hrinwhar's lunar surface rolled suddenly across my field of vision, rose to a vertical, and dropped away.

"We've got the cruiser cold!"

Those voices are from Corsarius, said the Monitor.

"Full spread!"

It sounded encouraging, but we got hit ourselves about then, and the *Stein* shook until I wondered how in hell it held together. On the bridge, the captain spoke almost casually to his officers as though nothing out of the way was happening.

A nuclear fireball, silent, blossoming, swept by us. Then: "We got the bastards. They're tumbling."

"Damage Control: report."

A cheer down on the deck. "Mutes have lost propulsion."

"Forward shield collapsed, Captain. We're working on it. Have it back in a few minutes."

"*Straczynski* has engaged the other two frigates."

"*Rappaport*, proceed to *Straczynski* assistance."

"Scopes all clear."

"Landing party stand by."

"*Rappaport* underway. ETA *Straczynski's* position approximately eleven minutes."

"The cruiser has broken apart." Another cheer.

"Captain, they've got nothing left to cover the heavy."

Through the plexiglass there was only black sky and pockmarked rock. On my screens, though, I could see it, an enormous illuminated barbell, its lights blinking out in a pathetic effort to avoid detection. It floated on tethers, within the spidery bays of its orbiting dock.

"Concur, Captain. No sign of tactical support."

"Acknowledged. *Stein* to Command. We have a heavy cruiser here. Permission to attack."

"Negative. Do not engage. Prepare to launch the assault teams."

Men and equipment were moving through the ship. *Sim will lead the ground force personally*, the Monitor said.

I listened to more exchanges, and then the landers were away. Now the two frigates, acting in concert, descended to attack. From my own visit, I recognized the cluster of domes set on the bleak moonscape.

A beam of pale light cut through the black sky. It appeared to be originating from a point north of the base. "Laser," said the intercom.

My displays locked on the source: a pair of dish antennas. We lobbed a plasma weapon of some sort in their general direction. The area erupted in a brilliant slow-motion conflagration, and the lights vanished.

After the ground assault had got well under way, we climbed back into orbit, where we were joined by *Rappaport* and *Straczynski*. It was a nervous time: we were now exceedingly vulnerable, and even I, who knew how it would all come out, waited anxiously, watching for the appearance of the enemy fleet on the scopes, listening to the reports coming back up from the landing force.

Resistance on the ground gave way quickly. Within ten minutes,

Sim's raiders had broken through the outer defenses, and entered the base proper.

"Monitor," I said, "how much of an advantage do the Ashiyyur have in close combat?"

You mean because of their telepathic capability?

"Yes."

Probably none. Experts don't think they can sort things out quickly enough to be of any real value in a combat situation. It may be fortunate that their capabilities are only passive in nature. If they could transmit, project thoughts or emotions into the minds of their enemies, things might have been very different.

The fighting turned quickly into a rout. Sim and his force moved almost at will through the enemy complex, collecting communication and tactical data, and destroying everything else: spare parts, supplies, weapons, intelligence systems, and command and control equipment.

"*Corsarius* to landing party: we urge you to finish up and prepare to return."

"Why?" It was the authoritative voice I'd heard earlier. I had no doubt who its owner was. "Is there a problem?"

"We're going to have company. We have line of sight readings on the mutes. They're coming fast."

"How long?"

"They'll be within maximum firing range in about thirty-seven minutes."

Pause. Then the voice from the ground again: "I thought we'd have more time, Andre. Okay: we'll be starting the *Stein* team up immediately. The rest of us will follow in about ten minutes."

"That's cutting it close."

"Best I can do. Release *Straczynski* and *Rappaport*. Tell them to withdraw. We're getting everything, Andre. Cross index on the entire fleet, breakout on cryptosystems, you name it."

"Won't do us any good if we don't get out."

I asked Monitor how long it would take for the *Corsarius* lander to rendezvous with its ship. The precise answer depended on a couple of variables, but it came down to approximately twenty-three minutes. That meant that we could get underway before the Ashiyyur began shooting, but we would be accelerating from orbital velocity. They'd overhaul us pretty quickly. Long before we could make the jump into hyper. Unless I was missing something, we were going to get blown up.

Blips appeared on my long range scan. Destroyers and frigates. We weren't tracking the big stuff yet, which meant they were probably having a hard time getting turned around and pointed in our direction. That would help.

Corsarius did not pass that extra bit of information along to the force on the ground.

The *Stein* lander reported that it was away. Moments later, we began to accelerate toward rendezvous.

The enormous bulk of Masipol hung in the western sky, an eerily lit purple blotch, an ill omen. I strained to see the lander, watched the giant planet, and kept an eye on the blips, which grew in size, and gradually defined themselves into forms I could read: a flotilla of destroyers here, a squadron of frigates there.

Again the voice from *Corsarius:* "Chris."

"We're moving as fast as we can."

"You're out of time."

"Acknowledged."

I could hear people breathing on the intercom. Someone was making course adjustments. Then a new voice: "Prepare the Phantom. Mask all systems."

"Enemy vessels will be within strike range in fourteen minutes. They have begun to decelerate."

"Fire the Phantom."

The ship trembled, and something dark leaped forward and disappeared immediately.

It's a decoy, said the Monitor. *We're running silent now, absorbing scans. The Phantom will simulate* Stein's *radiation patterns. The idea is to mislead the approaching force.*

"Will it work?"

For a few minutes. Incidentally, Corsarius *has also fired one.*"

I sat there sweating. How in hell could they possibly hope to outrun the Ashiyyur? Even with the fancy devices. I wasn't sure about these antiques, but a modern vessel, beginning from a standing start, would be overhauled within an hour.

"Chris?"

"We're leaving now. The mutes were trying to jury-rig a particle beam, and we had to take it out. Get moving. We'll rendezvous on the run."

He didn't sound as if he felt trapped. But the scanners were crowded with blips. They were going to be all over us.

"*Stein* lander alongside."

"Frigates leading the pack. They'll be the first ones here. Maximum firing range eleven minutes."

"Let's hope they chase the Phantoms instead of us. Rate of deceleration?"

"Slowing. It's back up to three percent."

"Operations reports the big ships are just now rising out of the flux. They haven't been able to reverse course yet, and will not participate in this action."

That meant they were still going the wrong way. I couldn't see how it would matter, though. The cloud of blips across my scopes was very close.

"Frigates are tracking the Phantoms."

It is difficult, Alex, for enemy sensors to pick up vessels as small as these, especially against a lunar background.

"Ground force aboard."

"Casualties?"

"Three. Plus Koley. Didn't make it back, sir."

"Get them to sick bay. Status on *Corsarius?*"

"Three minutes to rendezvous with her lander."

"Set course and speed to run parallel with *Corsarius* after pickup. Prepare for departure."

The oncoming fleet was settling behind the horizon now. I assumed Sim was planning to put the bulk of Hrinwhar between us and our pursuers, though that seemed to me to offer no hope.

"Destroyers are still locked on the Phantoms."

"Dumb bastards."

We'd shut down all nonessential systems and reduced power in others to cut radiation leakage. We were behind the moon now, invisible, secure. Temporarily. Still, it was a good feeling.

"*Corsarius* team on board."

"Very good. Lock in exit course. Wait for execute."

We waited. My God, we waited. But there was no hint of panic in the voices on the intercom, or among the bridge crew. We continued in our orbit: I watched the horizon ahead, waiting for the lights of the Ashiyyur. When we emerged from our hiding place, we would be within easy range of their weapons.

"What the hell are we doing?" I asked no one in particular.

"They're turning away from the Phantoms. They've figured it out."

"Scanners are locked on. They've found us."

"Doesn't matter now," came Sim's voice over the intercom.

"Let's clear out. Execute exit maneuver. Execute."

The webbed seat swung to face the direction of acceleration, and a moment later I was slammed flat. The moon was gone, the giant planet rolled across the top of the sky. I was damned if I could figure out what was going on. Lifting out of orbit now meant that we'd be heading in the direction of the two suns. *Toward* the oncoming force.

And then I pictured the scene in the Ashiyyurean ships: the poor sons of bitches frantically applying their brakes, while we roared directly at them. Their few hurried shots went hopelessly wide, and then we were among them where the risk was too high to fire. We nailed a destroyer on the way out.

Down below, on the bridge, and on the intercom, there was a collective sigh.

It was followed by Sim's voice: "Well done, friends," he said. "I think we've given them something to think about today."

VIII.

A good man's name has been dragged unjustly through the streets. If we can, in some small measure, help rectify this condition, then we will have served a worthwhile purpose. And if, along the way, we can pass an hour in quiet friendship, embellished by an appropriate toast or two, why so much the better!

—Adrian Coyle
Address at the founding
of the Ludik Talino Society

MACHESNEY HAD COME THROUGH. Though I was positive the reference was to Rashim Machesney, dead these two hundred years (like all the other principal actors in this curious business), I instructed Jacob to contact everybody on the net who owned that last name.

There weren't many.

We found no one who'd ever heard of Gabriel Benedict, and no one who seemed to have any ties to the Resistance: nobody who'd written about it, no old-time war buffs, no antique collectors. (There was some difficulty in acquiring this information, because persons owning that famous name tended to assume a prank when we started asking about the Resistance.)

My next step was to learn what I could about the great man himself. But if the problem with Leisha Tanner had been a paucity of data, in Machesney's case there was a tidal wave of crystals, books, articles, scientific analyses, you name it. Not to mention Machesney's own works. Jacob counted some eleven hundred volumes written specifically *about* him, treating his diplomatic and scientific achievements; many times that number included him in their indices.

Rashim Machesney had been a physicist, probably the most eminent of his time. And when the war broke out, while most of his colleagues urged restraint, he'd warned against the common danger and announced his intention to support the Dellacondans "to the limits of my strength." His home world tried to stop him (creating an embarrassment it hasn't yet lived down), but Machesney escaped, took some of his associates with him, and joined Sim.

His value to the Confederate cause had been, as far as anyone knew, primarily diplomatic. He lent his enormous prestige to the effort to induce neutrals to join the unequal struggle. He campaigned across half a hundred worlds, wrote brilliant tracts, addressed planetary audiences, survived assassination attempts, and in one memorable escapade was actually captured by the Ashiyyur, and rescued a few hours later.

Most historians credited Machesney for the ultimate intervention by Earth.

But I was overwhelmed by the sheer amount of material. "Jacob," I said, "there's no way I can go through all this. *You* do it. Find the connection. I'm going to try another approach."

"What precisely am I looking for, Alex?"

"Hard to say. But you'll know it when you see it."

"That's not much of an instruction."

I agreed that it wasn't, told him to do the best he could, and linked to the institution that had been created in Machesney's memory.

The Rashim Machesney Institute is a temple, really, in the classical Hellenic vein. Constructed of white marble, adorned with graceful columns and statuary, it stands majestically on the banks of the Melony. In the rotunda, the great man's likeness has been carved in stone. Overhead, around the circular roof, is his remark to the Legislature on Toxicon: "Friends, the danger awaits our convenience."

The Institute housed an astronomical data receiving station, which acted as a clearing house for telemetry relayed from a thousand observatories, from Survey flights, from deep space probes, and from God knew where else. Primarily, though, the Institute was a showcase for science and technology, a place where people took their families to see what life was really like out in the cylinder worlds. Or how computers and the pulsar Hercules X-1 combine to create Universal Standard Time. There was a simulation of a ride into a black hole running at the theater.

In addition, the library and bookstore were good sources on Machesney. I would have liked to run a search of the library files to see whether Gabe had ever checked anything out, but the clerk insisted it wasn't possible to obtain that kind of information. "Best we can do is look outside the net. We have better records on off-line materials that he'd have to check out physically. If he was late returning anything, we'd have it. Otherwise—" He shrugged.

"Don't bother," I said.

I'd gone there hoping to find an expert of some sort, take him aside, and get a fresh point of view on the problem. But in the end I could think of no way to formulate a question. So I settled for picking up some off-line material, copied it into a blank crystal, and added it to Jacob's pile.

Jacob reported no progress yet on the first batch. "I am processing at a slow rate, to allow better perception. But it would help if you could define the parameters of the search."

"Look for suggestions of a lost artifact," I said. "Preferably a puzzle for which we might reasonably expect Dr. Machesney to have had a solution. Or something that got lost, that *we* might consider an artifact."

I became something of an expert myself on Rash Machesney. He risked everything in that war. The scientific community blackballed him; his home world conducted criminal proceedings and sentenced him *in absentia* to two years in prison. The peace movement blasted him, one of its spokesmen declaring that his name would be linked with Iscariot. And the Ashiyyur denounced him as a prostitute, using his knowledge to create advanced weaponry. That was a charge he never denied.

He was also accused of being a crank, a womanizer, and a man who enjoyed his liquor. I acquired a distinct affection for him.

But I got nowhere, and gave up after several nights. There were no indications of anything valuable missing, and no connection with the Veiled Lady. That nebula was far from the scene of the war. It was a site for no battles, and no targets hid within its winding folds. (Strategic interest in the Veiled Lady was a creature of relatively recent development, springing from the expansion of the Confederacy into that region. During Sim's time, there would have been no point in advancing through the nebula because there were easier routes into the heart of the Confederacy. Today, however, matters were different.)

Chase offered to help. I accepted, and she got a sack of reading and viewing material. It didn't matter very much.

When the Ludik Talino Society held its next monthly meeting at the Collandium, I was there.

Jana Khyber was right: it was to be a social rather than an academic evening. The conversation in the lobby was good-humored, full of laughter, and everyone was clearly prepared for a party.

It felt a bit like going to the theater. People were well-dressed, waving to one another, mixing easily. Not at all the sort of crowd you might have expected at a gathering, say, of the local historical society, or the Friends of the University Museum.

I wandered inside, traded a few trivialities with a couple of women, and secured a drink. We were in a series of connected conference rooms, the largest of which was set up to seat about three hundred. It was just adequate.

There was money in the establishment: thick carpets, paneled walls, crystal chandeliers and electric candles, carved bookshelves, paintings by Manois and Romfret. Talino's image was displayed on a banner in the main room. And Christopher Sim's harridan device had been mounted on the podium.

There were exhibits of relevant works by the members: histories, battle analyses, discussions of various disputed details of that much-disputed war. Most had been privately produced, but a few bore the imprint of major publishers.

Above the speakers' platform, Marcross's *Corsarius* appeared again.

An agenda was posted. Panels would evaluate the validity of assorted historical documents, examine the relationship between two people I'd never heard of (they turned out to be obscure women who *might* have known Talino, and, in the opinion of many of those present, had quarreled over his favors), and look into some esoteric aspects of Ashiyyurean battle tactics.

On the hour, we were gaveled to order by the president, a large, hostile woman with a stare like a laser cannon. She welcomed us, introduced a few guests, rambled on about old business, accepted the treasurer's report (we were showing a pretty good profit), and introduced a red-faced man who moved to invite an Ashiyyurean "speaker" from the Maracaibo Caucus.

I whispered into my commlink and asked Jacob what the Maracaibo Caucus was.

"It's composed of retired military officers," he said. "Both ours and Ashiyyurean, and dedicated to keeping the peace. It's one of the few organizations in the Confederacy with alien members. What's going on there anyway? What's all the racket?"

The audience was voicing its discontent with the suggestion. The red-faced man shouted something above the noise, and was roundly hooted. I wondered whether there was any place in the Confederacy where feelings ran more strongly against the Ashiyyur than in the inner sanctum of the Ludik Talino Society.

The president reasserted herself, and the red-faced man turned away in disgust and descended into the crowd. A cheer went up, followed swiftly by laughter, and a hoisting of glasses. It was a game. Or a ritual.

The president quieted the audience with a cautionary glance, and launched into an introduction of the first speaker of the evening, a tall, balding man seated beside her, who was trying not to look impressed with the traditional flow of compliments. When she'd concluded and announced his name—it was Wyler—he ascended to the lectern, and cleared his throat. "Ladies and gentlemen, I'm delighted to be with you tonight." He lifted his jaw slightly, and struck a pose that he must have assumed to be one of considerable dignity. In fact, he was an ungainly individual, all elbows and odd angles, with wiry eyebrows and a nervous tic. "It's been a good many years since I've been in these rooms. A lot has changed. I wonder, for one thing, whether we're not closer to war. We're certainly closer to destabilization. Every place I go, there's talk of independence." He shook his head, and thrust one hand forward, waving it all away. "Well, it doesn't matter, really. Tonight, we're all here together, and I suspect whatever happens *out there*, the Talino Society will continue to serve as a bulwark of civilization!" His eyes brightened, and he jabbed a finger at the chandelier. "I remember I was sitting right over there—" I glanced in the direction he pointed, looked back toward the speaker, and realized suddenly that I'd seen someone I knew.

When I looked again, when I focused on the woman whose face

had drawn my attention, I saw only a stranger. Yet there was something familiar in the graceful curve of throat and cheekbone, or perhaps in the almost introspective expression, or the subtle grace with which she lifted her glass to her lips.

I *knew* the face. But I could not give her a name, and she was far too attractive to have forgotten.

". . . I was quite a young man when I first came to Rimway. I was even then fascinated by the puzzles surrounding the life and death of Ludik Talino.

"Here was a man who had fought for the Dellacondans against Toxicon, and before that against Cormoral, and before that against the Tuscans. He had received damned near every award for valor that his world could offer. He had nearly been killed on at least two occasions, and had once cast himself from the open hatch of a disabled ship to assist an injured comrade. With no assurance that help would come in time for them.

"Do you have any idea what it means to be *adrift* out there, with nothing between you and the void but the thin fabric of a pressure suit? No tether to home but the weak signal of a helmet radio? Believe me, it isn't the act of a coward."

Across the room, the woman was aware of me: she concentrated her attention on the speaker, and looked occasionally to her right, but never in my direction. Who the hell was she?

"How, I asked myself, could such a man have abandoned his post at so critical a moment? The only answer was that he could not. There had to be another explanation.

"So, as a young graduate student I was excited to have the opportunity to come here to look for that explanation in the place where Talino had spent most of his life, to study the documents firsthand, to walk where *he* had walked, to get a sense of what he must have felt during those final years. You won't be surprised to know that, on my first day in Andiquar, I visited the Hatchmore House where he died."

He fumbled behind the podium momentarily, found a glass, and filled it with ice water. "I can remember standing outside the second-floor bedroom, where they have cordoned it off, and thinking I could almost feel his presence. Which shows you what imagination will do. I've had a lot of time since then to look at the truth of matters. And the truth is that the man who died on Rimway a hundred and fifty years ago, proclaiming his innocence, was *not* Ludik Talino."

The audience stirred. The woman, possibly startled by the statement, looked directly at me. And I, irritated by an assertion I knew to be untrue, suddenly realized who she was! She'd been a girl, not quite arrived at adolescence when I'd last seen her. Her name was Quinda, and she used to come with her grandfather to visit Gabe.

Wyler pressed on: "He was in fact Jeffrey Kolm, an actor. Kolm had, in his day, guarded the throne in *Omicar*, played an emissary who was murdered almost the moment he set foot on stage in *Caesar and Cleopatra*, and delivered the critical message in *Trinity*. It could not have been a very satisfying career, and it was certainly not lucrative. Kolm held down a variety of jobs, mostly state-sponsored positions for people without skills. And it is therefore not difficult to suppose that he was looking for some more subtle challenge, some role that would perhaps yield a substantial profit.

"He found that role in Ludik Talino.

"Think of it: after Rigel, there was only confusion. Sim was dead, the Dellacondans scattered, the war apparently lost. No one knew precisely what had occurred, nor what might happen next. The worlds of the Confederacy, and the neutrals whom they'd been protecting, were scrambling diplomatically and militarily to survive, and no one was paying much attention to the details of what had happened at Rigel.

"It was chaos. People thought Tarien had died with his brother, and there were some among the Dellacondans who were trying to make peace with the Ashiyyur. What more critical moment for a *new* hero to step forward?"

Wyler did not use notes. His voice had dropped, and he spoke with cool certainty, waggling the fingers of his right hand at his audience to emphasize each point. "Remember that no one knew yet that Sim had been betrayed."

The lights dimmed, and two holographic faces appeared behind and above the speaker. They were dark, handsome, blessed with the sort of features that you might almost think of as noble. One was bearded, one clean-shaven; there was about fifteen years difference between the two. Still, the resemblance was striking. "Talino is on the right. The other man is Kolm. It's a publicity still, and shows him as he appeared in *The Deeps*." Both images faded, to be replaced by a third: this one was also bearded, but there were streaks of gray now in the black hair, and the eyes were troubled. "And this," Wyler said, "is from a holo of Talino made after Rigel. Which of the two men is it?'' He drummed his fingers against the podium.

I momentarily forgot Quinda.

"Kolm may well have recognized the need of the times. And the opportunity to play a bona fide hero in a real life role must have appealed to him. So he stepped forward, presenting himself as Talino the lone survivor, somehow blown clear of the *Corsarius* in those final moments."

He chuckled. "It must have come as a terrible surprise when the story of the betrayal surfaced. Sim's crewmen had fled. And what more natural for the general public to assume but that the man who claimed to have miraculously survived was in fact a liar? Particularly when that man's account of events varied so considerably from the official version. So Holm, expecting to enjoy the fruits of another man's heroism, instead found himself in the role of a miscreant."

He shrugged, and held up his hands, palms out. "So why did he continue? Why not go back to his old life?

"We'll never really know. Talino could easily have been allowed to vanish, and none would have ever known. But he stayed on, continued to play the part, addressed after-dinner groups. It might have been that it was more profitable to play the disgraced hero than to return to the anonymity of an unsuccessful acting career.

"But *I* wish to propose an infinitely stranger possibility: that Holm played Talino so well, identified with him so closely, that he literally *became* Talino. That he felt driven to defend the name he had adopted.

"Whatever the explanation, Ludik Talino lived on.

"And if his bitter denials that he had abandoned his captain ring so convincingly in our ears, it is because they are the cries of a man who was indeed innocent."

Briefly, he summed up the evidence. There wasn't much: inconsistencies in statements attributed to Talino/Kolm, the disappearance of the actor at about the same time that the Rigel action was fought, two statements by persons who had known Kolm maintaining that he had indeed masqueraded as Talino. And so on. "Individually," the speaker observed, "none of these amounts to much. But taken as a whole, they point clearly to one conclusion."

He looked around for questions. "What happened to Talino himself?" asked a young woman in front.

Quinda turned as casually as she could, and glanced in my

direction. She appeared deep in thought.

"I think we can argue," Wyler said, "that of all the crewmen, only he remained loyal. It's my opinion that he died with his captain."

"I don't believe a word of it," I remarked in the general direction of some people who were standing in front of me. One of them, a tall white-haired man with carefully honed diction and the bearing of a philosophy department chairman, turned and fixed me with a disapproving stare. "Wyler is a solid researcher," he said solemnly. "If *you* can demonstrate an error, I'm sure we'd be happy to hear from you." He laughed, jammed his elbow into the ribs of one of his companions, and finished off his drink with a flourish.

"Pity when you think about it," a woman behind us said. "A man stays and gives his life while everyone else runs, and what does he get?" Her eyes misted briefly, and she shook her head.

Quinda was talking with a young man, her back toward me. It *was* her; I was sure of it. The grandfather had been Artis Llandman, one of Gabe's colleagues. I could not recall the girl's last name. I started in her direction, pushing past snatches of conversation that suggested everyone wasn't as affected by Wyler's remarks as I: ". . . Stripped him of his tenure, it's a damned shame, well I can tell you we won't stand for it—" and, ". . . Wish to hell they could get their act together before real estate values go into the toilet around here—"

"Quinda," I said, coming up behind her, "is that you?"

She swung around with that appearance of vague defensiveness people display when they encounter a familiar face but can't put a name to it. "Yes," she said tentatively, as though there might be some doubt as to the facts of the matter. "I *thought* I knew you."

"Alex Benedict."

She smiled politely, but gave no sign of recognition.

"You and I used to go down and look at the Melony. Remember? My uncle lived in Northgate, and you came sometimes to visit us with your grandfather."

Her brow furrowed briefly, and then I saw an ignition in her eyes. "Alex!" she breathed, discovering the name. "Is it really you?"

"You've grown up very nicely," I said. "You were mostly pixie last time I saw you."

"She still is," said her companion, whose name I've long since forgotten. He excused himself moments later, and we drifted into one of the clubrooms, and fell into reminiscences of other days.

"Arin," she said, when I asked about her last name. "Same as it was." Her eyes were cool and green; her hair was cut short, framing expressive features; and she owned a comfortable smile which formed readily and naturally. "I always enjoyed those visits," she said. "Because of you, mostly, I think."

"That's nice to hear."

"I wouldn't have recognized you," she said.

"I've had a hard life."

"No, no. I don't mean that. You didn't have a beard then." She squeezed my arm. "I had a crush on you," she confided, with the slightest emphasis on the verb. "And then one time we went and you weren't there anymore."

"I went off to make my fortune."

"And did you?"

"Yes," I said. "In a way." And it was true: I'd enjoyed my work, and made a decent living from it.

She waited for me to elaborate. I let it pass. "What did you think of him?" she asked, noting my reticence and indicating Wyler, who was still lecturing a group of admirers.

"Of the speaker?"

"Of his notion."

"I don't know," I said. The fact that the audience had taken him seriously had left me off balance. "At this distance, how can anyone really know *what* happened?"

"I suppose," she said doubtfully. "But I don't think you'll find anybody who'd buy his story."

"I've already found someone."

She canted her head and smiled mischievously. "I don't think you quite understand the nature of the Talino Society, Alex. And I'm not sure I should spoil all this for you, but I'd be very much surprised if Dr. Wyler believes any of his arguments himself!"

"You're not serious."

She looked quickly round the room, and fastened her attention on a stout, middle-aged woman in a white jacket. *"That's* Maryam Shough. *She* can demonstrate conclusively that the actor Kolm was in fact one of the Seven."

"You're right," I said. "I *don't* understand."

Quinda suppressed a giggle. "The true purpose of the Talino Society is never spoken of. Never admitted."

I shook my head. "That can't be right. The Society's goal is clearly stated on the plate beside the doorway downstairs. 'To clear the name and establish a proper respect for the acts of Ludik Talino.' Or something to that effect."

"'Faithful navigator of the *Corsarius*,'" she concluded, with mock solemnity.

"So what's the secret?"

"The secret, Alex, is that there's probably no one in the room, except perhaps you and one or two other first-time guests, who takes any of this seriously."

"Oh."

"Now, why don't you tell me about your uncle? How is Gabe? How long have you been back?"

"Gabe was on the *Capella*."

Her eyes fluttered shut, and then: "I'm sorry."

I shrugged. "The human condition," I said. I knew that her grandfather, Llandman, was also dead. Gabe had mentioned it years before. "Explain to me why people come here and listen to hoaxes."

It was several seconds before she recovered herself. "I liked Gabe," she said.

"Everybody did."

We drifted over to the bar, and got a couple of drinks. "I wouldn't know how to explain this exactly," she said. "It's a fantasy, a way to get away from bookkeeping, and stand on the bridge with Christopher Sim."

"But you can do that with the simulations!"

"I suppose." She grew thoughtful. "But it isn't really the same. Here in the Talino Society clubrooms, it's always 1206, and the *Corsarius* still leads the defenses. We exercise some control over history: we can change it, make it ours. Oh, hell, I don't know how to explain it in a way that would make any sense." She smiled up at me. "The point is, I suppose, that Wyler's idea *might* be right. It's possible. And that possibility gives us room to breathe and move about during Resistance times. It's a way of becoming *part* of it, don't you see?" She watched me for a moment, and then shook her head with a flick of good humor. "It's okay, Alex. I doubt that any sensible person would."

I did not want to offend her. So I said of course I understood, and that I thought it was a fine idea.

If I'd been a stranger, she might have been irritated. As it was, I could see her decide to tolerate me. "It's okay," she said. "Listen, I have friends to attend to. Will you be coming back?"

"Yes," I said. "Probably." Meaning, of course, no.

She nodded, understanding.

"How about dinner instead?" I asked. "Maybe tomorrow evening?"

"Yes," she said. "I'd like that." We settled the details, and I moved on.

I found a few people who had known John Khyber. They liked him. But there seemed nothing extraordinary about the man, at least nothing that would have drawn Gabe's interest. Only one or two seemed to be aware that he was dead.

The Talino Society maintained a Trophy Room which was a permanent feature (and curiosity) of the Collandium. It opened off one of the conference areas, and was filled with visitors when I strolled into it.

It was dominated by exquisite matched portraits of Talino and Christopher Sim. Certificates and plaques were mounted on the walls. They were awards to persons whom I assumed were members, citing various achievements in scholarship: forays into naval tactics at Grand Salinas, analyses of Ashiyyurean psychology as it affected the attack on Point Edward, the publication of a collection of aphorisms attributed to Tarien Sim, and so on. I wondered how much was real, and how much was part of the illusion.

There were also photos of men and women in the light and dark blue uniforms of the early Confederacy; portraits of staid, middle-aged types who were among the founders of the Society; and a large platinum cup which had been awarded to a Society-sponsored kids' ramble team.

There were other trophies, some decorated with gleaming frigates or sunbursts. One particularly prominent silver plaque featured a black harridan. Some sixty names were engraved on it, outstanding members of the Talino Society, one chosen each year.

The Trophy Room included a data bank and two terminals. I waited until one became accessible, and then sat down. It was an offline system, of course, linked to data banks elsewhere in the building, but not tied in with the general net. Input was either verbal or by keyboard; responses were posted on the display. I brought up the menu, opened a channel to "Archives," entered

"John Khyber," and requested available biographical information. There wasn't much:

KHYBER, JOHN
CODE 367L441

His name, and the number by which he could be reached on the net.
  I asked for duties performed with the Talino Society. The unit responded:

CHAIRMAN, FINANCE COMMITTEE
1409–10
MEMBER, MEMBERSHIP COMMITTEE
1406–08
MEMBER, MATERIEL SURVEY COMMITTEE
1411–12
NAVAL ADVISOR, SIMULGROUP, RIGEL
1407
MASTER OF CEREMONIES, NUMEROUS OCCASIONS,
1407–PRESENT

DO YOU WISH DETAILS?
"No. Has he ever spoken at the meetings?"
YES. DO YOU WISH DETAILS?
"Yes. Titles of addresses, please."

TRIAL AND ERROR AT IMARIOS: CORMORAL
REACTS
3/31/02
BATTLE CHARACTERISTICS OF CORMORAL'S
CRUISERS
4/27/04
THE TWILIGHT WAR: THE FRIGATE COMES OF AGE
13/30/07
ALCOHOL AND THE ASHIYYUR
5/29/08
THE DANCING GIRLS AT ABONAI LOSE THE WAR
8/33/11
SMALL FORCE TACTICS: SIM AT ESCHAT'ON
10/28/13

THE GUERRILLAS COME TO STAY: SIM AT SANUSAR
11/29/13
ROOTS OF VICTORY: DELLACONDAN CRYPTOLOGY
3/31/14

PRINT COPIES ARE AVAILABLE.
"Please provide copies of everything."
I listened to the barely audible whirr of the printer, which was concealed in a cabinet beneath the terminal. I'd come here hoping that somewhere I'd find the reason Khyber was riding with Gabe. But, in this morass of game-playing, what was it possible to believe?

"Computer," I said, "has Gabriel Benedict ever been here?"
PLEASE BE AWARE THAT THE COMINGS AND GOINGS OF THE GENERAL MEMBERSHIP, AND OF THEIR GUESTS, IS NOT RECORDED. HOWEVER, THERE IS ONE KNOWN OCCASION ON WHICH GABRIEL BENEDICT ATTENDED A MONTHLY MEETING.

"When was that?"
THE FIRST MEETING OF THIS YEAR, PRIMA 30.
"Was he alone?"
NO DATA.
"Was Khyber here the same night?"
NO DATA.
I thought it over. What did I want to know? "Did Mr. Benedict speak? To the group, that is?"
NO.
There must have been something special about that one meeting. "May I see the program for the evening?"

403RD MEETING OF THE LUDIK TALINO SOCIETY
PRIMA 30, 1414
2000 HOURS
GUEST SPEAKER: LISA PAROT
"CONSPIRACY: WAS SIM MURDERED BY CONSPIRATORS
PRIOR TO RIGEL?"
FEATURED SPEAKER: DR. ARDMOR KAIL
"A PSYCHOLOGIST LOOKS AT THE TALINO RECORDINGS."
DINNER: VEAL MARCHAND
TEMERE SALAD
VEGETABLES

Something I'd overlooked occurred to me. "You said that attendance at these sessions is not routinely recorded."

THAT IS CORRECT.

"How do you happen to know that Gabriel Benedict was here on Prima 30?"

BECAUSE HE CONSULTED ME.

Ah! "About what?"

TWO ITEMS. HE WISHED INFORMATION CONCERNING JOHN KHYBER'S BACKGROUND.

"Did he see anything on that subject that you have not shown me?"

NO.

"What was the other item?"

HE REQUESTED A COPY OF AN ADDRESS GIVEN TWO AND A HALF YEARS AGO.

"Please provide a copy of the address."

A single page dropped into the tray. I picked it up and read through it.

It was hard to see a reason for Gabe's interest. This one was little more than a diatribe. "(Talino) has been betrayed by history," the speaker said, "and I am happy that there are still some who care about the truth. Time may prove you correct. Talino, and indeed his unfortunate comrades, are victims of a set of circumstances which took from them something far worse than their lives. I know of no similar miscarriage of justice in all the ages. And I wonder whether we'll ever succeed in correcting the record."

That was really the essence of the speaker's remarks. He said it several different ways, he laced it with redundancies, and he poured on the dramatics. Why was Gabe interested in it?

I stopped puzzling when I saw the name of the speaker. It was Hugh Scott.

IX.

(Human) interstellar polities are, by their nature, transitory. They are accidents, a kind of St. Elmo's fire ignited by economic upheaval, outside threat, or perhaps the charisma of an ideologue. When the night has passed, and normal conditions return, they flicker and vanish. No civilization devised by us can hope to stretch across the stars.

—**Anna Greenstein,**
The Urge to Empire

I'D NEVER READ *Man and Olympian.* Like probably every other kid in the Confederacy, I'd been exposed to it by the schools. And I can remember struggling through the chapter on Socrates for a college history class. But I'd never really *read* the book.

There was a bound copy on one of the shelves in Gabe's bedroom. (I didn't sleep there myself. I was using a room in the back of the house on the second floor.)

On the way home from the Talino Society meeting, I decided it was time to look at Sim's classic again.

It's one of the standard works, of course: a history of the Hellenic Age, from the Persian wars to the death of Alexander. My assumption had always been that it owed its reputation to the fame of its author rather than to any innate value; but that was a prejudice

110

grounded on a child's collision with a serious book.

I opened it approximately in the middle and read in both directions, expecting, I suppose, quiet excursions into Greek philosophy, and a tired rehashing of the Persian and Peloponnesian wars.

What I got instead was volcanic energy, sulphurous opinions, and sheer brilliance. One does not drift leisurely through a few political analyses, or stare at a few arrows on a battle map. Not with Sim. The statesmen in his book pound tables; one can smell the Mediterranean and the planks of the Athenian triremes. And the terrible issues of freedom and order, of mortality and the spirit, are achingly alive.

We are all Hellenes, he says in his introduction. *Dellaconda and Rimway and Cormoral owe all that they are to the restless thinkers along the Aegean, who, in the most exquisite sense, took the first steps to the stars. Only the mind is sacred. That notion was a dazzling insight in its time. Wedded to the observation that nature is subject to laws, and that those laws can be understood, it was the key to the universe.*

I read through the day, well into the late afternoon. Occasionally, Jacob fussed in the background, noisily grilling hamburgers or mixing drinks, or breaking in to suggest that I take advantage of the good weather for a stroll.

There were some surprises. Sim disapproves of Socrates, whose doctrines embody admirable values (he concedes); but which nevertheless disrupted Hellenic society. *The unfortunate reality about the execution of Socrates,* he writes, *is not that it happened; but that it happened too late.*

The early pages of *Man and Olympian* are filled with Xerxes' rage ("O Master, remember the Athenians"), Themistocles' statesmanship, and the valor of the troops who stood at Thermopylae. I was struck, not only by the clarity and force of the book, but also by its compassion. It was not what one would ordinarily expect from a military leader. But then, Sim had not begun as a military leader: he'd been a teacher when the trouble started.

The book is well named: Sim's views are essentially Olympian. One cannot escape the impression that he speaks for History; and if his perspective is not always quite that of his colleagues, or those who have gone before, there is no doubt where the misperceptions lie. His is the final word.

The prose acquires a brooding quality during his account of the destruction of Athens, and the needless loss of life during the effort to defend the Parthenon. His most memorable passage blasts the Spartans for allowing Thermopylae to happen: *They knew for years that the Persians were coming, and, in any case, had advance intelligence of the gathering of the invasion army; yet they prepared no league, and set no defenses, until the deluge was on them. Then they sent Leonidas and his men, and their handful of allies, to compensate with their lives for the neglect and stupidity of the politicians.*

It was a grim coincidence: those words were written before the Ashiyyur launched their war, and, in a broad sense, it fell to Sim to play the role of Leonidas. He led the holding action for the frontier worlds, while Tarien sounded the alarm and began the immense task of forging an alliance that could stand against the invaders.

In the morning, while I ate, Jacob told me he had hold of something else that was strange. "The *Corsarius* seems to have got around pretty well. For example, if we can believe the accounts, two days after the raid on Hrinwhar, it was reported to have driven off an Ashiyyurean destroyer near Onikai IV. Onakai is *eighty* light years from the Spinners. Four days in hyper alone. It attacked a capital ship at Salinas on the same day that Sim was winning at Chapparal. Again, an impossible flight. There are numerous other instances."

"What did the Ashiyyur have to say about all this?"

"They aren't very communicative, Alex. As nearly as I can make out, they've simply denied the stories. But their records have never been made available."

"Maybe," I said, "we should try talking to them."

"How do you plan to do that? There are no diplomatic contacts."

"There's one," I said. "The Maracaibo Caucus."

Thirty-six standard years ago, a small group of senior military officers broke with long-standing custom, and invited a noted Ashiyyurean naval strategist to address the Maracaibo War Academy, on Earth. The speaker, whose name no one seemed to be able to pronounce, was the first of her species to be admitted legally onto a Confederate world in more than a century.

The invitation became traditional, and from the annual meetings an unusual special interest group developed: retired military officers, both human and Ashiyyurean, who were dedicated to establishing a permanent peace. The group, naturally, remained small. It was never a popular movement. Members—at least the human ones—absorbed political punishment and suspicion for their activities.

When I tried to link in, I got only an AI, who explained that officers of the Caucus did not accept unsolicited calls. What was my business?

I told it who I was, and explained that I was doing some historical research. I wondered if I could talk with someone who was reasonably knowledgable about the Resistance in general, and details of the naval war in particular.

There was a delay, presumably while it sought instructions. Then: "It is not our policy to receive private visitors."

"I would be grateful for an exception." I explained that numerous questions remained unanswered, that an account of the war from the point of view of the Ashiyyur would contribute to mutual understanding. Needed to get information from the horse's mouth. Etcetera.

It listened politely, excused itself, and let me wait about ten minutes. "Very good, Mr. Benedict," it said on returning. "One of our staff will be pleased to entertain your questions. But we request that you come personally."

"You mean physically?"

"Yes. If that is not too great an inconvenience."

That seemed curious. "You want me to actually come down here?" I was at the moment seated opposite the AI in what I supposed was one of the suites at Kostyev House, where the Maracaibo Caucus maintained its offices.

"Yes. If you wish."

"Why?"

"Personal contact is always best. The Ashiyyur are uncomfortable with headband technology."

I shrugged and made my appointment. Two hours later I arrived outside Kostyev House, a former embassy building near the capitol. It was, on the afternoon of my visit, ringed with demonstrators, who circled a holo depicting an alien with burning eyes. Demonstrations, I learned later, were almost constant outside the grounds. Their intensity and numbers fluctuated in proportion to the current level of mutual hostility. Things were bad just now, and I was roundly jeered as I hurried past, gave my name to security, and entered the ancient gray structure.

I rode a tube up to the third floor, and turned into a thickly carpeted, paneled corridor. Carved doors appeared irregularly; and long murals depicted men and women in sedate tableaus, contemplating storm-threatened landscapes, dallying at overladen picnic tables, or browsing through markets. There were no windows, and the only illumination was gloomily cast by occasional electric candles. The effect was that the far end of the passageway seemed to stretch into a guttering infinity.

There were doors on both sides of the hallway. Most were unmarked. I passed a legal firm, and a shipping company, and, in two or three cases, offices designated only by names.

Eventually I arrived in front of a pair of double doors, and a plate reading *Maracaibo Caucus*.

I knocked and stepped inside. I'm not sure what I was expecting: I'd been thinking about representatives of a civilization much older than my own; of telepaths; of a species intellectually our superiors, and yet whose technological accomplishments trailed our own. The cost of easy communication, some had theorized. Vertical information storage, *writing*, came quite late.

Anyhow, whatever exotic sort of chamber I'd been anticipating from the Maracaibo Caucus, I'd walked into something that might have been a shipping office. The furnishings were tasteful, but mundane: a square-cut uncomfortable-looking couch, a couple of carved chairs, and a low table on which a row of worn books were haphazardly piled. Large square windows admitted blocks of pale sunlight. The titles of the books were vaguely familiar, though I'd read none: *An Urge to Empire, Green Grass and Silver Ships, Last Days*. There were several biographies of persons, both human and Ashiyyurean, who had tried over the millennia to prevent the outbreak of mass violence.

I discovered a copy of Tanner's *Extracts from Tulisofala*, and picked it up. It was a hefty volume, the sort you lay out as eyewash, but never expect to open.

I was paging through it when the sensation that I was not alone in the room, that I was indeed being watched, settled over me. I peered carefully from desk to cabinet to terminal to the entrance to another door that led (I presumed) to an inner office.

Nothing that I could see had changed.

Still, something that was *not me* moved.

I felt it. In the office. In the still warm air.

Back behind my eyes.

Simultaneously, I heard footsteps in the adjoining room. The connecting door opened, away from me. Whoever had hold of it did not immediately enter, but hung back as though in conversation with someone. There was no sound.

I began to sweat. My vision darkened, and white blossoms expanded in the gauzy light. I must have retreated to a chair. Someone entered the office, but I was too busy trying not to be sick to worry much about it. A hand touched my wrist, and a cool cloth was pressed against my forehead.

The thing that I had sensed stirred in measured cadence to the visitor's movements.

"It's all right, Mr. Benedict," he said. (It was a male. I had glimpsed that much.) "How do you feel?"

"Okay," I said, shakily. Something *turned* in my head, twisted away from the light, burrowed deep. Another wave of nausea swept over me.

"I'm sorry," he said. "Perhaps it would have been best to attempt the commlink after all."

That's what I was thinking. And of course he *knew* that. Still, I tried to look on the positive side: chance to meet an Ashiyyurean. How the hell could I forego that? And of *course* I'd heard the stories. But I'd dismissed them as hysterical.

I tried to concentrate on externals: desk and lamp. Sunlight. The creature's long, curiously human hand.

"My name," he said, "is S'Kalian. And if it's any consolation, you should know that your reaction is common." I couldn't see where the words came from: undoubtedly a device concealed within his loose sleeves.

I was able to sit up now. He placed the cool cloth he'd been using in my hand. "If you wish, I can withdraw, and have someone, a human, come and help you back to the street."

"No," I said. "I'm all right." S'Kalian retreated a few steps, and leaned casually against the desk. He dwarfed the furniture. You've seen holos of the Ashiyyur, but you have no idea of the presence they project until you've been in a room with one. I felt overwhelmed.

He wore a plain, long garment, belted round the waist; and a skullcap. His face, which deviated from a human's just enough to be unsettling (particularly, the large, arched eyes, and the canines that always chilled the smile), registered concern.

There was a sense of serene ferocity about those eyes. I pulled free of them, and tried to collect my wits. He looked young. And his appearance had just the correct strain of the exotic to render him attractive. In an unnerving sort of way.

"I'm grateful," I said, "that you agreed to talk to me."

He bowed, and I felt all the secrets of my life spill out into plain view. *He is a telepath!* I'd believed I could control myself, ask my few questions, and get out. His face showed no reaction. But I knew, *knew*, he was reading everything.

What was there for him to see?

The tilt and flow of Quinda Arin's breasts.

My God! Where had that come from?

I fastened on the Hrinwhar raid, the *Corsarius*, that magnificent plunge into the Ashiyyurean fleet.

No. That wasn't so good either. I squirmed.

More women drifted into mind. In compromising positions.

How does one converse with a creature who seizes the newborn thought?

"You seemed so insistent," he said, joining his hands beneath the folds of his robe, and giving no indication he was aware of any mental turmoil in the room. "How may I be of service?"

It would be incorrect to say that I was frightened, even though I knew that some people had suffered psychological damage from encounters with the Ashiyyur. Fear would come later, when I was safe. For the moment I was only ashamed, humiliated, that nothing I knew or felt was concealed from this other self, from the incurious eyes that casually glanced over my shoulder and focused somewhere behind me.

"Need I speak?" I asked. "You know why I am here." I looked for a fleeting smile, a nod, a physical sign that he understood my discomfort.

"I am sorry, Mr. Benedict," he said, "but I am no more able to avoid penetrating your *coelix*, than you would be to avoid hearing an orchestra playing in the next room. However, you should be happy to know that it is not at all easy to sort out." His lips never moved. But there was animation in the eyes. Interest. A trace of compassion. "Try to ignore the penetration, and speak as you would normally."

My God, how the rubble of a lifetime boiled to the surface: an act of cowardice committed long before in a schoolyard; a failure to speak honestly to a woman for whom all passion had expired; an unspoken satisfaction taken, for no discernible reason, in a friend's misfortune. Small, contemptible things. The baggage that one hauls through a lifetime, the acts that one would change—

"If it is of any assistance to you, please be aware that the experience is even more difficult for me."

"Why?"

"Are you sure you wish to know?"

It struck me that he possessed remarkably poor insight into human psychology to put the question that way. I wasn't at all sure I wanted to hear the answer. Nevertheless: "Of course."

"You have evolved without telepathic abilities. Consequently, you—your species—has never seen a direct need for imposing order, and very little for restraining the more violent passions. The intensity of your hates and fears, the sudden gales of emotion that may erupt without warning in a human mind, the dominance of your appetites: all of these create discomfort." He inclined his head slightly, and the wisp of a sad smile played about his lips. "I'm sorry, but you are greatly handicapped by the conditions of your environment."

"S'Kalian, *do* you know why I'm here?"

Apparently confident now that he would not have to come to my rescue, S'Kalian slipped off the desk, and dropped into an armchair. "I'm not sure *you* know, Mr. Benedict."

"Christopher Sim," I said.

"Yes. A great man. Your people are right to hold him in reverence."

"Our records on the war are incomplete and contradictory. I would like to clarify some points, if it would be possible."

"I am not a historian."

Quinda popped back into my mind. Quinda's shoulders, soft and naked in candlelight. I cringed, and tried to concentrate on the *Corsarius*, on the Tanner volume that lay on the table.

S'Kalian remained quietly attentive.

What would sex be like with a female Ashiyyurean? What happens to mating habits when minds are completely open?

"It's all right, Mr. Benedict," said S'Kalian. "This sort of thing invariably happens. There's no need to be embarrassed. Thought is, by its nature, unpredictable and, even among us, perverse. You and I can bring anything into each other's mind, in glittering color and full animation, merely by mentioning it."

"You're not a retired officer, are you?" I asked, close to panic.

He inclined his head. "Thank you. No. My function is to assist in communications, and to act as a cultural advisor. I'm trained to conduct conversations with humans. But not very effectively, I fear." Again he smiled, reassuringly. I wondered whether that particular gesture might turn out to be universal among intelligent species. At least, among those physically equipped to produce it.

"Can we talk about the Ashiyyurean perspective on some aspects of the Resistance?"

"Of course," he said. "Although I doubt that I know enough to help you. By the way, *we* call it the Incursion."

"Does that matter now?"

"I suppose not. But perceptions are important. Some would even say they *are* the true reality."

"When you mentioned Christopher Sim earlier, you described him as a great man. Is that view generally shared by the Ashiyyur?"

"Oh, yes. I don't think there's any question about that. Of course, if he had been one of our generals, we would have executed him."

I was shocked. "Why?"

"Because he violated all the rules of civilized behavior. He attacked without warning, refused to meet his opponents in open combat, waged war in a thousand unorthodox ways. When the war was clearly lost, he nevertheless continued to sacrifice lives, both those of his own people, and ours, rather than admit defeat. No: many died in a struggle that was needlessly prolonged."

I laughed at him. In the exposed position in which I found myself, it seemed the only proper response. Still, he maintained his equanimity, and even chuckled lightly himself.

"About the *Corsarius*," I said. "Our records place it and Sim at the scene of various engagements which happened too far apart and within too narrow a time frame to allow him to travel the distance between. For example, the actions fought in the Spinners, at Randin'hal, the first engagements in the Slot, and Sim's appearance at Ilyanda all occurred within twelve standard days of each other. The distances involved here are considerable. Hrinwhar in the Spinners is almost sixty light years from Randin'hal. If a modern warship were to succeed in re-entering linear space *at precisely the target area*—which is damned near impossible—it would still take three to four days to get from one place to the other. Sim appears to have done considerably better."

"Our records contain essentially the same time frames."

"There are other, similar, discrepancies. Other times and places."

"Yes."

"How do your historians account for it?"

His eyes slid shut. "Like yours, they can only speculate."

"And what are their speculations?"

"That there were actually three other vessels masquerading as the *Corsarius*. This proposition will not come as a surprise to your own analysts. It is the simplest explanation, and consequently the most likely.

"After all, who knows where he really was? All we can be sure of is that a ship with a supposedly unique symbol appeared in various places. Sim's intention in creating that symbol was clearly to wage psychological warfare. It was never the act of simple bravado which has found its way into the popular consciousness. And it was effective: that vessel was seen everywhere, and the effect of its appearance became, in time, quite demoralizing.

"You may be interested in knowing, Mr. Benedict, that there is a myth among our people that Sim was an *alien*. A *true* alien, that is, a member of a species unknown to us both.

"It was this aura, even more than his capabilities as a strategist, as a psychologist, and as a battle commander, that made him so dangerous, and so widely feared.

"Incidentally, there is reason to suspect that one of the duplicate *Corsariuses* was destroyed at Grand Salinas, and at least one, and maybe two, during the long series of engagements in the Slot."

"What you're telling me is that nobody really knows."

"That is correct. I can confirm that our information tallies with yours in most essentials. In fact, your historians and ours have long since collaborated on these matters, despite a distinct lack of official enthusiasm. But we are talking about wartime, and there was considerable confusion. It seems likely the whole truth in these matters will never be known." He shifted his position. "Is there anything else I can help you with?"

"Yes," I said, picking up the *Extracts*. "What do you know of Leisha Tanner?"

"Early translator of Tulisofala. Quite good, by the way."

"She also opposed the war."

"I know. That is a position that has always bothered me."

"Why?" I asked, thrown momentarily off stride.

"Because she had obligations to her species that outweighed the essential morality of the struggle. Once the war was underway in earnest, the risks for both sides were great, and the right or wrong of it, from a philosophical point of view, ceased to matter."

"Philosophers make the best generals," I said, drily.

"I understand the jest. But it is quite true. There comes a time when one must choose. Whatever we would prefer for ourselves, we must choose for the common good. Even if that means we must support an immoral cause. Had I been human, I would have fought with the Dellacondans."

This was all disconcerting. "You represent an organization dedicated to finding ways to keep the peace," I said.

"And we will. But it is not easy. If I can say this in all honesty, there are those on both sides who wish war."

"Why?"

"Because many of us who have looked into your minds are terrified by what we see there. It would be very easy to conclude that our only real safety lies in reducing your species to impotence. And among your own people, there are many who believe, and perhaps rightly, that enmity with us is the cement that binds your Confederacy together."

I grunted some sort of response.

He stood up, and adjusted the folds in his robe. "However that may be, Alex, you may be certain that you have a friend among the Ashiyyur."

X.

Nine persons died on the Regal: *her crew of eight, and Art Llandman.*

—**Gabriel Benedict,**
Uncollected Letters

*. . . These wine-filled hours
That will not come again . . .*

—**Walford Candles,
"Marking Time"**

I DREAMT THAT night: dark, savage dreams unlike anything I'd known before. Jacob woke me twice; the second time I lay a long while staring at the ceiling, and then showered and went out.

I walked past houses subtly shifted in the moonlight, through a wind that was subdued, but cold. Gravel crunched satisfyingly underfoot, and after a while streaks of gray appeared in the east. I was down by the Melony, watching chunks of ice float by, when the sun came up.

The community began to stir a short time later: people piled their kids onto the airbus, and lingered to talk with one another. Skimmers lifted into the sky and floated upriver, headed for Andiquar. Doors banged and voices drifted in the sharp air.

121

It felt good. Reassuring.

When I got home, Jacob had breakfast waiting. I ate too much, threw a log on the fire, and settled in front of it with a cup of coffee. I was asleep within fifteen minutes.

This time, there were no dreams. At least none that I remembered.

I spent the afternoon with *Man and Olympian,* and then went downtown to keep a dinner date with Quinda.

If I needed any additional dose of physical reality to offset the experience of the previous day, Quinda supplied it. She was resplendent in white and green, her blouse and sash matching her eyes, her hair loose over her shoulders. Neither of us was immediately hungry, so we spent an hour strolling along the Riverwalk. We poked into bookstores and art galleries, and stopped to get our portraits done by one of the imagists who will scrawl your likeness on an electronic sheet and scribble a legend beneath it. I still have hers. She looks stunning, even in this three-minute effort. The eyes retain a kind of wistfulness; the lips are soft and full, perhaps a shade exaggerated from reality; and the hair curls against the long, lean throat. It is all that remains of her. The legend reads: "Once in a lifetime." Curious that the artist should have said that.

By the time we got to the cheese and wine, we were deeply engrossed in her favorite subject, and I was describing my reaction to *Man and Olympian*. She listened patiently while I babbled on, nodding encouragingly from time to time. "You're coming to it late, Alex," she said, when I'd finished. "I think they make a mistake using it in the schools. It's not a book for kids; but if you discover it as an adult, without too many preconceptions, it can grab you by the throat."

"It's not really *about* ancient Greece," I said.

Lights were coming on across the river, in private homes, in boathouses and piers and restaurants. "I'm sure you're right," she said. "He was writing about his own time. But then, that's always true of a good history."

"Unity," I said. "He was worried about the inability of the human worlds to confederate."

"I suppose." Her eyes were lost somewhere. "I think it goes deeper than that. He seems to have wanted us to recognize a common heritage. To unite in some far deeper way than merely establishing a political bond. To recognize ourselves as Hellenes, and not simply Athenians and Corinthians." An expression of sadness crept into her features. "It'll never happen," she said.

Sim tells a story about two Greek colonies, I forget their names, that were planted on the African coast. They were surrounded by savages who regularly attacked both. Despite that, the colonies could never cooperate, and eventually they went to war against each other. *There is a deep and pervasive spirit in our species,* he says, *which would far rather pursue the emotional phantoms of the moment than survive! And when you recognize that, you have grasped the heart of what sociologists fondly call group motivational theory.*

I refilled both glasses. Quinda raised hers. "To our days along the Melony," she said.

"To the little girl of those days. Did she ever find the sea?"

"You remember." She brightened with pleasure.

"Yes, I remember." We'd talked of building a raft, and following the river across the continent. "You got angry with me when I tried to explain why we couldn't really do it."

"You promised, and then you took me back to the house."

"It never occurred to me that you would take it seriously."

"Oh, Alex, I wanted so much to make that trip. To watch the banks drift by, and"—Her green eyes fastened on me, and she smiled deliciously—"to have you with me."

"You were a little girl," I said.

"And I wanted to cry when you took me home. But you promised that when I was old enough, we'd do it. Do you remember?"

"I remember."

She only smiled, and left it hanging. That'll teach you, her eyes said.

Later, we walked through the malls and gardens, mixing with late evening strollers, talking about the Talino Society, and my life as a dealer in antiquities, and how lovely the night was (the stars were bright in the plexidome). And about Gabe and her grandfather. "He always liked you," she said. "He was disappointed when you left. I think he wanted you to follow in your uncle's footsteps."

"He wasn't alone." Art's image drifted into my mind. Round-faced, short, with a constantly bemused expression. Art Llandman had always looked as if he were trying to sort out some difficult puzzle. "I'm sorry if he was disappointed. I liked him: he was one of the few people who worked with Gabe who knew I existed. I was out with him on digs a couple of times: at Schuyway, and I think he was on Obralan. Yes, I'm sure he was. At Schuyway, he used to take time to walk with me through the ruins. He'd point out the treasury, and the scorched walls, and the place where they'd thrown convicts—and a few politicians—into the sea.''

"That sounds like him,'' she laughed. '' 'And over here is where they chucked him in.' When *was* that?''

"Before your time. I was about eight or nine.''

"Yes.'' She stared through me. "He was happy then.''

"He was unlucky,'' she explained, later. It was almost midnight, and we were back at the house in Northgate, with a low fire sputtering in the grate, a bottle of wine in an ice bucket, and a Sanquoi violin concerto drifting through the warm rooms. She was looking at the assorted materials I'd acquired at the Talino Society and the Machesney Institute, and had presumably concluded (since I'd offered no explanation) that I was even more of a buff than she was. "They recovered one of the Dellacondan frigates, you know. He and Gabe. It was intact, the archeological find of a lifetime. My grandfather put fifteen years into the search. Toward the end, he got Gabe involved. And together they found the *Regal*.

"It was lost at Grand Salinas.'' Her eyes glittered with satisfaction. "To locate it, they pored over old records and calculated trajectories and God knows what else. I was just old enough to know what they were looking for, and to have some idea that it was very important. The trick was to reconstruct the engagement to the extent that you could calculate all forces, course, speed, impact, later attempts by the crew to compensate, and whatnot.''

"Sounds impossible.''

"They were able to narrow things down. Gramp told me there were literally dozens of ships blown in all sorts of directions, still drifting out there, and recoverable if you just knew where to look. But two hundred years is a long time. Things get pretty well scattered.''

"Tell me about the *Regal*.''

"The Ashiyyur hit it with an electronic pulse of some sort. It didn't penetrate the hull, but it knocked out the ship's systems. From what Gramp said, it was the crew that blew a hole in the forward section, trying to recover power. Five were sucked out. The other three were trapped and couldn't get help. The research team found them in an airtight compartment.

"But the ship itself was in good condition."

"Gabe told me about it," I said. "There was an accident."

"Shortly after they got on board, it blew up. Someone on the team touched something. No one ever did figure out what happened. It never came out publicly, but Gramp said he thought the mutes were responsible. There was a man along named Koenig that they decided later was probably in the mutes' pay. They thought he did it."

"Why would the Ashiyyur care about a two-hundred-year-old wreck?"

She looked at me searchingly. Her eyes narrowed, while she made a decision. Then she said: "Gramp didn't know, but I guess there'd been other incidents all along that implied someone did not want the expedition to succeed."

"What happened to Koenig?"

"Died shortly after. Heart problem. He was still quite young, with no history of coronary disease." She sipped her wine, and peered at the glass stem. "I don't know: maybe there's something to it.

"But whatever the truth of that was, my grandfather was never the same. To have had *that* sort of prize in his hands, and have it slip away—" She sighed. "He died not long after Koenig."

"I'm sorry," I said.

"Gabe did what he could to help. I was never sure what caused more damage: losing the artifact, or getting laughed at by the entire profession. What frustrates me now is that I've gotten to know a lot of them as individuals. They aren't vindictive people. But they never understood how he felt, or maybe they didn't care because they had problems of their own. But Llandman and his frigate made such a great story. It was as if Harry Pellinor had discovered the ruins on Belarius, and then forgot where they were."

The Resistance-era materials I'd been gathering were all stacked on a couple of tables in the den. She pored over them, nodding with satisfaction at the simul crystals and the Candles volumes and the other assorted pieces. "I didn't realize," she said, leafing through Tanner's *Notebooks,* "you were so deeply involved in all this, Alex."

"It seems to have caught hold of me. Are you familiar with her?" I asked.

"With Tanner?" Her face glowed. "Yes! One of the most fascinating characters of the period."

"She started out as a pacifist," I said. "And ended up in the war. What happened? Do you know?"

Quinda crossed one leg over the other and bent forward energetically. I could see Tanner would be a favorite subject. "She was *never* a pacifist, Alex. She felt the war was unnecessary, and wanted to see a serious attempt made to negotiate. The Sims weren't much interested in that approach."

"Why not?"

"Because they believed any attempt at conciliation, while the mutes had the upper hand—*really* had the upper hand—would be interpreted as a sign of weakness. Against a human opponent, they'd have been right. But against the mutes, maybe not. Tanner knew as much as anyone did then about the enemy, and *she* thought they could be talked to."

"How did she end up in Sim's navy?"

"That's easy. Somehow, she got to Sim, I don't know how, and persuaded him to let her try to negotiate with the mutes. The fact that he went along should tell you that she was reasonably persuasive."

"But obviously things didn't work out."

"He agreed to let her meet with the mute commander, Mendoles Barosa.

"The site was a crater on an unnamed moon in a fringe system that neither side cared about. Tanner was the only one the Confederates had who'd traveled among the mutes, the only one who could communicate with them, and, most important, the only one who could guard her thoughts against them.

"Sim and Barosa circled overhead while she met with a mute negotiator. Tanner reported later that she and the mute envoy were very close to working out an agreement within the restrictions Sim had imposed on her, when she learned that the mutes would accept no deal that did not include the surrender of Christopher Sim for assorted barbarities and war crimes.

"They got nowhere on that issue, and Sim broke off the meeting. The mutes responded by attacking, and occupying, two nominally neutral worlds which had, in reality, been supporting the Dellacondans with weapons, crews, and money. A lot of people died. And Tanner was left feeling responsible for it all.

"She reacted by throwing herself wholeheartedly into the

common defense. Maurina Sim, in her diaries, says that Tanner never forgave the mutes. And that no one prosecuted that war with a more unrelenting fury.''

It was well into the early morning when we climbed into the skimmer and started back across the city. We were both tired by then, and the conversation dwelt on trivialities. I could see that her thoughts were far distant. At the end of the flight, as we circled down onto the roof of her apartment complex, I brought her abruptly back into focus: "Quinda, I spoke with one of the Ashiyyur yesterday. In person.''

All the warmth drained from her face. "You're not serious,'' she said, in a voice that was deadly flat.

I hesitated, confused by her reaction. "Yes,'' I said, my own temper going up a notch or two. "One of the people from the Maracaibo Caucus.''

"Alex, you didn't really *do* that.'' She radiated shock, anger, disappointment.

"Why *not?*'' I asked. "What's wrong?''

"My God, Alex,'' she whispered. "What have you done?''

XI.

We frequently refer to Imarios' revolt as "fateful," presumably in the sense that, without it, these two centuries of unremitting hostility and occasional war would not have happened. But consider the rough technological balance between the two cultures, their mutual expansionist tendencies and assumptions of destiny, and the personal antipathy inevitably experienced by individuals of either species in the presence of the other: how could it have been otherwise? If ever two societies were intended by nature to confront each other, and to settle the issue in Darwinian combat, those two societies are Ashiyyurean and human.

—Gasper Mendez,
The Long Twilight

"AND YOU DID not ask her to explain why she was upset?"

"No, Jacob. She didn't really appear to be in a mood to respond to questions."

"I see *one* connection. Remember the claim that Artis Llandman's expedition was destroyed by the machinations of the Ashiyyur. It appears to me that your Quinda Arin is concerned that you may have exposed information of consequence."

"But what? I don't know anything."

"I would say she thinks you do. In any case, I have some news. We may be able to get more information on Tanner. Maybe find out what she was doing during the missing years. Please attend the monitor."

The lights dimmed, and a message formed:
ANG/54/Y66133892/r 261 MARNET PLACE, TEUFMAN-OIL

MR BENEDICT. I HAVE MATERIAL ON LEISHA TANNER THAT YOU MAY FIND OF INTEREST. I AM IN POSSESSION OF A CERTIFIED COPY OF HER JOURNALS COVERING THE YEARS 1202–1219. I WILL NOT COPY THE DOCUMENT, NOR WILL I ALLOW IT OUT OF MY HANDS. IF YOU ARE INTERESTED IN EXAMINING IT, WITH A VIEW TO PURCHASE, PLEASE RESPOND TO ROUTING CODE ABOVE.

HAMEL WRICHT

"It came during the night. It's a response to a general query I sent out several days ago. But somebody's going to have to go get it."

"Why? Let's just link in and get a look at it."

"I've already suggested that." Jacob flashed a second message on the screen, the gist of which was: YOUR SUGGESTION WOULD EXPOSE THE ARTIFACT TO POSSIBLE COPYING. REGRET I CANNOT COMPLY.

"That doesn't make sense." I said. "We could only copy what we could see. It wouldn't be much."

"Do you wish to send another message?"

"I'll talk to him myself."

"He's not on the net, Alex. You can't reach him directly. Except maybe on the transcom."

"Do it," I said. "Where's the closest terminal?"

"At a hotel in Teufmanoil. I expected you would wish to respond, so I've already tried them. They say the address is outside town somewhere and they'd have to send someone out to get him and bring him in. They don't sound anxious to do it."

"A recluse," I grumbled. "Is this something other than the *Notebooks*? Did she keep journals, too?"

"Apparently she did," offered Jacob.

"All the writing she seems to have done, it's a wonder she had time for anything else. Find out how much Wricht wants for the thing, and buy it."

"Alex." Jacob adopted a tone that suggested he was about to

talk sense with me. "Artifacts of this nature, as you very well know, are inordinately expensive. And there's quite a good chance it isn't even legitimate." The message blinked off. "I don't wish to tell you your business—" he said.

"Thank you, Jacob. Where's Teufmanoil?"

"In the Sulyas."

He couldn't entirely hide his amusement. The Sulyas are halfway around the globe. "Okay," I said. "I'll go see him."

"Good," said Jacob. "I've booked the late afternoon flight."

I crossed two oceans, and landed about midnight local time at Wetherspur on the eastern flank of the Sulya Ridge. It was quite cold, high in the northern hemisphere. When I stepped out of the intercontinental, the air was literally heavy with frost. It was like walking into a wall.

I caught an airbus and, by morning, I was in Teufmanoil. It was a resort town, a skiing village. Despite the frigid weather, the snow on the slopes was thin. The sun was bright in a cloudless sky, and the streets were packed with people on their way to the slopes.

The tourist center was located in the lobby of the depot.

A middle-aged woman welcomed me energetically to the Silver Peak Ski Valley, and placed a cup of coffee in front of me.

I accepted, and gave her Wricht's address. She punched it into the computer, and a blue star appeared on the wall map behind her, just off a trail about six kilometers west of town. "Marnet Place," she said. "Who are you looking for?"

"Hamel Wricht. An antiquities dealer, probably."

"Oh, yes," she said. "I don't know about antiquities, but he has a small lodge out there. Anything else you need?"

"No," I said. "Thank you."

I rented a snowbike and, a few minutes later, I arrived outside Wricht's hotel, which was a white and red three-story lodge with a lot of glass, and about a dozen pairs of skis stacked on its porch.

Several people came out while I watched. They were kids, mostly, college students. Several waved as they passed, and one young woman, who appeared to have had a bit too much to drink, invited me to join them.

I walked up onto the porch, and knocked.

The door opened, revealing a trim, bearded young man who didn't seem to be much older than the group which had just left.

"I'm looking for Hamel Wricht," I said.

He bowed slightly, and stepped back to make room for me. "Do I know you?"

"My name's Benedict," I said expectantly. "I came about Leisha Tanner."

"Who?" He looked genuinely puzzled. And he also didn't look like someone who was likely to have an interest in the finer things of this world.

"You have a copy of her journals," I insisted.

"I have no idea what we're talking about, sir."

Plainly, I had the wrong man. "Is there another Hamel Wricht here somewhere?" I asked. "Your father, perhaps?"

"No." He was starting to pull away.

"Didn't you respond to a request for material on Leisha Tanner? You said you had a copy of her journals."

"You've got me confused with somebody else," he said. "I don't do anything like that. I rent apartments. Did you want one?"

Outside again, I called Jacob on the link and told him what had happened. He said it seemed unusual.

"Is that the best you have to say?" I asked.

"Apparently the transmission was faked. You may wish to be careful."

That was an uncomfortable thought.

"Someone wanted you away from here," Jacob continued. "Need I point out that we're dealing with people who have already shown no reluctance to indulge in breaking and entering. If indeed the objective toward which your uncle was working has some intrinsic value, it's possible that someone wants you out of the way."

"Why send me halfway round the globe to do it?"

"Accidents happen," he said. "And accidents are especially likely when one is traveling. I'm probably being alarmist; but please be careful."

Aircraft schedules weren't good, and it was a full thirty hours before I got back to Andiquar. No one made any attempt on my life, though I discerned any number of suspicious persons among my fellow travelers. I even found myself wondering whether "they" (as I had now begun to think of my antagonist) would be willing to destroy the intercontinental and everyone on board to get at me. I considered that possibility off and on, while listening periodically for some warning that the magnets were about to quit, or a wing to fall off.

I even considered, wildly, the possibility that Gabe had been murdered.

No. I put the thought away from me. Ridiculous.

Nevertheless, I was glad to get my feet back on solid ground.

It was late evening when my taxi crossed the Melony and started its descent into Northgate. As soon as the house came into view, I knew something was wrong. The windows were dark. Jacob liked light. Anyway, he was programmed to keep the living room cheerfully illuminated when I was out.

"Jacob," I said into the commlink. "Lights, please."

No response. Not even a carrier wave.

"Jacob?"

The pad was in total darkness, out of range of the streetlights. We landed on a newly fallen layer of snow. The meter calculated the fare, and returned my card. "Thank you, Mr. Benedict," it said. "Good evening."

I was out before the door was fully open, walking hastily along the side of the house, climbing onto the porch. The door opened to my touch. That meant the power was off.

I fumbled my way to the kitchen, found a portable lamp, and went down to the utility room. It was cold down there. A few flakes were blowing in through a broken window.

Several electrical cables had been pulled out of their jacks. Just like last time. Who would have thought they'd come back?

I reinserted the lines, felt the reassuring hum of power in the walls, saw lights come on upstairs, and heard Jacob's voice: "Alex, is that you?"

"Yes." I climbed back up into the kitchen. "I can guess what happened."

"We did not take precautions."

"No," I said. "I meant to, but I never got around to it."

"We did not even reset the burglar alarm. This time, the thieves were able to work at their leisure."

"Are you all right? They didn't try to get at you again?"

"No. Apparently not. But I think we should consider providing me with a way to defend myself. Possibly a neuric system."

"I'll think about it."

"Just something to put them out of business. I wouldn't want to injure anyone."

"Are they gone? Is anyone still here?" I'd been listening for sounds in the upper levels.

"I don't detect any movement of large animals in the building. What time is it?"

"About nine," I said. "On the twelfth."

"I've been down for about eleven hours."

"What did they get?"

"I'm doing an inventory now. All data systems seem to have maintained their integrity. I don't think they took anything. At least, anything that's tied in with me. All cataloged items respond. Sensors show disturbance in your bedroom. Something happened there."

Upstairs and toward the back of the house. Jacob had every light in the place on by the time I arrived.

The bed was torn apart: sheets and pillows flung about, and the night table turned over. But nothing else was disturbed. "What?" I said. "What the hell's going on?"

"I can't imagine why someone would attack your bed, Alex."

The world seemed suddenly very stark, and very cold. "I think I'll sleep downstairs tonight, Jacob." I turned away, and then remembered something, and started back into the room.

"The book," said Jacob, understanding immediately.

Walford Candles's *Rumors of Earth* had been on the nightstand. But it was nowhere to be seen now. I got down on my knees and looked under the bed. "Do you see it anywhere, Jacob?"

"It is not in the house."

"How about the other Candles books?"

Pause. "They're here."

"This makes no sense. Is it a rare edition of some sort?"

"No. At least not that I'm aware of."

"Then it could be purchased without any real problem?"

"I'd think rather easily."

I straightened the nightstand, picked up a couple of pillows, and went downstairs. Crazier and crazier.

"Jacob, what do we know about the Llandman expedition?"

"I can provide numerous accounts. Several excellent books deal with the subject at length."

"I don't want anything else to read. Tell me what we know."

"Llandman was a respected archeologist for forty years. He made his reputation on Vlendivol—"

"That's okay. I think we can skip that. What about the loss of the *Regal?*"

"1402. Did you know your uncle was along on that one?"

"Yes. But I assumed they just lost an artifact. Apparently, it became a major problem."

"The only Dellacondan frigate known to have survived the war was the *Rappaport*. It's on display at the Hrinwhar Naval Museum on Dellaconda. In fact, to a considerable extent, it *is* the museum. But it's been the subject of considerable controversy. Propulsion and data processing systems and weapons are missing. They've always been missing. The theory is that museum officials removed everything to ensure that no one would, say, fire a nuclear charge into the personnel office."

"Reasonable enough position," I said.

"Yes. But unfortunately, whoever removed the pieces didn't save them. There's a lot that historians would like to know; but without the works, the *Rappaport* is just a shell. No help to anyone.

"Consequently, the recovery of a bona fide Dellacondan warship would be a marvelous find."

I thought about Llandman and the *Regal*.

Jacob guessed. "He was unfortunate," he said. "Nevertheless, finding the vehicle was a considerable achievement. He worked on the problem for forty years. When they found it, it was 175 billion kilometers from the battle site, which should give you a sense of the magnitude of the calculations."

"Quinda thought it was deliberately destroyed, Jacob. What do we know about what actually happened?"

"She may be right. Shortly after the research team boarded, one of the nuclear weapons armed itself and an ignition sequence started. Damaged systems, careless handling, sabotage: no one knew. Llandman almost lost his life trying to jettison the bomb, but none of them really knew much about the ship's systems."

"What happened afterward?"

"There was talk of another expedition for awhile. Another ship. But that died out. In the end, there was only laughter. Llandman became depressed, grew ill, and retired. He was a bitter man by the end of his life. Some of the mockery rubbed off on your uncle as well. But Gabe was tougher material. He told his critics what they could do.''

"What finally became of Llandman?"

"I'm looking at the record. He took an overdose of something. The autopsy was never released. He was suffering from a variety of medical problems, and no one was ever prepared to say it was suicide. There was apparently no note.''

"Why do you say 'apparently'?"

"Because a cousin claimed to have seen one. If so, the family never released it.''

"Understandable.''

"Yes. An unfortunate end for a talented man.''

I thought of him leading me through the lost places of dead cities. I could remember his smile, and his gnarled hand holding mine, helping me over slabs, past digging equipment.

"There were even rumors that he destroyed the ship himself. Deliberately.''

"That's crazy!''

"One would think so.'' Jacob's tone dismissed the idea as unworthy of further consideration. "On a different note, I came across more information on Matt Olander while you were gone.''

"*Who?*"

"Olander. Leisha Tanner's missing friend. It turns out he's buried on Ilyanda. I was reading through a travel guide put out by their tourist people. Did you know that Ilyanda is a very popular tourist site?''

No, I didn't.

"It's still mostly wilderness, unexplored country, great fishing and hunting, and some ruins that no one has yet explained. They have a strong affection there for Christopher Sim, judging by the number of boulevards, parks, and universities named after him. The reason, I gather, is that, during the darkest days of the Resistance, he saved them all.''

"The evacuation," I said.

"Yes. At the time of the war, the entire population of the world was concentrated at Point Edward. There were twenty thousand people, and Sim learned somehow or other that the Ashiyyur planned to bomb the city.''

"Another puzzle," I said. "Neither side attacked populated areas at that time in the war.''

"Except Point Edward. Maybe you could visit your friend S'Kalian again and ask why. In any case, Sim went in with everything he could collect, big commercial liners borrowed from Toxicon and Aberwehl, a fleet of shuttles, and his own frigates. They got just about everyone off. But for some reason or other, Tanner's old friend stayed behind. The Ilyandans have a tradition that he'd lived in Point Edward as a young man, and that he'd met his wife there."

"Jill," I said.

"Yes. Jill. Who died during the assault on Cormoral. Anyhow, the Ilyandans say that he remained at Point Edward because he knew the city was going to die, and he thought it should have a defender. His grave is inside the spaceport. They've made a memorial out of it, and turned it into a park.

"There's something else you might be interested in. I've been digging into transportation records. This is technically confidential, but there's a unit down at Lockway Travel that owes me a favor. Your uncle left here for Dellaconda about two months before the disappearance of the *Capella*."

"Dellaconda," I said. "Christopher Sim's home world."

"Yes. Furthermore, it appears that Gabriel went there several times over the past year and a half."

"Jacob, it all keeps leading back to the Resistance. But I've been over it and over it, and I can't imagine what connection there could be between a two-hundred-year-old war and the *Tenandrome*."

"Nor I. Perhaps some one made off with a payroll and hid it somewhere in the Veiled Lady."

"Well, dammit," I said. "Something happened. Maybe it's time to get a look at the combat area."

Jacob complied, the lights dimmed, went out, and a sprinkling of stars flicked into existence. "The battlefield can be defined as an area approximately one hundred twenty light years wide and forty deep, stretching roughly between Miroghol and Wendrikan." Two stars, floating near opposite walls, momentarily brightened, one blue, one white. "Minimum travel time between them, in hyper, would have been no less than six days."

"How about a modern vessel?"

"About the same. We've been using the Armstrong for about five hundred years, and you can't really speed it up. I don't know why, but I could produce an explanation if you wish."

"That's all right."

"We are looking at the area, by the way, from the human side. The leading edge of Ashiyyurean influence, as it was at the beginning of the war, is across the room." A bank of about a dozen stars glowed more fiercely, and then subsided. All but one: a dull red sun whose identity I could guess. "Yenmasi," said Jacob.

That was where it had started. A human colony, planted on Imarios, the fourth world of Yenmasi, had revolted over some trivial question of taxes. And there, nearby, was Mistinmor, the yellow sun which illuminated the skies of the parent world Cormoral, whose warships had intervened, and whose destruction had galvanized the frontier worlds.

It was all there: the blue supergiant Madjnikhan, home of the unfortunate Bendiri, who had sent their only ship to assist the Dellacondans; golden Castleman's, where several of Sim's frigates had been lost in the futile effort to save the City on the Crag; the solemn beauty of the dozen stars whose symmetrical pattern created a light-years-long cylinder known to history as the Slot, where a small force of allied vessels had inflicted a devastating defeat on an Ashiyyurean armada; the yellow sun Minkiades (so much like Sol), still despised because its two populated worlds, full of fear, had thrown in with the invaders; the white dwarf Kaspadel, home star to Ilyanda; and brilliant white Rigel, where Sim and his ship had died. . . .

"Let's see the Veiled Lady."

"Change of scale," Jacob said. The war zone shrank into a glittering cloud about the size of the fireplace, and retreated toward the windows. In the center of the room, a second luminous patch appeared. "The Veiled Lady. Distance from nearest point in the combat area to the nebula's leading edge is somewhat more than eleven hundred light years."

"Sixty days travel one way from Rigel," I said.

"More or less. It's a long way from the battle zone. I cannot imagine what sort of connection there could be between the Veiled Lady and that war."

"Somebody hid something out there," I said. "It has to be. Can't be anything else."

"I'm sorry to say, Alex, that I find it hard to imagine what sort of object could result in all this secrecy."

I was damned if I had any answers. But I kept thinking that somehow it had to do with the Seven. So I pushed back into the cushions and propped my feet up and stared at the nebula.

The lights came back up. "It's late, sir."

The room was warm and solid. The pictures, the books, the liquor cabinet, everything was familiar and reassuring. A world that one could encompass and understand.

I poured myself some brandy. The crystal which carried the half-dozen scenarios from the library lay in its case on a side table.

"I think it's time I saw Sim's end," I said.

XII.

It is a curious fact that Sim, who ranks in the august company of Alexander, Rancible, and Black George, should accomplish with his death what he was unable to achieve with all his brilliant campaigns.

—Arena Cash,
War in the Void

I LOADED THE crystal, sat down, and adjusted my headband. "Now, Jacob."

"You've had a long trip, Alex. Are you sure you wouldn't rather wait until tomorrow?"

"Now, Jacob."

Pause. "As usual, you have two options: participant or observer?"

"Observer."

"Historical or alternative?"

"Historical. Let's see it the way it happened."

"Keep in mind this is a reconstruction of events from best evidence. Some dramatization is involved. Do you wish to observe from *Corsarius* or *Kudasai?*"

I thought it over. Experiencing the final action aboard the doomed ship would make for high drama. And there would be the challenge of seeing whether I could ride it out until the program itself snatched me from danger. On the other hand, the view from Tarien Sim's battle cruiser would be more informative, and less subject to the imagination of the writers. *"Kudasai,"* I said.

The room darkened, and the texture of the cushions changed.

"The sons of bitches are out in force today." Wearing the uniform of the Resistance Confederacy, Tarien Sim stood before a large oval port, staring moodily at the swirl of boulders and dust circling the gas giant Barcandrik. Far in the distance, the rubble blended into luminous rings of haunting beauty, thick and full and bright as any I've ever seen. Three shepherd moons hung like antique lanterns along the track, one nearby, all equally spaced.

Sim's troubled features were silhouetted against the lower rim of the planet itself, whose yellow-green atmosphere churned in dazzling sunlight. There was no way to mistake him: the stark gray eyes of a man who had, perhaps, seen too much; the thick neck and stocky body, giving way to middle-age spread; the neatly trimmed, reddish brown hair and beard. Shorter than his brother, and (aside from the eyes) not one who would easily engage the attention. An individual of rather common appearance. Until one hears his voice.

It is a rolling bass, backed by unshakable conviction. It sounded like the real Tarien, and my blood heated a bit. (I've always felt I was immune to crowd-rousers and jingoistic appeals. Yet, the sound of that familiar voice stirred something too deep to grasp easily.)

His hands were clasped behind his back. On an overhead situation display, lights blinked in multicolored patterns.

Good evening, Mr. Benedict. The words came from a speaker on my display panel. It was male, controlled, clipped. *Welcome to Rigel. I am the program monitor, and I will be your guide through the simulation. You are on the bridge of the* Kudasai, *the lone battle cruiser possessed by the Confederates at this stage of hostilities. It was contributed by a private foundation on Earth, and is seeing its first action. It is at present hidden within the envelope of gas and dust circling Barcandrik, forming its inner ring. Ship's captain is Mendel LeMara. Tarien Sim is technically an observer.*

"Why's he here at all?" I asked. "Seems like he picked the worst possible time. This must have looked like the end for all of them."

That is why. He does not expect to survive Rigel. You should keep in mind that, at this point, it appears that all his efforts to acquire assistance have failed. Earth and Rimway continue to vacillate, no major power has yet declared an intention to intervene, and the Confederate navy is now down to a score of ships. The only good news in all this has been the revolution on Toxicon, which may be well on the way to placing a friendly government in power, and ending that world's war with Muri. In fact, help will come from that quarter soon, but the allies are out of time.

Consequently, Tarien has elected to share the fate of his brother and his comrades.

I counted approximately two hundred enemy vessels on my display. Most were escorts and destroyers; but three heavy battle cruisers anchored the force.

Arrayed against them were twenty frigates, a couple of destroyers, and the *Kudasai*.

Mendel LeMara was tall, copper-skinned, grim-featured in the half-light of the bridge. He stood by one of the tracking stations, his lean, muscular form outlined against the battle displays. The officers at their various posts were subdued, their emotions masked. Tarien Sim stared thoughtfully through his portal at the big planet, which was in its third quarter. He seemed detached from the tension on the bridge. He has accepted the inevitable, I thought. He swung suddenly, met my gaze, and nodded encouragement.

It just missed being a star, said the Monitor. *Seventy years from now, there will be an unsuccessful attempt to ignite it. It is the sixth planet in a system of eleven worlds. Abonai is the fourth, and it is near its closest point of approach.*

"Why not," I asked the Monitor, "just clear out now? What's so important about Abonai?"

Abonai is the last of the frontier worlds of the original Confederacy. All the others have fallen: Eschaton, Sanusar, the City on the Crag, even Dellaconda itself. Consequently it has enormous symbolic value. With its loss, the war ceases to mean anything; Sim and his allies become exiles, a band of nomads utterly dependent on the assistance of governments that have demonstrated their indifference, or their fear, time and again.

"We don't think," the Captain was saying over the intership link, "that they know about the *Kudasai*. They're only expecting the usual mixed bag of frigates and destroyers. It's been a long time since we had any real firepower in this war, and we just may be able to deliver a hell of a punch today." He sounded almost exhilarated.

Around the bridge, the officers exchanged sober glances.

"We have some other advantages," he continued. "Volunteers from Toxicon skirmished with the Ashiyyurean main body, and drew a substantial number of escorts off. They will not arrive in time to participate in the general action." He took a deep breath. "I know you've heard the rumors that Earth has announced its intention to intervene. I have to tell you that we have been unable to confirm the story. I have no doubt it is only a matter of time before they do so, but we cannot expect any help at present.

"The frigates will engage within a few minutes. Contact will be at a range of about a million and a quarter kilometers from our position. Our units will try to make it look good, and then they'll break off and come this way. We expect the mutes to follow." The bridge illumination dimmed, and a holographic projection of Barcandrik appeared. The gas giant floated amid its wispy rings. Half a dozen satellites were visible. The contending fleets appeared as points of light, the Ashiyyur white, the Dellacondans scarlet. The three big cruisers blazed among their escorts.

The two fleets approached each other on the other side of the planet, well beyond its system of rings and moons. The Confederate frigates were moving rapidly toward the enemy flank, while the Ashiyyur formation rearranged itself to receive the attack.

"We are not visible to the approaching ships," said LeMara. "And we are not alone." One of the monitors brought up the *Corsarius*. It glittered silver and blue in the hard sunlight. "With a little luck," he continued, "we will be among them before they know their danger."

I'd become completely absorbed. I knew that the people around me were simulats, and the ships and worlds mockups, but I put the knowledge aside. I could feel my heart beating, and I wondered what Mendel LeMara's combat experience was, and whether he would still be on the bridge when the *Kudasai* gets blown up in a few weeks. And I thought about Sim's mysterious crew of drifters and deserters, who were now on board the *Corsarius*.

The Seven.

I watched the attack. And though I knew it, knew it well by now, I was caught up in the drama all the same.

A squadron of ten frigates and four destroyers skirmished with the leading elements as planned, relying heavily on a moderate technological advantage to offset the sheer numbers of the Ashiyyur. The enemy vessels were bunched too closely for combat.

They were consequently more cautious in using their firepower; no mute captain wanted to be charged with damaging a friendly ship. The Dellacondans, on the other hand, as at Hrinwhar, could hardly fail to find inviting targets. And for several minutes they ran wild among their enemy.

But two destroyers disappeared suddenly off the screens. And then, in quick succession, a pair of frigates.

I waited for the withdrawal, but they held on. For seventeen minutes they raced among the mute warships, and when the signal to retreat finally came, only five ships broke out. They dropped back toward Abonai, which, thanks to good planning and some luck, lay directly through Barcandrik's dusty system.

Clouds of destroyers and frigates wheeled to pursue.

Toward us.

One of the cruisers, unable to maneuver easily, was left describing an arc that would keep it well out of range for the duration of the action.

I knew what was coming: Abonai was about to fall, and the Dellacondans would dissolve as a fighting force. But the Ashiyyur would pay a heavy price for this victory. The death of Christopher Sim would sweep away neutralists on world after world. As a result of Rigel, the modern Confederacy would be born, and its first act would be the creation of an allied navy that, within a year, would turn back the Ashiyyur, and ultimately drive them across the Arm and beyond the Perimeter from which they had come.

The *Kudasai* would survive another few weeks, just long enough to see the intervention. At Arkady, it would die fighting alongside the first units from Earth. It would take Tarien Sim with it.

The crew of the *Kudasai* prepared for battle. Weapons went to full power, hatches closed, and the power cells built up a full charge. Voice circuits were busy, though I could understand little of the traffic.

LeMara strapped himself into the command chair. He looked over at Sim, who still stood by his port. "Best resume your seat, sir," he said gently.

Tarien's eyes were hooded, but he touched the communicator stud on the arm of his chair, and glanced at the Captain. LeMara nodded, and he opened a channel. "This is Tarien Sim," he said. "I want you to know I am proud to be with you. There are many who are saying that the future rides with us today. If it does, it couldn't be in better hands. God bless you.''

Beside us, swimming silently out of the dust, came the *Corsarius*.

Someone was calling off ranges.

Rigel was feeble from this distance, and the dust and gas through which we floated was illuminated by Barcandrik's gloomy light.

In the actual battle, said the Monitor, *the time lapse between the beginning of the retreat and the arrival of the Dellacondans within visual range of the* Kudasai *was several hours. We've compressed things a bit. If you look at the infrared monitor, you'll notice a cluster of stars brightening rapidly. Our ships are quite close now.*

One blew up almost immediately. *Only seven of the warships will survive this engagement. Contrary to common opinion, Sim committed a series of errors at Rigel in both planning and execution. Nowhere else, incidentally, did he directly confront a major enemy force. His strength throughout the war lay in his hit-and-run tactics. Time after time, when enemy units came out of hyper, Sim was waiting. His usual technique was to pick off a couple of victims, and then withdraw before Ashiyyur crews recovered from the disorientation that occurs during the jump.*

He may have felt that he simply had no choice at Rigel. And he never before possessed a warship with the firepower of the Kudasai. *It must have been very tempting to want to use it.*

By now, he and his allies have been losing for three years. We spoke earlier of the symbolic importance of Abonai, as the last of the Confederate worlds. Fortunately, the Ashiyyur do not share human perceptions, and may not have recognized the significance of their intended conquest. Had they done so, they would have come with everything they could assemble. Instead, they hurriedly created a couple of task forces and sent them in.

The deep-throated rumble of power being allocated to engines and weapons continued to build.

"So Sim staked everything on a single roll of the dice."

Yes.

"And he lost."

Only his life.

Yes: he won the war here. But how much satisfaction could that have been?

Activity on the bridge was picking up and, at a command from LeMara, we began to move.

Under actual combat conditions, of course, the observation ports would be closed. We're leaving them open for you. It won't matter much: the ships are too distant, and events happen too quickly. But we've tried to make adjustments for purposes of intelligibility.

"Mute destroyers in the area," said a voice in the commlink. "They seem to have got here first."

"Let them go."

I could see moons now, blobs of thick light drifting in the clouds.

We were accelerating.

"Captain, we have a readout on the leading pursuit elements: two cruisers, seventeen destroyers, nineteen or twenty escorts. Additional vessels are straggling, but should not be a factor in the first phase."

The two forces were clearly visible in infrared: a fountain of stars forming over the big planet, needling through the dark. It looked like a pair of comets.

"Destroyer squadron is positioned and ready to join us on signal."

The two cruisers were each screened by six or seven escorts, and were now close behind their targets.

From *Corsarius* came the voice of Christopher Sim, directed to his fleeing force: "Spirit, this is Truculent. Squadron will brake full thrust on my command. Allow the head of the line to overtake you, engage, and prepare to maneuver out as planned. We'll extract the sting."

We rose out of the debris. The enemy line was immediately in front of us.

We watched them pass, the Ashiyyur. Their ships were clean points of light, sparkling against the dust and detritus, and the void beyond Barcandrik. "They haven't seen us yet," said the navigator. "Everyone lock down."

We continued to accelerate. I could feel the gentle push of the engines.

I checked my harness. The Monitor was silent. I understood some of what was happening. The velocities of the Ashiyyur were so great, that even if they discovered us prematurely, there would be little they could do to prevent our getting a few good shots at the cruisers. On the other hand, we'd get no second chance if we missed, since that same velocity would carry them quickly out of range. Total firing time available to us, according to my screens, would be about eight seconds, with less than half that amount considered a quality opportunity.

I tried to relax, wondering why I was reacting as though the issue were in doubt. The Dellacondans would succeed in taking the cruisers by surprise. *Kudasai* would destroy one, and the *Corsarius* would cripple the other. But a series of strikes would strip her of her screens. And, while the *Kudasai* hurried to her assistance, the mortally wounded mute warship would finish her off. With a nuke.

Tarien was absorbed in thought. I watched the *Corsarius* take station about a kilometer away. Briefly, sunlight flashed on the hull. In some trick of perception, the black harridan strained forward. Her weapons clusters were primed and ready, her sensor dishes rotating slowly, the lights on her bridge dimmed. For all that, there was something almost insubstantial about her, as though she were already part phantom.

A klaxon sounded, its deep-throated shriek echoing through the ship.

"Something behind us," said one of the deck officers. She was barely able to conceal her surprise. "Coming fast. Looks like twelve, maybe thirteen destroyers."

"Confirmed," came another voice. "They've locked onto us."

"How the hell'd they manage that?" growled the Captain. "Plotting: what's their arrival time?"

"If present rate of deceleration continues, eleven minutes."

I listened to the ship's background noises. My overall impression was that the *Kudasai* was holding its collective breath.

I was a bit nonplussed myself. I'd had no idea they'd run into this sort of problem. And I wondered how, under the circumstances, they could possibly have executed their designs on the main body of the pursuers. Which, historically, they did.

Christopher Sim's voice shattered the stillness. "Mallet, this is Truculent. Break off attack. Withdraw."

"Wait a minute," I said. "Monitor, there's something wrong here."

"Mendel." Sim's voice was strained. "It's essential that we save the *Kudasai*. Get it out of here. I'll try to cover."

"No!" Tarien's big fist came down on the arm of his chair, and he glared at the overhead screen, across which the oncoming destroyers were swarming. "Proceed with the attack, Chris. We have no choice!"

"Can't do it," said his brother. "They'll catch us long before we can get close to the targets. We're going to fight destroyers today whether we want to or not, and we'd better concentrate on choosing our ground. They've got too much here for us to risk getting caught in the open. Head for Barcandrik.''

"Wait a minute," I objected. "This isn't the way it happened."

Please do not interfere, Alex.

"Well, what the hell is going on here, Monitor? I don't recall ever having heard about a destroyer attack at the last minute.''

You were not there. How do you know what really happened?

"I've read the books."

LeMara's voice: "Stand by to divert power to Armstrong units. If we have to, we'll jump out."

Tarien shook his head fiercely. "That'll be the end," he rumbled. "Don't do it."

We moved away hard, and I was crushed into my seat. The environmental support system, which supplies artificial gravity, also negates most of the inertia caused by acceleration. But it apparently wasn't quite as good as the equipment they have in the modern interstellars.

"Alex?" It was Tarien's voice on my link. It was also something of a surprise: participants aren't supposed to converse with an observer.

"Yes?" I said, struggling to form the words. "What is it?"

"We aren't going to survive this. Save yourself, if you can." He looked up at me, gave me a bail-out signal with his hand, and then turned back to his display.

That did it. "Monitor, pull me out."

Nothing.

"Monitor, where the hell are you?"

I was getting scared now.

The captain went to battle mode. I've found out since that ships of the period, during emergencies, could boost power temporarily. Systems drained more quickly, but for a limited time you could pour a lot of juice simultaneously into weapons, shield, and propulsion.

The planetary atmosphere in which we hoped to lose our pursuers looked hopelessly far away. We were picking up speed quickly. But on the displays, the destroyers were coming fast, and fanning out into a wedge.

I pressed my headband. It was wet with perspiration. "Monitor, get me out."

Still nothing.

A carapace closed over my observation port. Lights dimmed.

The instructions tell you that if everything else fails, you can escape from the software simply by removing the headband. You're not supposed to do it, because it's hard on the equipment, or the head, or something. I don't remember. But I pulled it off.

Nothing changed.

I shut my eyes, and tried to feel the overstuffed sofa in the downstairs living room. I was prone on that goddam sofa, but the only connection I had between this world and that was the headband. Even my clothes were different. (I wore the uniform of the Dellacondans; and they'd given me two silver circlets. I was an officer.)

Our own rear batteries opened up. The ship shuddered under the discharge. What the hell was going to happen here?

What I knew: if the ship were ripped open, if I were severely injured in the scenario, or killed, my physical body would certainly go into shock. It had happened occasionally. And people had died. ''Jacob! Are you there?''

''Destroyers commencing evasive maneuvering. At least, we'll pick up some time.''

On the overhead, I could see that *Corsarius* was still with us. Another screen sketched the paths of whatever the *Kudasai* had fired. Someone was reading off power projections. But most of the talk on the commlink had stopped.

The weapons tracks passed harmlessly among mute ships.

''All miss. Charged for second volley.''

''Wait,'' said the Captain. ''Hold it until they get closer. I'll tell you when.''

For a long time after that no one spoke. The only sounds came from the electronics and the life support ducts and the throbbing of power deep within the ship. The combat officer reported that the destroyers had fired, and that we had enacted countermeasures. They were using nuclear-tipped photels, which travel at lightspeed and had, fortunately, already missed.

''We'll be into the hydrogen in about four minutes,'' said the Captain.

There was a second exchange of salvos, and two of the destroyers blew up. Another wobbled out of formation. Someone cheered.

''Might make it yet,'' said a woman's voice on the commlink.

The Captain was frowning. Tarien was watching him curiously. ''What's wrong?'' he asked after a moment.

"*Corsarius* hasn't fired yet."

"Captain," said the navigator, "check the port screen."

We all looked. It was a visual of *Corsarius,* and though I saw nothing unusual, everyone else seemed to. At first, there was perplexity, then anger, and finally dismay.

I looked again: and I understood. The weapons clusters were pointed at us!

The Captain hit a switch on his chair. "*Corsarius,*" he said, "What the hell's going on?"

No response.

"Ridiculous," said Tarien, leaning over his own link. "Chris!"

"Full power to port shield," said the Captain. "Evade. Go to autolock. Break the commlink with *Corsarius*. At my command, come to zero three eight, mark six."

"No!" roared Tarien. "We need to talk to him. Find out what's happening."

"We'll talk later," said LeMara. "For now, I don't want a beamrider honing in on us." He turned impatiently to the officer at his right. "Helmsman, execute!"

The ship moved under me. I was flattened again.

"She's still with us." The long bullet shape of the *Corsarius* remained directly outside my viewport.

"That's got to be physically impossible." I breathed the remark into the link, expecting no response. But the voice of the Monitor was back.

You are correct, he said. *It is. Ask the Ashiyyur. They will tell you that the* Corsarius *is not bound by physical law, and that Christopher Sim is far more than human*.

Sim's ship rotated, bringing still another line of weapons into play.

"Pulsers," said the Captain.

A distant voice commented: "Point blank range."

There was no warning flash. The bolts traveled at lightspeed, so there was only the harsh gutting of metal, sudden darkness, and the howl of escaping atmosphere.

A scream rose and cut off. A sudden blast of cold ripped through the cabin, there was no air, and something slammed into my ribs. I became intensely aware of the arm of the chair in my right hand. The ship, the cabin, the trouble I was having breathing, everything focused down to that piece of fabric-covered metal.

"The bastard's getting ready to shoot again."

XIII.

A mob is democracy in its purest form.

—**Attributed to Christopher Sim,**
The Dellacondan Annals

MY FOREHEAD WAS cool. Something moved against it, a cloth, a hand, something. I listened to the rhythm of my breathing; a mild vertigo gripped me when I tried to move. My ribs hurt, and my neck. There was light against my eyelids.

"Alex, are you all right?"

Chase's voice. Far away.

Water dribbled into a basin.

"Hello," I said, still afloat in the dark.

She took my head in her hands, and pressed her lips against my forehead. "Nice to have you back."

I reached clumsily for her, to collect a second round, but she pulled back and smiled. The gesture didn't reach her eyes, though. "How do you feel?"

"Terrible."

"Nothing seems to be broken. You're beat up a little. What were you doing in there?"

"Finding out what happens to bystanders," I said.

"Do you want medics?"

"No. I'll be okay."

"Maybe you should. I'm not much at this kind of thing: for all I know, you could have internal injuries."

I looked up into her gray eyes. She was no Quinda Arin, but at that moment she looked very good. "I'm fine," I said. "How'd you get here?"

"Jacob called me."

"Jacob?"

"It seemed like a good idea," said Jacob.

"He noticed you were having problems."

"You were flushed," Jacob said. "And you were breathing irregularly."

"So he took a look and brought you out." She produced a glass of water.

"Thanks." I sipped it, and tried to sit up. But everything hurt too much. "How'd it happen?"

"We're not sure. The simul was defective."

I laughed my way into a spasm with that.

"Alex," said Jacob, "I've looked at all the scenarios. Much the same thing would have happened no matter which you used. Even the Spinners. Had you gone back to Hrinwhar with Sim's raiding party, you'd have discovered the plan to draw the Ashiyyur away doesn't entirely work, and the Dellacondans get decimated. These are *not* the same simulations that we copied."

"The burglar," I said.

"Yes," observed Jacob.

I was still trying to sit up, but Chase eased me back. "Maybe that explains why they threw the sheets around and stole the book."

"I don't think I see a connection," said Jacob.

"What about the sheets?" asked Chase, who looked as if she hadn't heard correctly.

"We had a burglar yesterday who did some strange things with the bedding, and stole a collection of Walford Candles."

"It was a distraction," she said. "To hide the real reason for the break-in. Somebody wants you dead."

"I disagree," said Jacob. "I broke off the simul as soon as I became aware of the situation. But, had I not done so, the program would have acted to rescue you within a few more moments anyway. The same is true with all the simuls. It was not the intent that you should die."

"Sounds as if they're trying to scare you, Alex," said Chase.

They had. I could see from the way she was looking at me that she knew it as well as I did. "It has to be connected with Gabe."

"Undoubtedly," said Jacob.

I was wondering how I could back out gracefully without having Chase write me off as a coward. "None of this is worth getting killed over," I said.

Jacob was silent.

Chase nodded. "It's safest," she agreed, after a long moment. She looked disappointed.

"Well, what do you want from me?" I demanded. "I don't even know who the sons of bitches are. How can I protect myself from them?"

"You can't."

Things got very quiet after that.

Chase stared out a window, and I put my hand to my head and tried to look battered.

"Still," she said, eventually, "it's a pity the bastards will get away with it."

"Someone," said Jacob, "must think you're on the right track." He sounded mildly reproachful.

"Does anybody know anything about these?" I asked, fingering the crystal in which the simuls were loaded. "How difficult is it to reprogram one of these scenarios? What kind of expertise does it take?"

"Moderate, I would think," said Jacob. "One needs not only to rewrite the basic program, but to effect a disjunction that would negate the Monitor's primary response package, which is aimed toward ensuring the safety of the participant. And it would be necessary to disconnect a series of backup precautionary systems as well. A properly equipped home system could do it."

"Could *you?*"

"Oh, yes. Rather easily, actually."

"So someone learned, probably from the library, which scenarios we'd copied. Then they acquired a duplicate set, reprogrammed them in *this* crystal, and substituted it."

Chase crossed her legs, and kept her eyes averted. "We could query the library and find out who else has been interested in this series of engagements. No one need know we've done that."

"It wouldn't hurt," I said.

"I've already taken the step, Alex. An identical set of scenarios was borrowed two days ago."

"Okay," I said, reluctantly. "By whom?"

"The record says Gabriel Benedict."

Next morning, Jacob commented offhandedly that he'd been reading about Wally Candles, and had uncovered some information during the night. "He wrote prefaces to all his books. Did you know that?"

"We have—or had—all five of them here," I said. "I don't recall any prefaces."

"That's because they're extremely long. Nearly as long as the books themselves. Consequently, they are never included with the actual volumes. But they were collected and annotated a number of years ago by Armand Jeffries, who is a prominent Candles scholar."

I was enjoying the heat from a thermal-wrap against my bruised ribs. "What's the point?" I asked.

"I came across a description by him of the reaction on Khaja Luan after the occupation of the City on the Crag. There's an interesting portrait of Leisha Tanner in action. Apparently she was a woman of considerable courage."

"How do you mean?"

"You remember she mentioned the mobs? Apparently she wasn't simply a bystander. I have the material set up, if you'd like to see it."

"Please," I said.

"On the screen?"

"Read it to me, Jacob."

"Yes." He paused. "There is quite a lot about the political situation."

"I'll look at that later. What does he say about Tanner?"

"On the evening after they heard that the City on the Crag had been taken, Candles was watching an interventionist demonstration on campus. But he kept a safe distance."

They were using the front portico of the dining hall as a stage. Seven or eight people were seated up there, all looking appropriately outraged, and all clearly prepared to cut a few throats in a just cause. Marish Camandero was speaking. She's head of the sociology department, attractive, big-boned, no-nonsense. Exactly the sort of person you need to teach sociology.

There were maybe two hundred demonstrators gathered in the Square. That may not sound like many, but they were loud. And active. They'd brought their own music, which was mostly clatter and shrieking, and they were constantly pushing and grabbing one another. There'd been a couple of fights, one young man seemed to be engaged in trying to couple with a marberry bush, and bottles were evident everywhere.

Camandero was whooping and flapping about mutes and murders, and the crowd had got pretty whipped up.

Into all this walked Leisha. Obviously she'd left her good sense at home. She strolled toward the rear of that mob, just about the time that Camandero was making the comment that history was replete with the corpses of people that would not, or could not, fight.

The crowd roared its approval.

She went on in that vein, how people were hiding their heads in the sand, and hoping the mutes would go away. "Now is the time," she said, "to take our stand with Christopher Sim." They caught his name and roared it skyward, this helpless mob whose entire world possessed little more than a couple of gunboats.

Somebody recognized Leisha and shouted her name. That caught everyone's attention, and the noise subsided. Camandero looked directly toward her. Leisha was standing on the edge of the crowd. Smiling broadly, Camandero jabbed an index finger in Leisha's direction. "Dr. Tanner understands the mutes better than we do," she said, with mock affability. "She has defended her friends in public before. I believe she assured us less than a year ago that this day would never come. Perhaps she would like to tell us what else we need not fear, now that the City on the Crag has been overrun?"

The crowd had not yet located her. It was her chance: she could have got out of there, but instead she stood her ground. It was a reckless, dangerous thing to do, against the ugly mood of the night. An energetic bookkeeper could have sent them to burn the capitol.

Leisha glared up at Camandero, gazed round her with undisguised contempt, shrugged, and strode toward the portico. I think it was less the act itself than the shrug that struck me. The crowd parted for her, but someone lobbed a cup of beer in her direction.

Camandero raised her arms in a pacific gesture, asking the spectators for calm and generosity, even to those who lack courage.

Leisha walked with regal disdain—it was lovely to watch, but frightening. She climbed the steps onto the platform, and confronted

Camandero. The last of the noise drained out of the crowd.

I could hear voices in the wind, and there was some traffic overhead. Camandero was by far the taller of the two women. They faced each other, drawing the moment out. Then she unhooked her throat mike, and dangled it from her fingers, in a way that would have forced Leisha to stretch for it.

The act broke whatever psychic link had connected the two. "I agree," Leisha said, in a clear and surprisingly amicable manner, "that these are dangerous times." She smiled sweetly, and turned toward her audience. Camandero let the mike drop to the platform. Then she stalked off the stage and plowed through the crowd until she broke out into the Square.

The mike lay where it had fallen.

Leisha pressed her advantage. "The war is very near," she said. "We aren't part of it yet, but that moment is now probably inevitable." A few scattered cheers broke out, but they died quickly. "The city tonight is filled with meetings like this. And we should take a moment to consider—"

A blast went off across the Square somewhere. More cheers.

"—To consider what it means. There's another species out there much like ourselves—"

That got a reaction. One person shouted they were nothing like us; others shrieked they were savages. Leisha just stood there, waiting for them to come back to her.

When they did, she said coolly, "They can think!"

The crowd reacted again. I was looking around for help, and wondering what I was going to do if they dragged her down off there.

"They have an ethical system," she continued. "They have universities where students gather at meetings like this and demand vengeance on us!"

"They had it today!" someone screamed, and the air was filled with threats, against the Ashiyyur, against the University, against Leisha.

"Yes." Leisha was visibly distressed. "I suppose they did. We lost a few ships, with their crews. And I understand the mutes shot a few people on the ground. And now, in our turn, we have no choice but to spill some blood ourselves."

The mob shook its torches.

"Bitch!" someone shouted.

"Damn right!"

"A lot of people have already died. What about them?"

I knew her answer to that. I'd heard it before: We owe nothing to the dead. They will not know whether we stay or go, whether we honor their names, or forget they ever walked among us. But she was prudent enough not to say that.

"There's still time," she said, "to stop all this, if we really want to do it. Or if not, at least we can keep out of it ourselves. Why isn't the Resistance getting any help from Rimway? Or Toxicon? Those are the systems that have the battle fleets! If the Ashiyyur are really a threat to us all, why haven't they come?"

"I'll tell you why," thundered a heavy-set man who was pursuing a doctorate in the classical literature program. "They want a general commitment from us! We're in the combat area, and if we won't help ourselves, why should they risk their own people?"

The crowd agreed loudly.

"You could be right," Leisha said. "But the plain truth is that Rimway and Toxicon mistrust each other considerably more than they mistrust the aliens."

I'd moved closer during all this. I'm not sure I was ever more fearful in my life than I was during those moments. I'd located a few security people in the crowd, but had that mob gone for her, they'd have made no difference.

"If you're serious about fighting this war," she continued, "we need to count what we have to fight with. As I understand it, Khaja Luan has one destroyer." She held out her hands, palms up. "That's it, folks. One destroyer. There are three or four frigates which last saw combat more than a half century ago. And there are a few shuttles, but they will have to throw rocks, since they're not armed. We do not have the facilities to build warships, so we'll have to buy them from someone.

"We're going to have to ram a hefty tax increase through the legislature. And eliminate state-paid educations." She paused and glanced back at the group of people seated behind her. Most prominent among them was Myron Marcusi, of the philosophy department. "I'm sure," she said, smiling brightly at him, "that Dr. Marcusi will be among the first to endorse whatever measures need to be taken to raise money."

"Damned right!" shouted someone in the rear of the crowd.

Marcusi rose to the occasion. "We're not concerned about money here, Doctor Tanner," he said, trying to speak loudly, but having trouble. "There's a great deal more at stake than a few scholarships. We're talking about lives, and possibly human survival, unless *we can unite against the common danger."*

He ended in a squeal, but he got a loud burst of applause.

And someone began to sing. Other voices picked up the rhythm, and Leisha stood watching, dejected. The song swelled and filled the Square. It was the ancient battle hymn of the City on the Crag. The "Condor-ni."

I spent the next few days linking in with university libraries and out-of-the-way archives, looking for whatever information might be available on Tanner. At night, I read myself to sleep with the works of Rashim Machesney. I managed a dinner with Quinda, and enjoyed myself thoroughly. For the first time, we did not pass the evening discussing the Resistance.

Several nights after my ride on the *Kudasai*, Chase called to say she'd found something. She wouldn't tell me what it was, but she sounded excited. That didn't exactly come as good news: I was beginning to hope I might have reached a blank wall, one that would allow me to back off with a clear conscience.

She arrived an hour later carrying a crystal and looking immensely pleased with herself. "I have here," she said, holding out the crystal, "the collected letters of Walford Candles."

"You're kidding."

"Hello, Chase," said Jacob. "Dinner will be ready in about a half hour. How do you like your steak?"

"Hi, Jacob. Medium-well."

"Very good. It's nice to see you again. And I'm anxious to examine what you've brought."

"Thank you. I've been talking to people at literature departments and libraries all over the continent. *This* was in the archives of a small school in Masakan. It was compiled locally, but the editor died, and no one ever formally published it. It includes a *holo* from Leisha Tanner, sent from Millennium!"

Millennium: the last entry in Tanner's *Notebooks*.

I inserted the crystal in Jacob's reader, and sat down in the wingback.

The lights dimmed.

Tanner's image formed. She wore a light blouse and shorts, and it was obvious she was operating from a warm climate.

Wally, she said, *I've got bad news*. Her eyes were troubled, and she looked frightened. The woman who had stood up to the mob in the Square on Khaja Luan had been badly shaken.

We were right: Matt was here after the loss of the Straczynski. *But the Dellacondans are trying to hide it. I've talked to a couple of the people who knew him, and either they won't discuss him at all, or they lie. They don't like him very much, Wally, but they pretend they do. I was talking to a computer specialist, a woman whose name is Monlin or Mollin or something. When I caught up with her she'd had too much to drink. I had learned by then not to approach the subject of Matt in any direct way, because when you do they pretend not to know anything at all. So I gradually led the conversation with Monlin around to how we had a mutual friend who'd mentioned her name to me once or twice. She looked interested, but when I named Matt, she lost her composure, and got so upset that she broke a glass and cut her hand. She literally screamed that he was a traitor, and a son of a bitch, and that she'd have gladly killed him if she could. I've never seen such venom. Then suddenly, as if somebody threw a switch, she stopped and wouldn't say any more.*

Next morning, I tracked her down at breakfast, but she told me it had just been the alcohol talking. She said she liked Matt, but claimed she'd never really got to know him very well. Sorry about his death, etcetera. That evening, she was gone. One of the officers told me she'd been sent on a temporary assignment. He didn't know where.

The thing that bothers me is this: Matt was always hard to get to know. But he's not the sort of person anyone could hate. *Wally, these people despise him. His name doesn't exactly excite a little irritation. These people—all of these people—would like to kill him.*

I suppose I should leave it at this and go home. I'm tired of talking to military types anyway. They hate rather easily. But my God I'd like to know the truth. I never knew anyone more loyal to Sim and his damned Confederates than Matt Olander.

This place is a madhouse now. It's overrun with refugees from Ilyanda, and it's hard to get near any of the groundside naval installations. I look around at these people, displaced from their homes, and I get very discouraged. Did you know that the Ashiyyur bombed Point Edward? How can they be such fools? I wouldn't say this to anyone else, but sometimes I wonder whether Sim isn't right about them. It's hard, Wally. It really is.

I've heard that Tarien will be making a speech downtown tomorrow, dedicating a housing area for the Ilyandans. I'm going to

*make an effort to talk to him there. Maybe he can be persuaded to
look into this business with Matt.*

I'll keep you informed.

The image faded.

"Is that it?"

"There's no other transmission," remarked Jacob, "with this
crystal."

Chase must have been sitting with her eyes closed, listening.
"That's all there is," she said. "The introduction indicates that
subsequent volumes were planned. But none of them got put
together. The editor died too soon."

"His name was Charles Parrini, of the University of Mileta,"
said Jacob. "He's been dead thirty years."

"Somebody else might have finished the project."

"Maybe." Chase straightened. "But if so, it never got published."

"It might not matter," observed Jacob. "Parrini must have
collected *some* source documents. Find them and you might get
your answers."

The University of Mileta was located in Sequin, the smallest of
Rimway's six continents, in the desert city Capuchai. Parrini had
been an emeritus professor of literature there for the better part of a
productive lifetime. The library overflowed with his books: the man
must have been extraordinarily prolific. His commentaries ranged
across every literary epoch since the Babylonians. He'd edited
several definitive editions of the great poets and essayists (including
Walford Candles). But, most interestingly, he'd translated a
shelfload of Ashiyyurean poetry and philosophy. Chase and I,
working from Gabe's study, spent an entire afternoon and part of
the next morning scrolling through the books.

Toward noon of the second day, Chase called me to her terminal.
"Parrini's *Tulisofala* is interesting. I've been looking at the
principals on which she bases her ethical system: *Love your enemy.
Return good for evil. Justice and mercy are the cornerstones of a
correct life; justice because it is demanded by nature; and mercy
because justice erodes the soul.*"

"Sounds familiar."

"Maybe there's only one kind of ethical system that works.
Although, with the mutes, it doesn't seem to have taken."

"Is this what you wanted to show me?"

"No. Just a minute." She scrolled back to the title page, and pointed to the dedication. *For Leisha Tanner.*

None of the librarians knew anything about Parrini. To them, he was simply a couple of crystals in the reference room, and three boxes of documents in a storage area on the third floor. (Or maybe there were four boxes. No one was sure.) At our request, they moved the boxes down to a viewing room and showed us the contents. We found student reports, grade lists, financial records that had been old when Parrini died, and invoices for furniture, art work, books, clothes, a skimmer. You name it.

"There has to be more," Chase said, after we'd removed our headbands and started on a hot lunch. "We're not looking in the right place. Parrini couldn't simply have accumulated the material for the first volume without simultaneously getting large chunks of material for the succeeding books."

I agreed, and suggested that the place to start was the literature department.

Jacob had a transmission code ready for us when we finished, and we linked into a shabby office with run-down furniture and two bored-looking young men who lounged at old terminals, their feet propped up and their fingers laced behind their heads. One was extremely tall, almost two and a half meters. The other was about average size, with clear, friendly eyes, and straw-colored hair. A monitor was running rapidly through blocks of text, but no one seemed to be paying any attention.

"Yes?" inquired the smaller of the two, straightening slightly. "Can I help you?" He really asked the question of Chase.

"We're doing some research on Charles Parrini," she said. "We're particularly interested in his work on Walford Candles."

"Parrini's a hack," said the other, without moving. "Schambly is much better on Candles. Or Koestler. Hell, almost anybody except Parrini."

The one who had spoken first frowned and introduced himself. "Korman," he said. "First name's Jak. This is Thaxter." Thaxter's lips parted slightly. "What do you need?" he asked, still talking to Chase. His eyes traveled swiftly down her anatomy. He looked pleased.

"Are you familiar," I asked, "with his translation of *Tulisofala?* Why did he dedicate it to Leisha Tanner?"

Korman smiled, apparently impressed. "Because," he said, looking in my direction for the first time, "she made the first serious effort to translate Ashiyyurean literature. Nobody really reads her anymore, of course. Modern scholarship has left her efforts behind. But she led the way."

Chase nodded in her best academic manner. "Have you read his work on Wally Candles?" she asked. Her diction was a bit more pronounced than usual. "The *Letters?*"

Thaxter inserted his foot into an open drawer and rocked it back and forth. "I know *about* it," he said.

"There were to be additional volumes. Did they ever get completed?"

"As I recall," Thaxter said, "he died in the middle of the project."

"That's right." Chase looked from one to the other. "Did anyone else finish what he started?"

"I don't think so." Thaxter drew the words out in a way that suggested he had no idea. He tried a tentative smile, got an encouraging response from Chase, and consulted his computer. "No," he said, after a few moments. "Only Volume I. Nothing after that."

"Dr. Thaxter," I said, bestowing a title I doubted that he owned, "what would have happened to Parrini's records after his death?"

"I'd have to look into that."

"Would you?" asked Chase. "It would be helpful."

Thaxter stirred himself enough to straighten up. "Okay, I can do that. Where can I find you?" He seemed to be talking to Chase's anatomy.

"Might you have an answer for us this evening?"

"Possibly."

"I'll be back," smiled Chase.

On his death, Charles Parrini's files passed into the hands of Adrian Monck, his frequent collaborator. Among other projects, Monck was to have completed the second and third volumes of the Candles letters. But he was working on the now-forgotten historical novel *Maurina,* an epic retelling of the Age of Resistance through the eyes of Christopher Sim's young wife. He didn't live to complete either the novel or the Candles collection, and *Maurina* was finished by his daughter. Parrini's papers were eventually donated by her to the University Library at Mount Tabor, where Monck had received his undergraduate degree.

Mount Tabor is located outside Bellwether, a relatively small city in the southern hemisphere eight time zones away. The university's name is a trifle misleading: the land around Bellwether is dead flat. The institution is church-affiliated, and "Mount Tabor" is a scriptural reference.

Moments after Chase returned from her conversation with Thaxter, we presented ourselves to the AI who maintained the University Library after hours. (It was just before dawn in Bellwether.) No unpublished materials were listed in the inventory under either Monck or Parrini.

In the morning, we were back when they opened. The young assistant whom we approached with our questions checked his databanks and shook his head after each entry. No Monck. No Parrini. Sorry. Wished he could help. It was exactly what the AI had said, but humans are easier to negotiate with.

We insisted they had to be there somewhere, and the young man sighed and passed us on to a dark-complexioned woman who was even taller than Chase. She was big-boned, with black hair and an abrupt manner that suggested her time was extremely valuable. "If anything *does* arrive," she told us peremptorily, "we'll get in touch with you immediately." She'd already begun to walk away. "Please leave your code at the desk."

"If they're not here now," I said, "they aren't coming. The Parrini papers were bequeathed to the university more than twenty years ago."

She stopped. "I see. Well, that's before *my* time, and obviously they're not here. You have to understand that we receive a great many bequests in the form you describe. Usually, they're materials that the heirs have no earthly use for. But in our grief, Mr. Benedict, we are inclined to exaggerate the importance of whomever has just passed on—You might wish to try the Literary Foundation."

"I would be *extremely* grateful if you can help us," I persisted. "And I'd be happy to pay for your time." I'd never tried to bribe anyone before, and I felt clumsy. I managed a glance at Chase, who was having trouble keeping a straight face.

"I'd be pleased to take your money, Mr. Benedict. But it really wouldn't do you any good. If it's not in the inventory, we don't have it. Simple as that."

I wondered aloud whether it might not create a disturbance if the Mount Tabor Board of Governors learned that the heritage of Charles Parrini had been treated so cavalierly by their librarians, and she suggested I should take whatever action I considered appropriate.

"End of the line, I guess," I told Chase when we were back in the study. She nodded, and we got up from the chairs in which we'd been sitting for the better part of two days. It was well past midnight.

"Let's get some air," she said, pressing her fingers to her temples.

Outside, we strolled gloomily along one of the forest footpaths. "I think it's time," I said, "to write the entire business off."

She looked straight ahead and didn't say anything. The night air was cold and had a sting to it, but it felt good. We walked for maybe a half hour. She seemed preoccupied, while my relief that it was finally over gradually gave way to an awareness of Chase's long-legged physical presence.

"I know how frustrating this must be for you," she said, suddenly.

"Yes." Her eyes were on about a level with mine, and I was very conscious of them in that moment. "I would have liked to get some answers," I said shamelessly.

"It would also be nice to catch up with whoever was playing games with you."

"That too." Like hell.

I tried to assuage my conscience by admitting that I was glad to turn my mind to other things, and I went on for some minutes about my responsibilities to Gabe's estate, and a few problems of my own, and whatnot. All lies, but it didn't matter. Chase wasn't listening anyway.

"I have a thought," she said, breaking in as though I'd said nothing whatever. "We know the documents were donated by Monck's daughter. The bequest might have been cataloged in *her* name, which would not necessarily have been Monck. The problem might just be that the library doesn't cross-reference very well."

She was right.

The materials themselves, like the documents at Mileta, were packed away in a plastic container in a storage room.

The tall dark-complexioned librarian argued briefly that the materials were not available for public viewing. But she conceded quickly when I threatened again to go to her superiors, this time with a considerably more detailed accusation.

She had the container delivered to a viewing room and, when we arrived, everything had been laid out on a couple of tables. The young assistant we'd met the previous day was assigned to us, to load data storage units, and hold things up to the light, and turn pages, and do the various other physical tasks that a headband projection cannot do for itself. He was very responsive and patient with a job that must have quickly become tedious for him, and was on the whole quite the opposite of his supervisor. I thought also that he was somewhat taken with Chase.

We spent two days going through the material. A substantial portion of it was correspondence originated by and sent to Walford Candles. It was on crystals; on some of the old spools and cylinders and fibres of various types that you don't see anymore; in lightpad memory systems; and on paper. "It's going to create a problem," said Chase. "We won't be able to read most of this stuff. Where would you find a reader that would accept this?" She held up a cube, turning it in the light. "I'm not even sure whether it's a data storage unit at all."

"The University will have the equipment," I said, directing the comment to the young man, who nodded vigorously.

"We have adapted readers for most systems," he agreed.

In all honesty, I have to confess that it was difficult to get through those letters. As Candles's reputation grew, his correspondence was no longer limited only to his band of friends. Parrini had found communications from both the Sims, from most of the people whose names live in the histories of the period, from statesmen and the men who fought the war, from weapons manufacturers and social reformers, from theologians and victims. There was even a description of a graduation on Khaja Luan at which Tarien Sim was a featured speaker. Under normal circumstances, he would have had the podium to himself, except that the Ashiyyurean ambassador also showed up to state his case. The alien's interpreter was Leisha Tanner!

"The woman," commented Chase, "really liked to ride tigers."

The event was described by Candles to a forgotten correspondent. It was dated a few weeks before the fall of the City on the Crag: *If a passion for ceremony signifies anything,* Candles comments, *our two cultures may be more alike than we wish to admit.*

Both formalize passages of various types, births and deaths and whatnot; sporting events; public displays of the arts; assorted political functions; and the ultimate ceremonial, war.

So, despite everything, the robed and hooded figure of the Ambassador, folded onto a bench well apart from the dignitaries on the parade stand, did not look entirely out of place. It sat quietly, its robe folded in a manner that suggested its forelimbs were placed on its lap. No face was visible within the hood. Even on that bright sunlit afternoon, I had the sense of gazing down a dark tunnel.

Leisha, who knows about such things, had informed me that this is an extremely trying experience for the Ambassador. Other than that it may well be in some physical danger, since the massive security forces surrounding the gathering can not really protect it from a determined assassin, it apparently also suffers from some sort of psychological oppression, induced by the presence of people in large numbers. I suppose I'd feel the same way if I thought they all wanted me dead.

There was a substantial amount of official talk about academic accomplishment and bright futures. And I wondered at the self-control of the Ambassador, stiff and erect among us.

I felt uncomfortable in its presence. In fact, if I aim to be honest, I must admit I did not like the creature very much, and would have been pleased to have it gone. I don't know why that should be. It has nothing to do with the war, I don't think. I suspect that we will never feel entirely comfortable when faced with intelligence housed in an exotic physical configuration. I wonder whether this isn't the real basis for our reaction to the aliens, rather than the sense of mental intrusion to which it is usually ascribed?

The University asked Leisha to act as interpreter. That meant reading the alien's speech. Everybody she knew advised her strongly not to do it, and a few people made it clear that she was behaving in a treasonable fashion, and that, if she persisted, they would see that she paid a price. Sometimes we forget who the enemy is.

I'd like to tell you that the friendship of those who threatened her in this way would not have been worth keeping. But unfortunately this is not so. Cantor was among the group. And Lyn Quen. And a young man whom I believe Leisha loved.

No matter. When the time came, she was up there beside the Ambassador, looking as cool and lovely as I've ever seen her. She's a hell of a woman, Connie. I wish I were younger.

Tarien Sim was there too, of course, resplendent among the notables. He has become a person of such incredible political dimension that one cannot but expect to be disappointed by his physical appearance. And yet—there is a sense of greatness about him that one can see and feel. Shafts of sunlight catch his eye, if you know what I mean.

His scheduled address was the reason for the Ambassador's appearance, actually. The Ashiyyur wanted equal time. But I knew it was a mistake. The contrast between Tarien, who is a father figure with a bright red beard and a voice that inspires revolution; and the silent, ominous, stick figure, could hardly have been greater.

There were more than four hundred graduates, counting those receiving advanced degrees. They sat in rows across Morien Field, where students have been listening to commencement oratory for almost four centuries. Behind them, a crowd of spectators—far larger than any I've seen during all the years I've been attending these things—overflowed the seating areas, and spilled into the athletic fields beyond. The press was out in force. And there was an army of security people, the University's own reinforced by city police and several dozen unmistakable narrow-eyed agents of one kind and another.

It was a restless afternoon. Everyone was looking for something to happen, anxious to see it when it did, but maybe a little scared to get caught in it.

The student speakers said the things that students always say at such times, and their remarks gathered polite applause. Then President Hendrik rose to introduce Sim. I understand there was something of a pushing match between the University and the government over the order of speakers. Hendrik wanted to give the final word to Sim, which would be his way of demonstrating publicly that he no more approved of the presence of the Ambassador than did the rest of the mob. But the government had insisted that the alien dignitary receive that honor.

The crowd stirred expectantly while Hendrik praised Sim's courage and abilities in these perilous times, and so on. Then they roared their applause when he rose and took his place at the podium. He shook hands with a couple of VIPs, pointedly not looking at the Ambassador. He stilled the clamor with a casual wave of his right hand, and surveyed his audience. "Graduations," he said, foregoing the customary preliminary greetings, "are about the future.

"It would be tempting to speak of the accomplishments of the *recent past. About the first serious efforts to abolish war, to unite the human family, to ensure security and a measure of prosperity for everyone. After all, these have been our goals for a long time, and they have proved more elusive than those who first proclaimed them would have believed."* Leisha sat motionless beside the Ambassador. Her features were strained, her limbs rigid. Her hands were closed in tight fists.

I wasn't alone in noticing. Others seemed fascinated by her presence at the Ambassador's side, as though there were something vaguely obscene in it. And I found it difficult myself to put to rest a similar notion. Please don't quote me or I'll deny it.

"Unfortunately," Tarien continued, "there's still much to do. More than my generation can hope to accomplish.

"Rather, it will be for you to succeed finally, to recognize that there can be no safety for any, until all are safe; no peace until those who would make war understand that there is no profit to be had—" Well, I could quote or paraphrase all of it, Connie. He was that good. If anybody can unite these bickering worlds into a Confederacy, he can. He spoke of remote places and courage and duty and the ships that carry ideals between the stars.

"In the end," he said, "it will not be arms that decide our destiny. It will be the same weapon that has destroyed oppressive governments and ambitious invaders time and again, since we built the first printing press. Or maybe carved a few symbols into the first tablet. Free ideas. Free ideals. Common decency.

"Time is on our side. The enemy with whom we contend, who would threaten, if it could, our survival, cannot with its warships overcome the power of a mind that thinks for itself."

The applause started slowly, and rippled swiftly across the cool grass, gathering momentum. One of the graduates stood, a tall proud young woman, whose dark eyes burned fiercely. I wasn't close enough to see tears, but I knew they were there. One by one others joined her, until they were all on their feet.

Tarien again signaled for silence, and got it. "It is better," he said, "that we recall those we have lost, for they have given us our future. They have bought time for us. But there will surely come an hour when we can celebrate together, when we have completed our task, and rolled back our oppressor."

They stood for several moments. The assemblage had become a large animal, and you could hear it breathe. Tarien bowed. "For my brother, and for all who fight in your name, I thank you."

Connie, I wish you had been there. It was magnificent! I doubt there was a single person in the square who would not gladly have traded his present station for some fighting skills, and a good deck underfoot. What more could one ask of this life than to join the Dellacondans?

Well, I can see you snickering: how Candles goes on. Must be getting old. But God help me, we're approaching the species' most critical test. And when years from now we look back on all this, I'd like to know that I made a contribution—

I felt sorry for the Ambassador, lone awkward mannequin, withering in the face of such a storm.

Hendrik, uncertain, frightened, came to center stage. We were all restless, wondering what was coming next.

"Honored Guests," he said, speaking flatly. "Faculty Members, Graduates, Friends of the University: our next speaker is the Ashiyyurean Ambassador, M'Kan Keoltipess."

Far away, almost on the horizon, a skimmer was rising above the tree line. I imagined I could hear the whisper of its magnetics.

The Ambassador rose awkwardly. It was clearly uncomfortable, whether from the local gravity (which was somewhat heavier than on Toxicon, where it had served until recently) or from its perception of the situation, I do not know. Leisha rose and stood beside it. She looked simultaneously defiant and unruffled. She had apparently used the time to get hold of herself. And this you'll like: she unnerved the crowd by offering the Ambassador her arm, and guiding it toward the podium.

It took its place, towering over Leisha. From within the robes came a sound like dried bones cracking. Leisha took a lightpad from her tunic. Obviously it contained the speech she was to read. But the Ambassador signaled her to put it away. I realized we were seeing the old human game of throwing away the prepared address. It fumbled with the folds of its hood, as a woman might with a skirt imagined to expose a bit too much. It raised both hands, shook the hood down to its shoulders, and stood uncovered, blinking in the bright sunlight.

It was very old. And its parchment features looked pained. The animal that Tarien Sim had created remained together, and it took a few psychological steps backward.

The Ambassador extended long desiccated fingers. They had too many joints, and the flesh was tight and gray. They danced in the *sunlight, and there was much in their frenetic, graceful movements that left me chilled.*

Leisha watched the fingers, and nodded. My impression was that she hesitated at translating its first "remarks," but obviously the Ashiyyurean insisted.

"The Ambassador thanks me," she said, "and wishes to say that he understands this is not easy for me. He also says: *I understand your anger at this hour.*" The hands weaved their intricate patterns. "*I wish to extend greetings to President Hendrik, to the honored Guests, to the Faculty, to the Graduates, and to their families. And especially—*" it turned toward Tarien Sim, seated far to its right, "*especially to the gallant representative of the Rebels, an opponent whom I would prefer to call 'friend.'*"

It paused, and I thought I could read genuine regret in its face. "*We wish you all good fortune. On an occasion such as this, when young ones go forward to test their knowledge, and to embrace their lives, we are particularly prone to realize that for them wisdom lies yet in the future. I can't help observing that, when one considers the conditions under which we meet today, much the same may be true of our two species.*"

Leisha's voice, which had begun with too high a timbre, and some trace of nervousness, had settled into its customary richness. She was, of course, no match for Tarien Sim, but she was damned good.

"*To the graduates,*" the Ambassador continued, "*I would point out that wisdom consists in recognizing what is truly important. And in treating with suspicion any cherished belief whose truth is so clear that one need not put it to the test. Among our people, we maintain that wisdom consists in recognizing the extent to which one is prone to error.*"

It paused, allowing Leisha a moment to catch her breath.

"*I would have preferred not to speak about politics today. But I owe it to you and to my own people to respond to Ambassador Sim. He has said there is a major conflict, and he is sadly correct. But the struggle is not between Ashiyyur and human. It is between those who would find a way to settle our difficulties peacefully, and those who believe only in resorting to a military solution. It is essential during the dark days that surely lie before us that you be aware that you have friends among us, and enemies among your own.*

"*Our psychological reactions to each other are intense, but not so much so that they cannot be overcome. If we wish. If we insist! In any case, I implore you not to use them as a basis to form a moral judgment. If we commit that crime against each other, we shall bear a heavy burden before history.*

"I can not agree more strongly with Ambassador Sim's remarks. For all our differences, of culture and physiognomy and perception, we share the one gift that really matters: we are thinking creatures. And on this day, under this sun, I pray that we will find ourselves capable of using that gift. I pray that we will pause in our headlong rush, and think!"

The entry, I noted belatedly, was earmarked for another book which was to have developed the influences on Walford Candles's early years. I was still thinking about it, wondering how events could have gone so wrong when everyone seemed to want to do the right thing. Weren't perceptions worth anything at all?

I have no answers, other than a suspicion that there is something relentlessly seductive about conflict. And that, after all these millennia, we still don't understand the nature of the beast.

Chase found more: a holo communication from Leisha, routed from Ilyanda, and dated thirty-two days after the earlier Millenium message. It was short: *Wally, I'm forwarding separately a written statement by Kindrel Lee which has things to say about Matt. It's a wild story, and I don't know what to believe. We need to talk about it when I get home.*

"I don't understand this," I said. I stared at the date, and consulted a text. "This thing was sent from Ilyanda *after* the evacuation. And probably after the destruction of Point Edward. What the hell's going on? Why would she have gone *there?*"

"I don't know," said Chase, who was searching through the piles of documents that we'd assembled.

"Where's the statement?"

"Forwarded separately," she said. "It doesn't seem to be included with this material."

XIV.

The destruction of Point Edward (after it had been evacuated) was an act of puzzling barbarity. Nothing could have more readily demonstrated the gap between human reason and alien spasm. In the wake of that destruction, men were sufficiently horrified that, for a moment, they drew together and came very close to recognizing their own common humanity and the peril it faced. Unfortunately, the moment passed quickly.

—Arena Cash,
War in the Void

THE CURIOUS THING about Matt Olander's grave is that it was waiting for the refugees when they returned to Ilyanda after the war. They found it in a weed-choked field that had once been a lawn, not twenty meters from the main terminal at the William E. Richardson Spaceport. It was marked by a single oblate white slab which had been cut out of the front of the building with a laser.

The slab was engraved, presumably with the same tool:

Matt Olander
died Avrigil 3, 677
No Stranger to Valor

The characters were crudely cut, the name and the last word written large. They tended a trifle toward the ornate, in the style of two centuries ago. The date, in Ilyanda's calendar, corresponded with the Evacuation.

The site lies within a grove. There are low hedges and flowering trees and seashell walkways. Overhead, a Dellacondan pennant, with its harridan sigil encased within the silver ring of the Confederacy, snaps fiercely in a cold stiff wind off the ocean. At the foot of the flagpole, the Point Edward Historical Society has erected a stone marker: a bronze plate, dated 716, carries Olander's name, and a remark attributed to him, reportedly spoken to a comrade during the final moments of the evacuation: *It is not proper that Point Edward should face the mutes without a defender.*

The base of the monument is engraved with a resolution of the Joint Chambers, that Matthew Olander *never be forgotten by the City he would not desert.*

The site is the sort of place people go to on holidays, to sit on benches and watch seabirds and floaters. On the midwinter day we were there (I'd brought Chase along), a troop of kids were flying brightly colored gliders, and a large tourist group had debarked from an airbus and were milling about. Ilyanda's white sun Kaspadei was breaking through a gray sky; and most of the older visitors were hurrying about, glancing at the inscriptions, and climbing back into the airbus, where it was warm.

It's a lonely place, despite its proximity to the Richardson terminal. Maybe the sense of isolation is spiritual rather than geographical. Standing beneath the canopy of shrub trees within an enclosure dedicated solely to one individual's courage, I kept thinking about the slippery quality of truth. How would Olander's comrades—the ones who had sneered at his memory and suggested to Leisha Tanner that he was a traitor—How would *they* have responded to all this? *No Stranger to Valor.*

Where *was* the truth? What had happened on Point Edward?

"Who put it here?" asked Chase. She looked solemn, thoughtful, almost oppressed. The wind pulled at her hair, and she brushed it back, out of her eyes.

"The park commission."

"No. I mean, who buried Matt Olander? Who cut the inscription on the tombstone? It says in the *Tourist Guide* that the grave was here when the refugees returned from Millenium after the war."

"I know."

"Who cut the inscription?" She thumbed through the publication. "According to this, the legend is that the Ashiyyur did it."

"I don't really know much about the Ashiyyur. But why not? Stranger things have happened in wars than people paying tribute to enemies."

A crowd gathered around the stone. Their breath was visible in the cold air. Some took pictures, others spoke hurriedly and moved on. "It *is* cold," said Chase, sealing her jacket and adjusting the thermals. "Why wouldn't the inscription be in their *own* written language?"

Hell, I didn't know. "What's the guide book say?"

"It says the experts disagree."

"Great. That's helpful. But I can think of another possibility. One that accounts for the burial, at least."

"Go ahead," she said.

"They tried to evacuate, what, twenty thousand people in a week? It couldn't be done without overlooking a few. There's always somebody who doesn't get the word. Anyway, Olander stayed behind, found them, and probably was with them when he died during the bombing. Maybe he did something to earn their admiration, shot down a mute ship with a hand weapon, rescued a child from a burning building. Who knows? Whatever it was, they admired him for it, and they gave him a proper sendoff. In the proper language."

I stared at the slab. "Leisha Tanner knew the truth," I said.

"Yes, I suppose so. Do you believe your own theory?"

"No. I don't know why, but it doesn't feel right. Neither does the notion that he didn't want to desert the city. That's pleasantly poetic. But it's more likely he got left behind. The Dellacondans got out of here a bare few hours before the enemy fleet arrived. They would have been in a hell of a hurry, cutting it that close."

"But that doesn't explain why his comrades reacted the way they did to Tanner."

We stood over the grave and tried to imagine what might have happened. "I wonder," I said, "if anyone's really buried here? Maybe the grave's empty."

"No. I was reading about it on the way out, Alex. They've taken pictures. There *is* a body down there, and dental records show that it *is* Olander's."

"Does it say how he died?"

"Not in the plasma drop, apparently. I guess there's evidence he got hit by a laser. They think a small, hand-carried weapon. Which supports one part of the legend."

"Which is—?"

"That the mutes sent in a landing party to try to take him alive."

"Maybe he was caught and executed."

"That," said Chase, "is a distinct possibility. But no one around here will accept it."

"Why not?"

"Because it's not very heroic. The image everyone prefers is Olander standing on the roof of the terminal with a pulser, surrounded by dead aliens, firing away until the bastards take him down. Anyway, how do you explain the inscription if he surrendered?"

"I guess that eliminates suicide too. Okay. Another question: if he stayed behind voluntarily, did his C.O. know about it? Or did he jump ship? If it was the latter, it might explain some of the irritation that Tanner ran into."

"I don't think Christopher Sim would have allowed anyone to stay behind to die. That wouldn't sound like him at all."

"How do you know?"

She looked momentarily confused. "We're talking about *Christopher Sim*, Alex." Our eyes locked, and she started to grin, but shook her head. "No," she said. "I don't believe it."

"Nor do I. I think if we could find out why Olander didn't leave with his ship, we'd be an appreciable distance toward understanding—" I hesitated.

"What?" prompted Chase.

"Damned if I know. Maybe Kindrel Lee can tell us."

We leased a skimmer at Richardson, keyed in the downtown hotel that had our reservations, and flew into Point Edward, which was a moderate-sized city of permearth, stone, and glass constructed over a dead seaside volcano.

The first view of it was a shock. There were no sweeping walkways or malls; no webbed parks connecting the upper levels. Point Edward was a city of clearly defined individual structures, heavy on the facing, with square-cut arches and ramparts, and plenty of statuary. The central area was rebuilt after the destruction of 677, employing the same architectural style throughout. The *Guide* described this as Uniform Toxicate. It must have seemed like a good idea at the time, but the result was to create a downtown of numbing stability and sobriety, of sharp corners and immovable purpose. It was life at ground level, in a city that felt like a fortress.

I wondered, as we settled onto the roof of our hotel, how much of this reflected the state of mind of a people who had barely escaped the fire.

An hour later, from Chase's room, we linked with the Bureau of Records and Vital Statistics. The clerk was an AI, cast in the appearance of an elderly male, with a full gray-black beard and sympathetic blue eyes.

"It would be easier if we had her ID number," he said.

"Sorry," I grumbled. "How many people named Kindrel Lee could have been living in a place with a population of, what, twenty thousand?"

"Mr. Benedict," he said, poking thoughtfully at his keyboard, "you understand, of course, that the records burned with the city in 677. We have very little preceding that date."

"Yes. But she—assuming Kindrel is a she—was still around after the attack. Must have been, if Tanner talked to her. So she might have married after that date. Or applied for some sort of exemption. Or got a job with the government. There should be *something* on her."

"Yes," he said agreeably. "I'm sure there must be." He bent to his task. "Are you sure of the spelling?"

"No. Actually it's guesswork."

"Is it possible she might have been born with a different name?"

"It's possible."

"You set a very difficult task, Mr. Benedict."

"Please do the best you can," I said. I tried to offer him money, but he refused it. Government rules. I was still feeling clumsy.

Chase took to prowling round the limited area allowed by the projector, while I watched the day's news reports follow each other across a monitor.

A recession had begun on Earth.

Along the frontier, shots had been exchanged between Ashiyyurean and Confederate warships again. No damage to our side, probably none to theirs.

"And forty years ago today—" A picture of a sailing yacht appeared on the terminal, "—the *Andover*, attempting to complete a round-the-world voyage, disappeared in southern seas."

"No," said the clerk suddenly. "There simply isn't any record."

"There *has* to be," I objected. "At the very least, she would have died."

"If she did, Mr. Benedict," he said, with a broad display of even white teeth, "she didn't do it on Ilyanda."

"I have another idea," I said, back in the apartment. "The *Andover*."

"I think we have enough mysteries, Alex. And I doubt that the *Andover* is involved in any of this."

"Of course not. But that was a forty-year-old clip we saw in there. How far back do the local newsgathering organizations go?"

Two syndicates were listed on the local net: Oceanic and Mega. Neither had been around much over a half century. That was Ilyanda time, where the years are about forty percent longer than at home, but it still wasn't enough. "It doesn't matter," a commtech at Mega told us. "Everybody uses centralized data storage anyhow. We have access to records that go back damned near three hundred years."

We tied in with Datalink, a central processing facility. It gave us what we wanted: access to Ilyanda's history, seen from a contemporary perspective.

Chase activated a terminal and poked in LEE, KINDREL.

The answer came back: NO ENTRIES.

She reversed the names: KINDREL, LEE

NO ENTRIES.

We tried every other way we could think of to spell the names, with no luck.

"What now?" Chase said.

"Olander." She punched in his name.

DO YOU WISH TO SEE AN INDEX? OR SHOULD I RUN ENTRIES?

"Entries," I said.

IN ANY PARTICULAR SEQUENCE?

"Chronological. From most recent."

WESCLARK MAN PLAYS OLANDER IN SPRING PAGEANT

"I don't think that's it," suggested Chase, touching the keyboard.

MATT OLANDER REMAINS POPULAR NAME FOR BOYS
OLANDER WAS PROBABLY BORN IN NEW YORK
MEDICAL ANALYSIS: OLANDER MAY HAVE BEEN DYING WHEN HE CHALLENGED ASHIYYUR

Stories piled up. There were literally dozens of them:

OLANDER ACADEMY SUED OVER CHILD'S DEATH
STANTON'S ANNOUNCES OLANDER LINE OF FASHIONS
MATT OLANDER AS SYSTEMS ANALYST: A MAN
AHEAD OF HIS TIME, EXPERTS SAY

I started working my way through the material, while Chase searched for references to Leisha Tanner. She eventually found a brief mention in a sixty-year-old book review.

"Sim's Lieutenants," she said. "Ever hear of it?"

"No. But it sounds like something we should get. Have them forward it to Jacob."

She shook her head. "It's off-line. Nearest copies available, it says here, are believed to be on Penthume."

"Where?"

"It's a long way. It was the author's home world. Maybe it doesn't matter. The reviewer says he got everything wrong, and the book's worthless. How are *you* making out?"

She was looking over my shoulder, so I keyed in another item:
MATT OLANDER TESTIFIES BEFORE DEFENSE COM-
MITTEE

I don't suppose she was in a mood for jokes: this Matt Olander was an expert in hyperspace stresses.

The second morning we expanded our search.

Late in the day we came across a curious entry, dated almost twenty years earlier:
DID SIM PROVOKE ATTACK ON ILYANDA?

The narrative argued that the Dellacondans had planned a trap at Ilyanda, but that a half-dozen battle cruisers, promised by Earth, had been withdrawn at the last minute.

There were other wild stories, especcially from the less reputable services that specialized in the sensational:
OLANDER MAY HAVE BEEN A WOMAN, and
OLANDER SEEN ALIVE ON TOXICON TWENTY YEARS
AFTER WAR

At the end of it, we still had nothing.

The plasma weapon that fell on Point Edward during an early autumn evening (the exact date is uncertain) in 677 seared the rocky basin in which the city rests, destroyed forest halfway out to Richardson, and removed the city itself as surely as though it had never existed.

The fact that Point Edward was deserted at the time of the attack, and that there was no way the aliens could not have known it was deserted, rendered the act the single most chilling event of the war. It demonstrated a fury with, and contempt for, all things human that must have terrorized the frontier worlds.

We were strolling listlessly along the waterfront area when I broke a long silence. "They were damned lucky there were so few people here. And Ilyanda's still relatively small. What's the population? Five, six million, tops. How many Lees can there be?"

"Not many," Chase agreed.

"We've been going about this backwards. Let's find a terminal."

There were fifty-six listings on the Ilyanda net for people named Lee, Leigh, Lea, and Li. We split them up.

We found Endmar Lee almost immediately.

One of his relatives described him as the family historian, and directed us to him. It was true: once he realized we shared his interest, his enthusiasm burgeoned. He brought out holos of individuals dressed in the somewhat stylized fashions of Resistance times on Ilyanda: Henry Cortison Lee, who had owned a souvenir shop at the Richardson terminal, and who had actually *seen* Christopher Sim; Polmar Lee, who would have stayed and faced the Ashiyyur in defense of his home, but who was drugged and taken off against his will. "And here's Jina," he said. "She was Kindrel's niece." Chase showed signs of impatience, but I frowned at her, and she sighed.

Endmar Lee was a short, almost fragile, man, spare of body and speech. He was young, yet he seemed to lack the energies and certainty of youth. "Ah," he said at length, projecting a holo into the middle of the room. "Here she is now. We think this was taken before the war."

She was attractive, lean with wide shoulders, her features perhaps a trifle nonchalant. Dark hair, worn long. Not someone who was likely to be hurried along by other people's concerns.

"What do you know about her?" I asked.

"There's not much *to* know," said Lee. "I don't think there's anything especially remarkable about Kindrel. She went through a lot very early in her life—"

"How do you mean?"

"Her husband died during the third year of their marriage. Freak boating accident of some kind. I don't know the details; they're lost. Then shortly after that, the war came."

"It might actually have made things easier for her," said Chase. "Forced her to concentrate on other things."

Lee hesitated. "Yes." The word trailed off, leaving something unsaid.

"Did she come back? After the war?"

"Yes, she did. She came back with the rest."

"Does the name *Leisha Tanner* mean anything to you?"

He thought about it, and shook his head. "I can't say that it does. Does she have some connection with Kindrel?"

"We don't know," said Chase. "Did Kindrel ever marry again?"

"No," he said. "Or at least she wasn't married when she left Ilyanda. After that we lost track of her. But she was well along in life by then anyhow. The last holo we have of her—" He worked the control device in his lap, "—is this one." She appeared again, almost elderly now, standing close beside Jina, her niece, who was by then middle-aged. The resemblance between the two was striking.

"Kindrel was a bit wild, I guess. She owned a yacht, and lived aboard it for years. Took long cruises, sometimes alone, sometimes with friends. There might have been a drug problem.

"She was very close to the niece. Jina died four years after this was taken, but she's not mentioned as having attended the funeral. That was in 707, and it suggests she was no longer on Ilyanda by then, though we know she was here in 706. That fixes the date of her departure pretty well."

"Yes," I said. Figuring it all in standard time, I decided Kindrel had left her home world almost forty years after the attack. "How do you know she was still here in 706?"

"We have a document dated by her."

"What's the document?"

"Medical certificate," he said, a trifle too quickly.

"Were there any children?"

"None that *I* know of."

Chase studied the woman in the holo: Kindrel at an advanced age. "You're right," she said, directing her comment to Lee.

"About what?"

"She looks as if she's had a difficult time."

Yes, I thought: she does. It was not simply that she'd grown older, that her early exuberance had faded, but that her expression had grown distant, distracted, wary.

Chase braced her chin on her fists, and studied the image. "What was her connection with Matt Olander?"

His expression didn't change, but there *was* a reaction: a tic, a brief flicker in the eyes, something. "I don't think I understand."

"Mr. Lee." I leaned forward and tried to assume a no-nonsense attitude. "We know that Kindrel knew Matt Olander. Why don't you tell us about it?" He sank deeply into his chair, exhaled, and fixed his attention on the holo. I strove for an attitude of disarming candor. "I'm prepared to pay for information." I mentioned a sum that I considered generous.

"Who are you, anyhow?" he asked. "Why do you care about any of this?"

"We're researchers from the University of Andiquar," I said. "We'd just like to know the truth. If you're worried about something getting out, you needn't be."

"Researchers don't have that kind of money," he said. "What's this all about?" The way he asked the question, I *knew* he had what we were looking for.

"The money's from a government grant. If you're not interested, there are other avenues open to us."

"Name one."

Chase's eyes narrowed. "I can see we're wasting our time here, Alex."

"No," Lee pressed the control device, and the holo faded. "Listen, you want my honest opinion about all this? I offer it free."

We waited.

"Olander died pretty much like everybody said, and the thing you're looking for is a fraud." He took a deep breath. "There's no story here." His eyes had grown small and hard.

"I can transfer funds now," I said. "What is it that's a fraud?"

"The money's fine," he said, "though that's not the point. I don't want to be made a fool of."

"Nothing like that," I said.

"I can tell you straight out I don't like what's in it, and I don't think it ought to get around. You follow me?"

"Yes," I said. "I understand."

"There's a statement by Kindrel. I shouldn't show it to anybody. But I let myself get talked into it once, so maybe once more doesn't matter. But you look at it here. Nothing leaves this house. No copies. If you're going to insist on giving me something, make it cash. I don't want a record.''

"Okay," I said.

"Because," he continued, "if anything comes out, I'm going to deny it. I'll deny everything.''

Chase leaned across and touched his arm. "It's all right," she said. "We won't cause you any trouble." She switched her position, glanced at me, and looked back at Lee. "Who else came here about this document?''

"Tall man. Dark skin. Dark eyes." He watched us for a sign of recognition. "About three months ago.''

"What was his name?''

He went back to his commlink, spoke briefly to it, and looked up. "Hugh Scott.''

XV.

There were few professional soldiers among the Dellacondans. Sim worked his miracles with systems analysts, literature teachers, musicians, and clerks. We tend to remember him primarily as a strategist and tactician. But none of that would have mattered, had he not possessed the capacity to draw, from ordinary persons, extraordinary performance.

> —**Harold Shamanway,**
> ***Commentaries on the Late War***

Attachment: THE STATEMENT OF KINDREL LEE

Point Edward
13/11/06

I'm not sure who will read this, if anyone. Nor have I any reason for setting down these facts, other than to accept in some visible fashion my own responsibility, which I cannot hope to shed in this life.

I will leave this with my niece, Jina, who is familiar with its contents, and who has been a friend and confidante throughout my ordeal, to do with as she sees fit.

> —**Kindrel Lee**

* * *

To me, Ilyanda has always seemed haunted.

There is something that broods over its misty seas and broken archipelagos, that breathes within its continental forests. You can feel it in the curious ruins that may, or may not, have been left by men. Or in the pungent ozone of the thunderstorms that strike Point Edward each night with a clocklike regularity that no one has yet explained. It is no accident that so many modern writers of supernatural fiction have set their stories on Ilyanda, beneath its cold hard stars and racing moons.

To the planet's several thousand inhabitants, most of whom live at Point Edward on the northern tip of the smallest of that world's three continents, such notions are exaggerated. But to those of us who have traveled in more mundane locations, it is a place of fragile beauty, of voices not quite heard, of dark rivers draining the unknown.

I was never more aware of its supernal qualities than during the weeks following Gage's death. Against the advice of friends, I took the Meredith *to sea, determined in the perverse way of people at such a time to touch once again a few of the things we'd shared in our first year, thereby sharpening the knife-edge of grief. And if, in some indefinable way, I expected to recapture a part of those lost days, it might have been from a sense that, in those phantom oceans, all things seemed possible.*

I sailed into the southern hemisphere, and quickly lost myself among the Ten Thousand Islands.

While Kindrel Lee tacked through warm seas, the war was getting close. And when she returned to Point Edward, she was mystified—and frightened—to find it deserted. Sim's evacuation fleet, unknown to her, had come and gone.

She describes her initial shock, her increasingly frenzied attempts to find another human being in the broad avenues and shopping areas. *No one's ever accused me of having an active imagination, but I stood puzzled out there, listening to the city: the wind and the rain and the buoys and the water sucking at the piers and the sudden, audible hum of power beneath the pavement and the distant banging of a door swinging on its hinges and the Carolian beat of the automated electronic piano in the Edwardian. Something walked through it all on invisible feet.*

The city's lights burned brightly. The air was filled with radio signals. She even listened to a conversation between an approaching shuttle and the orbiting space station, indicating that the regular early morning flight into the Captain William E. Richardson Spaceport would take place as scheduled.

Ultimately, she was drawn to Richardson, which was located twenty-two kilometers outside the city. Midway to her destination, she began seeing evidence of the withdrawal. In fact, she literally *ran* into some of it: at a place called Walhalla, she rounded a curve too fast and crashed into a city carrier that had run off the road and been abandoned.

The shuttle that she'd expected never came. Still unaware of what was happening, and by now in a state of near-panic, Kindrel raided a security office—in fact, the one in which her husband had worked—and armed herself with a laser. Shortly after that, high in the main terminal building, she encountered Matt Olander.

I'm not sure precisely when I realized I wasn't alone. A footstep somewhere, perhaps. The sound of running water, possibly a subtle swirling of air currents. But I was suddenly alert, and conscious of my own breathing.

My first impulse was to get out of the building. To get back to the car, and maybe back to the boat. But I held on, feeling the sweat trickle down my ribs.

I moved through the offices one by one, conscious of the weapon in my boot, but deliberately keeping my hands away from it. I was close to panic.

I'd stopped in a conference room dominated by a sculpted freediver. A holograph unit which someone had neglected to turn off blinked sporadically at the head of a carved table. A half-dozen chairs were in some disorder, and several abandoned coffee cups and light pads were scattered about. One would have thought the meeting had recently adjourned, and that the conferees would shortly return.

I activated the holo and some of the light pads. They'd been discussing motivational techniques.

As I turned away, somewhere, far off, glass shattered!

It was a sudden sharp report. Echoes rattled through the room, short pulses that gradually lengthened into each other, merged with the barely audible hum of power in the walls, and subsided at last into a petulant whisper.

Somewhere above. In the Tower Room, the rooftop restaurant.

I rode the elevator up one floor to the penthouse, stepped out into the gray night and walked quickly across an open patio.

In the fog, the Tower Room was little more than a gloomy presence: yellow-smeared, round crossbarred windows punched into a shadowy stone exterior; rock columns supporting an arched doorway; a waterwheel; and an antique brass menu board whose lighting no longer worked.

Soft music leaked through the doors. I pulled one partway open and peered in at an interior illuminated by computerized candles flickering in smoked jars. The Tower Room looked, and felt, like a sunken grotto. It was a hive of rocky vaults and dens, divided by watercourses, salad dispensers, mock boulders and shafts, and a long polished bar. Blue and white light sparkled against sandstone and silverware. Crystal streams poured from the mouths of stone nymphs and raced through narrow channels between rough-hewn bridges. Possibly, in another time, it might have been a relatively pedestrian place, one more restaurant in which the clientele and conversation were too heavy to sustain an architect's illusion. But on that evening, in the stillness that gripped the Blue Tower, the empty tables retreated into a void, until the glimmering lights in the smoked jars burned with the steady radiance of stars.

It was sufficiently cool that I had to pull my jacket about my shoulders. I wondered whether the heating system had given out.

I crossed a bridge, proceeded along the bar, and stopped to survey the lower level. Everything was neatly arranged, chairs in place, silver laid out on red cloth napkins, condiments and sauce bottles stacked side by side on the tables.

I could feel tears coming. I hooked my foot around a chair, dragged it away from the table, and sank into it.

There was an answering clatter, and a voice: "Who's there?"

I froze.

Footsteps. In back somewhere. And then a man in a uniform.

"Hello," he called cheerfully. "Are you all right?"

I shook my head uncertainly. "Of course," I said. "What's going on? Where is everybody?"

"I'm back near the window," he said, turning away from me. "Have to stay there." He paused to be sure I was following, and then retreated the way he'd come.

His clothing was strange, but not unfamiliar. By the time I rejoined him, I'd placed it: it was the light and dark blue uniform of the Confederacy.

He'd piled his table high with electronic equipment. A tangle of cables joined two or three computers, a bank of monitors, a generator, and God knew what else. He stood over it, a headphone clasped to one ear, apparently absorbed in the displays: schematics, *trace scans, columns of digits and symbols.*

He glanced in my direction without quite seeing me, pointed to a bottle of dark wine, produced a glass, and gestured for me to help myself. Then he smiled at something he had seen, laid the headset on the table, and dropped into a chair. "I'm Matt Olander," he said. "What the hell are you doing here?"

He was middle-aged, a thin blade of a man whose gray skin almost matched the color of the walls, marking him as an off-worlder. "I don't think I understand the question," I said.

"Why didn't you leave with everyone else?" He watched me intently, and I guess he saw that I was puzzled, and then he started to look puzzled. "They took everybody out," he said.

"Who?" I demanded. My voice went off the edge of the register. "Who took everybody where?"

He reacted as if it was a dumb question and reached for the bottle. "I guess we couldn't really expect to get one hundred percent. Where were you? In a mine somewhere? Out in the hills with no commlink?"

I told him and he sighed in a way that suggested I had committed an indiscretion. His uniform was open at the throat, and a light jacket that must have been nonregulation protected him from the chill. His hair was thin, and his features suggested more of the tradesman than the warrior. His voice turned soft. "What's your name?"

"Lee," I said. "Kindrel Lee."

"Well, Kindrel, we spent most of these two weeks evacuating Ilyanda. The last of them went up to the Station during the late morning yesterday. Far as I know, you and I are all that's left."

His attention returned to the monitor.

"Why?" I asked. I was feeling a mixture of relief and fear.

His expression wished me away. After a moment, he touched his keyboard. "I'll show you," he said.

One of the screens—I had to move the bottle to get a good look—dissolved to a concentric ring display, across which eight or nine trace lights blinked. "Ilyanda is at the center. Or, rather the Station is. The range runs out to about a half billion kilometers. You're looking at a mute fleet. Capital ships and battle cruisers." He took a deep breath and let it out slowly.

"What's happening, Miss Lee," he continued, "is that the Navy is about to blow hell out of the sons of bitches." His jaw tightened, *and a splinter of light appeared in his eyes.* "At last.

"It's been a long time coming. They've been driving us before them for three years. But today belongs to us." He raised his empty glass in a jeering salute toward the ceiling.

"I'm glad you were able to get people away," I said into the stillness.

He tilted his head in my direction. "Sim wouldn't have had it any other way."

"I never thought the war would come here." Another blip appeared on the screen. "I don't understand it," I said. "Ilyanda's neutral. And I didn't think we were near the fighting."

"Kindrel, there are no neutrals in this war. You've just been letting others do your fighting for you." His voice was not entirely devoid of contempt.

"Ilyanda's at peace!" I shot back, though it seemed rather academic just then. I stared at him, into his eyes, expecting him to flinch. But I saw only hatred. "Or at least it was," I continued.

"No one's at peace," he said. "No one's been at peace for a long time." His voice was very cold, and he bit the words off.

"They're only here," I said, "because you are, aren't they?"

He smiled. "Yes," he said. "They want us." He gripped the edges of his chair, propped his chin on his fist, and laughed at me. "You're judging us! You know, you people are really impossible. The only reason you're not dead or in chains is because we've been dying to give you a chance to ride around in your goddam boat!"

"My God," I gasped, remembering the missing shuttle. "Is that why the redeye never got here?"

"Don't worry about it," he said. "It was never coming."

I shook my head. "You're wrong. I overheard some radio traffic shortly after midnight. They were still on schedule then."

"They were never coming," he repeated. "We've done everything we could to make this place, this entire world, appear normal."

"Why?" I asked.

"You have the consolation of knowing we are about to turn the war around. The mutes are finally going to get hurt!" His eyes glowed, and I shuddered.

"You led them here," I said.

"Yes." He was on his feet now. "We led them here. We've led them into hell. They think Christopher Sim is on the space station. And they want him very badly." He refilled his glass. "Sim has

*never had the firepower to fight this war. He's been trying to hold off
an armada with a few dozen light frigates."* Olander's face twisted.
It was a frightening aspect. *"But he's done a job on the bastards.
Anyone else would have been overwhelmed right at the start. But
Sim: sometimes I wonder whether he's human."*

Or you, I thought. My fingers brushed the laser.

"Maybe it would be best if you left," he said tonelessly.

I made no move to go. *"Why here? Why Ilyanda?"*

*"We tried to pick a system where the population was small
enough to be moved."*

I smothered an obscenity. *"Did we get to vote on this? Or did Sim
just ride in and issue orders?"*

"Damn you," he whispered. *"You haven't any idea at all what
this is about, do you? A million people have died in this war so far.
The mutes have burned Cormoral and taken the City on the Crag and
Far Mordaigne. They've overrun a dozen systems, and the entire
frontier is on the edge of collapse."* He wiped the back of his hand
across his mouth. *"They don't like human beings very much, Miss
Lee. And I don't think they plan for any of us to be around when it's
over."*

"We started the war," I objected.

*"That's easy to say. You don't know what was going on. But it
doesn't matter now anyway. We're long past drawing fine lines. The
killing won't stop until we've driven the bastards back where they
came from."* He switched displays to a status report. *"They're
closing on the Station now."* His lips curled into a vindictive leer.
*"A sizable chunk of their fleet is already within range. And more
arriving all the time."* He smiled malevolently, and I can remember
thinking that I had never before come face to face with anyone so
completely evil. He was really enjoying himself.

"You said Sim doesn't have much firepower—"

"He doesn't."

"Then how—?"

A shadow crossed his face. He hesitated, and looked away toward
the monitors. *"The Station's shields have gone up,"* he said. *"No,
there's nothing up there of ours except a couple of destroyers.
They're automated, and the Station's abandoned."* The blinking
lights on the battle display had increased to a dozen. Some had
moved within the inner ring. *"All they can see are the destroyers,
and something they think is* Corsarius *in dock with its hull laid open.*

And the bastards are still keeping their distance. But it won't make any difference!"

"Corsarius!" I said. "Sim's ship?"

"It's a big moment for them. They're thinking right now they're going to take him and end the war." He squinted at the graphics.

I was beginning to suspect it was time to take his advice and make for the wharf, get the *Meredith*, and head back to the southern hemisphere. Until everything settled down.

"The destroyers are opening up," he said. "But they won't even slow the mutes down."

"Why bother?"

"We had to give them some opposition. Keep them from thinking too much."

"Olander," I asked, "if you have no ships up there, what's this all about? How does Sim expect to destroy anything?"

"He won't. But you and I will, Kindrel. You and I will inflict such a wound on the mutes tonight that the sons of bitches will never forget!"

Two monitors went suddenly blank. The images returned, swirls of characters blinking frantically. He leaned forward and frowned. "The Station's taken a hit." He reached toward me, a friendly, soothing gesture, but I stayed away from him.

"And what are you and I going to do to them?" I asked.

"Kindrel, we are going to stop the sunrise."

I found that remark a bit murky, and I said so.

"We're going to catch them all," he said. "Everything they've got here, everything out to the half-billion-kilometer ring, will be incinerated. Beyond that, if they see right away what's happening and get a running start, they have a chance." He glanced toward the computer. A red lamp glowed on the keyboard. "We have an old Tyrolean freighter, loaded with antimatter. It's waiting for a command from me."

"To do what?"

His eyes slid shut, and I could no longer read his expression. "To materialize inside your sun." He hung each word in the still air. "We are going to insert it at the sun's core." A bead of sweat rolled down his chin. "The result, we think, will be—" he paused and grinned, "—moderately explosive."

I could almost have believed there was no world beyond that bar. We'd retreated into the dark, Olander and I and the monitors and *the background music and the stone nymphs. All of us.*

"A nova?" I asked. My voice must have been barely audible. "You're trying to induce a nova?"

"No. Not a true nova."

"But the effect—"

"—will be the same." He looked eminently satisfied. "It's a revolutionary technique. Involves some major breakthroughs in navigation. It isn't easy, you know, to bring this off. Never been donè before."

"Come on, Olander," I exploded, "you can't expect me to believe that a guy sitting in a bar can blow up a sun!"

"I'm sorry." His eyes changed, and he looked startled, as though he'd forgotten where he was. "You may be right," he said. "It hasn't been tested, so they really don't know. Too expensive to run a test."

I tried to imagine Point Edward engulfed in fire, amid boiling seas and burning forests. It was Gage's city, where we'd explored narrow streets and old bookstores, and pursued each other across rainswept beaches and through candle-lit pubs. And from where we'd first gone to sea. I'd never forgot how it had looked the first time we'd come home, bright and diamond-hard against the horizon. Home. Always it would be home.

And I watched Olander through eyes grown suddenly damp, perhaps conscious for the first time that I had come back to Point Edward with the intention to leave Ilyanda.

"Olander, they left you to do this?"

"No." He shook his head vigorously. "It was supposed to happen automatically when the mutes got close. The trigger was tied in to the sensors on the Station. But the mutes have had some success at disrupting command and control functions. We couldn't be sure . . ."

"Then they did leave you!"

"No! Sim would never have allowed it if he'd known. He has confidence in the scanners and computers. Those of us who know a little more about such things do not. So I stayed, and disconnected the trigger, and brought it down here."

"My God, and you're really going to do it?"

"It works out better this way. We can catch the bastards at the most opportune moment. You need a human to make that judgment. A machine isn't good enough to do it right."

"Olander, you're talking about destroying a world!"

"I know." His voice shook. "I know." His eyes found mine at last. The irises were blue, and I could see white all round their edges. "No one wanted this to happen. But we're driven to the wall. If we can't make this work, here, there may be no future for anyone."

I kept talking, but my attention was riveted to the computer keyboard, to the EXECUTE key, which was longer than the others, and slightly concave.

The laser was cool and hard against my leg.

He drained the last of his wine, and flung the glass out into the dark. It shattered. "Ciao," he said.

"The nova," I murmured, thinking about the broad southern seas and the trackless forests that no one would ever penetrate and the enigmatic ruins. And the thousands of people to whom, like me, Ilyanda was home. Who would remember when it was gone? "What's the difference between you and the mutes?"

"I know how you feel, Kindrel."

"You have no idea how I feel—"

"I know exactly how you feel. I was on Melisandra when the mutes burned Cormoral. I watched them seize the Pelian worlds. They were irritated with the Pelians so they shot a few people. People who were like you, just minding their business. Do you know what Cormoral looks like now? Nothing will live there for ten thousand years."

Somebody's chair, his, mine, I don't know, scraped the floor, and the sound echoed round the bar.

"Cormoral and the Pelians were assaulted by their enemies!" I was enraged, frightened, terrified. Out of sight under the table, my fingers traced the outline of the weapon. "Has it occurred to you," I asked, as reasonably as I could, "what's going to happen when the mutes go home, and we go back to squabbling among ourselves?"

He nodded. "I know. There's a lot of risk involved."

"Risk?" I pointed a trembling finger at the stack of equipment. "That thing is more dangerous than a half-dozen invasions. For God's sake, we'll survive the mutes. We survived the ice ages and the nuclear age and the colonial wars and we will sure as hell take care of those sons of bitches if there's no other way.

"But that thing you have in front of you—Matt, don't do this. Whatever you hope to accomplish, the price is too high."

I listened to him breathe. An old love song was running on the sound system. "I have no choice," he said in a dull monotone. He glanced at his display. "They've begun to withdraw. That means they know the Station's empty, and they suspect either a diversion or a trap."

"You do *have a choice!" I screamed at him.*

"No!" He pushed his hands into his jacket pockets as though to keep them away from the keyboard. "I do not."

Suddenly I was holding the laser, pointing it at the computers. "I'm not going to allow it."

"There's no way you can stop it." He stepped out of the line of fire. "But you're welcome to try."

I backed up a few paces and held the weapon straight out. It was a curious remark, and I played it again. Olander's face was awash with emotions I couldn't begin to put a name to. And I realized what was happening. "If I interrupt the power supply," I said, "It'll trigger. Right?"

His face gave him away.

"Get well away from it." I swung the weapon toward him. "We'll just sit here awhile."

He didn't move.

"Back off," I said.

"For God's sake, Kindrel." He held out his hands. "Don't do this. There's no one here but you and me."

"There's a living world *here, Matt. And if that's not enough, there's a precedent to be set."*

He took a step toward the trigger.

"Don't, Matt," I said. "I'll kill you if I have to."

The moment stretched out. "Please, Kindrel," he said at last.

So we remained, facing each other. He read my eyes, and his color drained. I held the laser well out where he could see it, aimed at his chest.

The eastern sky was beginning to lighten.

A nerve quivered in his throat. "I should have left it alone," he said, measuring the distance to the keyboard.

Tears were running down my cheeks, and I could hear my voice loud and afraid as though it were coming from outside me. And the entire world squeezed down to the pressure of the trigger against my right index finger. "You didn't have *to stay," I cried at him. "It has nothing to do with heroics. You've been in the war too long, Matt. You hate too well."*

He took a second step, tentatively, gradually transferring his weight from one foot to the other, watching me, his eyes pleading.

"You were enjoying this, until I came by."

"No," he said. *"That's not so."*

His muscles tensed. And I saw what he was going to do and I shook my head no and whimpered and he told me to just put the gun down and I stood there looking at the little bead of light at the base of his throat where the bolt would hit and saying no no no. . . .

When at last he moved, not toward the computer but toward me, he was far too slow and I killed him.

My first reaction was to get out of there, to leave the body where it had dropped and take the elevator down and run—

I wish to God I had.

The sun was on the horizon. The clouds scattered into the west, and another cool autumn day began.

Matt Olander's body lay twisted beneath the table, a tiny black hole burned through the throat, and a trickle of blood welling out onto the stone floor. His chair lay on its side, and his jacket was open. A pistol, black and lethal and easy to hand, jutted from an inside pocket.

I had never considered the possibility he might be armed. He could have killed me at any time.

What kind of men fight for this Christopher Sim?

This one would have burned Ilyanda, but he could not bring himself to take my life.

What kind of men? I have no answer to that question. Then or now.

I stood a long time over him, staring at him, and at the silently blinking transmitter, with its cold red eye, while the white lights fled toward the outer ring.

And a terrible fear crept through me: I could still carry out his intention, and I wondered whether I didn't owe it to him, to someone, to reach out and strike the blow they had prepared. But in the end I walked away from it, into the dawn.

The black ships that escaped at Ilyanda went on to take a heavy toll. For almost three more years, men and ships died. Christopher Sim continued to perform legendary exploits. His Dellacondans held on until Rimway and Earth intervened, and, in the heat of battle, the modern Confederacy was born.

The sun weapon itself was never heard from. Whether, in the end, it wouldn't work, or Sim was unable afterward to lure a large enough force within range of a suitable target, I don't know.

For most, the war is now something remote, a subject for debate by historians, a thing of vivid memories only for the relatively old. The mutes have long since retreated into their sullen worlds. Sim rests with his heroes, and his secrets, lost off Rigel. And Ilyanda still entrances tourists with her misty seas, and researchers with her curious ruins.

Matt Olander lies in a hero's grave at Richardson. I cut his name into the stone with the same weapon I used to kill him.

And I: to my sorrow, I survived. I survived the attack on the city, I survived the just anger of the Dellacondans, I survived my own black guilt.

The Dellacondans: they came twice following the murder. There were four of them the first time, two men and two women. I hid from them, and they left. Later, when I'd begun to suspect they would not come again, a lone woman landed on one of the Richardson pads, and I went out in the sunlight and told her everything.

I expected to be killed; but she said little, and wanted to take me to Millenium. But I couldn't face that, so I walked away from her. And I lived outside the ruined city, in Walhalla where perhaps I should have died, pursued by an army of ghosts which grew daily in number. All slain by my hand. And when the Ilyandans returned at the end of the war, I was waiting.

They chose not to believe me. It may have been politics. They may have preferred to forget. And so I am denied even the consolation of public judgment. There is none to damn me. Or to forgive.

I have no doubt I did the right thing.

Despite the carnage, and the fire, I was right.

In my more objective moments, in the daylight, I know that. But I know also that whoever reads this document, after my death, will understand that I need more than a correct philosophical stance.

For now, for me, in the dark of Ilyanda's hurtling moons, the war never ends.

XVI.

What bleak thoughts carried him high onto that windy rock, we never knew—

—**Aneille Kay,**
Christopher Sim at War
(These words also appear on a brass plate at Sim's Perch.)

IN THE MORNING, when we sat over breakfast in the penthouse restaurant, warmed by a bright sun, it all seemed a little unreal. "It's a fraud," said Chase. "They couldn't count on having that ship materialize inside a planetary system, let alone inside a sun. It wouldn't work."

"But if it *were* true," I said, "it answers some questions. And maybe the big one: what's out in the Veiled Lady."

"The bomb?"

"What else?"

"But if the thing worked, why didn't it get passed on? Why put it out in the woods someplace?"

"Because the Dellacondans thought the Confederacy wouldn't survive the war, even if they won. Once the Ashiyyur were driven off, the worlds would go back to squabbling. And Sim may not have wanted that kind of weapon loose. Maybe not even among his own people.

"Maybe toward the end, when things were getting desperate, he saw only two options: destroy it, or hide it. So he hid it. But everyone who knew was killed off. And the entire business was forgotten."

Chase picked up the thread: "So now, two hundred years later, the *Tenandrome* comes along and stumbles on it. And they classify everything!"

"That's it," I said. "Has to be."

"So where's the weapon? Did they bring it back?"

"Sure. And right now, we're putting it into production. Next year at this time, we'll be threatening the mutes with it."

Chase was shaking her head. "I don't believe it," she said. "How would the *Tenandrome* recognize the thing for what it is?"

"Maybe it comes with an instruction book. Listen, it's the first explanation we've got that makes sense."

She looked skeptical. "Maybe. But I still don't think it's possible. Listen, Alex, star travel is *extremely* approximate. If I take a ship that's in orbit around this world, and jump into hyper—"

"—and come right back out, you might be a few million kilometers away. I know that."

"A few million kilometers? I'd be damned lucky if I could jump back into the planetary system at all. Now how the hell are they going to be so good that they can hit a star? It's ridiculous."

"Maybe there's another way to do it. Let's check out what we can. See if you can find an expert, a physicist or somebody. But stay away from Survey, and tell them you're doing research for a novel. Right? Find out what happens if we inject a load of antimatter into the core of a star. Would it really explode? Is there any theoretical way to accomplish the insertion? That sort of thing."

"What are *you* going to do?"

"Some sightseeing," I said.

Ilyanda has changed since Kindrel's time. No fleet of shuttles and cruisers and interstellars could hope to sneak in now and evacuate the global population. The old theocratic Committee that governed in Point Edward still exists, but it is now vestigial. The doors have long since opened to settlers, and Point Edward is now only one of a network of cities, and by no means the largest. But it has not forgotten its past: the Dellacondan Cafe stands on Defiance

Street across from the Matt Olander Hotel. Without looking hard, one can find Christopher Sim Park, Christopher Sim Plaza, and Christopher Sim Boulevard. The orbiting terminal has been renamed for him, and his picture appears on various denominations of Bank of Ilyanda credit serials.

And Matt Olander: a bronze plate bears his likeness and the legend "Defender" in the archway through which one enters Old City, the four-square-block tract of shattered buildings and gaping permearth which has been left untouched since the attack. Visitors stroll silently through the memorial, and usually stop to see the visuals.

I spent some time in the dromes myself, watching the holos of Sim's shuttles, during that desperate week when the Ashiyyur were coming, moving in and out of Richardson on silent magnetics. It was rousing stuff, complete with anthems and stern-eyed heroes and the sort of subdued commentary one expects with the portrayal of mythic events. My blood began to pound, and I was gradually caught up again in the drama of that ancient war.

Later, in a sidewalk cafe flanked by frozen trees, I thought again how easily one's own tides rise at the prospect of combat in a cause, even one whose justice may be suspect. The company of heroes: if Quinda was affected by it, so were we all. Our glory and our downfall. Embrace the terrible risks of war; drive home the spear (for all the proper reasons, of course). I sat that morning, watching crowds that had never known organized bloodshed, and wondered whether Kindrel Lee wasn't right when she argued that the real risk to us all comes not from this or that group of outsiders, but from our own desperate need to create Alexanders, and to follow them enthusiastically onto whatever parapets they may choose to blunder.

Who was the lone woman who had visited Kindrel Lee? Was it Tanner? Lee had described her as Dellacondan, but she was expecting Dellacondans.

It was easy to see why the Dellacondans might have lied about the manner of Olander's death: they would not have wished to reveal the existence of the sun weapon. So they'd simply made a hero out of the unfortunate systems analyst who'd stayed behind to ensure success and had thereby savaged Sim's plans. But anyone who knew the truth must have hated him. How many had eventually died because of Olander's act?

I could imagine them all, posted safely outside this system's oort cloud, watching the sensors, expecting to strike their decisive blow. No wonder they were bitter.

But Sim had fought on for another year and a half, and never used the solar weapon. I wondered about Kindrel Lee's idea that the weapon, after all, had been flawed, rendered unworkable by some quirk of nature, or incapable of execution at the Resistance Era level of technology. That she had, after all, killed Matt Olander for no reason.

Midway through the afternoon, I took the skimmer up into a stiff wind. Street traffic was heavy, and several giant holos of eminently good-looking models demonstrated winter fashions to a crowd gathered outside an emporium. I arced over the downtown area, gained altitude, and sailed into a gray sky.

During the evacuation of Point Edward, Christopher Sim had left his staff to direct the operation, and had busied himself with other matters. A curious thing then happened: his officers noticed that he rose well before dawn each day, and took a skimmer north along the coast from the city. His destination was a lonely shelf on a cliff face high over the sea. What he did there, or why he went, no one ever learned. Toldenya immortalized the scene in his masterpiece, *On the Rock*, and the place has been designated an historical site by the Ilyandans. They call it Sim's Perch.

I wanted to look at the war through *his* eyes. And visiting his retreat seemed a good way to do it.

The vehicle leveled off at about a thousand meters, and began a long swing toward the sea. I was feeling vaguely overwhelmed by the combination of peaks, city, ocean, and mist, when it occurred to me there was someplace else worth visiting.

I switched to manual, and turned back inland. The computer buzzed at me, insisting on a higher altitude. I went up until the noise stopped, and was near the clouds when I passed over the western edge of the city. That was also the western rim of the volcano. Safely dead, according to the literature. Taken care of by engineers centuries ago, and checked periodically by the Point Edward Environmental Service.

All the romance has gone out of life.

I descended toward the vibrant canopy of a purple forest. To the southwest, the land was divided into large farms. Two streams wound across the countryside, joining approximately eight kilometers beyond Point Edward, and disappearing into a mountain.

On the horizon, the spires of the spaceport looked fragile against the threatening sky. A curtain of water fell from the top of the Blue Tower. I watched a shuttle loop in from the far side, bank gracefully, and descend into the complex.

It took a while to find what I was looking for: the road that Lee had taken from Point Edward out to Richardson. It no longer existed in any real sense. All transport between the two points was by air now; and anyone living in the small towns that still dotted the landscape had damned well better have a skimmer.

But sections of the ancient track were visible. It skirted the edge of a cluster of hills, and ran parallel first to one river, and then the other. For the most part, it was little more than a place where the trees were younger.

I put the map on the overhead monitor, and looked through the atlas, trying to find the town where she'd crashed. Walhalla.

It was a small farming community, maybe a dozen houses, a hardware store, a food store, a city hall, a restaurant, and a tavern. Two men were atop a roof, installing a dormer. A few people were gathered on the deck outside the hall. No one glanced up as I passed overhead.

She'd described a sharp curve, which could only be the eastern side, where the trace wound down out of hilly country. There was no sign of a ditch or depression, but two hundred years is a long time. Somewhere here, it had happened. An unmarked, unknown spot on a world littered with memorials. And I wondered how different Ilyanda's history might have been had Kindrel Lee died out here that night.

An hour later, I flew out over the glassy waters of Point Edward's sprawling, island-studded harbor.

The city had spread up the sides of the surrounding ridges. It clung precariously to precipices, supported by a combination of metal struts and gantner light. Landing pads gleamed on rooftops and in grottos cut from the cliffside. Some public buildings arched across rock fissures. Seaway Boulevard, which follows almost the same route that it did during Resistance times, skirted the harbor, narrowed in the north to a two-lane, and climbed into the peaks.

Forest, rock, and snow: in both directions along the coastline, the craggy landscape turned gray-white, and disappeared into a hard sky. I flew in lazy circles over the area, admiring its wild beauty. And then, after a while, I turned north.

Point Edward fell behind. The coastal highway drifted inland and plunged into thick trees.

Mountains crowded together, and merged gradually into a monolithic gray rampart, smooth and reflective and timeless. The Ilyandans call it Klon's Wall, after a mythical hero who built it to protect the continent against a horde of sea demons. In its shadow, the air was cold. I stayed low, near the spray.

Sails stirred the mist and, well above me, skimmers and even an airbus plowed back and forth. A few gulls kept pace. They were ungainly creatures with scoop snouts and enormous wingspans and cackles like gunshots. Floaters drifted idly in the air currents.

Occasional trees clung to the cliff face. The computer identified some of these as *cassandras*, thought to possess a kind of leafy intelligence. Tests had proven inconclusive, and skeptics held that the tradition had developed because the web of branches tended to resemble human features, particularly when seen with the sun behind them.

Some were clustered along the rim. I turned the navigator's telescope in their direction. Their branches were entwined, and their broad spined leaves extended for whatever gray light they could capture. But there was no sun, and no face. As I neared Sim's Perch, a repeating message turned up on the commlink. "Full tourist facilities are available," it said. "Please return your vehicle to controlled guidance. Manual navigation is not permitted within eight kilometers of the park." I complied. The skimmer immediately swung out to sea, gained altitude, and began a long slow turn back toward the escarpment.

Three of us were lined up on the approach. A couple of kids waved from the skimmer immediately ahead, and I waved back. We were above the cliff rim now, approaching a blue and scarlet landing pad complex, which was atop the summit. Sim's shelf was about a third of the way down the cliff face.

It was marked by a complex of structures, cut from the rock. Among them was a gold-domed hotel, with mush courts and swimming pools. In Sim's time, the ledge must have been of modest proportions, a strip of rock barely wide enough to support a skimmer. But it's been braced and extended and broadened and fenced.

The voice on my commlink was young, female, and syrupy. "Welcome to the Christopher Sim Perch," she said. "Please do not attempt to leave the vehicle until it has completely stopped.

Quarters are available at the Sim Hotel. Do you wish to make a reservation?"

"No," I said. "I only want to see the shelf."

"Very good, sir. You can reach the Christopher Sim Perch by following the blue markers. The Resistance Committee reminds you that refreshments may be consumed only in designated areas. Please enjoy your stay."

I followed another vehicle onto a blue pad, turned the skimmer over to a service attendant, and took a tube down to the main level. That left me in the hotel lobby. But a blue arrow pointed toward a side door.

A few people, kids mostly, splashed in a fern-lined pool. There was a souvenir shop with Resistance Era dishware and glasses and pennants, models of the *Corsarius*, and a substantial array of crystals and books. Among the books was *Man and Olympian*, and a modest volume titled *Maxims of Christopher Sim*. Toldenya's magnificent *On the Rock* dominated the lobby. If you haven't seen it: Sim sits thoughtfully, and precariously, atop a rounded slab, peering out over an uneasy ocean, illuminated by a rising sun. Storm clouds are visible on the horizon.

He wears a loose jacket and floppy trousers, his gray-blond hair curling out from under a battered hat. His eyes are narrowed, and filled with pain. The green and white wing of his skimmer is visible on the left. (It was on this occasion that I learned the significance of the tree symbol on the aircraft: it is the Morcadian tree, and has been the official device of Ilyanda for four hundred years.)

I bought a copy of the *Maxims* and took it outside, onto the shelf.

I was almost alone. "Off season," one of the attendants told me. "We don't get many tourists this time of year. But a lot of people come out from the city for dinner and drinks. Tonight. There'll be a good crowd tonight."

The shelf was open to the elements. Everything else was sealed and heated, including an observation deck, which lay at right angles to the face of the promontory. A few people had found their way to it, and were manning a battery of telescopes. A young couple, wrapped against the chill of the afternoon, followed me out.

A few kids played near, and sometimes climbed onto, the low mesh fence which was all that separated them from a happier world. The ocean was a long way down, and I cringed, watching.

Overhead, a variety of pennants flew. A few seabirds wheeled nearby, and a couple of floaters drifted just out of reach beyond the fence. Their filaments rippled in the moving air. Even in the shadow of the mountain wall, the daylight, reflected through their amoebic sacs, maintained a deliberate cadence of shifting hues. They exist on so many worlds, these peaceful, slow-moving creatures that seem endlessly curious about us. They'd been worth saving, I thought. They and the gulls and the broad sea that had been here for how many million years?

How could Sim have even considered destroying all this? How could he have stood up here, beneath these timeless walls, and contemplated that kind of act?

I found a bench on the observation deck, and opened the *Maxims*. It had been privately printed, through the Order of the Harridan. Much of the material had been derived from Sim's one published work. But there were also excerpts from letters, court documents, comments attributed to him, public pronouncements, and so on.

The crisis, he tells the congress of the City on the Crag, *is upon us, and I would be less than candid if I did not admit to you that, before it ends, I fear we will have emptied many of the seats in this chamber.* And, in a note to a senator from that same body: *I have every confidence that whatever Power has brought us this immeasurable distance along the road from Akkad, it surely does not intend to abandon us now to this ancient, unimaginative race that so singlemindedly pursues our extinction.*

Toldenya's slab is located at the north end of the ledge. It is the largest of a group of rocks, wedged into the cliff face, jutting precariously out over the void. No one really knows where Sim stood when he was here, and I have to think that the notion he actually climbed out there is purely an artist's conceit.

His shelf had been narrow. At its widest point, it would have been just wide enough for a good pilot to set a skimmer down. Given a surprise—a sudden downdraft, say—and skimmer and pilot could have fallen a half kilometer into the ocean.

Why?

And why before dawn?

Yet how better to contemplate the star and the world he was about to destroy, than to catch them together in the magnificent symbiosis of an ocean sunrise?

And I wondered, while I considered what must have passed through his mind on those bleak mornings, whether he had not hoped for the sudden downdraft that might have shifted the decision to someone else's shoulders.

Had he perhaps, in the end, come to fear his own weapon? Christopher Sim was first and last an historian. Standing out here, watching what he believed to be the last few sunrises this world would have, he must have been terrified of the verdict of history.

I felt the certainty of it in a sudden shock: the ultimate warrior had shuddered under that knowledge. No wonder we never heard again from the sun weapon.

XVII.

The measure of a civilization is in the courage, not of its soldiers, but of its bystanders.

—Tulisofala,
Mountain Passes

(Translated by Leisha Tanner)

THE MIST BLEW off the sea in the late afternoon, and I retired to a table in a corner of the bar, to sit quietly sipping green lamentoes. After a while, as the sky began to darken and Ilyanda's rings took shape, I activated my commlink. "Chase, are you there?"

I heard it buzz, which meant she wasn't wearing it. I went back to my drink and tried again a few minutes later. This time I connected. "Shower," she explained. "It's been a long afternoon, but I've got some answers. Our boy's idea would work."

"The antimatter?"

"Yes. It should be antihelium, by the way, assuming the target has a helium core. Which is the case here."

"Who'd you talk to?"

"A physicist at a place called Insular Labs. His name's Carmel, and he sounds as if he knows what he's talking about."

"But it *would* work?"

"Alex, he said, and I quote: 'A shipload of that stuff would blow the son of a bitch to hell!' "

"Then Kindrel's story is at least possible. Provided you can get the stuff into the core. Did you ask him about that part of the problem? Could Sim have found a way to navigate in hyper?"

"I didn't mention Sim. We were talking about a novel, remember? But Carmel thinks that navigation in Armstrong space is theoretically impossible. He suggested another way: ionize the antihelium, and put it behind a powerful magnetic field. Then ram it into the sun at high velocity."

"Maybe that's the way they intended to do it," I said. "Could *we* do that now?"

"He doesn't think so. The antihelium would be easy to make and contain, but the technology for the insertion would be pretty advanced stuff.

"Theoretically, the only type of nonlinear space that permits physical penetration by three-dimensional objects is Armstrong. I still think it's a hoax."

"Yeah," I said, "Maybe. Listen, I'm at a nice spot. How about joining me for dinner?"

"The Perch?"

"Yes."

"Sure. Sounds good. Give me a little time to get myself together. Then I'll take a taxi out. See you in about an hour and a half?"

"Okay. But don't bother with the taxi. I'll send the skimmer back for you."

I tried to use my commlink to enter the return code into the skimmer's onboard computer. But the red lamp blinked: no connection. Why not? I made another unsuccessful effort, and patched through to the service desk. "I'm having problems with my automatics," I said. "Could you send an attendant to enter a code manually into my skimmer?"

"Yes, sir." It was a female voice, and it sounded vaguely annoyed. "But it'll take a while. We're shorthanded, and this is our busy night."

"How long?"

"It's hard to say. I'll send someone in as soon as I can."

I waited about twenty minutes, and then went up myself to the hangar area, which was located underground at the summit. The temperature had plummeted, and the rings, which had brightened the sky a half hour earlier, were now only a pale smear against a heavy overcast. Outside the hangar, I tried the service desk again. Still busy. Any time now, though.

"Can you tell me where my skimmer's located?"

A pause, then: "Sir, guests aren't allowed in the hangar area."

"Of course," I said.

A warning was posted on the door: AUTHORIZED PERSON-NEL ONLY. I pushed through it into a sprawling cave that would probably not have looked so big if I could have seen some walls. It was illuminated only by a string of yellow lamps burning morosely out in the gloom somewhere. While I tried to get my bearings, a set of overhead doors opened, and a vehicle descended through a shaft into the hangar. Its navigation lamps sliced across rows of parked vehicles. I got only a glimpse before the lights went out. But the skimmer's magnetics continued to whine, and its black bulk glided to floor level and accelerated. I felt the wave of cold air as it passed at high speed.

My own aircraft was green and yellow. A bilious combination, but one that would be easy to see if I could get reasonably close to it. I waited for my eyes to adjust, and then stepped cautiously through the door onto a permearth floor, and turned to my left, on the ground that there was a little more illumination in that direction.

Another skimmer dropped out of the shaft, lights blazing. I tried to get a good look around, but the lamps blinked off almost immediately. Then it accelerated down one of the corridors formed by the parked aircraft. I groped past a small airbus, and penetrated deeper into the hangar.

There appeared to be three shafts, and vehicles were coming in at an alarming rate. Maddeningly, there was never quite enough time to organize my search during the few seconds of illumination that each provided. I became an expert on the placement of running lights that evening, and formulated Benedict's Law: no two sets on any consecutive vehicles will point in the same direction. In the end, they only added to the confusion.

In addition, once they reached ground level, the skimmers, now lost in the dark, moved at high speed. I had a bad time of it: I stumbled past wing struts and tail assemblies, banged a knee, and fell on my face.

At one point, I was kneeling immediately in front of a skimmer rubbing a knee when I heard the magnets energize. I scrambled to one side as the thing rolled forward, but a wing caught me anyway and knocked me flat.

I was by then having a few misgivings, but I'd lost my fix on the door, so I couldn't retreat. I considered calling the service desk again to ask for help, and was about to do so—reluctantly—when I spotted a green and yellow fuselage.

Gratefully, I hurried over, climbed into the cockpit, and called Chase to tell her the aircraft would be a few minutes late.

"Okay," she said. "Anything wrong?"

"No," I grumbled. "I'm doing fine. Just a minor problem with the skimmer. Stay with me a second until I make sure it works."

"Make sure it works?" She sounded skeptical. "Listen, maybe I better take the taxi."

I've thought since, many times, yes, *there* was my chance to head it all off. It's what I should have done in the first place. And I never even considered it. Now, of course, I'd gone to too much trouble to take the obvious solution.

You have to work at it to shut down a skimmer response system inadvertently. On the bilious special I had, it was necessary to take off a plastic cover and push a presspad. Simple enough, but you had to make a conscious decision to do it.

How had it happened?

Careless attendant, presumably. Odd, since the attendants don't enter the aircraft unless there's a problem. Still, there it was. I promised myself there'd be no tip. My God.

I turned the systems back on, enjoyed the swirl of warm air in the compartment, tapped instructions in for the topside pads, and listened to the magnets engage. The vehicle lifted off the floor, paused while something sailed past, and entered the corridor. Then the skimmer accelerated, stopped (throwing me against the harness), and rose almost vertically into an exit shaft.

I rode it up, out over the summit, and down again into the landing area. I got out and reset the guidance system for the roof of the Point Edward hotel. "On its way," I told Chase, over the commlink. It lifted again, and accelerated seaward.

"Good thing," she said. "I'm getting hungry."

I watched it climb, its running lights blurring against the underside of a low cloud cover. It circled toward the south, and was swallowed in the night.

* * *

"Storm building," I told Chase a half-hour later from the hotel bar. "You'll want to dress for it."

"You're not going to be walking me through a lot of snow, are you?"

"No. But the Perch itself is outside. Unprotected."

"Okay."

I was seated in a padded armchair. Thick carpets cushioned a stone floor, and the wall-length window which faced the ocean was circumscribed by dark gray drapes. Resistance Era patriotic art decorated the walls, world seals and frigates framed against lunar surfaces and Valkyrie mothers juxstaposed with portraits of their sons. "It's lovely out here."

"Good." Pause. "Alex?"

"Yes?"

"I've spent the day thinking about antimatter and Armstrong units and whatnot. We've assumed that Kindrel's story might be true because *maybe* a sun weapon could have been built. But there's another possibility: maybe the story is true, but Olander was a liar."

I considered it. There was no reason I could find to dismiss the idea. Still it didn't feel right.

"You know what Kindrel Lee looked like," Chase continued. "Olander's sitting in that bar, probably half-tanked, and suddenly she's there with him. What more typical of a man than that he should begin immediately to exaggerate his importance?"

"That's a side of you I haven't seen before," I observed.

"Sorry," she said. "No slur intended. It's more or less the nature of things. Well, you know what I mean."

"Of course."

"The skimmer just came in. See you in a bit." She signed off. The wind was rising, whipping flakes against the window.

The storm arrived and began to build in intensity. I called the desk and reserved two rooms for the night. Not that the weather presented any serious danger to travelers: the skimmers were inordinately sturdy vehicles and, as long as the pilot stayed with the automatics, there was really nothing to fear. But I was drawn by the prospect of spending a stormy night on Sim's Perch.

I was enjoying a dark Ilyandan wine, lost in thought, when a hand pressed on my shoulder, and a voice that I knew cried, "My

God, Alex. Where've you been?" The voice was Quinda Arin's, and she held on tight. "I've been looking everywhere for you." There was snow in her hair and on the shoulders of her jacket. She was trembling, and her voice shook.

I stared at her in mild shock. "Quinda," I said, "what the hell are you doing *here?*"

Her face was pale. "Where's your skimmer?"

"Why?" I stood up intending to help her into a chair, but she waved me impatiently away.

"Where's the skimmer?" she demanded, in a tone that I could only characterize as threatening.

"Somewhere out over the ocean, I guess. It's bringing Chase Kolpath in from Point Edward."

She swore. "That the woman you brought with you?" Her eyes locked on mine: she looked wild, frightened. "You need to get in touch with her. Tell her to get off the skimmer. Keep everybody else away from it too." She was having trouble speaking and breathing. Her eyes lost their focus, and she wiped a damp brow with the back of her hand.

Things started to go cold. "Why?" I asked. "What's wrong with the skimmer? What's going on?"

She shook her head violently. "Never mind." She got up as though to leave, looked about, sat down again. "There's a bomb on board."

I could barely hear her, and I thought I'd misunderstood. "Pardon?" I said.

"A bomb! Get her off. For God's sake, call her. Get her off the goddam thing. Wherever you sent it, get everybody away from it."

"It's probably a little late for that now." I was slow to react: I couldn't quite get hold of things, and Quinda was on her feet, anxious to go somewhere, do something. "How do you know about the bomb?"

Her face was a white mask. Frozen. "Because *I* put it there." She glanced at her commlink. "What's her code? I'll call her myself. Why didn't you log onto the net while you were here so you could be found?"

"Nobody knows us on this world," I said. "Why the hell *would* we sign on?" I opened a channel and whispered Chase's name into my own unit.

Immediately, I could hear the hiss of the carrier wave, and the rattle of the wind against the aircraft. Chase said hello. Then: "Alex, I was going to call you. Order me a steak and baked. I'll be there in twenty minutes."

"Where are you?"

She responded with amused suspicion. "Almost halfway. Why? Something come up? Or someone?"

"Quinda's here."

"Who?"

"Quinda Arin. She thinks you have a bomb on board."

More wind. Then: "The hell she says."

Quinda was on her own system now. "I don't *think*. It's attached to one of the skids. It could go off any time."

"Son of a bitch. Who are you, lady?"

"Listen, I'm sorry. None of this was supposed to happen." I thought she was going to come apart. Tears started, but she shook them off. "It's *there*, Kolpath. Can't you see it?"

"Are you kidding? In this? There's a blizzard going on out there. Listen, I'm twenty minutes away. Is this thing about to go off or what?"

Quinda shook her head no. Not no that there was no immediate danger, but no that she had no idea, no that she could promise nothing. "It should have exploded an hour ago," she said. "Any possibility you could climb down and dislodge it?"

"Wait a minute." I heard Chase moving in the cockpit, struggling with the canopy, swearing softly. She got it open, and the wind howled. Then she was back, breathless. "No," she said. "I am not going down there." I caught a sense of panic around the edge of her voice. "How'd it *get* there?" she demanded in a voice whose pitch had risen sharply.

I tried to visualize the aircraft. It would be a long step from the cockpit out to the strut, and then she'd have to lower herself maybe two meters onto the skid. All this in the face of a storm. "How about if you stop the skimmer? Can you hold it steady?"

"How about if *you* come up here and do some handstands on the skids? Who the hell is this woman anyhow? Which of us does she want to kill?"

"She's got to get rid of the bomb," said Quinda. "Or get out of the skimmer."

"Listen," said Chase. "I'm going to go to manual, and make for the summit. You'll have to come get me. But do it quick. After I get down, I'm going to get as far away from this thing as I can, and it's cold out."

"How far off shore are you?"

"About three kilometers."

"All right, Chase. Do it. But keep your commlink on. We're on our way."

"I can't believe you've done this," I told her.

Quinda was directing her skimmer to pick us up. She kept on until she'd finished, and then she turned on me in cold fury. "You dumb son of a bitch. You brought it on yourself. What right do *you* have, barging in and trying to grab things for yourself? And then blabbing to the goddam mutes. You're lucky you're not dead. Now let's get moving and we can argue about it later."

We were both on our feet now.

"You want to do something constructive?" she continued. "Call the Patrol. And tell Kolpath to activate her beacon." She was having trouble controlling her voice. "I never intended anyone should get hurt, but I'm not so sure now that was a good idea."

I notified the Patrol, and gave them the situation. They were incredulous. "Who the hell," demanded the official voice on the link, "would put a *bomb* on an aircraft?" Quinda was glaring at me. "On our way," he grumbled. "But we've got nothing in the immediate vicinity. Take a while. Maybe forty minutes."

"We don't have forty minutes," I told him.

"Alex," Quinda said, as we hurried through the lobby, "I'm sorry. I'm sorry I didn't just go to you, and I'm sorry you're such a damned fool. But why the hell couldn't you have minded your own business? I may wind up having *killed* somebody before this is over!"

"It was *you* all the time, wasn't it? You took the file, and you left the loaded simulation. Right?"

"Yes," she said. "Goddam shame you can't take a hint."

It was too much. I believe, had there been time, I'd have thrown her against a wall. As it was, we had things to do. "Where's your skimmer?"

"It's on its way."

"God help me, Quinda, if anything happens to her I'll pitch you into the ocean!" We went through the lobby on a dead run. There's a ballroom at the north end, which was corded off. The cord was flexible, and there was about twelve meters of it. I ripped it free, and coiled it as we ascended the shaft to the summit.

Snow was falling heavily onto the pads. Our headlong rush stopped at the end of a line. People stood with their heads bent against the storm, hands jammed into the pockets of their thermals. Quinda pealed back the sleeve of her jacket, and glanced at her watch.

No trace of the hangar was visible from the landing pads. We watched an aircraft rise out of the trees, and float in our direction. Overhead, a couple of incoming skimmers circled, waiting their turns to land.

An airbus drifted in and docked.

"This isn't going to work," she said, looking anxiously around. "Where *was* it supposed to go off?"

"In the hangar. But something went wrong."

"Another warning?" She turned toward me. It's the only time in my life that I can remember seeing violence in a woman's eyes. "Quinda, why did you disconnect the automatics?"

"To prevent anyone from using it," she said stiffly. "Who would have thought you'd go down there to get the thing?"

"What triggers the bomb?"

"A timer. But either I didn't set it properly, or it's defective. I don't know."

"Wonderful."

The storm beat down on us. I felt suddenly very tired. "Don't you have any idea," Quinda asked, "of the risk you're running? For all of us?"

"Maybe you should tell me."

"Maybe you should just leave it alone. Let's get your partner, and the two of you can go back to Rimway and *leave it alone*." She spoke into her commlink: "Control, we have an emergency. My name's Arin. I need my skimmer immediately. Please."

They were slow to answer. "Your aircraft is on the way," a computer voice said. "There is nothing we can do to hurry matters."

"Can you supply a vehicle?" I asked. "This is an emergency."

"Just a moment, please. I'll put you through to my supervisor."

The bus passengers filed out, and hurried through the storm. When they were gone, the vehicle lifted, swung ponderously over the trees, and descended into the hangar. Moments later, a sleek, luxurious skimmer rose over the same grove and turned in our direction. It was steel blue, with inlaid silver trim, and tapering ingot wing mounts. A Fasche. An elderly couple hurried forward out of the shelter of the tube station.

I considered trying to commandeer the Fasche, but Quinda shook her head. "Here it comes," she whispered.

A new voice from Control: "What is the nature of your problem, please?"

"Aircraft in trouble." Quinda gave them Chase's code.

Our skimmer lined up behind the luxury aircraft. Both floated toward us.

Control again: "We are notifying the Patrol. We do not maintain rescue facilities here."

"We don't need rescue facilities," said Chase. "Just a skimmer."

"I understand."

My commlink beeped. I opened a channel. "Yes, Chase?"

The wind was loud at both ends, drowning her voice.

I turned away from the weather. "Say again!"

"I think the damned thing has just blown." She was struggling to keep her voice under control. "I've lost the son of a bitch. It's going down."

"Do you still have power?"

"Yes. But part of the tail's gone. And something big came through the cockpit. The canopy's popped and I have a hole in the deck big enough to fall through." The wind screamed in the link.

Quinda: "Are you all right?"

Chase's voice hardened. "Is *she* still with you?"

"We're going to be using her skimmer," I said.

"*Going to be?* You mean you're not *started* yet?"

"Starting now. Are you okay?"

"I've been better." There was a sharp intake of breath. "I think my left leg's broken."

"Can you make the summit?"

"No. I'm above it now, but I'm losing altitude too fast. If I try it, I'll probably hit the wall."

"Okay. Stay clear."

Quinda turned worried eyes toward me, and put her hand over my wrist, covering the commlink. "The ocean's cold. We have to get to her quickly."

The Fasche settled into its slot on the pad. Its owners passed us, walking backward against the storm. The man looked up, and took in the sky with a broad sweep of his hand. "Hell of a night," he said. "Isn't it?"

Chase's voice again: "I'll try to stay in the air as long as I can."

"You'll be okay."

"Easy for you to say. Where the hell's the survival equipment in these things? There isn't even a lifebelt."

"They're not supposed to crash," I said. "Listen, we may get there before you hit the water. If not, we'll only be a couple minutes behind. Stay with the skimmer."

"Suppose it sinks? This one's got a very big hole in it."

Our vehicle settled onto the pad, and we clawed the canopy open and scrambled on board. *Hurry.* Quinda didn't say it, but her lips formed the word. *Hurryhurryhurry—*

"Losing power," Chase said. "The magnetics are making a lot of noise. I don't have much forward motion, and I'm still pretty high. Alex, if they quit, I'm going to take a long fall." Something banged.

"What happened?"

"The cockpit's coming apart, Alex."

"Maybe you ought to go lower."

"I'm *going* lower. Have no fear. When are you going to get here?"

"Twenty minutes."

The voice from Control broke in: "Arin, you have emergency priority. We've returned control of your aircraft to you. Good luck."

Chase: "I'm getting knocked around a lot up here. This thing may just flat-out disintegrate."

We lifted. Slowly. As soon as we got above the windbrakes, the storm hit us. It was going to be a rough ride. I patched the signal from Chase into the tracking system, and put a display of the target area on the monitor.

We were beginning to accelerate. Quinda rang up a hundred eighty kilometers on the control. Top speed. I doubted the thing could manage that kind of velocity.

A blue light came on near the right side of the target display, pinpointing Chase's position. I opened the channel. "How are we doing?"

"Not good," came Chase's voice.

"Any sign of the Patrol?" I didn't really expect they'd be there that quickly, but it was a way to sound hopeful.

"Negative. How far away are you?"

"Thirty-eight kilometers. What's your condition?"

"Dropping faster. I'm going to hit pretty hard." The words came one at a time, broken up by the noise, and maybe a little fear. I could sense her, pressed against her seat in the shattered aircraft, looking down into a void.

"Quinda?"

"We're going as fast as we can." She punched up numbers on the display. Other than Chase's aircraft, and the Fasche (which was rapidly dropping behind us), there were two blips.

I put them on the scopes. One was an airbus, headed out from Point Edward toward Sim's Perch. The other looked to be a private skimmer, just leaving the city, headed our way, but at a greater range than we were. I wondered where the hell the Patrol was. "Chase, I'm going to leave the circuit open. We'll be right here."

"Okay."

I opened a channel to the bus. "Emergency," I said. "Skimmer in trouble."

A woman's voice crackled back: "This is the Sim's Perch Express. What's happening?"

"There's a skimmer going down about four kilometers ahead of you, and a few degrees to your starboard. Present altitude about two hundred meters."

"Okay," she said, "I have the blip."

"One pilot, no passengers. There's been an explosion. Pilot may have broken her leg."

"Bad night for it," she said. Then: "Okay. I'm notifying the Patrol that I'm diverting to assist. There are several aircraft coming off the Perch. Which one are you?"

"The one in front."

"You'll want to get here quick. This thing isn't maneuverable in the best of circumstances, and nobody's going to be able to set down without getting swamped. You better think about how you're going to handle this."

"Okay," I said, pulling on the cord to test its strength, which seemed substantial. "I've got some rope."

"You'll need it."

"I know. Do what you can. Stay with her."

Quinda bent silently over the controls, urging the skimmer

forward. Her face was immobile in the pale light of the instruments. Despite everything, she was lovely. And, I thought, now forever beyond reach.

"Why?" I asked.

She swung toward me, lifting her eyes. They were filled with tears. "Do you know what you've been looking for? Do you have any idea what's out there?"

"Yes," I said, and took my best shot. "There's a Dellacondan warship."

She nodded. "Intact. Everything intact. Alex, it's a priceless artifact. Can you *imagine* what it would mean to walk her decks, to read her logs? To bring her back? I think it's one of the *frigates*, Alex. One of the frigates—"

"And you were willing to take chances with our lives to get the damned thing."

"No. You were never in danger. I wouldn't have—But—the—goddam—bomb—didn't—trigger." She squeezed the words out. "And then I couldn't find you to warn you. I couldn't get to you."

"Where's the Tanner file?"

"I hid it. You have no right to it, Alex. I've been working on this for years. Your uncle is dead, and there's no reason why you should just walk in and pick everything up."

"But how'd you get involved?"

"Didn't it ever occur to you that Gabe wasn't the only one wondering about the *Tenandrome?*"

Another blip appeared on the display. It was the rescue craft. But it was too far away. Chase would be in the water a long time before it arrived on the scene.

"Hey, Skimmer." It was the bus pilot. "I got a glimpse of the bird. The weather closed in again right away, but I saw her. She's not exactly falling, but she's coming down too fast."

"Okay. Chase, you copy?"

"Yeah. Tell me something I don't know."

"Anything you can do?"

"I'm open to suggestions."

"I understand, Chase. We'll be there quick."

"I don't see anything here that'll float except maybe the seats, and they're anchored."

"Okay. You can hang on for a couple minutes. We're making our descent now. Coming fast."

"I can see the bus. She's following me down."

"Good."

Quinda again: "Chase, you won't have any trouble getting out of the skimmer, will you?"

"No," she said, her tone softening slightly. "I'll be all right."

"Chase? Is that your name?" It was the bus pilot.

"Yes."

"Okay, Chase. We're going to stay right with you. And your friends are coming. You'll be all right."

"Thanks."

"I can't get you out of the water. Ocean's too rough for me to come close enough to try to reach you."

"It's okay."

"I mean, I've got twenty people on board."

"It's all right. Who are you?"

"Hoch. Mauvinette Hochley."

"Thanks, Hoch."

"Water coming up. You're going to hit in about twenty seconds."

We were down near the surface now. The boiling sea unrolled, and the wind screamed. Quinda had gone quiet again. I was starting to coil the cord.

One of the monitors blinked on. "Feed from the bus," Quinda said. We were looking at the stricken aircraft from slightly above and nearby. The bus was angled so that its running lights illuminated the scene. We could see Chase in the cockpit, pushed back into her seat, clinging to the yoke. The skimmer was shredded, undercarriage gone, holes punched in the fuselage, tail crumpled, one of its stubby wings shattered.

"How much longer?" I asked.

"Three, maybe four minutes."

"There's no way," I whispered, covering the commlink with my hand so Chase wouldn't hear.

"We'll get there," Quinda said.

She hit hard. The skimmer slapped down into a trough and the ocean rolled over it.

We were all calling Chase's name, but nothing moved in the cockpit.

"It's sinking," said Hoch.

The skimmer wallowed in white water; a wing lifted momentarily, and broke off, its lights still burning brightly.

"We're right overhead," said Hoch. "I wish to hell there was a hatch on the bottom of this son of a bitch.'' She sounded distraught.

Quinda's breath was coming in short sharp gasps. ''She's not getting out,'' she said. ''Alex—'' Her voice started up the scale. ''She's not going to get clear.''

The bus pilot whispered her name. ''Come on, Chase. Get your ass out of there.''

Nothing. The wreckage slipped beneath the water.

We hurtled across the heaving, white-flecked ocean.

''Hey!'' It was Hoch's voice. ''What are you doing back there?''

Another outside camera switched on. We had a view of the bus's main hatch. A crack of yellow light appeared around it, and then the door swung outward. A woman who'd been pushing on it nearly fell out.

There was a burst of profanity from Hoch.

A man—his name was Alver Cole, and I'll remember it all my days—appeared in the doorway, hesitated, and jumped out into the ocean. He vanished immediately into the black water.

Quinda hit the braking jets. ''About a minute,'' she said.

One of the bus's lights stabbed down and picked up Cole, who had surfaced and was struggling toward the cockpit.

Hoch increased her magnification on the scene in the water. Swimmer and wreckage were lifted high on a wave. ''I don't know,'' said the bus pilot, ''whether you can see this on your screen or not. But it looks as if he's reached her.''

''Hoch,'' I said. ''Your door's still open. You're not going to let anybody else jump, are you?''

''I damn well hope not.'' She directed someone to see to it. Moments later, the light vanished.

''Patrol coming fast,'' said Quinda. ''Be here in four or five minutes.''

A cheer went up in the bus. ''He's waving,'' said Hoch. ''He's got her.'' Hoch continued to maneuver the big vehicle, trying to keep her winglamps on the water.

''We're seconds away,'' said Quinda. ''Get ready.''

She pushed the braking jets to full throttle, and the skimmer went into a mild spin. But we stopped hard. I released the canopy lock and pushed it up out of the way. Snow and spray poured in, and I looked out across a slippery wing surface into blazing lights and rough ocean.

Quinda rotated the rear seats, and depressed their backs, giving us two couches. "Over to your left," came Hoch's voice.

"There," said Quinda. I looked just in time to see two heads vanish beneath a wave.

Uncurling my cord, I crawled out onto the wing. It was icy, and my hands froze to it. A sudden burst of wind struck me, and I skidded wildly, sliding toward the ocean. But I got hold of a lamp, a flap, something, and ended up twisted over on my side, both legs dangling, still headed for the water. Quinda was out the door immediately, sprawled across the wing, holding me by an arm and a leg. I could hear Hoch's voice over the shrieking of the storm, but I couldn't tell what she was saying. The ocean was turned on its side, and my legs were tangled in the cord.

Quinda shifted around to get a better grip. A wave pounded into the skids, rocking the skimmer violently and sending cold spume into the air. "I've got you," she said.

"Hell of a rescue team," I grumbled, finally getting my balance, and rolling clumsily back into a sitting position.

"Okay?" she asked.

"Yeah. Thanks."

She gave me a thumbs-up, and ducked back inside just as we got hit again. The skimmer lurched, and icy water washed across the wing. Quinda produced strips of cloth from something and passed them out to me. I wrapped my hands in them.

I could see Chase and the man from the bus. But it was a long way down to them. Maybe eight meters. "Take it lower," I shouted.

"I think we're already too low," Quinda said. "A couple more minutes of this and we'll be swamped."

"A couple more minutes of this and it won't matter." I went flat on my belly, wishing there was a way to jettison the skids. The swimmers were almost directly below me. Chase was either unconscious or dead. Her rescuer was doing his best to hold her head out of the water. Her leg floated at an odd angle. I watched it bend as they disappeared again into the turbulence.

In that moment, I could have killed Quinda Arin.

The man with Chase hung on. She coughed and threw her head back.

Alive, at least.

He seemed at the end of his strength.

I threw the line toward him. It fell close by, but his hands were frozen. He couldn't get hold of it. I tried to drag it closer. He got it finally, and looped it around Chase. Quinda appeared beside me again. "Stay at the controls," I said.

"They're on automatic."

"That won't help if the ocean knocks us sidewise."

"That's going to be dead weight coming up. You want to handle it alone?"

The man in the water waved. Okay.

We pulled the line tight. The ocean lifted her toward us, and then fell away. I heard encouragement from Hoch as Chase came out of the water. We were both on our knees now, taking advantage of what purchase we could get, hauling hand over hand.

Chase's arms hung loosely at her side, and her head lolled on her shoulders.

When she was close enough, I reached down and grabbed her jacket. Her face was deathly white, and splinters of ice crystals clotted her hair and eyebrows. "Watch her leg," said Quinda.

We got her up onto the wing, and I got the line off her and threw it back into the ocean. Quinda climbed inside the cabin, and I passed Chase through. "Hurry," said Hoch. "You're losing the other one." I left her for Quinda to move to the far couch, and went back for her rescuer.

He was trying to hold onto the line, and not having much luck. Too cold. He held one arm weakly toward me, and slipped under.

Quinda was back.

I handed her the end of the line, and was about to slide over the side, but she shook her head vehemently. "How do you expect me to haul him out of there? Or you afterward?"

"Maybe we should just let him drown," I said.

"Thanks," she said bitterly. And then, before I knew what she intended, she was gone. She plunged into the waves, sank, came up choking and gasping, looked around her, went under again.

The man from the bus surfaced moments later on his own. Quinda reached for him, and the sea broke over their heads. But when I saw them again she had him.

I'd retrieved the line and dropped it to her. She looped it quickly under his arms and signaled.

I hauled up.

Dead weight. And a lot heavier than Chase had been.

There was no place to plant my feet. When I tried to pull the line in, I simply slid across the wing surface.

I climbed back inside the cabin, and tried from there. But it was too cramped. He was just too damned heavy.

"Hoch," I cried.

"I see your problem."

"Can you have your people open that door again?"

"They're doing it now."

"Quinda," I shouted. "Hang on. Hang onto him. We're going to bring you both up." I was tying the line around the seat anchor.

She shook her head. I couldn't hear her, but she pointed at the line. It wouldn't be strong enough to support both. To emphasize the point, she pushed away from him, and shouted something else. Over the roar of sea and wind, I understood: "Come back for me."

I scrambled into the cockpit and took the skimmer up.

Hoch rotated her bus to cut down on my maneuvering. A big warm circle of yellow light opened in her hull. Behind me, Chase made a noise, more whimper than groan.

I got above the bus, and started down. "Tell me when," I said. "A lot of this is guesswork."

"Okay," she said. "You're doing fine. Check your monitor: you should be getting a picture now, but just keep coming the way you are, coming down, maybe a few meters forward—Okay, keep coming—"

On the screen, I was looking back along the hull of the bus. Several sets of hands gripped the sides of the aircraft around the opened door. "A little lower," said Hoch.

The line stretched tight out through my own door and over the leading edge of the wing.

Arms reached out of the bus, seized the man by his legs as soon as he was close, and hauled him inside. "Okay," said Hoch. "We've got him."

"I need the line back."

"You got it."

I lurched away. "Keep the door open," I said. "I've got another one in the water. Let's do it the same way."

"Okay," said Hoch. And then, somberly: "Hurry."

Hurry.

When I got back out on the wing, she was gone. I stood there, trailing the cord, calling her name, not even certain where she'd been, until the Patrol vehicles circled in and took station overhead.

They searched until dawn. But there never was any hope.

XVIII.

To lack a grave matters little.

—Virgil,
Aeneid, II

THERE WAS A gathering for Quinda on a hill outside Andiquar. It was advertised as a commemoration of her life rather than a memorial service. They set a table, and hired a band. The guests sang loudly, if not particularly well, and everyone drank a good deal.

There were maybe two hundred people present, some of whom I recognized from the Talino Society. They toasted her frequently and energetically, and regaled each other with reminiscences. The wind played over the flickering gantner shield that protected them from the temperatures of the winter afternoon.

Chase and I stood off to one side. She leaned on a crutch, moodily silent. When most of the food had been cleared away, the guests gathered around a circular table. And they came forward, one by one, to sum up her life in quiet sentences: she was not known ever to have injured anyone, they said. She was a friend, she was unfailingly optimistic, she'd been a good daughter, and we would not see her like again.

All cliches. And I reminded myself that this was a woman who'd twice broken into my home, who'd shown a reckless disregard for *my* life, who'd damned near killed Chase, and who was, finally, a victim of her own ruthlessness.

Toward the end, I noticed Cole, Chase's rescuer and the man Quinda had saved, standing quietly off by himself, beside a tree. We walked over and stood with him.

A young man who looked startlingly like Quinda approached us, introduced himself (he was her brother), and thanked us for coming. He knew us, understood that we had been with her at the end, and asked whether I would speak to the assembly. I hesitated. Principle seemed to demand that I forego that particular hypocrisy.

But I agreed nonetheless, and walked through the crowd to take a place at the table. The brother introduced me by name.

"You've already heard all the important things there are to know about Quinda," I told them. "I knew her only at the beginning, and again at the end, of her short life. And maybe the only thing I can add to what has been said here this afternoon is that she did not hesitate to sacrifice that life for a man whose name she never knew."

An hour later, in possession of a court order, I reluctantly visited Quinda's quarters accompanied by her executor, and searched for the Tanner file. It was not there.

I hadn't thought it would be. We never *did* learn what she'd done with it.

I inquired of the executor, and later of the family, whether I could have access to her private papers. It was a difficult request to honor, in light of the fact that I'd forced myself on them with a court order. They understandably refused, and a few days after her death, certain designated private documents, according to the wishes of the deceased, were burned.

I suspect they contained indirect evidence of her conniving: possibly some record of the preparation of the bogus simulations. In any case, I consoled myself with the knowledge that the location of the artifact was not being burned too: she obviously had known no more about that than I did.

That evening, there were two pieces of news. Patrols in disputed areas were being beefed up as a result of another clash near the Perimeter. Some observers thought the scare was being fanned by a government anxious to stem the political power of separatists throughout the Confederacy.

The other item came in the form of a message from Ivana: Hugh Scott's house on Fishbowl had been sold.

The proceeds had been deposited in an account on Dellaconda! What more appropriate for the driven Scott than that he be found at last on Christopher Sim's home world.

I was off again.

XIX.

The legend that Maurina was scarcely more than a child when she married Christopher Sim is demonstrably untrue. She was, in fact, his instructor in classical Greek and Platonic philosophy. And her mastery of those difficult disciplines on a frontier world do not suggest extreme youth.

Their wedding took place in the shadow of sporadic clashes with the Ashiyyur. And when those clashes eventually flared into all-out war, Christopher left to join his brother Tarien, promising his bride that only God could prevent his return.

As events fell out, neither brother ever again saw the wintry peaks or the wide rivers of Dellaconda. When, after more than three years, news came of the disaster at Rigel and the loss of her husband, Maurina took to wandering the lonely mountain trails. She appears never to have lost hope that he still lived, and that he would return. Even when the war ended, and the men and women who had fought it, the handful of Dellacondan survivors, came home, she persisted. Her family and friends lost patience and, in time, shunned her.

She became a familiar sight to nocturnal travelers, who were startled by her slim form, passing across the packed snow under the hard moonlight, wrapped in a long silver cloak.

And, as everyone had supposed would happen, there came a night when she did not return. They found her in

*the spring, at the foot of the escarpment that now bears
her name.*

*Today, townspeople claim that her spirit continues to
wander the high country. And more than one villager,
returning late to his home, has seen the lovely apparition.
She stares at the sky, it is reported, and asks a question,
which is always the same: "O Friend, is there news yet of
the* Corsarius?"

—Ferris Grammery
Famous Ghosts of Dellaconda

DELLACONDA IS A small, heavy, metal-rich world circling the
ancient, brick-red star Dalia Minor. In relatively recent times—
about twenty thousand years ago—it is believed to have been
involved in a near-collision, possibly with the object that is now
its moon. Today it describes an erratic looping orbit around its
central luminary, much as its own satellite rolls in a wild ellipse.
(The moon will break free eventually, but that event is still ten
million years away.) The orbit is gradually correcting itself, and
current estimates are that within several hundred thousand years
the world will have acquired a pleasant, backyard sort of climate.

In the meantime, the habitable parts of Dellaconda are afflicted
with brutal winters, blazing summers, and a capricious weather
machine punctuated by terrifying storms. People tend to live
inland, well away from the cyclonic winds that regularly rake its
coasts. It is a world of rock and desert, of vast plains frozen during
much of the year, of impenetrable forests and impassable rivers.

The cities are protected by gantner fields, though some people
still claim they prefer the old days ("when you got a real change of
seasons"). It's all too predictable now, they say: every day is
twenty degrees and pleasant. Ruins the young people. But the
occasional measures introduced into Council to disconnect are
always resoundingly defeated.

There were one hundred seventeen listings in various
Dellacondan cities under the name "Scott, Hugh." I called them
all. If any of them was the Scott I was looking for, he didn't admit
to it.

I tried the Grand Bank of the Interior, which held the account into which the proceeds from the sale of the house had been placed. They listened politely, and explained that they regretfully could not provide an address. Furthermore, it was against their policy to take a message.

So I was left to search a planetary population of thirty-odd million for a man who didn't want to be found.

The most likely place to start was Christopher Sim's home. It's a museum now, of course: a modest, two-level permearth house in Cassanwyle, a remote mountain town whose population during the Resistance was about a thousand. It isn't really a whole lot bigger today, excluding tourists.

Still, this tiny, exposed collection of well-kept but ancient buildings constitutes the lodestone of the Confederacy. The great symbols are here: the harridans haunt its forested peaks; the Signal glows forlornly in an upstairs window of Sim House; and (in Tarien's modest cottage across the wooded valley) a computer still carries within its memory early versions of the phrases that would eventually find their way into the Accord.

I got there late in the afternoon. To maintain old world charm, the Dellacondans had, at that time, refrained from erecting a shield over the town. That's no longer the case, as you may be aware; but when I visited it during the late spring, in the Dellacondan year 3231, it was exposed to the elements. It was a brisk day, as I recall, with a temperature that, in mid-afternoon, could get no higher than twenty below. There was a steady current of frigid air across the mountain slopes, and through downtown Cassanwyle.

But the visitors came, wrapped against the weather, and generally subdued in this holiest of Confederate shrines. The Dellacondans had built a tourist shelter several hundred meters downslope of Sim House. From there, people were ferried by airbus to all the major historical sites in the area.

But the wait at the holding station could be long. I was there almost an hour before a group of about twenty of us were taken the final distance over a field of hard-packed snow to our transportation.

Sim had lived in a three-story farmhouse with an enclosed veranda on two sides. Our bus circled the area while we looked down at the various points of interest: the little cemetery in back where Maurina was buried; Sim's own skimmer, now permanently moored beneath a gantner shield just north of the property; the Bickford Tavern, visible at the foot of the east slope, where the first strategy meetings had been held after the fighting broke out.

We stayed aloft until everyone in a previous airbus had loaded; then we descended to our assigned place on the landing pad. The guide informed us we would have ten minutes inside, and opened the exit doors.

We filed out and, despite the severity of the climate, most people paused along the walkway in front of the house to absorb the moment, and to look up at the bedroom windows. It was the middle of the day, so the Signal was not particularly evident, but the soft yellow glow was visible nonetheless in the curtains.

We moved inside. The veranda was heated, and furnished with rockers and thick-armed, heavily padded chairs. A chess board had been set up, and a bronze plate explained that the position had been taken from a recorded game actually played between Christopher Sim and one of the townspeople. I gathered from the comments of the visitors that Sim, who had the black pieces, had the stronger position.

The view from the veranda was stunning: the long valley with its wandering frozen river; broad white slopes broken only by occasional houses or patches of forest; the cold peaks, lost in wisps of cloud; and the warm defiance of Cassanwyle, its hundred or so buildings clustered against the wilderness.

The interior of Sim House is stiff and formal, in the manner of its era: richly embroidered rugs and vaulted ceilings and boxy, uncomfortable furniture. A central hallway divides the living room and library, on one side, from casual and dining rooms on the other. As so often happens in historical buildings, the intended effect of preserving a sense of another age, of how it must have been, is lost; instead there is only the mustiness of arrested time. Despite the photos and personal items and books placed carefully about to suggest that the owners had just stepped away (perhaps to discuss the wisdom of intervention), there is no life.

A visitors' log had been placed in the library. I scrolled quickly through it, throwing its pages on the monitor, and drawing the attention of one of the security guards. He wandered over to ask whether he could be of assistance.

I replied pleasantly that, for me, the visitors' log was always the highlight of a visit. "You can learn a great deal from what people have to say about a place like this," I observed, searching the

remarks columns for pithy comments. There were observations on
the quality of the food at the various inns, and suggestions that the
bathroom facilities at the tourist shelter were inadequate. "Just
married" appeared beside one couple's name, and "Kill the
mutes" beside another's.

"I know," said the guard, losing interest.

Well back in the entries I found what I was looking for: Hugh
Scott's name! How long ago had he been here? The dates were
written in the Dellacondan calendar, which I cranked into my
commlink: I was, at most, four months behind him.

In the section reserved for his address, he had marked
"Dellaconda." And the comment block was blank.

I'd have liked to look around the house a bit, but the tour
completed its rounds and headed for the door. The guide signaled
me toward the exit, and I reluctantly fell in with my fellow
visitors.

My next stop was Wendikys Academy, where Sim had been an
instructor.

The school is a replica. A whiteout destroyed and scattered the
original shortly after the war, and no building stood at the site for
almost a century.

All but one of the classroom spaces are now devoted to other
purposes: souvenir shop, washrooms, projection areas, restaurant. The one that remains is Sim's: displays are set up for a
history lesson on the Persian wars, using materials and a lesson
plan from his files. A holo of a fully armed Spartan hoplite,
resplendent in polished armor, stood by the door.

The title of the lesson flickered on one of the displays:
LEONIDAS IN THE PASS.

A silver plaque is mounted on the wall outside the classroom. It
lists those former students who eventually fought by their teacher's side. The names of twenty-seven are inscribed, only two of
whom ever returned.

Like Sim House, Wendikys Academy maintained a visitors'
log, and again Scott's name was there. Same date, and this time
he'd added an observation that was pointedly disquieting: "In the
end it made no difference. . . ."

Assuming he would only sign in once at each site, I concluded
he might be an occasional visitor. I looked around, scanning the
crowd: we stood jammed together in roped-off portions of the
building. Some were watching the battle of Thermopylae, others

tried to see Sim's control console, still others sat at terminals bringing up data that, according to the Parks Department, had been devised and entered by Sim himself.

Monuments and markers are everywhere. One can see Mora Poole's cottage, with the black harridan which she defiantly painted on her roof at the height of the Occupation; and the plaque containing Walt Hastings's response on learning that all five of his sons and daughters had died at Salinas: *I count myself the most fortunate of men, to have known such children!;* and the memorial to the nameless Ashiyyurean officer who was slain by partisans while participating in a midwinter search for a lost child.

But the most celebrated is the Signal.

At dusk each evening, it shines forth from the front window on the second floor of Sim House: a warm yellow cone glittering across the snow. It's Maurina's beacon to her lost husband, an ancient lamp which, according to legend, has burned every night since the news came from Rigel two centuries ago.

And Maurina Sim: there's a name that goes to the heart of the tragedy of those days. One always thinks of her as she appears in the Constable engraving, staring out at a wild quarter moon, lovely, young, black hair loose, dark eyes stained with agony.

Her wedding took place in the shadow of approaching war. She made no effort to dissuade her husband from joining Tarien and his volunteers, who were resolved to assist Cormoral. That expedition must have seemed suicidal at the time, though many thought the Ashiyyur would back off rather than slaughter a force that was more mob than navy.

But Cormoral burned before the Dellacondans got there. And that melancholy action changed everything. What was to have been little more than a demonstration became unrelenting war.

In time Maurina went to war herself. She was present at the defense of the City on the Crag and at Sanusar. She is known to have manned a weapons console at Grand Salinas. But she functioned also as an ambassador, traveling the neutral worlds with Tarien, pleading the cause of Confederacy. And it happened that she was on Dellaconda when that world was seized by the Ashiyyur.

She was stranded until the invaders withdrew near the end of the long struggle. Curiously, despite their telepathic abilities, they seem never to have realized the prize they had in their hands. Or if they did, they chose to ignore the fact.

She is said to have been in her bath when news came of her husband's death. A young townsman, whose name was Frank Paxton, was the carrier, pounding tearfully on the door until she understood what had happened.

The Signal was still burning in the upstairs window on the night that she left her home for the last time. The townspeople have never allowed it to die.

I picked up Hugh Scott's track again at the Hrinwhar Naval Museum, in Rancorva, Dellaconda's capital. I'd always been puzzled by the remark attributed to him that he was "going to Hrinwhar." He'd come to the museum, while *I* had gone a couple of hundred light years to look at the asteroid and battle site for which it was named.

He was listed as a supporting member of the Naval Society. No address was given, but there *was* a code. It was local, and I connected on the first try. "Mr. Scott?"

"Yes?" His voice was not unfriendly. "Who is this?"

I felt a rush of elation. "My name is Benedict. Alex. I'm Gabe's nephew."

"I see." His tone flattened. "I was sorry to hear about your uncle."

"Thank you." I was standing in the members' room, looking through a glass panel at an exhibit of period naval uniforms. "I wondered if we might have dinner together? I'd enjoy an opportunity to talk with you."

"I appreciate the invitation, Alex. But I'm really quite busy."

"I read your remarks at the Talino Society. Were they *all* innocent?"

"All of whom?"

"The crewmembers of the *Corsarius?*"

He laughed, but the sound had a dull ring to it. "I know you don't take that place seriously," he said.

"How about dinner?"

"I really haven't the time, Mr. Benedict. Maybe we can get together at some future date. But not just now." He broke off, and I was listening to a carrier wave.

I gave him about ten minutes, and tried again. "You're being a nuisance, Mr. Benedict," he said.

"Listen, Hugh. I've been all over the Confederacy. My house

has been robbed and my life threatened, a woman has drowned, the Ashiyyur may be involved, and I get stone walls everywhere. I'm tired. I'm really tired, and I want some answers. I'd like to buy you dinner. If you won't go for that, I'll find you some other way. It might take a while, but Rancorva isn't all that big."

He heaved a deep sigh. "Okay," he said. "If I see you, will you go away afterward and leave me alone?"

"Yes."

"You understand I will have nothing more to say to you than I did to your uncle?"

"I'll settle for that."

"All right then. Can you find the Mercantile?"

He was an old man. His face was deeply lined, and his movements were strained. His hair had grayed, and his frame sagged with the weight of too much roast beef over too many years.

He made no effort to look pleased at the tactics I'd used to get him to the table. He was already seated in a corner staring gloomily out at the city when I walked in. "No point delaying it," he said, when I commented on his promptness. He ignored my offered hand. "You'll forgive me if I pass on the food." A drink stood before him. "What exactly do you want of me?"

"Hugh," I said, as casually as I could manage, "what happened on the *Tenandrome?* What was out there?"

He did not react: he had known the question was coming, but I still caught a tremble of uncertainty in his throat, as though he'd decided to test the chemistry of the evening before deciding how to reply. "You've made up your mind there's a secret, I take it?"

"Yes."

He shrugged as one might when a conversation has taken a tiresome, and inconsequential, turn. "You got this idea from your uncle?"

"And from other sources."

"All right. You've come all this way, I assume, to speak to me. And you will not believe me when I tell you that there was nothing unusual about that mission, except the breakdown of the propulsion system?"

"No."

"Of course. Very well, then: will you believe me when I tell you that we had good reason to keep the secret of what we found? That your persistence in asking difficult questions can do no good, and may do a great deal of harm? That the decision to say nothing was unanimously supported by the men and women on the mission?''

"Yes," I said carefully, "I can believe that."

"Then I hope you will have the good sense to break off your present course and go home and stay there. If I know anything at all about Gabriel Benedict, I suspect he left you a considerable sum of money. Yes? Go back to Rimway and enjoy it. Leave the *Tenandrome* alone." He'd stiffened while he was speaking, and the air had grown tense.

"Is this what you told my uncle?"

"Yes."

"You didn't tell him you'd found a Dellacondan warship?"

That hit home. He caught his breath and looked round to see if anyone might have been close enough to overhear. "Alex," he protested, "you're talking nonsense. Let it drop. Please."

"Let me try it another way, Hugh. Why are *you* here? What are you looking for?"

He stared into his drink, his irises round and hard and very black. "I'm not sure anymore," he said. "A ghost, maybe."

I thought of my long-ago conversation on Fishbowl with Ivana. *He's a strange one.* "Her name wouldn't be Tanner, would it?"

His eyes rose slowly and caught mine. There was pain in them, and something else. His big hands twisted into fists, and he pushed himself out of the seat. "For God's sake, Alex," he hissed. "Stay out of it!"

XX.

Poetry is vocal painting.

—Attributed to Simonides of Ceos

ALWAYS IT CAME back to Leisha Tanner.

"She's the key," Chase observed. "Where was she during the missing years? Why is she at the center of whatever it is that's driving Scott? And she was significant enough that Gabe named the file for her." She was stretched out on the sofa with an electronic brace strapped to her leg. It hummed softly, stimulating the healing process. "The missing years," she said. "Why did she keep dropping out of sight for years at a crack? What was she doing?"

"She was," I said slowly, "looking for whatever it was the *Tenandrome* found."

Yes, that might fit: if the sun weapon had been hidden, lost, it might have been a nervous prospect. Both Sims dead, and no one knew where it was. So Tanner had led the hunt. "It's possible," she said. "Where do we go from there?"

"We have Tanner looking for a frigate, and two hundred years later, Gabe is looking for the same frigate. And he is extremely interested in Tanner. What does that suggest?"

"That she found it, and recorded its location somewhere?"

"But she couldn't have found it. Or it wouldn't still be out there for the *Tenandrome* to run across. I mean, what was the point of

234

the hunt if she was just going to go away again and leave it?"

"Truth is," said Chase irritably, "after all we've been through, things still don't make sense."

I was up out of my seat and prowling the room. "Let's try it from a different angle. There must have been a piece of information of some kind to guide her. Otherwise, she's got an impossible job. Right?"

"Okay."

"What form would that piece of information have taken? Maybe she went along when they went out to the Veiled Lady. In that case, she would have known the length of the voyage. Or maybe she didn't go, but had a half-remembered heading from a crewman."

"Good," she said. "But where would Gabe have got hold of that kind of information? We've read through all the stuff we could find on her, and there's nothing. And anyhow, if we're right in assuming she was out there for years and never found whatever it was, then what good could her information *be*? I mean, if *she* couldn't find it, what could she tell *us*?"

What could she tell us? There was an echo in that remark, and I played it through again. Who *had* she told?

"Candles," I said.

"Pardon?"

"Candles. She'd have told Candles!" And, son of a bitch, I knew right where it was. I took down the copy of *Rumors of Earth*, with which I'd replaced the stolen volume, and opened it to "Leisha." "It's even named for her," I said. "Listen:

> Lost pilot,
> She rides her solitary orbit
> Far from Rigel,
> Seeking by night
> The starry wheel.
> Adrift in ancient seas,
> It marks the long year round,
> Nine on the rim,
> Two at the hub.
> And she,
> Wandering,
> Knows neither port,
> Nor rest,
> Nor me!

"I've never been strong on poetry," Chase said, "but that sounds pretty bad."

I had Jacob display the critical work that had been done on the poem: discussions of the ancient mystical significance of the number nine (nine months in the birth process, nine knots in the Arab love whip, and so on) with the yin/yang implications of the dual stars at the axis. Leisha emerges as a symbolic representation of the all-mother, making (apparently) some sort of cosmic adjustment after the death of her equally symbolic son at Rigel. The hero becomes Man, enmeshed in the wheel of mortality.

Or something.

"Hell," said Chase, "it's a constellation. It's obvious."

"Yes. And I think we've got the answer to something else. *Rashim Machesney had come through.* Gabe meant the databanks at the Machesney Institute! They must have run a search for him!"

A half-smile touched the corners of Chase's mouth.

"What's so funny?"

"Quinda."

"What do you mean?"

"When she stole your copy of *Rumors of War:* she had the answer in her hands."

Jacob set up an appointment with one of the administrators and we linked in within the hour.

He was a thin freckled youth with a long nose and a quiver in his voice. His shoulders were hunched in a defensive fashion, and he seemed unable to respond to any question without first consulting his monitor. He made no effort to rise from behind his desk to greet us; and he kept it between us like a fortification. "No," he said, after I explained the purpose of our visit. "I'm not aware that we've done any special projects for someone named, uh, Benedict. Which of our channels would it have come through?"

"I beg your pardon?"

"Research requests are received from a variety of government, university, corporate, and foundation sources. Which would your uncle have used?"

"I don't know. Possibly none."

"We don't accept requests from individuals." He seemed to read that directly off his monitor.

"Listen," I said. "I've no way of knowing how he might have arranged it. But it's important, and I have no doubt he'd have been seen around here himself at one point or another. *Somebody* was working with him."

The administrator tapped his fingertips against the polished desktop. "That would be entirely against the rules, Mr. Benedict," he said. "I wish I could help." That was intended as a signal that the interview was ended.

"My uncle died recently," I said. "The reason I'm here is that he was quite pleased with the job that your people did for him, and he wished to express his appreciation in some substantive way." I flashed a congratulatory smile.

The administrator's expression softened. "I see," he said. There was much about the man that was birdlike: his slightness; the quick, perfunctory moves; the sense that his attention flitted about the office, never resting more than a few seconds in one place.

"Unfortunately, my uncle neglected to identify the person who helped him, and I have no direct way of doing so. I need your help." I produced a photo. "This is my uncle."

The administrator squinted at it, and shook his head. "I don't know him."

"How many professionals do you have on your staff?"

"That depends on how you define the word."

"Define it any way you please. At least one of them will recognize the photo. Of course, I'd need to be sure I had the right person, so I'll expect him, or her, to be able to describe the project."

"Very well," he said, tossing the photo into a stack of paper. "I'll see what I can do."

"I couldn't ask for more." I lifted my left wrist ostentatiously, and spoke into the commlink. "Jacob, we'll be making the transfer now." And to the administrator: "I'll need an account number."

He was only too happy to comply. I named the sum for Jacob, who acknowledged, and announced he was prepared to execute. About a week's pay for the administrator, I guessed. "It's yours. There's as much more if you find the person I'm looking for."

"Yes," he said, gaining interest. "I'm sure I can find him."

"By tonight."

He nodded. "Of course," he said. "Where can I reach you?"

Eric Hammersmith was sandy-haired, bearded, overweight, and he drank too much. I liked him immediately.

"I never really got to know your uncle," he said. We were in a pub downtown, huddled over a bottle of tomcat rum, and eying the gravity dancers while we talked. "He was kind of secretive. He kept pretending the search he wanted me to do was part of a statistical study of some sort."

"Okay," I said.

"You'll forgive my saying so," he pinched my sleeve between thumb and forefinger. "But he was a lousy actor."

There was a loud dinner party in an adjoining room, and a fair amount of noise in the bar, so we had to lean close together to be heard.

Hammersmith was propped up on an elbow. He'd walked in sufficiently flushed that I suspected he'd done some early celebrating. "What," he asked, with an engaging smile, "was he up to?"

"He was trying to locate an archeological site, Eric," I said. "It's a long story." And I hoped he wouldn't insist I tell it.

"With a constellation?" His eyebrows arched.

I drank my rum, and adapted an ignorant bystander attitude. "I guess it *is* strange. Fact is, I really didn't pay much attention to the details." The dancers were distracting him. "Anyway, he wanted to be sure you understood he was grateful for your help."

"I'm glad to hear it," he said. "It wasn't exactly by the book, you know."

"What wasn't?"

"What I'm trying to say is that I had to bend a few regulations. We're not supposed to use the equipment for private purposes."

"I understand." I repeated the process of setting up a transfer, this time for about six months' salary—as best I could guess.

"Thanks," said Hammersmith, his smile broadening. "Let me buy the next round."

I shrugged. "Okay."

He was waiting for me to transfer the money. When I didn't, he signaled the waiter, and we refilled our glasses. "I assume," he said, "you don't know any more than I do."

I was startled. Was I really *that* transparent? "You mean about the wheel?"

"Then you *do* know!"

Bingo. Results at last. "Of course." Somewhere in the Veiled Lady, there was a world in whose skies that circular constellation appeared. *Nine on the rim, two at the hub.* "By the way," I said, trying to sound nonchalant, "he used to talk about this quite a lot.

Where is it, exactly, the world he was looking for?"

"Oh, yes." The dancers pursued each other erotically through a halo of soft blue light. "It took several weeks to find," he said, "because we're just not programed to perform that kind of search. And the computers often weren't available. Actually,"—he lowered his voice—"it's the first time I've taken a chance and broken the regulations. It's worth my job if anyone finds out."

Sure, I thought. That explains how the administrator was able to locate you so easily.

"It was a big job, Alex. There are 2.6 million stars in the Veiled Lady, and, without a very specific configuration, drawn by a computer, with precise angles between the stars, and exact magnitudes, he would be very likely to get a substantial number of possibilities. I mean, what's a wheel look like? Is it perfectly formed? If not, how much variance is there from the base line of arc? Are there really only nine stars? Or are there nine *bright* stars? We had to set some parameters, and the result was, to a large extent, guesswork."

"How many possibilities did you get?"

"Over two hundred. Or twelve thousand if you become a little liberal with the parameters." He watched me sympathetically, enjoying the frustration he imagined I was feeling. But I was thinking how Jacob and I had looked at the starship patterns weeks ago, and cut the search area down to ten thousand stars or so. Given those numbers, it should be easy to eliminate most of Hammersmith's targets. I was briefly tempted to buy a round for the house.

"Can you give me a printout?"

He reached into his jacket. "I brought it along in case you wanted proof." He delivered a broad grin.

"Thanks," I said. I completed the transfer, and got up. "You've been helpful, Eric."

We were both tossing cash onto the table. "Thank *you*," he said. "And Alex—?"

"Yes?"

"Gabe asked me not to say anything about this. To *anyone*. I wouldn't have, if he were still alive."

"I understand."

"I'd like a favor. If you ever find out what this is all about, would you come back and tell me what it is?"

Our eyes met. "If I can," I said, and walked out into a pleasant, late winter evening.

The primary target was located about thirteen hundred light years from Saraglia, in a region of the Veiled Lady that carried only coordinates and no name. "Two months, at least," Chase said. "One way. It's a long way out."

XXI.

A starship is no place for a man in a hurry.

—Nolan Creel,
The Arnheim Review, LXXIII, 31

WE RODE THE *Grainger* out to Saraglia. *Grainger* was the *Capella's* sister ship, and I thought a lot about Gabe while we drifted down the long gray tunnel.

The observation ports were, of course, shuttered. The view outside is a bit hard on the comfort level for most people; but there are a few places on the ship where a curious passenger who wants to see the nether world can indulge himself. One of them was a lounge called the Captain's Bar at the forward section of the topmost deck.

Chase and I retreated there after I recovered from the plunge into hyper. My reaction, by the way, seemed to be getting worse with each successive trip. And I sat there that first evening, refusing to say very much to anyone, morosely recalling my pledge to myself—it seemed a long time ago now—that I was returning to Rimway to travel no more.

We drank too much. Starship bars always do very well. And, with too much time to think, I got to wondering why the research team on the *Tenandrome* had agreed that they would say nothing of their find. And I worried about that.

I didn't eat well, and after a while even Chase seemed to grow moody. So we worried our way through the formless flux of a dimension whose existence, according to some, was purely mathematical in nature.

Eight days later, ship time, we made the jump back into linear. The passengers, as they recovered from the effects of the transit, crowded around the ship's viewports, which were now open, to gape at the spectacle of the Veiled Lady.

At this close range, it bore no resemblance to anything on a human scale. Even the nebular structure was no longer recognizable. Rather, we were staring at a vast congregation of individual stars, a blazing multitude of dazzling points of color spearing the soul, a river of light passing ultimately into infinity. How poor had Jacob's representation been in the study at home.

After a while, when I could stand it no more, I went into the bar. It was crowded.

The longest part of the flight now lay before us: the journey from the re-entry point to Saraglia itself, which, in the event, required two and a half weeks. I read a lot, and took to playing cards in the Captain's Lounge with a group of regulars. Chase frolicked in the gym and the pool with a young male whose name I've forgotten.

A pair of shuttles rendezvoused with us at the beginning of the third week. They carried passengers and cargo for the next phase of the *Grainger's* flight, and removed everyone bound for Saraglia. Chase said good-bye to her friend, and I was surprised to discover a sense of well-being at our departure.

Saraglia is a construct approximately the size of a small moon, orbiting the collapsed remnant of a supernova. Its mission was to serve as an observation station. But its proximity to the super dense star led to its development as a commercial center, specializing in a wide range of processing services for manufacturers whose products required the application of ultra-high pressures for extensive periods of time.

The station looks a trifle haphazard: the original structure was little more than a platform. But that's been long since encased within environmental pods, manufacturing shells, power extraction nets, loading and docking facilities and automated factories.

A substantial dust cloud—held in place by artificial gravity— orbits the complex, providing a shield against the harsh light of the Veiled Lady. Once inside the perimeter of the cloud, an observer is struck by the relatively soft illumination of the cylinder world, which spills out of a hundred thousand windows and ports and transparent panels and receiving bays. If Saraglia is on the edge of man's universe, it is also the warmest of his habitats.

We rode our shuttle into one of the bays, disembarked, and checked into a hotel. Chase immediately began preparations for the second phase of the journey.

I needed some recovery time though. So I went sightseeing among the forests and glades, and even spent a couple of afternoons enjoying one of its seacoast lodges.

Several days after our arrival, we were on our way again, in a leased Centaur. It wasn't as large as the vehicle that Gabe had authorized, and the accommodations were (as Chase pointed out with some asperity) rather Spartan for a long trip. But I hadn't got accustomed yet to controlling large amounts of money, and the price for the Centaur was sufficiently exorbitant.

As soon as the engines had built up a sufficient charge, we made the jump back into Armstrong.

"We'll make our re-entry in fifty-seven days," she said. "Shipboard days. Also, we have a decision to make."

"Go ahead."

"This is a long flight. Confederate regulations don't really apply out where we're going, but we're supposed to abide by them anyhow. If we follow the guidelines, we will allow three hundred A.U.s for re-insertion back into linear. Factoring in our inability to be precise, we might find ourselves very easily five or six hundred A.U.s off the target. Now, a Centaur's a lot slower in conventional space than a big commercial liner. If we aren't lucky, we could find ourselves with a long trip to get where we're going. Best bet would be to just go ahead and jump back in as close to the target as we can."

"Hell, no," I exploded. "We've waited all this time. I don't mind a little patience now."

"How about a lot of patience?"

"Oh," I said. "How much time are we talking?"

"Possibly the better part of a year."

"I don't think," I said, "you mentioned this before."

"I was making assumptions about how you'd want to handle it. Alex," she smiled and assumed her most soothing manner. "The chances of our actually materializing inside something are virtually nil. There's an enormous amount of empty space within the entry area we'd be using. You'd be safer than flying a skimmer at home.''

Her smile widened.

"That's not exactly reassuring," I said.

"Trust me," she beamed.

I've always been careful to ration my exposure to electronic fantasy. But that long ride out into the Veiled Lady provided the perfect excuse to dispense with old inhibitions. I retired to my cabin rather early in the voyage.

I traveled extensively through the ship's library, vacationing in a dozen different luxury spots. Some of them actually existed, some did not, some never could. There was always at least one lovely woman on my arm. And their characters, of course, were amenable to my programing.

Chase knew. She stayed up front in the cockpit most of the time, reading and staring out into the gray tunnel which opened endlessly before us. She said little when I wandered up periodically to crash into a seat beside her. It was always mildly embarrassing, and I didn't know why. So I grew irritated with her.

Eventually I tired of the standard travelogues. I'd brought along some archeological puzzle scenarios from Gabe's collection. These were elaborate adventures, set in mythical ruins against exotic locales: find and identify a curious artifact in a submerged temple peopled with grotesque, animated statuary; translate a set of three-dimensional symbols afloat within a cluster of translucent pyramids on a frozen tundra; piece together the meaning of an ancient sacrificial ritual which seems to hold the key to explaining how the original inhabitants produced, within a few generations, a savage race.

There was in all this a surprise.

When I got in trouble trying to get through a water-filled passageway in the temple, I was rescued and dragged into a stone basin by an exquisite, half-naked woman whom I remembered but was slow to pinpoint.

Ria.

The woman in the photo in Gabe's bedroom.

She showed up again as a lovely savage in the ruined city, and among the pyramids as a magnificent wind-born creature with wings. Always she was there to rescue the adventurer and inform him he had lost the game; and on the one occasion that I got through to the end, she was waiting.

Her name was always Ria.

I became increasingly absorbed until, on one occasion while I was being stalked by an invisible thing through a mountain fortress that seemed to have no exits, the sequence dissolved, and I was on my back in a bunk in a dark space.

For a long time, my heart pounded while realization gradually set in that I had returned to my cabin. And then I felt movement, detected a silhouette.

"Chase?"

"Hello, Alex," she said. Her voice sounded different, and I could hear her breathe. "How about some reality?"

On the seventeenth day, we saw a shadow on the Armstrong scanners. Only momentarily, and then it was gone.

"It was nothing," Chase said.

But afterward, she was frowning.

XXII.

Man is fed with fables through life, and leaves it in the belief he knows something of what has been passing, when in truth he has known nothing but what has passed under his own eye.

—Thomas Jefferson,
Letter to Thomas Cooper

THE TARGET STAR was a dull red type-M dwarf. It floated benignly in one of the dustier regions of the nebula, about one thousand three hundred light years from Saraglia. We had no idea how many worlds circled it, nor have I ever learned.

Chase brought us out into linear space at a sharp angle to the plane of the planetary system, within about ten days travel time. It was a piece of extraordinarily good fortune (or good navigating) to get so close.

We held a party in the cockpit that night, toasting the red star and congratulating one another. For the first time since I'd known her, Chase drank too much. And for several hours, the Centaur lacked a pilot. She was passionate and sleepy by turns, and several times I looked away from her at the myriad stars, wondering which was the general direction from which we'd come. Odd that the vast political entity of several hundred worlds and a thousand billion human beings could disappear so utterly.

Two planets floated within the biozone. One seemed to be in a primitive stage of development: its nitrogen atmosphere was filled with dust thrown up by global rings of volcanoes. Its surface was ripped by continual quakes and convulsions. But the other: it was a blue and white globe of unsurpassing loveliness, like Rimway and Toxicon and Earth, like all the terrestrial worlds on which life is able to take hold. It was a place of vast oceans and bright sunlight and countless island chains. A single continent sprawled atop the north pole. "I suspect it's cold down there," said Chase, peering through the scopes at the land mass. "Most of it's covered with glaciers. No lights on the dark side, so I don't think anyone lives here."

"I'd be surprised," I said, "if anyone did."

"It looks comfortable in the temperate zones. In fact, downright balmy. What say we get out the capsule, and go down for a swim? Get away from walls for a while?" She stretched, enticingly, and I was about to reply when her expression changed.

"What's the matter?"

She passed her hand across the search control, and a blip sounded. "There's what we came for," she said.

It rose out of the dark, above the terminator, indistinguishable from the blazing stars.

"It's in orbit," whispered Chase.

"Maybe it's a natural satellite."

"Maybe." She keyed analyses onto the screens. "Its reflection index is pretty high for a rock."

"How big is it?"

"Can't tell yet."

"Or it could be something the *Tenandrome* left behind," I said.

"Like what?"

"I don't know. A monitor of some kind."

She shielded her eyes and peered into the scope. "We're getting some resolution," she said. "Hold on." She put the starfield on the pilot's monitor, filtered out most of the glare, and reduced the contrast. A single point of white light remained.

Over the next hour we watched it take shape, expanding gradually into a cylinder, thick through the middle, rounded at one end, flared at the other. There was no mistaking the forward battle bridge, or the snouts of weapons, or the classic lines of Resistance Era design. "We were right," I breathed. "Son of a bitch, we were right!" And I clapped her on the shoulder. It was a good feeling. I wished Gabe could have been with us.

By the standards of modern warships, it was minuscule. (I could imagine it dwarfed beside the enormous girth of the *Tenandrome*.)

But it had a hell of a history. It was the kind of ship that had leaped the stars during the early days of the Armstrong drive, that had carried Desiret and Taniyama and Bible Bill to the worlds that would eventually become the Confederacy. It had waged the endless internecine wars. And it had fought off the Ashiyyur.

"I have its orbit," said Chase, with satisfaction. "I'm going to lay us in right alongside her. Right under her port bow."

"Good," I said. "How long will it take?"

Her fingers danced across the instruments. "Twenty-two hours, eleven minutes. We'll have a close pass in about an hour and a half, maybe a hundred kilometers. But it'll take a few orbits before we can match course and speed."

"Okay." I watched the image in the monitor. They were lovely ships. We've had nothing like them, before or since. We were in sunlight, and this one was a rich silver and blue. Her lines curved gently: there was about her a sense of the ornate that one does not see in the cold gray vessels of the modern age. The parabolic prow with its sunburst, the flared tubes, the swept-back bridge, the cradled pods—all would have been of practical use only to an atmospheric flyer. But she possessed an aura that was gently moving: whether it might have been the sheer familiarity of a type of vessel that symbolized the last great heroic age; or whether it was some sense of innocence and defiance designed into her geometry; or the menacing thrust of her weapons, I could not say. It reminded me of a time when I'd been very young.

"There's the harridan," said Chase, centering our long-range telescope on the bow. I could almost make it out, the dark avian form caught in furious flight against the burnished metal, as though it would draw the ship itself hurtling down its track. She tried to increase magnification, but the image grew indistinct; so we waited, while the range between the two ships shortened.

Chase's attention was diverted by a blinking light on one of the panels. She listened to an earphone, looked puzzled, and threw a switch. "We're getting a signal!" she said. Her eyes had widened.

It got very quiet in the cabin. "From the derelict?" I whispered.

She was holding the phone against her ear, but shaking her head. "No. I don't think so." She hit a switch, and an electronic whine fluttered through the sound system.

"What is it?"

"It seems to be coming from the surface. There are a couple of them, in fact. But no visual."

"They're beacons," I said. "Left by the *Tenandrome*."

"Why are they still running? Does it mean they cleared out in a hurry?"

"Not really. They could be any number of things. Most likely geological sites. Survey uses transmitters to send different types of pulses through the planet over extended periods of time. The devices make a record, which gives you a pretty good picture of its internal dynamics. Anytime a ship enters the area, the record is automatically broadcast. There are probably other signals too if you can find them." She smiled, embarrassed by her tendency to jump to nervous conclusions.

"How do you know so much about these missions?" she asked.

"I've done a lot of reading about them over the past couple of months." I was about to say more when Chase's complexion went bone white.

The antique ship had been drawing closer, growing larger in the overhead monitor. I followed her gaze toward its image, but saw nothing. "What's wrong?" I asked.

"Look at the sigil," she whispered. "The harridan."

I looked, and I saw nothing unusual, just the prow, with its feathered symbol—

—Enclosed by a curving slice of light—

—A silver crescent.

—*So the enemy can find me*.

"My God," I said. "It's the *Corsarius*."

"Impossible." Chase was scrolling through old accounts of the final battle, stopping periodically to point out specifics: . . . *Destroyed while Tarien looked on helplessly . . . Sim's operational staff and his brother watched from the* Kudasai *while the* Corsarius *made its desperate run, and vanished in nuclear flame* . . . Et cetera.

"Maybe," I said, "the Ashiyyur were right: there was more than one."

She surveyed her instruments. "Axial tilt's about eleven degrees.

And it's rolling. I think the orbit is showing signs of decay." She shook her head. "You'd think they would have corrected that, at least. The *Tenandrome*, I mean."

"Maybe they couldn't," I said. "Maybe there's no power after all this time."

"Maybe."

Images flickered across the command screen, tail sections and communication assemblies and lines of stress factors. The ship itself was beginning to pull away again. "If it can't move on its own, they'd have no way to get it home. I mean, even if they could get it into a cargo bay, which I doubt, how the hell could they secure it? And the goddam thing could blow up at any time. Remember the *Regal?*

"Chase," I said, "that's why Gabe wanted the extra pilot. And had Khyber along. To try to take it back!"

She looked doubtful. "Even if the drive's okay, you'd be taking a hell of a risk. If something came loose somewhere, say during the jump—" She shook her head.

The quality of light was changing: we were moving into the early evening, the *Corsarius* dwindling quickly, falling through the dusk, plunging toward the terminator. It glowed against the encroaching dark. I watched it during those last moments before it lost the sunlight, waiting, wondering perhaps whether it wasn't some phantasm of the night which, with the morning, would leave no trace of its passing.

The object dropped into the planetary shadow. It grew dimmer, but—

"I can still see it," said Chase, tensely. "It's glowing." Her voice dropped to a whisper. "Where the hell is the reflection coming from? There aren't any moons."

It shone with a steady, pale luminescence. A cool damp hand groped its way up my spine. "Running lights," I said. "Its running lights are on."

Chase nodded. "The *Tenandrome* people must have done it. I wonder why?"

I couldn't believe that. I knew enough about the way professionals operate with technological artifacts: if possible, until studies are complete, they get left the way they're found. I wondered briefly whether the people from *Tenandrome* had boarded the ship at all.

An hour or so later, we followed the *Corsarius* down the nightside. By then it was only a dull star.

"That's enough for me," Chase said, getting up. "Maybe we should take Scott's advice and go home. Barring that, I think it would be a good idea if one of us remains in the cockpit at all times. I know that's a little paranoid, but I'll feel a lot better. You agree?"

"Okay." I tried to look amused, but I favored the proposal.

"Since this is your expedition, Alex, you draw the first watch. I'm going back and try to get some sleep. If you decide to drop this whole business, you'll get no argument from me. And while you're thinking about it, keep an eye on the goddam thing." She let herself out through the cockpit hatch. I listened to her moving around back there, running the dispenser, closing doors, and finally turning on the shower. I was glad she was there. Had she not been, I doubt I'd have gone any further.

I depressed the back of my seat, adjusted my cushions, and closed my eyes. But I kept thinking about the derelict, and periodically I raised myself on an elbow to look out at the night sky, to make sure something wasn't sneaking up on us.

After an hour or so of that, I gave up trying to sleep, and switched on a comic monologue from the library. I didn't much care about the humor, which was weak and obvious. But the delivery was casual, energetic, studded with one-liners and awash with audience laughter. It was a good sound, reassuring, soothing, encouraging. There is this about comedy: even when it's bad, it provides a sense of a secure existence, in which things are under control.

Eventually the cockpit drifted away from me. I was vaguely aware of the absolute stillness in the after living quarters—which meant Chase was asleep, and that I was, in a sense, alone—of the smooth liquid rhythm of a cinco band, and of the occasional flicker of instrument lights against my eyelids. When I came out of it, it was still dark. Chase was back in the pilot's chair, not moving, but I knew she was awake.

She'd tossed a spread over me.

"How are we doing?" I asked.

"Okay."

"What are you thinking?"

The instrument lights caught in her eyes. Her breathing was audible; it was part of the pulse of the ship, one with the muted bleeps and whistles of the computers, and the occasional creak of metal walls protesting some minor adjustment of velocity or course, and the thousand other sounds which one hears between the stars. "I keep thinking," she said, "about the old legend that Sim will come back in the Confederacy's supreme hour of need." She was looking through the viewport.

"Where is it?" I asked.

"Around the curve of the planet. The scanners won't pick it up again for several hours. We'll have dawn in about twenty minutes, by the way."

"You said last night we should leave it alone. Did you really mean that?"

"To be honest with you, Alex, yes. I'm queasy about all this. That damned thing shouldn't be out here. The people on the *Tenandrome* must have reacted to it the same way we have. Which means they rendezvoused and went aboard, and then they pulled out and went home and swore everyone who knew anything about it to keep quiet. *Why?* Why in God's name would they do that?"

"Leave now," I said, "and sleep no more."

"It might be a no-win situation. From what you've told me about Scott, he's become a driven man. Is that what's going to happen to us after we board her tomorrow?" She shifted her weight, and stretched her long legs (lovely in the pale green glow of the instruments!). "If I could arrange to forget this thing, erase the record, go somewhere else, and never come back, I believe I'd opt for it. That thing out there, I don't know what it is, nor how it could be what it seems; but it doesn't belong in this sky, or *any* sky. I don't want anything to do with it."

She tapped the keyboard, and a stored image of the stranger ship unfolded on the monitor. She homed in on the bridge. It was dark, of course. But it looked as alert and deadly as it had in the simulations of the raid on the Spinners, and the action at Rigel. "I was reading his book during the night," she said.

"*Man and Olympian?*"

"Yes. He was a complex man. I can't say I always agree with him, but he has a forceful way of stating his position. He comes down rather hard, for example, on Socrates."

"I know. Socrates is not one of his favorite people."

Her lips formed a half-smile. "Man had no respect for anybody."

"His critics agreed. But of course Sim blasted them, too, in a second book that he didn't live to finish." *Critics have all the advantage*, he'd once said, *because they wait until you've died, and then they get the last word.*

"It's a pity." She sat back and locked her hands behind her head. "They never present this side of him in the schools. The Christopher Sim that the kids get to see comes off as perfect, preachy, and unapproachable." Her brow furrowed. "I wonder what he'd have made of that thing out there?"

"He'd have boarded. Or, if he couldn't board, he'd have waited for more information, and found something else to think about in the meantime."

Her hull was seared and blistered and pocked. It had a patchwork quality imposed by the periodic replacement of plates. Navigational and communication pods were scored, shields toward the after section of the ship appeared to have buckled, and the drive housing was missing. "Nevertheless," said Chase, "I don't see any major damage. There *is* one strange thing, though." We were approaching from above and behind in the Centaur's capsule. We were wedged in pretty tight. The capsule itself isn't much more than a plexibubble with a set of magnetics. "The drive housing wasn't *blown* off. It was *removed*. And I'm not sure, but it looks as if the drive units themselves are missing." She pointed toward two pod-shaped objects that I'd assumed were the Armstrongs. "No," she said. "They're only the outer shells. I can't see any cores. But they should be visible."

"They have to be there," I said. "Unless someone deliberately disabled the ship after it arrived."

She shrugged. "Who knows? The rest of it doesn't look too good either. I'd bet there's a lot of jury-rigging down there."

"Unfinished repairs," I said.

"Yes. Repairs made in a hurry. Not the way *I'd* want to take a ship into combat. But, except for the Armstrongs, it looks servicable enough." The aguan solenoids, through which *Corsarius* had hurled the lightning, protruded stiff and cold from an array of mounts. "So do they," she added.

But the chill of age was on the vessel.

Chase sat in the pilot's seat, perplexed, and perhaps apprehensive. The multichannel was open, sweeping frequencies that would have been available to *Corsarius*, as though we expected a transmission. But we heard only the clear hiss of the stars. "The histories must be wrong," I said. "Obviously, it wasn't destroyed off Rigel."

"Obviously." She adjusted the image on the monitors, which

needed no adjusting. The Centaur's computers were matching schematics of the derelict with ancient naval records of *Corsarius*, again and again, in endless detail. "It makes me wonder what else they might have been wrong about."

"Does this mean Sim might have *survived* Rigel?"

Chase shook her head. "I'm damned if I know what it means."

I pursued the thought. "If he did, if he lived through it, why would he come out here? Hell, this was a long way from the war zone anyhow: could *Corsarius* even have made this kind of flight?"

"Oh, yes," Chase said. "The range of any of these vessels is only limited by the quantity of supplies they can get on board. No: they could have done it. The question is why they would want to."

Maybe it *wasn't* voluntary. Maybe Sim and his ship somehow fell into the hands of the Ashiyyur. Was it possible that he lived through the Rigel action, but that he was injured in some way, and wandered off afterward, not knowing who he was? Ridiculous. Even if there was something to the notion of the duplicate ships, what would any of them be doing *here?* Who would have had time, in the worst days of the Resistance, to come so far with a warship that must have been desperately needed at home?

We drifted out over the bow, past the fierce eyes and beak of the harridan, past the weapons clusters bristling in the ship's snout. Chase turned us in a narrow loop. The hull fell sharply away, and the blue sun-splashed planetary surface swam across the viewports. Then it too dropped off, giving way to the broad sweep of black sky.

We talked a lot. Chattered really. About how well Chase's leg had healed, about how good it would be to get home, about how much money we would probably make from all this. Neither of us seemed to have any inclination to let the conversation die. And meanwhile we drew alongside the derelict. Chase took us the length of the hull, and stopped by the main entry port. "In case you had any doubts," she said, raising her voice to indicate there was something significant to say, "she's blind and dead. Her scopes have made no effort to track us."

We put on the helmets to the pressure suits we were wearing, and Chase drew the air from the cockpit. When the green lights went on, she pushed up the canopy, and we drifted out. Chase moved to the entry port, while I paused to look at a set of Cerullian characters stencilled on the hull. They were the ship's designation, and they matched the characters on the *Corsarius* of the simulations.

* * *

The hatch rotated open, and a yellow light blinked on inside. We stumbled clumsily into the airlock. Red lamps glowed on a status board set into the bulkhead.

"Ship's on limited power," said Chase, her voice subdued over the commlink. "There's no gravity. I would guess that it's in some sort of maintenance mode. Just enough to keep things from freezing."

We activated our boot magnets. The closing cycle for the outer hatch didn't work. The stud lit up when I touched it, but nothing happened. Worse, the lamps blinked to orange, and air began to hiss into the compartment. Chase tugged on the outer door, pulling it shut. We locked it tight.

Air pressure built up quickly, the bolts on the inner assembly slid out of their wells, the warning lights went to white, and the door into the ship swung noiselessly on oiled hinges.

We looked out into a dimly lit chamber. The interior of the most celebrated warship in history! Chase held out one gloved hand, took mine, and squeezed. Then she stood aside to let me pass.

I ducked my head and stepped through.

The room was filled with cabinets, computer consoles, and large storage enclosures loaded with gauges and meters and electronic wrenches. Pressure suits hung near the airlock, and a computer diagram of the vessel covered one wall. At each end of the room, we could see a sealed hatch of the same design as the one through which we had entered.

Chase glanced at the gauge she wore on her wrist. "Oxygen content is okay," she said. "It's a bit low, but it's breathable. The temperature's not quite three degrees. A trifle cool." She released the studs that secured her helmet, lifted the headpiece, and cautiously inhaled.

"They turned down the heat," I said, removing my own.

"Yes," she agreed. "That's precisely what it is. Somebody expected to come back." I was having a hard time keeping my eyes off the hatches, as though either of them might swing open at any moment. She advanced on the row of pressure suits, one cautious step at a time, the way someone enters a cold ocean from a beach. When she reached them, she stood counting and then announced there were eight. "They're all there," she added.

"You didn't expect that?"

"It was possible that survivors of whatever disaster overtook this ship went outside to make repairs, and were swept away."

"We need to look at the bridge," I said. "That's where we'll get some answers."

"In a minute, Alex." She released the after hatch, pulled it open, and passed through. "I'll be right back," her voice said on the commlink.

"Keep a channel open," I said. "I want to hear what's happening."

I listened to her footsteps for several minutes thereafter, and then the heavy clank of more hatch bolts sliding back. Considerations of what my position would be were something to happen to Chase left me listening anxiously for her return, wondering whether I should go after her, and trying to recall the steps necessary to pilot the Centaur. My God, I suddenly realized I didn't even know which way the Confederacy was.

I wandered among the assorted black boxes and cable and God knows what else, stuff I couldn't even begin to identify, circuit boards, glass rods, and long poles with a greenish viscous liquid in them.

Some of the cabinets seemed to belong to individual crew members. Names were stenciled on them: VanHorn, Ekklinde, Matsumoto, Pornok, Talino, Collander, Smyslov. My God: the seven deserters!

Nothing was locked. I opened the cabinets one by one, and found oscillators, meters, wire, generators, and coveralls. Not much else. Lisa Pornok (whose photo I had seen in the records somewhere, and who was a tiny, dark-skinned woman with huge luminous eyes) had left an antique commlink that would have had to be carried in a pocket, and a comb. Tom Matsumoto had hung a brightly colored period hat on a hook. Manda Collander had owned a few books, written in Cerullian. I approached Talino with awe, but there were only a half-dozen journals, filled with fuel usage and shield efficiency reports, a workshirt (he was apparently considerably smaller than I'd been led to believe), and several data clips that turned out to be concerts.

I found only one photo. It was of a woman and a child, left by Tor Smyslov. The child was probably a boy. I couldn't be sure.

Everything was secured in bands, clamps, or compartments. Nothing to rattle around loose. Equipment was clean and polished. It might have been stowed the day before.

I heard Chase approaching long before she stepped through the hatch. "Well," she said, *"there's* one theory blown."

"What was that?"

"I thought maybe they'd gone down to the surface, and there'd been an accident of some sort. Or maybe the lander just quit on them and they couldn't get back."

"Hell, Chase," I said, dismissing the idea, "they wouldn't *all* have left the ship."

"No. Not if there were a full crew on board. But maybe there were only a couple of survivors." She threw up her hands. "Damn, I guess that doesn't make any sense either. It seems to me they must have come here to hide. The war was lost, and the mutes were probably taking no prisoners. And then the drive quit on them. Battle damage maybe. They couldn't get home. If the radio was knocked out, it could have happened in a way that no one would have known. In fact, in this kind of ship, the radio's probably not capable of extreme long-range communications anyhow. So if they got into trouble, they couldn't get help. At least not from any human world.

"Something else, too: I was right about the Armstrong units. They're missing. There's nothing here but housings. This goddam thing has no stardrive. It's got magnetics for linear propulsion, but you wouldn't want to do any long distance traveling in it. The thing that's really strange is that they had to patch the overhead when the units came out. That's heavy duty work. It couldn't have happened here."

"Then how'd the ship *get* here?"

"I have no idea," she said. "By the way, the lander's still in its bay. Pressure suits are all accounted for. How'd the crew get off?"

"There might have been a *second* ship," I said.

"Or they're still here. Somewhere."

Most of the luminous panels had failed. The corridors were filled with shadows which retreated before the beams cast by our hand-held lamps. None of the elevators worked, and there was a trace of ozone in the air, suggesting that one of the compressors was overheating. One compartment was full of drifting water-globes; another was scorched where an electrical fire had burned itself out. From somewhere deep in the ship came a slow, ponderous heartbeat. "It's a hatch opening and closing," Chase said. "Another malfunction."

Progress was slow. Getting around in null gravity is cumbersome, and we had trouble with most of the hatches. All were shut.

Some responded to their controls; others had to be winched open. Chase tried twice to establish normal power from auxiliary boards, but had no luck on either occasion. Both times the green lamps went on, indicating that the functions had been executed, but nothing happened. So we continued to clump about in the semi-dark. One hatch resisted our efforts so fiercely that we wondered whether there wasn't a vacuum behind it, although the gauges read normal. In the end, we went down one level and bypassed it.

We talked little, and we kept our voices down.

"Chow hall."

"This looks like an operations center. Computers seem to be working."

"Private quarters."

"No clothes or personal gear."

"There wasn't much back in the storage units either. They must have taken everything with them when they left."

It's been a good many years now since Chase and I took that walk through the belly of the ship. The chill that lay heavy in *Corsarius* on that occasion pervades my nights still.

"Showers."

"Damn, look at this, Alex. It's an armory."

Lasers, disruptors, beam generators, needlepoints. Nukes. There were a dozen or so fist-sized nukes.

We stopped in front of another closed hatch. "This should be it," she said.

And I wondered also whether, like Scott, I was about to become a driven man.

The door responded to the controls and opened.

Stars were visible in a wraparound plexiglass viewport, and lamps blinked in the dark.

"Christopher Sim's bridge," one of us whispered.

"Hold on a second," said Chase. The lights came on.

I recognized its type immediately from the simuls: the three stations; the overhead bubble like the one in which I'd sat during the raid on Hrinwhar; the banks of navigation, communications, and fire control equipment.

"Primitive stuff," said Chase, standing near the helmsman's position. Her voice bounced off the walls. I walked over and stood behind the command chair, the seat from which Sim had directed engagements that had become legendary.

Chase thoughtfully inspected the consoles, and she brightened when she found what she wanted. "One gee coming, Alex." She tapped in a sequence, and frowned when there was no response. She tried again: this time something in the walls whined, sputtered, and took hold. I felt blood, organs, hair, everything settle toward the deck. "I've turned the heat up too," she announced.

"Chase," I said, "I think it's time to hear what Captain Sim has to say for himself."

She nodded vigorously. "Yes. By all means, let's find out what happened." She experimented with one of the control boards. The lights dipped, the ship's monitors glowed, and external views of the vessel appeared. One tracked to the Centaur, and stayed with it; another showed us the capsule which had brought us over. "Battle control, probably," she said. "Don't touch anything. I'm not sure about the condition of the weapons, but everything looks operational. It might not take much to vaporize our ride home."

I put my hands in my pockets.

I tried to visualize the bridge as I'd seen it on the *Stein:* quiet, efficient, illumination spotted only where it was needed. But things had been happening too quickly for me to observe procedures. I had no idea who did what. "Can you bring up the log?" I asked.

"I'm still looking for it. I don't know any of these symbols. Bear with me." The ship's general communication system snapped on, snapped off.

"They might have taken it," I said, thinking of a *Tenandrome* boarding party.

"Computer says it's all here. Just a matter of finding it."

While she looked, I diverted myself with an examination of a command center designed by a people who clearly possessed a deep and abiding love for the arc, the loop, and the parabola. The geometry was of the same order as the exterior of the ship: one would have been hard-pressed to find a straight line anywhere. It was also clear that the Dellacondans had never worshipped the utilitarian gods who dominate our own time. The interior of the ship possessed a richness and luxuriance that suggested an inclination to go to war in style. It seemed an odd affectation for a people traditionally thought of as having their roots in tough frontier mountain country.

"Okay, Alex, I've got it. These are final entries." She paused momentarily to heighten the tension, or perhaps to allow me to entertain second thoughts. "The next voice you hear—"

—Was certainly not that of Christopher Sim. *Zero six fourteen twenty-two*, it said. *Abonai Four. Repair categories one and two completed this date. Repair category three as shown on inventory. Weapons systems fully restored.* Corsarius *returned to service this date. Devereaux, Technical Support.*

"That's probably the chief of a maintenance crew," I said.

"If they're returning command of the ship to its captain, there should be more."

There was. Christopher Sim had delivered few speeches, had never spoken to parliaments, and had not lived long enough to make a farewell address. Unlike Tarien's, his voice had never become familiar to the schoolchildren of the Confederacy. Nevertheless, I knew it at once. And I was impressed at how cleverly it had been reproduced by actors.

Zero six fourteen thirty-seven, it said in a rich baritone. Corsarius *received per work order two two three kappa. Note that forward transformers check out at nine six point three seven, which is not an acceptable level for combat. Command understands that the port facility is under pressure just now. Nevertheless, if Maintenance is unable to effect repairs, they should at least be aware of the deficiency.* Corsarius *is hereby returned to port. Christopher Sim, Commanding.*

Another round of entries announced restoration of transformer power, and Sim's crisp voice accepted without comment. But even over the space of two centuries, one could read the satisfaction in his tone. He loved having the last word, I thought, amused.

"This would be the completion of repairs at Abonai," I said. "Just shortly before the crew mutinied."

"Yes. The dates check."

"My God," I said. "The mutiny, the Seven, we've got everything. Run the rest of it!"

She turned slowly toward me, with a pale smile. "That's the last entry," she said. "There *is* nothing after it." Her voice was hollow, and beads of sweat had appeared on her upper lip, despite the fact that the air was still cool.

"Then the *Tenandrome* people *did* take it!" I said, a little too loudly.

"This is a ship's log, Alex. It can't be erased, can't be doctored, can't be removed, can't be changed in any way without leaving a trail. The computer says it's intact." She bent over it, stabbed at the keyboard, looked at the results, and shrugged. "It's all here."

"But *Corsarius* went into battle shortly after that! There must have been log entries! Right?"

"Yes," she said. "I can't imagine a naval service trying to function with arbitrary log-keeping. For whatever reason, Christopher Sim took a volunteer crew into the climactic battle of his life, and neglected to enter any of it into his log."

"Maybe he was too busy," I suggested.

"Alex," she said, "it could not have happened."

She settled herself with some diffidence into the captain's chair, and punched fresh instructions into the computer. "Let's see what we get if we back up."

Christopher Sim's voice returned. —*I have no doubt that the destruction of the two battle cruisers will focus enemy attention on the small naval bases at Dimonides II, and at Chippewa. It can hardly do otherwise. Those sites will be perceived by the enemy as a bone in their throat, and will be attacked as soon as they can concentrate sufficient power. The Ashiyyur will probably divert their main battle group to the task—*

"I think this is early in the war," I said.

"Yes. It's good to know at least that he uses his log."

We listened while Sim described the composition and strength of the force he expected, and launched into a detailed description of enemy psychology, and their probable attack strategy. I was impressed that he seemed to have got most of it right. Chase listened a while. Then she got up, and announced that she wanted to explore the rest of the ship. "Want to come along?"

"I'll stay here," I said. "I'd like to hear more of it."

Maybe that was a mistake.

After she left, I sat in the half-light listening to projections of energy requirements and commentary on enemy technology and occasional crisp battle reports, describing Sim's hit-and-run tactics against the big enemy fleets.

No wonder Gabe had been excited! I wondered whether he had known precisely what he was stalking.

Gradually, I was drawn into the drama of that long-ago struggle, and I saw the monster Ashiyyur formations through the eyes of a commander who consistently succeeded in scattering, or at least diverting, them with a handful of light warships. I began to understand the importance of his intelligence-gathering capabilities, the listening stations along enemy lines, fleet movement analysis, even his awareness of the psychology of individual enemy commanders. It appeared they could not void themselves without Sim's knowledge.

The individual accounts were riveting.

Off Sanusar, the Dellacondans, assisted by a few allied vessels, ambushed and destroyed two heavy cruisers at the cost of a single frigate. I listened to Sim reporting his coup in the Spinners. There were other actions, many of which I had never heard. But always, despite the long line of victories, the result was the same: withdraw, count losses, regroup. The Dellacondans could never stand and fight: time and again, Sim was forced to pull back because he lacked the sheer force to exploit victory.

And then came Ilyanda.

We think we can beat them here, he announces cryptically. *If not here, then I fear it will be nowhere.* In that moment, I understood that Kindrel Lee's story was true.

He names, but does not describe, the instrument of execution. *Helios.*

The sun weapon.

He pauses, almost uncertain. *As surely as I sit in this chair, history will judge harshly what I am about to do. But, God help me, I can see no other course.*

At Ilyanda, the evacuation goes slower than anticipated. *Some people are resisting, demanding their right to stay behind. I cannot permit it and, where necessary, we are resorting to force.* And later: *It's unlikely that we will succeed in getting everyone off. We will do what we can. But whatever our circumstances when the mutes arrive, we will detonate on schedule!*

Tension mounts, and units of the Ashiyyurean armada appear among the outer worlds. *We must have everything away from here and all unusual movement stopped before they get within scanner range.* There's talk of sacrificing some frigates to delay matters, but Sim concludes that he cannot allow the Ashiyyur to guess that their presence has been detected. Meantime, some of the hoped-for transports have not arrived. The Dellacondans respond by padding the freight compartments of the shuttles (which are, of course, capable only of interplanetary travel) with blankets and mounds of clothing. Then they load the final evacuees, and clear out.

With luck they won't be seen. They'll get hungry, and a few of them may get blistered. But they have a chance.

With five hours remaining to his escape deadline, Sim withdraws the operations teams that have been coordinating the evacuation and salvaging as much of the art and literature of Ilyanda as possible. *Tarien says no price is too high to stop the mutes. I suppose he is right.*

At the last minute, more people are found at Point Edward. They are hustled up on the remaining two shuttles. Sim's small fighting force has been leaving in single units, in an effort to create the smallest possible scan target. Finally, only *Corsarius* remains. Most of the late arrivals are packed on board, and they are quickly underway.

I hurried through the next few entries. *Corsarius* withdraws to a distance of about a half parsec, where they pause to watch. The Ashiyyurean fleet closes in, transmits warnings to the Dellacondans, and offers Sim a chance to surrender.

Sim captures the recording for his log: *Resistance is useless,* the voice of the enemy says. It is mechanical, matter-of-fact, eminently reasonable. There is no hint of exultation. *Save the lives of your crews.*

I looked around the bridge. Hard to realize it had all happened here. Outside, the planetary rim, hazy in bright sunlight, was coming into view. Where would Talino have been while they waited?

The station has opened fire on the enemy ships with its meagre batteries. The weapons are taken out quickly, and Sim reports that several destroyers have accomplished a forced docking.

Now, he adds. And there is an unspoken question in his tone. *Now.*

It is a bad moment, and I can read his anguish.

And I thought: Matt Olander is sitting in a bar at the spaceport. He has taken the trigger off automatic, and his attention has been distracted.

The *Corsarius* debarked its passengers on Millenium four days later. I checked the tables. A modern liner, traveling between Ilyanda and Millenium, would spend about eight and a half standard days in Armstrong space alone. How had he done it?

There was something else, another log entry following a series of maintenance reports: *We have to find out what happened. The thing might still go off. It has to be disarmed and made safe.*

After that, the record garbles. I was trying to read it when Chase came back. "There are no remains anywhere," she said.

I told her what I'd found. She listened, made an effort of her own to clear the transmission, and shook her head. "It's a security code of some sort. He didn't want just anybody to read it."

"The phrasing bothers me," I said. "'Disarmed and made safe.' It's a redundancy. Sim is usually very precise. What does one do after disarming a sun weapon to make it safe?"

We looked at one another, and I think it struck us both at the same instant. "He's talking about security," Chase said. "No one is to know they have the weapon."

"Which means they have to explain the evacuation." I sat down in Sim's command chair. It was a bit tight for me.

"Wasn't it fortunate," she said quietly, "that the mutes acted so untypically at Point Edward. It saved Sim from having to answer so many questions."

She looked at me a long time. And I understood, finally, why there had been an attack against the empty city. And who had conducted it.

I found more log entries further on. Sim and the *Corsarius* were plunged again into engagements in a dozen different places across the Frontier. But he had changed now, and I began to read, first in his tone, and then in his comments, a despair that grew in proportion with each success, and each subsequent retreat. And I heard his reactions to the defeat at Grand Salinas, and the loss, one by one, of the allied worlds. It must have seemed as though there was no end to the black ships. And eventually, there came the news that Dellaconda, too, had fallen. He responded only by breathing Maurina's name.

Through all this, there was no further mention of the sun weapon.

He railed against the shortsightedness of Rimway, of Toxicon, of Earth, who thought themselves safe by distance, who feared to rouse the wrath of the conquering horde, who perceived each other with deeper-rooted jealousies and suspicions than those with which they regarded the invader. And when he paid for his victory at Chapparal with the loss of five frigates and a light cruiser manned by volunteers from Toxicon, he commented that *We are losing our finest and bravest. And to what point?* The remark was followed by a long silence, and then he said the unthinkable!: *If they will not come, then it is time to make our own peace!*

His mood grew darker as the long retreat continued. And when two more ships from his diminished squadron were lost at Como Des, his anger flared: *There will be a Confederacy one day*, he says wearily, *but they will not construct it on the bodies of my men!*

It is the same voice that indicted the Spartans.

XXIII.

Solitude holds the mirror to folly. One cannot, in its cold reflection, easily escape truth.

—Rev. Agathe Lawless,
Sunset Musings

WE RETURNED TO the Centaur for a meal, and some sleep. But the sleep came late: we talked for several hours, speculating on what had finally happened to the captain and crew of the *Corsarius*. Had the *Tenandrome* found remains on board? And possibly conducted a funeral service? A ritual volley, report home, and forget it? Pretend none of it ever happened?

"I don't think so," said Chase.

"Why not?"

"Tradition. The captain of the *Tenandrome* would have been bound, if she took such action, to have closed out the *Corsarius's* log with a final entry." She looked out at the old warship. Its running lights glowed white and red against the hard sky. "No: I'd bet they found her the same way we did. She's a dutchman." She folded her arms tightly across her breast as though it were cool in the cabin. "Maybe the mutes captured the ship, spirited away the crew, and left it here for us to find and think about. An object lesson."

"Out *here?* How would they expect us to find it?"

Chase shook her head, and closed her eyes. "Are we going back over?"

"We don't have any answers yet."

She moved in the dark, and soft music crept into the compartment. "There may not be any over there."

"What do you think Scott's been looking for all these years?"

"I don't know."

"He found something. He went through that ship, the same as we did, and he found something."

While we talked, Chase took us out another few kilometers, smiling ruefully, but admitting that the derelict made her nervous.

I could not get out of my mind the image of a Christopher Sim in despair. It had never occurred to me that he, of all people, could have doubted the eventual outcome of the war. It was a foolish notion, of course, to assume that he'd had the advantage of my hindsight. He turns out to be quite human. And in that despair, in his concern for the lives of his comrades, and the people whom he tried to defend, I sensed an answer to the deserted vessel.

There will be a Confederacy one day; but they will not construct it on the bodies of my men.

Long after Chase had gone to sleep, I tried to tabulate everything I could recall or guess about the Ashiyyur, the Seven, Sim's probable state of mind, and the Rigellian Action.

It was difficult to forget the guns of the *Corsarius* turning in my direction during the simul. But that, of course, was *not* how it had happened: Sim's ploy had worked. *Corsarius* and *Kudasai* had succeeded in surprising the attacking ships. They'd done some serious damage before *Corsarius* had been incinerated in its duel with the cruiser. That at least was the official account.

It obviously hadn't happened *that* way either. And I wondered, too, why Sim had changed his strategy at Rigel. During his long string of successes, he'd always led the Dellacondans personally. But on this one occasion, he'd preferred to escort *Kudasai* during the main assault, while his frigates drove a knife into the flank of the enemy fleet.

And *Kudasai* had carried the surviving brother to *his* death only a few weeks later at Nimrod. But Tarien lived long enough to know that his diplomatic efforts had succeeded: Earth and Rimway had joined hands at last, had promised help, and Toxicon had already joined the war.

The Seven: somehow it connected with the tale of the Seven.

How did it happen that their identities were lost to history? Was it coincidence that the single most likely source of their names, the log of the *Corsarius*, was also mute on the subject, and in fact mute on the battle itself? What had Chase said? *It could not have happened!*

No: it could not.

And somewhere, along the slippery edge of reality and intuition that precedes sleep, I understood. With a clear and cold certainty, I understood. And, had I been able, I would have put it out of my mind, and gone home.

Chase slept fitfully for a couple of hours. When she woke, it was dark again, and she asked what I intended to do.

I was beginning to grasp the quandary of the *Tenandrome*. Christopher Sim, however he might have died, was far more than simply a piece of history. We were embroiled with the central symbols of our political existence. "I don't know," I said. "This place, this world, is a graveyard. It's a graveyard with a guilty secret."

Chase looked down at the frosty, cloud-swept rim of the world. "Maybe you're right," she said. "All the bodies are missing. The bodies are missing, the names are missing, the log entries are missing. And the *Corsarius*, which *should* be missing, is circling like clockwork, every six hours and eleven minutes."

"They intended to come back," I said. "They put the ship into storage. That implies someone expected to come back."

"But they didn't," she said. "Why not?"

During the entire history of Hellenic civilization, I know of no darker, nor more wanton crime, than the needless sacrifice of Leonidas and his band of heroes at Thermopylae. Better that Sparta should fall, than that such men be squandered. "Yes," I said, "where are the bodies?"

Through a shaft in the clouds, far below, the sea glittered.

The Centaur's capsule was designed to permit movement from ship to ship, or from orbit to a planetary surface. It was not intended for the sort of use I proposed to put it to: a long atmospheric flight. It would be unstable in high winds, it would be cramped, and it would be relatively slow. Still, it could set down on land or water. And it was all we had.

I loaded it with supplies, enough to last several days.

"Why?" asked Chase. "What's down there?"

"I'm not sure," I said. "I'll keep the videos on."

"I have a better idea: let's both go."

I was tempted. But my instinct was that someone should stay with the ship.

"They're all a long time dead, Alex. What's the point?"

"Talino," I said. "And the others. We owe something to them. The truth should have *some* value."

She looked dismayed. "What am I supposed to do," she objected, "if you get in trouble? I won't be able to come down after you to bail you out."

"I'll be all right. If not, if something happens, go for help."

She sneered, thinking how long it would take to make the round trip. "Be careful."

We ran through the various systems checks. "Don't go to manual until you're down," she said. "And probably not then. The computers will do all the tricky stuff. You're just along for the ride." She'd been staring at me.

I reached for her, but she stiffened and drew away, shaking her head. "When you come back," she said, so softly I could barely hear.

I climbed into the vehicle, pulled the canopy down, and secured it. She rapped on it twice, gave me a thumbs-up, turned quickly, and left the bay. I watched the lights change over the exit door, signaling that the chamber was sealed.

Her image popped onto my display. "All set?"

I smiled gamely and nodded.

Red lamps in the bay went purple, then green. The deckplates opened beneath the capsule, and I was looking down at wisps of cloud and a gem-blue ocean. "Thirty seconds to launch, Alex."

"Okay." I locked my eyes on the instrument panel.

"It'll be late afternoon when you get down there," she said. "You'll have about three hours until dark."

"Okay."

"Stay in the capsule tonight. You have no idea at all what sort of place this is. In fact, you should probably stay aloft. Keep off the ground altogether in the dark."

"Yes, Mom."

"And Alex—?"

"Yes?"

"Do what you said. Keep the cameras on. I'll be with you."

"Okay."

The capsule trembled as the magnets took hold. Then I fell away, down through the clouds.

It was raining over the ocean. The capsule descended into gray overcast and leveled off at about a thousand meters. It turned southwest on a preset course, which would parallel the overhead track of the *Corsarius*.

There were thousands of islands scattered through the global ocean: no way I could hope to search them all. But *Corsarius* had been left in orbit.

I was certain now that there had been a conspiracy. Its shape and form was unclear, but I had no doubts who the principal victim had been. But why abandon the ship? To torture him, perhaps? Or as a sign they would come back for him? Whichever it was, the conspirators, with an entire planet to choose from, would have placed him somewhere along its track, close beneath its orbit.

Within the womb of the bubble cockpit, I felt warm and safe. Rain splattered in large sluggish drops on the plexiglass.

"Chase?"

"Here."

"Islands ahead."

"I see them. How're you doing?"

"Ride's a bit rough. I don't know what this thing'll be like if it gets windy."

"The capsule's supposed to be reasonably stable. But it's small. They really don't expect you to go joyriding in it, Alex." She still sounded worried. "You might want to cut the search area down."

I was planning to look at everything in an eight-hundred-kilometer-wide band centered on a line drawn directly beneath *Corsarius's* orbit. "It's probably too narrow already."

"You're going to be busy."

"I know."

"You'll run out of sandwiches long before you run out of islands. You're lucky you don't have to track across the continent."

"That wouldn't matter," I said. "It's too cold there." It must have seemed a cryptic remark to her, but she didn't press me.

The first group of islands lay dead ahead. They looked sterile, sand and rock, mostly, with scattered brush and a few withered trees.

I flew on.

* * *

Toward sunset, the storm had fallen behind. The skies purpled, and the sea became smooth and transparent and still. A school of large, black-bodied creatures glided below the surface; and towers of sun-streaked cumulus drifted on the western horizon.

The ocean was studded with white, sandy reefs; lush, fern-covered atolls; and ridges, bars, and islets. There were thousand-kilometer-long island groups, and solitary fragments of rock lost in the global sea.

Chase's voice, exasperated: "If I knew what you were looking for, maybe I could help."

"Sim and the Seven," I said. "We're looking for Christopher Sim and the Seven."

I saw no birds anywhere, but the skies were filled with schools of floaters. They were bigger by far than their cousins on Rimway and Fishbowl, and indeed larger than any I had seen anywhere. These living gasbags, variations of which could be found on so many worlds, gamboled through the air currents. They rose and dived in synchronized movements, and swirled in wild chaos like balloons in a sudden gust.

All the floaters I'd ever heard about, though, were animals. These seemed different, and I learned later that my first guesses about them were correct. Their gas sacs were green; and they possessed a vegetable appearance. The larger ones tended to be less mobile. Long tendrils trailed from a stem and, on the more sedentary creatures, floated on the surface. I saw no indication of eyes or any of the extrusions associated with animals. I suspected this was one of those ecologies which produces *animates*, species not possessing the clear distinction between plant and animal which adheres on most living worlds.

A few approached the capsule; but they could not keep up, and though I was curious, I resolved not to slow down. Keep moving. Tomorrow maybe.

I passed over a group of desert islands while the last of the sunlight was fading. They were strung out at remarkably constant intervals, alternately to my left and right. *Footprints of the Creator*, Wally Candles had said of a similar chain on Khaja Luan. (By then, I had become something of an expert on Candles.)

Candles and Sim: how much had the poet known?

Our children will face again their silent fury,

> *And they will do it without the Warrior,*
> *Who walks behind the stars*
> *On far Belmincour.*

Yes, I thought: Belmincour.
Yes.

I crossed into the southern hemisphere in the late afternoon of
the following day, and approached a wedge-shaped island dominated by a single large volcano. It was a place of luxuriant growth:
of purple-green ferns and broad white flowers and vast green webs
that clung to every piece of rock. Placid pools mirrored the sky, and
there was a fine natural harbor, complete with waterfall. It was an
ideal site, I told myself, setting down on a narrow strip of beach
between the jungle and the sea.

I climbed out, cooked my dinner over an open fire, and watched
Corsarius pass overhead, a dull white star in a darkening sky. I had
a steak that night, and beer. And I tried to imagine how it would
feel if the capsule (whose cabin lights glowed cheerfully a few
meters away) were gone. And if Chase were gone.

I kicked off my boots and walked beneath the stars toward the sea
and into the surf. The tide sucked the sand from around my soles.
The ocean was very still, and the immense isolation of that world
was a physical thing I could touch. I activated the commlink.

"Chase?"

"Here."

"I can see the *Corsarius*."

"Alex, have you thought about what you're going to do with it?"

"You mean the ship? I'm not sure. I suppose we should take it
home."

"How? It has no Armstrongs."

"There must be some way to manage it. It got here. Listen, you
should see this beach."

"You're out of the capsule," she said, accusingly.

"I'm sorry you're not here."

"Alex, I have to watch you every minute! Do you have anything
down there to defend yourself with? I didn't think to pack a
weapon."

"It's okay. There are no large land animals. Nothing that could
be a threat. By the way, if you look at the sky a little to the north,
you'll see something interesting."

I heard the sound of movement over the commlink, and then she caught her breath. Wally Candles's wheel. The cluster of stars seemed almost to spin in the heavens: a blazing halo dominating the night, a thing of supernal beauty.

I went back to the capsule and extracted two blankets from the utility box. "What are you doing, Alex?"

"I'm going to sleep on the beach."

"Alex, don't do it."

"Chase, the cockpit is cramped. Anyhow, it's lovely out here." It was: the surf was hypnotic, and the moving air tasted of salt.

"Alex, you don't know the place. You could get *eaten* during the night."

I laughed—the way people do when they want to suggest that someone is being unnecessarily alarmist—stood in front of one of the capsule's cameras, and waved. But her concern was sufficiently infectious that I would probably have retreated back into the cockpit, if I could have done so graciously.

With a suspicious glance at the black line of jungle which was only a dozen or so meters away, I spread one of the blankets on the sand. The spot I'd picked was only a few quick steps from the capsule. "Goodnight, Chase," I said.

"Good luck, Alex."

In the morning, I crisscrossed the island for an hour, but there was nothing. Disappointed, I set out again, over a wide expanse of unbroken ocean. About midmorning, I ran into a sudden squall. I went higher, to get over the storm. There were patches of heavy weather throughout most of the rest of the day. I inspected more sites, sometimes in bright sunlight, sometimes in cold drizzles. There were plenty of floaters, which sheltered from the storms under trees or on the lee side of embankments and rock walls.

My instruments were most effective at shorter ranges, so I stayed within fifty meters of the surface. Chase urged me to go higher, arguing that the capsule was subject to sudden violent air movements, and a sharp downdraft could easily drive it into the ocean. Still, there was no sign of turbulence, despite the numerous storms.

I looked at probably twenty islands that third afternoon. None seemed promising. I was approaching one more (which was big, and a lot like the island with the volcano), when something odd caught my eye. I wasn't sure what it was, though it was connected with a cloud of floaters which were milling aimlessly just off the surface, about a half kilometer north of the island.

I switched over to manual, and cut air speed.

"What's wrong?"

"Not a thing, Chase."

"You're losing altitude."

"I know. I was looking at the floaters." Several of them reacted in a way that suggested they were aware of my presence, just as they had the day before. But they must have decided I was no threat.

No wind blew. The ocean was calm.

I could not shake the feeling that something was wrong in the picture: sea, sky, animates.

A wave.

It was on the far side of the floaters, approaching: green and white, its crest breaking and reforming, it rolled through the silent sea.

The island was long and narrow, with a high rocky coast at the eastern hook, sloping down into bright green forest and white beach. Quiet pools lay within sheltered glades.

"My kind of place," said Chase, not without irritation.

I drifted down through the heavy afternoon air, and settled onto the sand just beyond the water line. The sun, approaching the horizon, was almost violet. I pushed the canopy back, climbed out, and dropped to the ground. The surf was loud.

I looked out across that ocean over which no ship had ever sailed. It was a lovely, warm, late summer day, with just enough bite in the salt air. *Here.* If there was an appropriate place on this world for the conspiracy to come to its climax, it should have been *here.*

But I knew it was not so. The scanners had shown no evidence of previous habitation. No one else had ever stood on that beach.

Out beyond the breakers, some of the smaller floaters played in the air currents.

The wave kept coming. It was somehow not in sync with the surface: too symmetrical, too purposeful, and perhaps too quick. It was in fact accelerating.

Curious.

I walked down toward the waterline. A couple of huge shells, one almost as big as the capsule, were lolling gently in the shallows. A small creature with a lot of legs sensed my presence and burrowed swiftly into the sand. But it left its tail exposed. Something else, a quick flicker of light, moved in the water and was gone.

Some of the floaters turned toward the wave, and it dissipated.

They exhibited uncertainty. Most drifted as high as they could without lifting their tendrils out of the ocean. A few, smaller, brighter colored, probably younger, were nudged loose altogether and rose into the afternoon sky.

I watched, fascinated.

Nothing happened.

One by one, the floaters settled back toward the surface, until, eventually, almost the entire herd was down on the water again. I assumed they were feeding on the local equivalent of plankton.

The ocean stayed quiet.

But I could feel their uneasiness.

I was about to return to the capsule when the wave reformed. Much nearer.

I wished I'd brought the binoculars with me, but they were in a storage bin behind the seats, and I didn't want to take the time to go back to the aircraft, which was about two hundred meters down the beach.

The wave was headed directly toward the floaters, approaching on a course more or less parallel to the coastline. Again, it seemed to be gaining velocity. And getting bigger. A thin line of foam developed at its crest.

I wondered what sort of sense organs the floaters had? Anything with vision would have been clearing out, but they only bobbed nervously about on the thin strands that resembled nothing so much as tethers, as if the creatures were tied to the ocean.

The wave rushed toward them.

There was a sudden squeal, a shrill keening that seemed just on the edge of audibility. The floaters erupted skyward simultaneously, in the manner of startled birds. They were apparently able to pump air through the central gas bag, and they were doing that vigorously, trying to gain altitude, but the larger ones were slow.

Nevertheless, the entire colony would, I thought, be well clear of the water when the wave passed; why then did their cries sound like panic?

The wave acquired a sharp angular shape as though its essential fluidity had hardened. And it passed, harmlessly, I thought, beneath the retreating floaters.

But several of the creatures were abruptly jerked down toward the surface, and were hauled twisting and flailing in the wake of the disturbance. Two got tangled in each other's tendrils. And the wave changed direction again. Toward shore.

Toward where I was standing.

Chase's voice: "Alex, what the hell's going on?"

"Feeding time," I said. "There's something in the water."

"What? I can't get a good look at it. What is it?"

Her questions were coming closer together, tumbling over one another. The onrushing wall of water climbed higher. It was long, almost as long as the beach itself, which would have taken fifteen minutes to walk across.

I broke for the capsule, which seemed impossibly far away. The sand was thick and heavy underfoot. I churned through it, fixing my eyes on the aircraft, listening for a change in the dull roar of the surf. I lost my balance and pitched forward, but came up running, pumping wooden legs.

Chase had gone silent. She would be watching through the videos, and that thought caused me to reflect (as if everything were happening in slow motion) that my dash across the beach displayed a degree of terror that would embarrass me later. If there was to be a later. I could sense her holding her breath; and so my flight became even more frenzied.

I rehearsed what I would have to do to lift off. Open the canopy. (My God, had I *shut* the son of a bitch? Yes! There it was, dead ahead, gray and gleaming and *closed*.) Activate the magnetics. Energize internal systems. Pull back on the yoke.

I could activate from where I was by whispering the instruction into the commlink, but I'd have to slow down to do it, get my breathing under control. That would lose time, and anyhow my body was running on its own. No way I'd be able to stop it.

The wave was entering the breakers now. But it was enormously higher, and heavier, than the combers it rolled over. Goddam tidal wave. But there was an odd lack of fluidity to it: the sense of the thing was not that something enormous lurked within, but that the wave itself was somehow alive. The water that composed it seemed a deeper green than the ocean, and, in the sunlight, I discerned a dark, fibrous strain. A network. A web.

Through all this the shrill ululation of the entangled floaters had been rising in pitch, but diminishing in volume. As, presumably, they were dragged into the churning water.

There were tidal pools near the capsule. Thick brown water ran into them, and they began to overflow their banks. A long, slow mud-colored wave broke on the shore and rolled high up the beach.

It came my way, and I splashed through it. It clung to my boots, pulled at me, and tried to suck me into the sand. I broke free and ran on.

I ran blindly. Something hissed past me, a thin fibrous strand. The beach made for slow, ponderous going. I couldn't get my breath and fell headlong. Some of the water got onto my right hand: I felt a stab of pain that brought tears. I wiped the flesh against dry sand, and ran again. Ahead, the tide swirled over the skids and around the ladder. I was slogging through it, one heavy step at a time, wrenching each boot free before moving on.

In the shallows, the wave broke, and roared across the beach.

Only one of the trapped floaters was still in the air. It whipped in tight little circles, squealing ceaselessly, fueling my own panic.

The sun was blocked off now.

Chase's voice exploded into the tableau: "Come on, Alex. Run!"

I plunged desperately across the last few meters. The depth of water underfoot was increasing, and my lower clothes were wet and beginning to burn, and they slid clammily over my flesh. Another strand, fibrous and green and *alive,* arced around one foot, and pulled tight. I tumbled against the ladder, held on, and kicked free of the boot. I scrambled up, hit the release, waited in sheer panic while the canopy opened, fell into the cockpit, started the magnetics, and stabbed at the computer panel to activate the rest of the systems. Then I yanked back on the yoke and the capsule jerked into the air. The wave hit the struts and skids, the vehicle rolled sharply on its side, and nearly dumped me out. I dangled over the boiling water, and for a terrible moment, I thought the capsule was going to flip completely over. More filaments whispered toward me. The tip of one brushed my foot. Another wrapped around the undercarriage.

I scrambled into the cockpit and pulled the canopy shut. In the same moment, the vehicle lurched and dropped. I looked around for a knife, thinking wildly about climbing back outside. I was lucky: there was none. It forced me to take a moment to think.

I pushed the yoke quickly forward. The capsule fell a few more meters, and then I kicked in full thrust and jammed it back. We leaped up and ahead; shuddered to a quick, bone-ripping halt, and then lurched free.

I didn't know it then, but the undercarriage was gone.

I threw most of my clothes out after it.

Below, the thick, gummy water had rolled over much of the island.

And I shuddered for Christopher Sim and his men.

After that, I no longer considered tropical islands as likely candidates for my search. Surely, I thought, the conspirators would have been aware of the dangers. They would have looked for something else.

Mid-morning of the next day, while I cruised somberly through a gray rainy sky, the monitors drew a jagged line across the long curve of the horizon. The ocean grew loud, and a granite peak emerged from the mist off to my right. It was almost a needle, worn smooth by wind and water.

There were others, a thousand towers rising from the dark water, marching from northeast to southwest on a course almost directly parallel to the orbit of the *Corsarius*. The storm beat against them, and buffeted the small craft in which I flew. Chase urged me to go higher, get above them.

"No," I said. "This is it."

The winds drove me among the peaks. I navigated with as much caution as I could muster. But I quickly got confused, and lost track of where I'd been, where I wanted to go. Chase refused to help from the Centaur. Eventually I was forced to take it up a few thousand meters and wait for the storm to end. In the meantime it got dark.

The red-tinged sun was well into the sky when I woke. The air was cold and clear.

Chase said good morning.

I was stiff and uncomfortable and I needed a shower. I settled for coffee, and drifted back down among the towers. "It's here, somewhere," I told her.

I said it over and over, as the day wore on.

The spires glittered blue and white and gray. And the ocean broke against them. Occasionally, on the sheer walls, a tree or a bush had taken root. Birds screamed at the heights, and patroled the boiling sea. Floaters, perhaps fearing the combination of sudden air currents and sharp rock, were not to be seen. Smarter than I was, maybe.

In all that wilderness, there seemed hardly a place where a human could set foot.

"Straight ahead," said Chase, galvanized. "What's that?"

I put down the binoculars to look at the screens she was using. She blanked all but one: a peak of moderate size, utterly without any unusual characteristic. I should note that I was expecting to find something with its top lopped off. A place that had been thoroughly flattened and made habitable.

That was not the case here. Rather, what I saw was a wide ledge, about a third of the way down the precipice.

Déjà vu.

Sim's Perch.

It was far too level, and too symmetrical, to be natural. "I see it."

I eased up the magnification. A round object stood on the widest part of the shelf. A dome!

I stared through the scopes: there had been no way on or off, up or down. Not that it mattered.

Odd that a man who had owned the light years should eventually play out his life confined to a few hundred square meters.

Other than the shelf and the dome, there was no sign of the hand of man. The scene possessed almost a domestic aspect. I imagined how it must have looked at night, with lights in the windows, and its illustrious tenants possibly seated out front idly discussing their role in the war. Awaiting rescue.

"I don't understand." Her voice trembled.

"Chase, at the end, Sim lost heart. He decided to save what he could, to make terms."

It was very quiet on the other end. Then: "And they couldn't allow that."

"He was the central figure of the war. In a way, he *was* the Confederacy. They could not allow surrender, not while there was still a chance. So they stopped him. In the only way they could, short of killing him."

"Tarien," she said.

"Yes. He would have had to be part of it. And some of his senior staff officers. Maybe even Tanner."

"I don't believe it!"

"Why not?"

"I don't know. I just don't think they'd have done that. I don't think they could have."

"Well. Whatever. They faked the destruction of the *Corsarius*. Brought it out here. And marooned Sim and the crew. They must have intended to come back. But most of the conspirators died within a few weeks. They were probably all on board the *Kudasai* when it was destroyed. If there were any survivors, they might have had no stomach for facing their victims. Except Tanner, maybe. However it happened, she knew what they had done, and she knew about the Wheel. She saw it; or someone else did and described it to her."

I drifted in over the shelf.

"I wonder," said Chase, "if Maurina knew?"

"We know Tanner went to see her. It would be interesting to have a copy of that conversation."

Chase murmured something I couldn't make out, and then: "Something's wrong here. Look at the size of the dome." It was small, far smaller than I'd realized. "That thing would never support eight people."

No. And I understood with sudden, knife-cold certainty how terribly wrong I had been, and why the Seven had no names.

My God! They'd left him here alone!

Two centuries late, I floated down through the salt air.

The wind blew clean and cold across the escarpment. No green thing grew there, and no creature made its home on that grim pile. A few boulders were strewn about, and some loose rubble. Near the edge of the promontory, several slabs stood like broken teeth. The flat-sided peak towered overhead, its walls not quite sheer. The ocean was a long way down. Like at Ilyanda.

I landed directly in front of the dome.

Damage sustained in the fight with the sea animate—a bent undercarriage and a missing skid—gave the capsule a distinct lean to the pilot's side. I set the cameras, one on the dome, the other to track me, and I climbed out.

"It's a lot like the two-man survival unit we have on board the *Centaur*," said Chase. "If it were properly stocked, he could have survived a long time. If he wanted to."

A makeshift antenna was mounted on the roof, and curtains were drawn across the windows. The sea boomed relentlessly against the base of the mountain. Even at this altitude, I imagined I could feel spray.

"Alex." Her tone had changed. "You'd better get back up here. We're getting visitors."

I looked up, as though it might be possible to see something. "Who?"

"Looks like a mute warship. But I'm damned if I can understand what's going on."

"Why?"

"It's on a rendezvous course. But the damned thing's coming in at relativistic speed. No way it can stop here."

XXIV.

For me, sex is second. I'd rather catch an enemy in the cross hairs anytime.

—**Alois of Toxicon**
(Address at the Dedication of the Strategic Studies Center)

"I NEED A few minutes here. How much time do we have?"

"About a half hour. You can't make it back by then anyway. But I don't see what difference it makes. Only thing he can do is wave as he goes by. It's going to take him several days to get turned around and come back."

"Okay." I was more interested in the shelf just then. "Keep him on the scopes."

I had no extra boots, and the sun was heating up the rock. I pulled on a pair of socks, and advanced on the dome.

It was discolored by weather, streaked in some places, faded in others. Falling rock had creased it, and earth movements had pulled it askew.

Christopher Sim's tomb.

The shelf was so very like the one on Ilyanda, where he had suffered a death of another kind. It was not a very elegant end, on this granite slab, under the white star of the ship that had carried him safely through so much.

The door was designed to function, if need be, as an airlock. It was closed, but not sealed, and I was able to lift the latch, and pull it open. Inside, the sun filtered through four windows and a skylight to illuminate living quarters that appeared surprisingly comfortable, in contrast to the sterility of the dome's exterior. There were two padded chairs of starship design anchored to the floor, several tables, a desk, a computer, a stand-up lamp. One of the tables was inlaid for chess. But there was no sign of the pieces.

I wondered whether Tarien had come on this long flight out from Abonai, whether there had been a last desperate clash, perhaps in this room, between the brothers! Had Tarien pleaded with him to continue the struggle? It would have been a terrible dilemma: men had so few symbols, and the hour was so desperate.

They could not permit him to sit out the battle (as Achilles had done). In the end, just before Rigel, Tarien must have felt he had no choice but to seize his brother and dismiss the crew with some contrived story. (Or perhaps an angry Christopher Sim had done that himself, before confronting Tarien.) Then the conspirators had invented the legend of the Seven, concocted the destruction of *Corsarius*, and, when the engagement was over, they'd brought him and his ship here.

I stood in the doorway and wondered how many years that tiny space had been his home.

He would have understood, I thought. And if, in some way, he could have learned that he'd been wrong, that Rimway *had* come, and Toxicon, and even Earth, he might have been consoled.

There was nothing on the computer. I thought that strange; I'd expected a final message, perhaps to his wife, perhaps to the people he had defended. But the memory banks were empty. And in time I felt the walls begin to close, and I fled the place, out onto the shelf that had defined the limits of his existence.

Chilled, I walked the perimeter, skirting the slabs at the north end, striding in the shadow of the wall, and returning along the edge of the precipice. I tried to imagine myself (as I had on the island a couple of nights before) marooned in that place, alone on that world, a thousand light years from anyone with whom I could speak. The ocean must have seemed very tempting.

Overhead, *Corsarius* flew. He could have seen it moving among the stars, hurtling across the skies like an errant moon every few hours.

And then I saw the inscription. He had cut a single line of letters into the rock wall, just above eye level, at one end of the shelf. They were driven deep into the limestone, hard-edged characters whose fury was clear enough (I thought), though I could not understand the language in which they'd been written:

$$\hat{\omega}\,\pi o\pi o\hat{\iota}\,!\,\hat{\omega}\,\Delta\eta\mu o\sigma\Theta\acute{\epsilon}\nu\eta\varsigma\,!$$

"Chase?"

She was slow to answer. "I'm watching."

"Can we get a translation?"

"Trying. I'm not sure how to enter a visual into the computer. Give me a minute."

Greek. Sim had remained a classicist to the end.

My heart hammered against my ribs, as I contemplated what his final days, or years, must have been. How long had he endured this shelf, beneath the ecliptic of the endlessly circling link with home?

It would have been a reflexive choice, when the *Tenandrome* flashed its news to Fishbowl and Rimway, to keep it quiet. I could imagine the hurried meetings of high-ranking officials, already burdened with a disintegrating government. Why not? What good could come of such a revelation? And the men on the *Tenandrome*, themselves shaken by what they'd seen, had readily agreed.

"Alex. The computer thinks it's classical Greek."

"Good. What else?"

"That's it. It says there are only a few languages in its library, and all of those are modern."

"The last word," I said, "looks like *Demosthenes*."

"The orator?"

"I don't know. Maybe. But I can't imagine why he'd go to the trouble to carve the name of a dead Greek on a wall. In these circumstances."

"Makes no sense," said Chase. "He had a computer available in the dome. Why didn't he use *that?* He could have written whatever he wanted. Why go to all the trouble to carve it in rock?"

"The medium's the message, as someone once said. Maybe an electronic surface wouldn't express his feelings appropriately."

"I have a link with the computer on *Corsarius*. There are only two references to 'Demosthenes.' One is the old Greek, and the other was a contemporary wrestler."

"What's it say about him? The Greek, I mean."

"384-322 B.C. Old Style. Greatest of the Hellenic orators. Said to have been born with a speech impediment which he overcame by placing pebbles in his mouth and speaking against the sea. His orations persuaded the Athenians to make war against Macedonia. The best known were the three Philippics and three Olynthiacs. All dating from around 350 B.C., give or take a few years. The Macedonians won despite Demosthenes' efforts, and he was driven into exile. Later, he died by his own hand."

"There's a connection," I said.

"Yes. Tarien was an orator too. Maybe it's a reference to him."

"I wouldn't be surprised," I said. I'd noticed another inscription on the rock, at its base, in letters of a different sort: *Hugh Scott, 3131.* Cut with a smaller laser.

"That's Universal time," said Chase. "It equates to either 1410 or 1411, Rimway." She sighed. "At the end, Sim might have forgiven his brother. Maybe he even realized he was right."

"Considering the circumstances, that would take a lot of forgiving." My feet hurt. The socks weren't all that much protection, and I had to keep moving to prevent being burned. "Where's our visitor?"

"Still coming. Still accelerating. They're really piling it on." The air was still. "Alex?"

"Yes?"

"Do you think she found him? In time, I mean?"

"Leisha?" I'd been thinking about little else since I'd set down. Tanner had hunted for years. Candles's *lost pilot.* And Sim,
> *Who walks behind the stars,*
> *On far Belmincour.*

"She didn't have the resources of the Machesney Institute. My God, she must have been out here all that time, taking pictures and running them through computers, trying to recreate that constellation."

"What do you think?"

"I don't know. But I suspect that's the question that haunts Hugh Scott."

I'd resisted the temptation to cut my name in the rock alongside Scott's, and wandered back toward the capsule. I was climbing into the cockpit when Chase's voice took on a note of urgency. "Alex," she said, "I hate to break in with bad news, but there's another one! And it's *big!*"

"Another *what?*"

"A mute ship. Battle cruiser, I think. I should have seen it before, but I was watching the little one, and not paying much attention to the scan."

"Where?"

"About ten hours out. Also on an approach vector. It's coming fast, but braking hard. Must be raising hell with the crew. Anyhow, it should be able to slow down enough to get into orbit. I think you'd better get back here so we can clear out."

"No," I said. I was sweating. "Chase, get out of the *Centaur*."

"You're crazy."

"Please," I said. "There's no time to argue. How far away is the destroyer?"

"About five minutes."

"That's how much time you have to get aboard the *Corsarius*. If you don't make it by then, you're not going to make it at all."

"*You've* got the capsule."

"That's why we shouldn't be standing around talking. Move. Get over there any way you can, but get there!"

I saw the flash high in the western sky: a brief needle of light.

"Chase?"

"I'm okay. But you were right. The bastards just blew the *Centaur* to hell."

I tried to pick the destroyer up with the capsule's scopes, but it was already out of range. Chase, who had a picture of it on *Corsarius's* monitor, hadn't figured out yet how to relay it down to me. It didn't matter anyway. "I'm on my way," I said. "See you in a couple of hours. You might want to invest the time learning how to run Sim's bridge. Can you get a message off to Saraglia?"

"I've already done that. But if they ever receive it, I'll be amazed. This thing isn't equipped for *that* kind of long-range transmission. Alex, I think we're stuck here."

"We'll manage," I said. "They've *got* to have a stardrive." I lifted off the shelf, and locked onto the numbers that Chase transmitted.

In the soft cool womb of the cockpit, over the late afternoon of the world, I thought about Sim and Scott. And it was Scott's melancholy fate that caught at me.

Maybe because Christopher Sim was too remote.

Maybe because I knew Scott's obsession would become my own.

* * *

I rendezvoused with *Corsarius* several hours later. By then I knew that Chase had been able to get the magnetics working. We'd be able to move, at least. The capsule wasn't designed to fit in the warship's bay, so I secured it to the hull outside one of the hatches. I wasn't quite ready to cast it adrift, until I had a better idea how things stood.

Chase opened the hatch for me. "Okay," I said, as soon as I had my helmet off, "let's get out of here."

She looked unhappy as we headed back toward the bridge. "We can't outrun them, Alex."

"This is the *Corsarius*," I said.

"It's also two hundred years old. But that's not the problem. Listen: we've been through all this. We don't have a stardrive. The computers are behaving as if we do, but we don't—"

"We have to assume it's there. If not, nothing else will make much difference."

"Okay. But even if we've got Armstrongs hidden back there somewhere, we need time to get a sufficient charge to make the jump—"

"How much time?"

"That's what's strange. The readout should be precise on that. But the computer says between twenty-five and thirty-two hours."

"I don't think this is a time to worry about details."

"I suppose. Anyhow, I started to power-up as soon as I came on board."

"When will the mutes be here?"

"In about six hours."

"Then let's get moving."

"They'll catch us long before we can make the jump. Even if we assume the most optimistic numbers." She'd got the internal systems working. Each of the hatches opened as we approached, and closed behind us. "I thought it best to keep the individual compartments sealed, until we're reasonably sure of internal integrity."

"Yeah," I said. "Good idea. How come we can't outrun them? I thought this thing was, supposed to be fast."

"It probably is. But they're already at a high velocity; we'll be moving out from a start-up."

I tried to visualize the situation. It sounded like Sim's problem at Hrinwhar. Enemy ships bearing down, and no real chance to accelerate away. What had he done? "How long before we can vector out on a head-on course?'' I asked.

''You mean go out to meet them?''

''In a manner of speaking.''

She frowned. ''Why make it easy for them?''

''Chase,'' I said. ''What happens if we run right past them? How long does it take them to get turned around?''

''Hell.'' Her face brightened. ''They'd never catch us. Of course, they'll probably shoot a big hole in us as we go by.''

''I don't think so,'' I said. ''They're going to a lot of trouble for this ship. The whole point of the attack on the Centaur was to try to prevent our getting aboard *Corsarius*. I can't believe they'll risk destroying it.''

''They might if they think we're going to get away with it.''

''Then we'll have to take our chances. You have a better idea?''

''No,'' she said, sitting down in the pilot's seat. ''You'll be happy to hear the magnetics test out. We'll have full-thrust linear anyhow. If necessary, we can ride *them* home. Only take about fifty centuries.''

''Let's see the mute,'' I said.

There was a large, wraparound display set over the viewports. It darkened to the color of the night sky, and the alien appeared. I'd never seen anything like it before, and I wasn't at first certain that it was a vessel at all: at least, whether it was capable of carrying a crew. It appeared to be a cluster of approximately twenty hyperboloids of varying sizes and design, slowly orbiting each other in a manner that suggested they were not physically connected. There was only a stylized resemblance to the alien vessels of the Resistance era. For purposes of comparison, a silhouette of the *Corsarius* appeared in the lower right corner. We were scarcely larger than the smallest of the alien's components.

''Are we sure it's a mute?''

Chase shook her head. ''Damned if I know. Only thing I'm certain of is that it's not ours. The *destroyer* was certainly a mute.'' She pushed back from the pilot's console, and swung to face me. ''You really want to try running past that thing?''

''Yes,'' I said. ''I don't think we have any other option.''

''Okay,'' Chase said, loading instructions into the computers. ''We'll start to leave orbit in about fifty minutes. How close do you want to go?''

I thought about it. ''I'd like to stay out of firing range. Any idea what that might be?''

''None.''

"Okay, let's try for a minimum of ten thousand kilometers. That should make for a tough shot, at least. And still give them a long turn."

"Okay," she said. "Locked in. By the way, this thing's really building up an operational power reserve. We've got enough juice to run a big interstellar. And it's still climbing. I suspect, if it comes to a fight, we've got a substantial kick ourselves."

"It's not going to blow up, is it?" I was thinking of the *Regal*.

"Your guess is as good as mine."

Minutes later, the engines of the *Corsarius* took hold. Chase looked up at me from the navigator's console. "Historic moment, Alex. You want to execute?"

"No," I said. "Go ahead."

She smiled, and pressed the keys. I felt the ship move.

"Once we leave orbit," I said, "give us everything we've got. Full throttle."

"Alex," she said, "the *Corsarius* can accelerate a lot faster than you and I can. We'll move pretty quickly, but it'll be well below what this ship can do."

The alien was getting bigger. It had begun to pulse with a soft blue-green glow, reminiscent of Christmas lights.

"Operational power levels are still building," Chase said. "I've never seen anything like it. This son of a bitch might actually have enough of a punch to knock that monster over. If we have to."

"I'd rather outrun it," I said.

We lifted out of orbit within the hour, and, with our prow turned toward the enemy—for that was certainly how we both thought about the other ship—we accelerated. Almost immediately, Chase reported that the other vessel had begun to change course. "To get closer," she said.

"Veer off. Try to keep that ten-thousand-kilometer range at closest approach."

"I'll do what I can." She looked grim. "But I wish to hell one or the other of us knew what we're doing."

Chase was right: the pressure of constant acceleration wore us down. She looked exhausted after an hour, and I became acutely conscious of my heartbeat. We increased oxygen content, and that helped for a while.

Meantime the distance between the two ships narrowed. "Coming fast," Chase said.

"They won't shoot. The only reason they're here is to salvage the *Corsarius*."

But I wasn't really all that confident, and Chase knew it. So we waited, while the computers counted down the time.

The alien's components seemed to be moving within themselves: whirling lights and orbiting topological shapes. It looked ghostly, insubstantial. "Closest point of approach," said Chase. "Mark."

The computer announced in a burgundy female voice: "They are tracking us for laser fire."

"Hang on, Chase."

"Goddam it, Alex, we forgot something—"

She was interrupted by a blast. The ship lurched violently: metal tore, and something exploded. Klaxons howled and warning lights blinked on. Chase unleashed a series of expletives. "The magnets," she said. "They just wiped us out, first punch." She looked gloomily at me, and at the image of the alien as it reached maximum size, and began to diminish. Red lights across the status boards were switching to purple. "The ship's sealing itself, but we've got problems." She shut the alarms down.

"What happened?" I asked. The pressure of acceleration had eased. Considerably.

"That's not my doing," she explained. "They cut a hole in our propulsion system. And unless you're an expert at repairing magnetic drive units, we're going to be down to a slow walk."

"Well, we'll keep moving at our current velocity, right?"

"Actually, we'll do a little better than that. But that isn't very good, when the other guy keeps accelerating. What will happen now is that they'll continue on, loop around the planet and come get us. Pretty much at their leisure. And what really irritates me is that it needn't have happened!"

"Why? What do you mean?"

"The problem is neither of us knows anything about combat. We've *got* a shield. But we never activated it!"

"Son of a bitch."

"Now you know why Gabe was bringing John Khyber along. The old naval systems expert. He damned well wouldn't have overlooked anything so obvious!" Her eyes filled with tears. All we'd been through, and it was the first time I'd seen her so discouraged.

"What about the stardrive? Any damage to that?"

She took a deep breath and flicked switches. "Stardrive ignition is still no less than twenty-three hours away. But I'm damned if I can imagine what's going to ignite. Son of a bitch, we had plenty of time. You know what we had up? Standard navigational meteor screens! We're lucky we didn't get nuked. Dumb!''

''No point worrying about that now. How much time do we have before they catch us?''

Chase tapped the computer. ''About fourteen hours.'' She slumped in her seat. ''I think,'' she said, ''it's time to run up a white flag.''

She was right. The giant vessel swung round the world that had been Sim's prison, and hurtled after us.

We went into the after section and looked at the magnetics. Three of the series were fused. ''It's a wonder we've got any acceleration at all,'' Chase said. ''But it's not going to be enough to make a difference.''

We used our remaining time as prudently as we could. First thing we did was get an explanation from the computer on the ship's system of shields. I would have liked to run a test, but I decided it might be a better idea not to let the mutes see it. Maybe they assumed it was no longer operational. After all, what other explanation could there be for not using it in a situation which so clearly called for defenses? Then, having assured ourselves, perhaps too late, that we would not stand completely naked to the bastards, we started to look to our firepower.

While we watched them come, we studied schematics, and talked to computers. We learned details about a bewildering tangle of weapons systems, which were operated from four different consoles. And I began to understand why the frigates required an eight-man crew. ''We couldn't hope to fire more than one or two of these damned things,'' complained Chase. ''If we had more people, people who knew what they were doing, and everything worked, I think even now we could put up a decent fight.''

''Computer,'' I said, ''can the mute detect our power build-up?''

''Unknown.''

''Can we read power levels on board *their* ship?''

''Negative. We can detect external radiation only, and I can draw inferences from mass and maneuvering characteristics. But they would be estimates whose only real use would be to provide absolute minimum values.''

''Then *they* can't read ours?''

"Unknown. We lack data on their technology."

"Alex, what are you getting at?"

"I'm not sure. But I'd prefer they think we're helpless."

"What's the difference?" asked Chase. "Their screens are up. They're assuming we're dangerous."

"Computer, what can you tell us about enemy capabilities?"

"*Corsarius* was struck by an enhanced laser of extremely narrow concentration. The energy required to produce the effect we witnessed, at their extreme range, implies power which exceeds ours by a multiple of at least six point five. Analysis of ECM and physical structure suggests the generation of a quasi-magnetic energy field for defensive, and perhaps offensive, purposes. Probably an amplified version of our own shields. We would be wise to assume considerable difficulty in penetrating defensive systems.

"Propulsion appears to be standard. Armstrong symmetries are detectable in radiation pattern, as is a magnetic track of the type one would expect for a linear drive system—"

And so on.

For several hours, we continued to widen our lead over the mutes. But they were accelerating at a much higher rate than we were. And eventually, Chase informed me quietly that they had exceeded our speed, and were now beginning to close.

Its blue-green lights grew brighter on the screens. And, as it drew near, it began to slow down, presumably to match our course and speed.

We were both chilled by the precision of the long-range laser shot which had destroyed the engines, and neither of us held any illusions about the outcome should we be forced to fight.

Nevertheless, we concentrated on our own weapons. We had nukes and accelerated particle beams and proton rams, and half a dozen other devices I'd never heard of. The most promising (which is to say the easiest to aim and fire) seemed to be a weapon that Chase referred to as the scattershot: a wide-band energy beam consisting of gantner photons, hot electrons, and a kind of "particle soup." Its effect, according to the computers, was to destabilize matter at short range. "But you have to get in close," the computer warned. "And you have to knock out the defensive systems first. It won't give you any penetration at all of the shields."

"How do we *do* that?" asked Chase.

The computer replied with a complex strategy requiring quick maneuvering and operators at three of the weapons consoles.

"One console," I said. "We can only man one. Or two if we dispense with the pilot."

"Why don't we just give them the ship?" said Chase. I could see fear in her eyes, and I doubt that I was doing a good job hiding my own emotions. "That's what they want, and it's our best chance to get away from here with our heads."

"I don't think," I said, "that we should surrender the *Corsarius*. Under any conditions. Anyhow, you saw what they did to the Centaur. I don't think we have any choice but to fight. Or run, if we can."

"It's suicide," she said.

I couldn't argue with that. Still, we had a hell of a ship. And *they* wanted it very badly. That might give us an advantage of sorts. "Computer, if the alien's shield was down, what would be the logical target for the scattershot?"

"I would recommend," it said, "either the bridge or the power plant. I will inform you if I am able to locate them."

Chase looked out the viewport at the mute, whose shadow now filled the sky. "We might as well throw rocks," she said.

We shut down what was left of our magnetics, and coasted now at a constant speed. The alien settled into a parallel orbit, about a kilometer to starboard. Chase watched them a while, and then shook her head hopelessly. "They can't see the capsule," she said. "How about if we put a timer on one of the nukes, blow the ship to hell, and get out? We might still be able to make it back to the planet."

"You'd spend the rest of your life there if you did," I said.

"First things first." She hunched her shoulders, and turned back to the screen. "I wonder what they're waiting for."

"My guess is they're trying to figure a way to get us out of here without damaging the ship. Maybe they're waiting for the destroyer to come back. Where is it, by the way?"

"Still headed out of town. I'd say another standard day and a half before they can even turn around. Anyway, what would they need a destroyer for?"

She looked through a viewport at the giant ship floating off our beam.

"Their shields are still up?"

"Yes. This would be a good time for an idea." Her face clouded.

"I just had an uncomfortable thought. Can they read our minds from there?"

"I don't think so. They have to be reasonably close. A few meters, judging by my experience with them. And by the way, if they do get inside your head, you'll know it."

"Unpleasant sons of bitches, aren't they?" She tapped the keyboard. "Energy levels have finally stopped rising. I think we're about as combat ready as we're going to get. If any of this stuff still works."

"Assume everything's fine. That's what we'll need to survive, so assume it. If there's a problem somewhere, knowing about it in advance won't help us any."

"So what do we do now?"

"Wait," I said. "Keep the scattershot primed. If we get a chance to use it, we're going to shoot, and run like hell."

"Limp like hell," she corrected.

"Benedict."

The sound spilled out of the ship's commsystem. "It's coming from the mute," said Chase.

"Don't acknowledge," I said.

"Alex." The voice was warm, understanding, reasonable. And familiar. "Alex, are you all right? I've been worried about life support over there. Is there anything we can do?"

It was S'Kalian. Defender of the peace. Idealist. *Friend.* "I'm sorry about the loss of the Centaur. The destroyer was only supposed to prevent anyone's boarding the artifact."

"Stay on the trigger," I told Chase.

"What do I aim at?"

"Pick your target," I said.

"Preferably toward the center," said the computer. "Without specific knowledge, the most probable location of the power plant would be a centralized position within the configuration."

S'Kalian again: "Alex?"

Chase nodded. "Locked in. Now's your chance to ask him to take down the screens."

"Alex, you can hear me. We have an opportunity to settle this peacefully. There need be no bloodshed."

I opened a channel. His image appeared on one of the auxiliary monitors. He looked solicitous, compassionate. "You can't have the *Corsarius*, S'Kalian."

"We already have it. Fortunately for both our peoples, *we* have it."

"Why?" I asked. "Why is it so valuable to you?"

"Surely by now you have guessed, Alex." His tone dropped an octave. "Sim's secrets will be safe with us. We are not an aggressive species. Your people have nothing to fear."

"That's easy to say."

"We don't have your bloody history, Alex. War is not a normal condition of life among us. We do not kill our own kind, nor would we have killed yours if it could have been avoided. We still live today with the memory of that terrible war."

"That was two hundred years ago!"

"And there," he said, sadly, "lies the difference between us. For the Ashiyyur, yesterday's tragedy remains painfully fresh. It is not merely *history*."

"Yes," I said. "We've seen how violence upsets you."

"I'm sorry about the attack on the Centaur. But we wished very much to avoid the situation which has now arisen. However, we cannot permit the *Corsarius* to be returned to its creators. The sad truth of all this is that we may yet be forced to take your lives."

"What do you want?"

"Only the ship. Turn it over to us. I'm prepared to provide safe passage home for you, and to compensate you generously for the loss of the artifact."

I looked at him, trying to read sincerity into those too-thoroughly composed features. "What's involved in the surrender? How do you propose to do it?"

"It's *not* a surrender, Alex," he said smoothly. "It's an act of courage under difficult circumstances. But we would simply send over a boarding party. As for you, all we ask is that you signify your consent by leaving the vessel. Both of you, that is." He nodded, expressing content that we were moving toward a prudent course. "Yes, simply leave the vessel. Come here to us. You have my solemn guarantee that you will be well treated."

"And released?"

He hesitated. It was brief, a moment's reluctance. "Of course." He smiled encouragingly. Somehow, during the conversation we'd had at Kostyev House, the fact that his lips never moved had been less disconcerting, perhaps because I could see the communication device by which he spoke, or maybe because the circumstances had changed so drastically. Whatever it was, the dialogue was thoroughly unnerving, and carried with it a sense of direct mental contact. I wondered whether I had underestimated him, whether he was in fact reaching across the void and penetrating my mind. "Are you prepared to leave?"

"We're thinking about it." Chase stared at the overhead.

"Very good. We will watch for you. In deference to your feelings, we will make no effort to board the ship until you have arrived safely here.

·"By the way, Alex, I know this is difficult for you. But the day will come when our two species will stand united in fast friendship. And I suspect you will be remembered for your contribution to that happy moment."

"Why is it so important?" I asked. "Why do you want the ship?"

"It is a symbol of the evil time. I think, in all honesty, that it could not have been found at a worse period. We are again close to war, your people and mine. *This vessel,* with all the memories it will stir, could well be the catalyst for a tidal wave of hostility. We cannot, in conscience, allow that to happen."

Who's he kidding? Chase asked with her eyes.

"This is not an easy decision for us," I said.

"I understand."

"Please give us a moment to think about it."

"Of course."

"Do it!" Chase said, as soon as his image had faded. "It's a way out. And they'd have nothing to gain by killing us."

"The sons of bitches *would* kill us, Chase. They aren't going to turn us loose."

"You're crazy," she said. "We've *got* to trust them. What other choice do we have? I don't want to give my life for a derelict. You know as well as I do that if they can't have this thing, they'll just blow it up and us with it. And any notions we have of fighting that goddam monster are just so much fantasy. I mean, this antique wouldn't have a chance against that son of a bitch, even if it had a full crew and Sim himself sitting in that chair."

"That's not what you were saying a few minutes ago."

"A few minutes ago I didn't think we had a choice."

My mouth had gone dry, but I tried to sound calm. "I don't agree, Chase. They want this ship, and as long as we stay *in* it, I think we're safe. They can't board, and they won't destroy it."

"Why not? If all they want is to keep us from getting back home with it, they can blow us up any time they please."

"Then why haven't they already done so?"

"Maybe because they don't want to kill anyone if they don't have to."

"You believe that?"

"Damn it, Alex, I don't know."

"Okay." I was out of the command seat now, rattling around the bridge, trying to think. "If you're right, then why did they attack the Centaur? They had no compunctions about our lives. They wanted to keep us from getting on board because then they'd have to *talk* us out."

"Maybe you're right," she said angrily. "I just don't know. But I don't want to get killed over it."

"Then we stay right where we are. How much time before the Armstrongs activate?"

"There *are* no Armstrongs," she said, desperately.

"Come on, Chase," I said. "How much time before whatever we've got activates? Before we can jump into hyper?"

There were tears in her eyes. "About a half day. You think you can stall them that long?"

"I think it's our best chance." I took her by the shoulders, and hung on to her. "You with me?"

She looked at me a long time. "You're going to get us both killed," she said.

"I regret that you feel compelled to pursue a course that can only result in bloodshed." S'Kalian did indeed appear upset. "Is there nothing I can say to dissuade you?"

"The hell with you," I said. "You're going to have to blow up your artifact. So go ahead and do it!" I broke the link.

"You were persuasive," Chase said, glumly. "I hope he doesn't take you up on it."

The mute drifted closer. The slow oscillation of its component parts accelerated. "Best analysis," said the computer, "suggests everything we can see is part of an energy deployment system."

Chase swore softly. "Where's the operational center? Where are they vulnerable?"

"At present, insuffucient information is available to draw conclusions."

"Your guess is as good as his," I said.

"I think it's time to put up the shields."

"No," I said.

"Why not?"

"We don't gain anything by it. We can't run, and we can't fight. The shields would only delay the inevitable. Let's try to keep a surprise available." Something had been bothering me about my conversation with S'Kalian, and I suddenly realized what it was. "Why were they being so nice to us?" I said.

"What do you mean?"

"Why did they want to wait for us to go over there before they dispatched a boarding party?"

Chase shook her head. "I still think maybe they're telling the truth."

"No," I said. "I'll tell you what it is: they don't trust us. We're bushwhackers in their eyes, and they want us where they can keep an eye on us. That means they think we can do them some damage. How?"

Chase's eyes closed briefly, and then she nodded. "I can give you a good guess. Their boarding party: they have to lower their screens to pass them through. For a few seconds, they'd be vulnerable."

I felt a simultaneous rush of elation and fear. "They don't trust us," I repeated. And I found myself thinking about Sim's chessboard. "Maybe we can turn it to our advantage."

"Go ahead," Chase said. "I'm open for ideas."

"I need you to go back and get two of the pressure suits. Put them inside the capsule, and inflate them. Try to make them look like us. And rig the capsule so we can operate it from here."

"Why? What good will that do?"

"I'm not sure how much time we have, Chase. Just do it. Okay? Let me know when it's ready, and then get back here."

"All right," she said, getting up, and extending her hand. "And by the way, if I don't see you again, it's been a hell of a ride, Alex." There was a catch beneath the flippancy, but she left quickly. In the general silence of the ship, I could follow her progress back through the hatches.

"Movement," said the computer. "Something's happening."

The ovoid dance of the alien vessel changed its pattern, and its colors deepened. It glowed fiercely in the eternal dark, its tiny lights swirling. Luminous insects in the mouth of a cannon. It went on for several minutes.

"Psychology," I told the computer. "They're playing mind games with us."

"I'm not sure what that means. But I detect a familiar metal shape within the configuration. Plasma missile launcher, probably. Eight tubes. This type weapon is intended for use against a relatively stationary target. High velocity projectile designed to penetrate thick armor, and burn out interior. Analysis indicates that only one of the tubes contains a weapon."

Hell. "What," I asked, barely able to speak, suddenly aware that I didn't know how to put the shield up if I wanted to, "will be the effect on *Corsarius?*"

"How much energy to defensive screens?"

"None."

"Total destruction."

I thought about calling Chase, to warn her, to get her back. But I let it go. What the hell.

I could hear her banging around in the after section. A red lamp lit up on the status board. Outside hatch open.

"They've locked on," said the computer.

I squeezed my eyes shut and waited.

"Missile away."

In that final moment, what I thought about was that we had not fired a single shot in our own defense.

The thing blasted through our metal skin and set off a windstorm below decks. The klaxons let go again, and all the rest of the ship's systems that warn of immediate and serious danger. But we were still alive!

"What the hell's going on up there?" demanded Chase, with the mild echo that indicated she was inside a pressure suit.

"They just fired on us. You okay?"

"Yeah. You think maybe it's time now to put up the shield?" She sounded shaky.

"Are you finished yet?"

"Almost. But maybe we ought to evict the dummies, and you and me get in there and clear out."

"Get back here quick," I said. "Computer, damage report. How come we're still on the premises?"

"The missile did not detonate. I don't know why, unless it was an empty shell. Impossible to be certain, since it passed completely through the ship."

"Where'd it hit?"

"The compartment directly below the bridge. We will require repairs on both bulkheads as soon as you can get a damage control crew down there. In the meantime, I've sealed the area off."

S'Kalian's voice again: "Alex: there is still time." He held out his arms in a gesture of appeal.

"You are a son of a bitch," I said quietly.

"I admire your restraint, under the circumstances. Please understand: we can punch holes in your vessel, and I believe we can do it without damaging critical systems. Now, what further demonstration do you need of my concern for your welfare? Get out of there, while you can. Your death, and that of your, uh, woman, will accomplish nothing."

Chase opened the rear hatch and came in. "Ready to go," she whispered.

The computer broke the link with the enemy ship. "Captain," it said, "another missile has been loaded."

"If you've got an idea," said Chase, "this is the time."

"Computer, get the mute back."

S'Kalian's image reappeared. "I hope you have made the wise decision," he said.

"I don't think you're going to like it much." I paused for effect, and tried to look moderately demented. "I'm going to arm one of the nukes and I'm going to sit here and blow the *Corsarius* to hell."

"I don't believe you."

"Believe what you want."

"I've *seen* your psyche, Alex. In a sense, I've *been* you. You don't believe strongly enough in anything to commit such an act. Your will to survive is very strong—"

I shut him off. "That's it," I told the computer. "I don't want to receive any more transmissions from the other ship. Nothing. Refuse everything."

"It's useless," said Chase. "What are you trying to do? They don't believe you. They'll be looking for a trick." Her eyes widened. "Hey, you weren't by any chance serious, were you? I have no interest whatever in going up in a fireball."

"No. Of course not. And they won't believe it either. That's what I'm counting on. Stay by the scattershot. In six minutes, we're

going to send the capsule for a ride. Shortly after that their shield
should come down. You'll get green lights on the status board.
Then pull the trigger. Aim into the center somewhere, and fire
everything we've got." I began counting off the time.

"What if the shields don't come down?"

"Then we'll have to think of something else."

"I'm happy to know we have a plan."

"Are you ready to launch the capsule?"

"Yes," she said. We waited. The minutes ticked off.

"I want it moving away from the alien. It should be on a course
back toward the planet."

She frowned, understood, and smiled. "They won't buy it," she
said. "We're too far away from the planet now. They'll know we
couldn't make it."

"Do it," I said. "Now."

She pressed a stud on the console. "Capsule away."

"They won't know," I said. "They probably don't know a
damned thing about its capabilities. And if they *do* know, they'll
assume *we* don't. The only thing they're going to be thinking about
is the two of us trying to cut and run. And the nuke that's ticking
away in here. Tricky humans."

She put the capsule on one of the monitors, and we waited. It
looked good: two people in pressure suits, one bent over the
controls. "You look drunk," Chase said.

"It's okay. It's good enough to fool them."

She agreed. "And I wish I were on it."

"No, you don't. We're going to come through this okay. Try to
maneuver it in the shadow of the ship. We want it to look as though
we're trying to keep out of sight. But make sure they can see it."

"Right," she said uncertainly.

"Enemy missile is locked on the bridge," said the computer.

"I hope this thing has enough of a charge to take them out." She
looked doubtful.

"Be ready," I said. "We're only going to get a couple of
seconds. As soon as the green lamps go out—"

"Captain," said the computer, "the enemy ship is signaling
again."

"Don't respond. Tell me when it stops."

"They should be able to see the capsule now, Alex."

"Okay. Any time now. It'll happen quick."

"Captain, the signal from the mute has broken off."

"Alex, are you sure this is going to work?"

"Of course not."

We watched the consoles, the green lamps, waiting.

"Activity in one of the ovoids," said the computer. We got several simultaneous views on the screens, in close. A portal had opened, and the silver prow of a launch vehicle was visible. It looked armored.

"Here we go," I said. "It's the bomb disposal unit."

Chase heaved a sigh of relief. "They've got guts."

The lamps flickered and died. "Their shields are down."

Chase pulled the trigger.

We bucked and rolled, and a deep-throated roar shook the bulkheads.

I stabbed at a row of keys, and our own shield activated.

Blinding light spilled through the ports; the screens blanked out. Chase was pitched out of her chair, but held the firing stud down. Course correction jets fired.

Something hammered us. The ship shook, and the lights dipped.

"Proton burst," announced the computer. "Shields holding." One of the monitors came back and we were looking again at the mute ship: its lights flared and swirled in a frenzy. Patches of darkness appeared among them and expanded. The oscillations abruptly collapsed and broke apart. A few fireballs erupted and died in showers of sparks. When it was over, there remained only a blackened network of spheres and tubing.

Chase shut off the scattershot. "I think we're depleted," she said. The silver launch and its assault team had spurted past us and was still going, hoping (I assumed) not to be noticed in the general melee.

Another blast hit us. "A second proton burst," said the computer. "This one was well off target. No damage."

"Computer, arm a nuke."

"Alex, this is our chance to run." Something else blew up out there. Whether it was the warship disintegrating, or continuing to fire on us, I couldn't tell.

"In a minute."

"Armed and ready to fire, Captain."

"Alex, what are you doing? It's over. Let's get out of here."

"The sons of bitches tried to kill us, Chase. I'm going to finish them while we can."

I listened to the sounds of the bridge: the reassuring throb of power in the bulkheads, the cadences of the data processing systems, the soft murmur of the intership commlink. Chase's breathing.

"There's no need," she said.

I locked in the target angle.

She stared at me. "I liked the earlier Tanner," she said. "The one who offered her arm to a mute."

Electrical fires raged throughout the stricken ship.

"Captain, it has begun to move away."

"Let them go," urged Chase. "Let's try to do things right this time."

I sat with my finger on the presspad.

"They'll know you could have killed them, and didn't. They'll always know that."

"Yeah," I said. "For all the good it'll do anybody."

We watched them limp off into the dark.

XXV.

Boundaries have no existence save on charts or in small minds. Nature does not draw lines.

—Tulisofala, **Extracts, CCLXII, vi**
(Translated by Leisha Tanner)

I THINK SOMETIMES about Christopher Sim's observation that Thermopylae need not have been fought.

My war with the Ashiyyur seems to fall into the same category. It would not have happened had I not spent an afternoon revealing everything I knew to S'Kalian at the Maracaibo Caucus. That visit may not have been the dumbest act of all time, but it's certainly up there among the top ten. We came desperately close to losing the *Corsarius* and all she contained.

Chase was right about the Armstrongs: there weren't any. But a far more sophisticated propulstion system stood in their place. And, about ten hours after the incident with the mute warship, the computers gave us a few minutes warning, and the *Corsarius* took us home.

It was not the sickening dive into multi-dimensional space, and the dreary two-month ride down the gray tunnel that we'd endured on the way out.

It was more like a blink.

Stars blurred, and reappeared. (If we'd been watching closely, we'd have seen the constellations change, the Great Wheel vanish, the familiar configurations of Rimway's nighttime sky emerge from the moment of confusion.) Belmincour's sun was gone, and we were approaching lovely, blue-white crescented Rimway. The comm system crackled with traffic, and a quarter moon floated off to starboard.

There was only the briefest physical sensation: a moment during which there had been no deck underfoot, no air to breathe. It passed so quickly that I was unsure it had happened at all.

Under the pressure of that desperate war, someone, certainly Rashim Machesney and his team, had solved a series of theoretical problems related to gravity waves and derived a practical application. Recognizing that gravity, like light, is dualistic in nature, that it is both wave and particle, they had drawn the obvious conclusion: gravity can be quantized.

A wide range of implications rises from this simple fact. The one most significant for Chase and me, sitting in our ancient frigate, feeling not confident of ever getting home, was this: large physical objects are capable of the quantum jump of the electron. That is, it is possible to move them from point to point without crossing the intervening space.

The *Corsarius* was equipped with a tunable gravity wave collector, enhanced by hyperconductive magnets designed to reduce electrical resistance to a negative factor. The result: the ship was able to achieve displacement in the time/space fabric with a zero time interval.

Well, you already know all that. But that's how it happens that Chase and I are not still out on the far side of the Veiled Lady.

The quantum drive.

Range isn't unlimited, of course. It's a factor of the nature of the drive, and of available power. Energy is stored in a hyperconducting ring, and must be applied within excruciatingly exact limits at the moment of transition. And a ship can't move freely even within that range. The minimum distance it will cross is slightly longer than a light-day. After that, intervals are reduced by infinitesimal, but steadily increasing, variables. It's somewhat like stations. All this is apparently tied in with statistics and quantum logic and the Hays Certainty Principle. But the result is that the method isn't practical for voyages that are either very short, or very long.

We have a better understanding now of what relations among the various human worlds really were during the War against the Ashiyyur. (Or at least Chase and I do.) Though we had always known they hadn't trusted one another, it came as a shock that the Dellacondans withheld their discovery from their allies. And that it was consequently lost for two centuries after Rigel.

A lot has changed since we brought the *Corsarius* back from Belmincour.

Political unity on a grand scale has become practical, and the Confederacy appears to be stabilizing. We may make it after all.

I've also been happy that the drive has not been used in any particularly offensive way against the Ashiyyur. I owe them no love, and yet, if there is a lesson in all this, I think it points in that direction. We own an immense technological advantage now. Tensions have eased, and some experts claim you can't have a serious rivalry without a military balance. Maybe we're looking toward a new era. I hope so.

The Maracaibo Caucus is still open down at Kostyev House. I've never gone back, but I wish them well.

You can still see Matt Olander's grave outside Point Edward. The Ilyandans dismissed Kindrel Lee's story out of hand.

There's talk now of an intergalactic mission. Power remains a problem; the voyage would have to be made in a series of (relatively) short jumps. Recharging is slow; and the experts estimate that a trip to Andromeda would consume the better part of a century and a half. But we're coming. There've already been some improvements on Machesney's basic design; and I hope to live long enough to crack a bottle across the prow of the first intergalactic survey ship. (Promises have been made.)

The reputations of the Sims have suffered no lasting damage. In fact, most people dismiss the Belmincour story and believe firmly that the hero died off Rigel.

There's a theory that has gained some status among scholars that I've found interesting: the notion that there was a final confrontation on the shelf, and that the brothers ultimately embraced, and parted in tears.

Which brings us to the inscription on the rock:

$$\hat{\omega} \pi o \pi o \hat{\imath} ! \; \hat{\omega} \; \Delta \eta \mu o \sigma \Theta \acute{\epsilon} \nu \eta s !$$

The first section is a cry of anguish, used often by the hero in classical Greek tragedy. Then: *O Demosthenes*. Most historians read that cry as a tribute by Christopher Sim to his brother's oratorical abilities and hence as a demonstration of forgiveness: *I am in agony, O Demosthenes*, it seems to say. This also supports the view of the final parting on the shelf, attended by all the comcomitant bitterness and affection that such an event would have generated.

But I have my doubts. After all, Demosthenes persuaded his countrymen to fight a pointless and suicidal war against Alexander the Great!

If *we* have not understood the remark, I think Tarien would have.

We've always wondered about Tanner and Sim, why she searched so relentlessly for so many years. Somehow, there seems to have been more than simple compassion or loyalty in that quest. Chase would inject a romantic note: *She loved him*, she has told me on occasion, when the wind blows hard outside, and the fire leaps high. *And she found him. I am sure of that. She would not have given up—*

Maybe.

I've always suspected that Tanner was part of the original plot. That it was she, and not a nameless staff officer or crewman, who saw the Wheel. And that it was guilt, rather than love, that drove her.

And anyhow, we *know* he didn't come back. Christopher Sim was never heard of again, after Rigel. Sometimes I think about him on that rock, and I want more than anything else in my life to believe that she came down out of the clear blue sky. And that she took him away.

I like to think it. But I don't believe it.

And finally, Gabe.

Today, the logs of the *Corsarius*, and a personal notebook in the hand of Christopher Sim, are on display at the Center for Accadian Studies. In the Gabriel Benedict Wing.

EPILOGUE

THE SKIMMER ARCED in over the rim of St. Anthony's Valley, circled the abbey, and set down on the visitors' pad near the statue of the Virgin in front of the administration building. A tall, dark-skinned man climbed out of the cockpit, blinked in the sunlight, and glanced round at the cluster of dormitories, the library, and the chapel, which seemed to have been scattered over the landscape in no very orderly fashion.

A young man in red robes had been standing off to one side, near the Virgin, watching. Now he walked swiftly toward the visitor. "Mr. Scott?" he inquired.

"Yes."

"Welcome to St. Anthony's. I'm Mikel Dubay, the Abbot's representative." Usually, Mikel broke the formality of the announcement with the additional observation that he was a novice. But Scott's manner did not encourage spontaneity.

"Ah." He was looking past Mikel's shoulder.

"We've prepared a room for you."

"Thank you. But I won't be staying overnight."

"Oh." That was puzzling. "I understood you had intended a retreat here."

"That's true," Scott said, suddenly aware of the novice. "In a way. But it will take only a half hour or so."

Mikel's jaw tightened, but he did not reply until he was sure he could keep the ice out of his voice. "The Abbot wished me to see that you receive whatever assistance you require."

* * *

With his heart hammering, Hugh Scott followed his guide behind the residence halls and past the recreation area. Shouts from a group of young ballplayers drifted on the late afternoon air. A couple of white-clad priests came from the other direction, greeted Mikel and his charge cheerfully, and continued on. The portion of their conversation that Scott had caught seemed to have something to do with high energy physics.

The chapel bell tolled. A large avian flapped wildly in one of the trees, and fell out. It hit the ground with a shriek, got up, and galloped away on enormous wedge-shaped feet. "It followed one of the fathers home from a mountain novena a few weeks ago," the novice explained. "We've been trying to catch it so that we can take it back."

"I've never seen anything quite like it," Scott said reflexively, looking uphill, perhaps not thinking of the creature at all. Indeed, he might not even have been aware of its existence.

"It's a mowry bird," continued Mikel, falling into silence thereafter.

The walkway curved past groves of flowering bushes and dwarf trees. They turned uphill. On the ridge, behind an iron fence, Scott could see rows of white markers.

He slowed his pace. It was a lovely day, an afternoon to enjoy, a moment to savor! And the blood rushed in his veins!

Marble benches were set near the entrance, intended obviously as places where one might with profit contemplate the brevity of a lifetime. His glance swept past them to the arch, beneath which the fathers pass on their final journey. A cross stood at its apex, and it was inscribed: *He that would teach others how to die, must know how to live.* Yes, Scott thought. Sim had *known!*

"Back there." Mikel pointed toward a section shaded by ancient trees. Scott walked down the rows of plain white markers, and it struck him that this was probably the first time in his adult life that he'd visited a graveyard and not succumbed to gloomy imaginings about his own mortality. Something more important today.

"Here, sir." The novice stopped by a marker utterly undistinguishable from the others. Scott approached it, and read the inscription:

> Jerome Courtney
> Died 11,108 A.D.

Scott checked his commlink. The date equated to 1249 on the Rimway calendar. Forty years after the war! Tears filled his eyes, and he went down on one knee.

The grass rippled in the warm afternoon breeze. Water was moving somewhere, and voices floated in the sunlight. He was overwhelmed by the timelessness of the place.

When he recovered himself, and got back to his feet, Mikel was gone. A man stood in his place, bearded, stocky, wearing the flowing white cassock of the Disciples. "I am Father Thasangales," he said, offering his hand. It was large and bony, roughened by labor.

"Do you *know* who he was?" Scott asked.

"Yes. The abbots have always known. I'm afraid the bishop knows too. But that was necessary."

"He was here *forty* years," Scott said, astonished.

"He was here *periodically* for forty years," said Thasangales. "He wasn't a member of the Order. Nor even of the Faith, for that matter; although there is evidence that he sympathized strongly with the Church." The Abbot gazed wistfully at the far hills. "According to the accounts we have, he came and went quite frequently. But we are pleased to know that St. Anthony's was his home."

"Do you have any documents? Did he make any statements? Did he explain what happened?"

"Yes." The Abbot drew his arms together, and looked pleasantly up at the taller man. "Yes, we have several documents of his, manuscripts really. One in particular appears to be an attempt to systematize the rise and fall of civilizations. He has, I believe, gone considerably further in the matter than anyone else. There are also several histories, a series of philosophical essays, and a memoir."

Scott's breath caught in his throat. "You have all this? And you never let the world know?"

"It was his request. 'Do not give any of it to them,' he said, 'until they come and ask.'" He peered intently into Scott's eyes. "I presume that hour has arrived."

Scott drew his fingers across the gravestone. Despite the coolness of the afternoon, it felt warm. "I believe I'll take that room you offered. And, yes, I'd be interested in seeing what he has to say."

THE ULTIMATE IN
SCIENCE FICTION AND FANTASY!

From magical tales of distant worlds to stories of
technological advances beyond the grasp of man, Penguin has
everything you need to stretch your imagination to its limits.
Sign up for a monthly in-box delivery of
one of three newsletters at

penguin.com

ACE
Get the latest information on favorites like
William Gibson, T.A. Barron, Brian Jacques,
Ursula Le Guin, Sharon Shinn, and Charlaine Harris,
as well as updates on the best new authors.

ROC
Escape with Harry Turtledove, Anne Bishop,
S.M. Stirling, Simon Green, Chris Bunch, and many
others—plus news on the latest and hottest in
science fiction and fantasy.

DAW
Mercedes Lackey, Kristen Britain, Tanya Huff,
Tad Williams, C.J. Cherryh, and many more—
DAW has something to satisfy the cravings of any
science fiction and fantasy lover.
Also visit dawbooks.com.

*Sign up, and have the best of science fiction
and fantasy at your fingertips!*